GWETHALYN GRAHAM WAS BORN in 1913. Her father was a prominent Toronto lawyer and her mother convened meetings to discuss the refugee crises in Europe. One grandfather was a professor of Hebrew, Sanskrit, and Oriental Languages, as the subject was known then. Graham was educated at Rosedale Public School, Havergal College, Pensionnat des Allières in Lausanne, Switzerland, and Smith College in Massachusetts.  She dropped out of college to elope with John McNaught, the son of her father's law partner. The couple had one child, but divorced. Graham moved to Westmount, where she became part of the literary and political community that included Hugh MacLennan, F. R. Scott, Philip and Margaret Surrey, Thérèse Casgrain, Mavis Gallant, and the young Pierre Trudeau. In 1947, she married David Yalden-Tomson, a professor at McGill. They lived in Virginia, but divorced. Graham returned to Montreal in 1958.

Graham published two novels, both of which won the Governor General's Literary Award: *Swiss Sonata* (1938) and *Earth and High Heaven* (1944). The latter was the first Canadian-authored book to reach number one on the *New York Times* bestseller list — where it stayed for the better part of a year — and in 1945 it won the Anisfield-Wolf Book Award, the American book award founded to bring recognition to books that expose racism or explore the richness of human diversity. Graham also wrote articles and essays for *The Canadian Forum*, *Saturday Night*, *Maclean's*, and *Chatelaine*, and other newspapers, magazines and journals. In these pieces, she tackled what she saw to be the issues of her day: immigration, politics, anti-Semitism, and the oppression of and discrimination against French Canadians. She wrote a dozen scripts for CBC television. Her correspondence with Solange Chaput-Rolland, which explored the tensions between English- and French-speaking Canadians, was published as her final book, *Dear Enemies* (1963).

Graham died in 1965, at the age of 52, the result of an undiagnosed brain tumour. She is the subject of a biography *Gwethalyn Graham: a Liberated Woman in a Conventional World* Barbara Meadowcroft.

EARTH AND HIGH HEAVEN

EARTH AND HIGH HEAVEN

GWETHALYN GRAHAM

Cormorant Books

Canada Council Conseil des Arts
for the Arts du Canada

 ONTARIO ARTS COUNCIL
CONSEIL DES ARTS DE L'ONTARIO
an Ontario government agency
un organisme du gouvernement de l'Ontario

 Canadian Patrimoine
Heritage canadien Canadä

The publisher gratefully acknowledges the support of the Canada Council
for the Arts and the Ontario Arts Council for its publishing program.
We acknowledge the financial support of the Government of Canada
through the Canada Book Fund (CBF) for our publishing activities,
and the Government of Ontario through the Ontario Media
Development Corporation, an agency of the Ontario Ministry of Culture,
and the Ontario Book Publishing Tax Credit Program.

Printed and bound in Canada

NATIONAL LIBRARY OF CANADA CATALOGUING IN PUBLICATION

Graham, Gwethalyn, 1913–1965
Earth and high heaven : a novel / Gwethalyn Graham.

Originally published: Toronto : J. Cape, 1944.

ISBN 1-896951-61-9

1. Title.

PS8503.R775E3 2003   C813'.54   C2003-904232-4

Cover Design: Tannice Goddard/Angel Guerra
Text Design: Tannice Goddard
Cover image: National Archives of Canada
Printer: Friesens

CORMORANT BOOKS INC.
215 SPADINA AVENUE, STUDIO 230, TORONTO, ON CANADA M5T 2C7
www.cormorantbooks.com

For
Joyce Tedman

Be still, my soul, be still; the arms you bear are brittle,
Earth and high heaven are fixed of old and founded strong,
Think rather, — call to thought, if now you grieve a little,
The days when we had rest, O soul, for they were long.

Men loved unkindness then, but lightless in the quarry
I slept and saw not; tears fell down, I did not mourn;
Sweat ran and blood sprang out and I was never sorry:
Then it was well with me, in days ere I was born.

Now, and I muse for why and never find the reason,
I pace the earth, and drink the air, and feel the sun.
Be still, be still, my soul; it is but for a season:
Let us endure an hour and see injustice done.

Ay, look: high heaven and earth ail from the prime foundation;
All thoughts to rive the heart are here, and all are vain:
Horror and scorn and hate and fear and indignation —
Oh why did I awake? when shall I sleep again?

— A. E. HOUSMAN, FROM "A SHROPSHIRE LAD"

I

One of the questions they were sometimes asked was where and how they had met, for Marc Reiser was a Jew, originally from a small town in northern Ontario, and from 1933 until he went overseas in September, 1942, a junior partner in the law firm of Maresch and Aaronson in Montreal, and Erica Drake was a Gentile, one of the Westmount Drakes. Montreal society is divided roughly into three categories labeled "French," "English," and "Jewish," and there is not much coming and going between them, particularly between the Jews and either of the other two groups; for although, as a last resort, French and English can be united under the heading "Gentile," such an alliance merely serves to isolate the Jews more than ever.

Hampered by interreligious distinctions to start with, relations between the French, English, and Jews of Montreal are still further complicated by the fact that all three groups suffer from an inferiority complex — the French because they are a minority in Canada, the English because they are a minority in Quebec, and the Jews because they are a minority everywhere.

Thus it was improbable that Marc Reiser and Erica Drake should meet, and still more improbable that, if by some coincidence they did, that meeting should in any way affect the course of their lives.

Leopold Reiser, Marc's father, had emigrated from Austria to Canada in 1907 and owned a small planing mill in Manchester, Ontario, on the fringe of the mining country five hundred miles away; Charles Sickert Drake, Erica's father, was president of the Drake Importing Company, a business founded by his great-grandfather which dealt principally in sugar, rum, and molasses from the West Indies. Marc was five years older than Erica; when she was beginning her first term at Miss Maxwell's School for Girls in Montreal, he was starting his freshman year at a university in a town about halfway between Manchester and Montreal. When he entered law school four years later, the original distance of five hundred miles had shortened to nothing; on the night of her coming-out party at the Ritz, he was within three blocks of her, sitting in his room in a bleak boardinghouse for Jewish students, hunting down the case of Carmichael vs. Smith, English Law Reports, 1905. They must have passed in the street or sat in the same theatre or the same concert hall more than once, yet the chances of their ever really knowing each other were as remote as ever, and it was not until ten years later, when Erica was twenty-eight and Marc thirty-three, that they finally met at a cocktail party given by the Drakes in their house up in Westmount.

During those ten years their lives had ceased to run parallel; some time or other, Erica had jumped the track on which most people she knew traveled from birth to death, and was following a line of her own which curved steadily nearer his. When she was twenty-one, her fiancé had been killed in a motor accident, two weeks before she was to be married; not long after, she awoke to the realization that her father's income had greatly shrunk as a result of the depression and that it would probably be a long time before she would fall in love again. She got a job as a reporter on the society page of the Montreal *Post* and dropped, overnight, from the class which is written about to the class which does the writing. It took people quite a while to get used to the change. In the beginning, there was no way of knowing whether she had been invited to a social affair in the ordinary way, or whether she was merely there on business, but as time went on, it was more often for the second reason, less and less often for the first. When, at the end of three years, she became Editor of the Woman's Section, she had ceased to be one of the Drakes of Westmount and was simply Erica Drake of the *Post*, not only in the minds of others, but in her own mind as well. She had no desire to get back on the track again, but it was not until the war broke out that she realized how far it lay behind her.

In June, 1942, she met Marc Reiser.

None of the Drakes had ever seen him before; he was brought to their cocktail party by René de Sevigny, whose sister had married Anthony Drake, Erica's older brother, two months before he had gone overseas with the R.C.A.F.

Almost everyone else had arrived by the time René and Marc got there. Having caught Erica's mother on her way to the kitchen, where the Drakes' one remaining servant was having trouble with the hot canapés, René had introduced Marc, then got him a drink and went off in search of Erica, leaving Marc with no one to talk to.

3

He found himself all alone out in the middle of the Drakes' long, light-walled drawing-room, surrounded by twenty or thirty men and women, none of whom he knew and all of whom appeared to know each other, with René's empty cocktail glass in one hand and his own, still half full, in the other. At thirty-three he was still self-conscious and rather shy, and he had no idea what to do or how to do it without attracting attention, so he stayed where he was, first making an effort to appear as though he was expecting René back at any moment, and when that failed, trying to look as though he enjoyed being by himself.

He finished his drink, having made it last as long as he could, and then attempted to get his mind off himself by watching the other guests gathered in small groups all around him. When you look at people, however, they are likely to look back at you. Marc hastily shifted his eyes to the plain, neutral-colored rug which ran the full length of the room, transferred one of the glasses to the other hand so that he could get at his cigarettes, and then realized that he needed both hands to strike a match. He put the package of cigarettes back in his pocket and went on standing, feeling more lost and out of place than ever.

He had had an idea that something like this would happen, and when René had phoned to ask him to the Drakes' he had first refused, and then finally agreed to go, only because René said that he had already told Mrs. Drake that he was bringing him. Marc disliked cocktail parties, in fact all social affairs at which most of the people were likely to be strangers; if the Drakes had been Jews he would have stayed home regardless of the fact that they were expecting him, but the Drakes were not Jews and that made it more complicated.

A dark girl of about twenty suddenly turned up in front of

him asking, "Aren't you George . . .?" then broke off, smiled and murmured, "Sorry," and disappeared just as Marc had thought up something in order to keep her there a little longer. There was another blank pause of indefinite duration, then a naval officer swerved, avoiding someone else and jarring Marc's arm so that he nearly dropped one of the glasses, apologized and went on.

The scene was beginning to assume the timeless and futile quality of a nightmare. He glanced at his watch and found to his amazement that it was only six minutes since René had left him, which meant that, adding the ten minutes spent in catching up with their hostess on her way to the kitchen and finding their way to this particularly ill-chosen spot in the middle of the room, they had arrived approximately a quarter of an hour ago.

What is the minimum length of time you must stay, in order not to appear rude, at a party to which, strictly speaking, you were not invited, and where it is only too obvious that no one cares in the least whether you stay or not?

"Excuse me," said Marc, backing up and bumping into an artillery lieutenant in an effort to avoid someone who had bumped into him. He turned and said, "Excuse me," again, and then identifying the lieutenant as a former lawyer who had been at Brockville on his O.T.C. in the same class as himself, although Marc could not remember ever having spoken to him, he said with sudden hope, "Oh, hello, how are you?"

The lieutenant looked surprised, said, "Hello," without interest or recognition and went on talking to his friends. It did not occur to Marc until later that if, like himself, the lieutenant had happened to be out of uniform, Marc would not have recognized him either. Having been turned down cold by the only human being in the room who was even vaguely familiar,

Marc abruptly made up his mind to go, only to find when he was halfway to the door that René had vanished completely and that Mrs. Drake was blocking his exit, standing in the middle of the hall talking to an elderly man in a morning coat. He would either have to wait until she moved, or until the hall filled up again so that he could get by her without being noticed. To return to the middle of the room and the lieutenant's back was unthinkable.

". . . glasses, sir?"

"What?" asked Marc, jumping.

"Would you like me to take those glasses, sir?" asked the maid again.

"Yes, thanks. Thanks very much." He put the two glasses on her tray, lit a cigarette at last, and having worked his way around the edge of the crowd, he finally reached the windows which ran almost the full length of the Drakes' drawing-room, overlooking Montreal.

The whole city lay spread out below him, enchanting in the sunlight of a late afternoon in June, mile upon mile of flat grey roofs half hidden by the light, new green of the trees; a few scattered skyscrapers, beyond the skyscrapers the long straight lines of the grain elevators down by the harbour, further up to the right the Lachine Canal, and everywhere the grey spires of churches, monasteries, and convents. Somehow, even from here, you could tell that Montreal was predominantly French, and Catholic.

"Hello, Marc," said René's sister, Madeleine Drake. "What are you doing here all by yourself?"

"I don't know, you'd better ask your brother. How are you, Madeleine?"

"I'm fine, thanks," she said, but she looked tired, and sat down on the window seat with a sigh of relief. She was twelve years younger than René, with fair hair and a quiet, self-contained manner; her husband had been overseas since late in January and she was expecting a baby in August.

"Where is René?"

"Out in the diningroom."

"Oh, so that's where they all went," said Marc. "I was wondering. Can't I get you a chair?"

"No thanks, don't bother. I can't stay long. Have you had anything to drink?"

"I had a cocktail when I came in. It's all right," he added quickly as she made a move to get up again. "I don't drink much anyhow, and I'd much rather you stayed and talked to me."

"You must be having an awful time," said Madeleine sympathetically. "These things are not amusing when you don't know anyone." Her parents had died when she was a small child and she had grown up in a convent, so that her English was more precise and less easy than her brother's. She smiled up at Marc and said, "It's a long time since you've been to see us — could you come to dinner on Tuesday next week?"

"Yes, thanks, I'd love to."

"About seven?" He nodded and she asked, "Have you met any of my husband's family?"

"Just Mrs. Drake. That's a Van Gogh over the fireplace, isn't it?"

"Yes, 'L'Arlésienne.'"

"It must be one of those German prints, it's so clear."

From the Arlésienne his eyes moved along the line of bookcases reaching halfway up the wall, across the door, past more bookcases and around the corner to a modern oil painting of a Quebec village in winter, all sunlight and colour and with a radiance which made him think of his own Algoma Hills in

Ontario. Walls, furniture, and rug were all light and neutral in tone; Marc liked their room so much that he knew he would like the Drakes when he got to know them. Apart from all the strangers clustered in groups which were constantly breaking up and re-forming as some of them drifted out into the hall and the dining room beyond, and others drifted back again, and apart from the fact that he would be stranded again with no one to talk to as soon as Madeleine left, he was beginning to feel quite at home. More at home than he had ever felt in the bleak rooming house for Jewish students where he had continued to live from a combination of inertia and indifference to his own comfort, ever since he had arrived in Montreal to go to law school thirteen years before. The rooming house was large and dusty, with high ceilings, buff walls trimmed with chocolate brown like an institution, and uncomfortable, leather-covered furniture; during the college term it was so noisy that he usually worked in his office downtown at night, and during holidays it was like a graveyard. About twice a year the place got on his nerves and he determined to do something about it, but after spending several evenings looking at other rooming houses which were worse, and apartments which were not much better and had the added disadvantage of having to be kept clean some way or other, he always gave up and went on living where he was. Now it was no longer worthwhile moving in any case, since he would be going overseas in a short time.

"It's nice to be in a house again," he said to Madeleine. "Most of the people I know live in apartments. I was brought up in a house."

Out in the hall, Madeleine's brother, René de Sevigny, was starting his fourth cocktail, while waiting for Erica to return from the kitchen. He was about Marc's age but looked older, with dark hair, an aquiline nose, and fine, highly arched eyebrows which gave him a slightly satanic expression. At the moment he was leaning against the staircase with his long legs crossed, staring thoughtfully into his martini and doing his best to overhear as much as possible of a conversation between two men and a woman in the doorway leading to the library. They were obviously English Canadians, not necessarily because they were speaking English, but because they had devoted most of the past quarter hour to a discussion of Quebec and the war in language extremely unflattering to French Canadians.

"I don't understand them," said the woman, who was wearing a red hat, which, René had already decided, would have looked much better on Erica, who was several inches taller, a great deal thinner, and who had hair which was naturally blonde. Except, thought René, sighing inwardly, that Erica took no interest in hats, even very chic red hats with coq feathers; she never wore one except in winter or on the regrettably rare occasions when she went to church. "Surely they must know that the war is going to be won or lost in Europe and the Pacific, so why all this ridiculous talk about being perfectly willing to fight for Canada provided they can stay on Canadian soil?"

"Because they don't want to fight for Canada," said the man on the right, yawning.

The man on the left was a young officer with a good-looking, but not particularly intelligent face. What he lacked in intelligence however, René realized, he made up in prejudice, and he now rendered judgment. "I'll tell you what's at the bottom of it," he said. "Quebec knows that the war isn't going to be lost if they don't fight. But, on the other hand, if enough English Canadians make suckers of themselves and get killed, then the French who had enough sense to stay home will be that much nearer a majority when it's over."

"Tiens," observed René admiringly to himself. "Now why didn't I think of that? Eric!"

"Yes?"

"Wait for me." He caught up with her just inside the drawing-room door and asked, "By the way, where's your father?"

"Upstairs in his study. He always gives up after the first half hour."

"Have you seen Chambrun?"

"Who on earth is Chambrun?" asked Erica, taking advantage of the pause to sit on the arm of a chair for a moment. She was one of the few women René had ever seen who could wear her hair almost to her shoulders and still look smart. Seven years of working on a newspaper with erratic hours had given Erica a strong preference for tailored clothes; she wore her fine, well-made suits on all possible occasions and on some which, like the recent large, and very formal wedding of one of his innumerable cousins, to René were definitely not possible.

"He's just arrived from Mexico — escaped from France two years ago on a coal boat."

"Why must it always be a coal boat?" inquired Erica, closing her eyes.

"He's a de Gaullist. I think he hopes to do propaganda in Quebec for the Free French."

"What an optimist," said Erica, and then asked hastily, "Friend of yours?"

"Well," said René cautiously, "I've met him a couple of times."

"Don't tell me you're committing yourself to something . . ."

"Certainly not," said René, looking amused. "Your mother knows him and said she was going to invite him today. I just thought you might have seen him around somewhere," he added with a vague gesture which included the drawing-room, the hall, the dining room, and the library.

"Maybe he's hiding," suggested Erica.

"Are you asleep?"

"Practically." She opened her green eyes wide, blinked, gave her head a shake, and asked, "What does he look like?"

"Like a Michelin tire with a drooping black mustache," answered René, after due consideration.

"Oh, there are dozens of those running in and out of the woodwork in the dining room," said Erica. "You might go and see if one of them is your Free Frenchman — and bring me back a drink, will you, René?"

"Rye and water?"

"Yes, please. You haven't got a 'Do Not Disturb' sign on you anywhere, have you?" He shook his head and she said sadly, "I was afraid you hadn't."

She stood up for a moment when René had gone, looking over the room to see if everyone had drinks and someone to talk to, then collapsed into the chair with her legs straight out, and closed her eyes again.

She was aroused a minute later by her mother's voice saying, "Oh, there you are, Erica. I've hardly seen you since you came in. I'm so glad you were able to get away in time for the party, darling."

"I have to go back to the office after dinner," said Erica, yawning. "Special Red Cross story — they sent us the dope but the morning papers will use it as it is, so we'll have to rewrite. After that there's a Guild meeting."

"I didn't know you'd joined the Guild," said her mother, looking startled.

"I joined last month, as soon as they really began organizing."

"Why?"

"Partly on general principles and partly because Pansy

Prescott fired Tom Mitchell after he'd been on the *Post* for ten years, because he went on a five-day drunk after his wife died of TB up at Ste. Agathe."

"Well, I suppose . . ."

"It wasn't because of the bat," interrupted Erica. "Or because Pansy doesn't like women interfering with his arrangements, even indirectly after they're dead — it was mostly because Tom was the chief organizer for the Guild. I thought if Tom could stick his neck out, so could I. The *Post* is all for unions provided their employees don't join any," she explained. "They have to put up with the linotype operators and the . . ."

"Mr. Prescott will object to your joining, then, won't he?"

"You bet," said Erica placidly.

"When I was your age, I didn't even know men like that existed!" remarked her mother irrelevantly. In appearance, although not in temperament or in outlook, she and her daughter were very alike. They were about the same height, and Margaret Drake was still slender, with light brown hair which had once been even fairer than Erica's and which she wore rather short and waved close to her head. She was intelligent, practical, and unusually efficient, born and bred in the Puritan tradition. She had very definite and inelastic convictions and had had the character to live up to them, and yet you could see in her face that somehow it had not come out quite right, although she herself was largely unaware of it, consciously at any rate. She never realized that the expression at the back of her blue eyes did not quite bear out what she said with such certainty and so little room for argument; it never occurred to her that there could be anything wrong with her system, but only, on the rare occasions when she had the time, and the still rarer occasions when she had the inclination, to think about Margaret Drake, that there must be something wrong with herself.

"You didn't know Mr. Prescott," said Erica.

"It seems funny to think of your joining a union. The Guild is a union, isn't it?"

"Oh, yes, it's a union. Or it will be someday if the *Post* doesn't fire us all first."

Her mother glanced over the room, remarking absently, "I'm glad you got home in time, Eric," and then remembering that she had said it before, she added, "I wouldn't know how to give a party without you any more. You don't know how much it means to Charles and me just to — just to have you around," she said, smiling down at Erica. "All the same, you can't spend the rest of the afternoon in that chair. Get up and be useful, darling."

"Where shall I start?" asked Erica without much enthusiasm.

"Start by doing something about that young man over there by the window. Madeleine was talking to him a while ago, but she seems to have disappeared."

"Who is he?"

"I don't know. He looks like the one René phoned about. His name sounded foreign so I suppose he's a refugee."

"I don't think René knows any refugees," said Erica.

"Well, do something about him, Eric!"

"All right," said Erica, struggling to her feet.

The strange young refugee was tall and very slender except for his shoulders; he had slanting greenish eyes, high cheekbones, a square jaw, and to Erica, looked more Austrian than anything else.

She said, "Hello, I'm Erica — one of the invisible Drakes. I'm afraid I got home rather late . . ."

"My name's Marc Reiser," he said, shaking hands.

"Austrian?"

"Native product," said Marc.

"Oh, *Reiser* — of course, you're René's friend, he's often talked about you." She sat down on the window seat and inquired, "Have you seen René recently?"

"Not since he disappeared half an hour ago."

"That's what I thought," said Erica. "How long have you been standing here?"

"Well, I . . ."

"And of course he didn't bother to introduce you to anyone, he never does." She said, looking amused, "Once he deserted me in the middle of an enormous party, all French Canadians, where I didn't know anyone, even my hostess . . ."

"What did you do?" asked Marc with interest.

"I just left. I don't think anyone would have noticed if René hadn't come to a couple of hours later and started running around in circles wanting to know where I was. I refused to phone and apologize the next day, so he had to, because they were rather important people and he'd made quite a fuss about bringing me. Now, whenever we go anywhere, he's scared to take his eyes off me, for fear I'll do it again. Wouldn't you like a drink?"

"Not if you have to go and get it. I've spent most of the past half hour trying to look like a piece of furniture and all I want is not to be left alone."

"All right, then, I won't leave you if I can help it," said Erica, smiling up at him.

There was a pause, during which he looked back at her with a curious directness, and finally he said, "This is an awfully nice room . . ."

"Yes, it — it is, isn't it?" said Erica, lamely. Something in the way he had looked at her had thrown her slightly off balance. He was leaning against the window frame, half-turned away from her, with his eyes back at the Van Gogh print over the fireplace again, and after another pause she asked, "You're a lawyer, aren't you?"

"Yes. I'm with Maresch and Aaronson. I was articled to Mr. Aaronson in my first year at law school and I've been there ever since."

"What about Mr. Maresch?"

"He's dead." Marc glanced at her and then said quickly, "I'm not doing much law at the moment, I'm just sort of hanging around at Divisional Headquarters waiting for my unit to be sent overseas."

"Army?"

"Yes, reinforcements for the first battalion of the Gatineau Rifles — unfortunately," he added.

"Why unfortunately?"

"We've just been pigeonholed for the time being, apparently. It doesn't look as though the first battalion is going to need us until they go into action somewhere. They've been sitting in England for almost three years doing nothing."

The naval officer and his wife were coming toward them and Erica got up to say goodbye. When they had gone, she remarked, "I didn't introduce you, because I never have seen any sense in it when people are just leaving."

"Cigarette?" asked Marc.

"Yes, thanks."

He felt through his pockets and finally produced a folder containing one match. As he held the flame to the end of her cigarette he said, "Your father isn't here today, is he?"

"He was here for a while at the beginning and then he evaporated. He always does. It's not shyness, exactly; he's just not interested in people in general, he's a rugged individualist. It's Mother who keeps up the social end of things. Charles can't be bothered, except at his club. Why? Do you know him?"

"I've seen him once or twice, I've never met him."

"If you'd like to meet him, I'll take you up to his study and introduce you to him . . ."

"Oh, no thanks," said Marc hastily. "I'm sorry," he added, rather embarrassed, "I didn't mean to sound rude, but I'm no good at meeting people, I never know what to say to them. The idea of barging in on your father just . . . well, I'd rather not, if you don't mind."

Erica was looking up at him with interest. Finally she remarked involuntarily, "You and René are not a bit alike . . ."

"Why should we be?"

"You're one of his best friends, aren't you?"

"No," he said, "I don't think so. I've known him for about ten years, but in all that time I doubt if we've ever had a really personal conversation. We usually talk law when we're together. He's a very good lawyer . . ."

"Not politics?" interrupted Erica.

"No, not politics," said Marc. "We stick to law. I suppose he's told you that he's going to run in the by-elections . . ."

"Is he?" asked Erica, surprised. She said with a faintly amused expression: "One of our difficulties is the fact that René refuses to stop being funny about everything that really matters. Probably it's just as well," she added reflectively. "I don't like quarreling with people."

"René wouldn't quarrel with you. He's too good a politician."

She could see René across the room talking — French, she realized by his gestures and his expression — to Mrs. Oppenheim, the Viennese refugee. Although she was not in love with him, the very sight of him moved her a little, and she said, her voice changing, "René's not just a good politician. He's really brilliant, he studied in France, and even though he disapproved of the French, it isn't as though he'd been stuck in Quebec all his life! He's an awfully good speaker and he knows what this war's all about . . ."

"Does he?" asked Marc.

"Don't you think he does?"

"I'm not sure," said Marc noncommittally.

Between the Drakes' house and the house on the street below, the steep slope was planted with rock gardens, squat pines and cedars, flowers and flowering shrubs, and halfway down there was a cherry tree in blossom. Beyond the cherry tree and the lower houses half hidden by green leaves, the skyscrapers and church spires were turning to gold and the city was full of long blue shadows.

"What a marvellous place to live," said Marc.

"Wait another hour when the lights are on and it isn't quite dark. I've lived up here all my life and I still haven't got used to it. I've been in love with Montreal ever since I can remember."

He was watching a ship which was moving slowly up the Lachine Canal, and thinking of Erica, only half hearing her voice as she went on talking, softly and unselfconsciously as though she had known him for years. She was not only lovely to look at, she was also the sort of person whom you liked and with whom you felt at ease from the first moment. Her character was in her fine, almost delicate face, in the way she talked and listened to what you had to say; there was nothing put on about her and nothing hidden. You could tell at a glance that she had a good brain, that she was generous, interested, and highly responsive. Her manner was neither arrogant nor self-deprecating; it was as though she had already come to terms with life and had made a good bargain, asking little on her side, except that she might be herself. She was wearing a grey flannel suit and very little makeup, sitting on the window seat with the light falling on her long fair hair, and he knew that she had stirred his imagination and that if he never saw her again, he would not forget her entirely.

Erica was staring at René, who, with his shoulders against the mantelpiece, his hands in his pockets, and his eyes squinting against the smoke rising from the cigarette in the corner of his mouth, was listening to the talkative Mrs. Oppenheim with a polite expression, but not much interest. She was actually thinking of Marc, however, for there was something not only preoccupied but remote about him, as though he had spent half his life learning how to withdraw into himself and observe the world from a safe distance. He had an unusually fine body and a physical grace which reminded her of her sister Miriam; he was obviously sensitive and very intelligent, and she realized instinctively that his disconcerting remoteness and preoccupation were both a kind of defence. Defence against what?

Another thing that was interesting about him was the structure of his face. High cheekbones usually went with a light skin, but Marc Reiser was rather dark; his eyes were the same greenish mixture as her own but set quite differently, and although he did not look particularly Jewish nor particularly foreign, at the same time, it would have been a shock to discover that his name was Brown, or Thomas.

"Where do you come from?" she asked suddenly.

"From Manchester. It's in northern Ontario."

Erica had spent a night in Manchester once, it was on the transcontinental line, but all she could remember was the sweetish smell of rotting lumber down by the docks, the brilliant blue of the lake with the sun cutting across the outer islands from the west, and the magnificent sculptured forms of the Algoma mountains, lying across a stretch of fields and bush behind the town. Of Manchester itself, she had only a hazy recollection of an interminably long main street which looked like all the other main streets of North America — the inevitable collection of groceterias, hardware and drug stores, gas stations, vacant lots, show windows containing approximately ten times too many unrelated objects, soda fountains, airless beer parlors, and three-storey office buildings.

She made an entirely unsuccessful effort to visualize the obviously civilized individual beside her, against a background of hardware stores, beer parlors and vacant lots, and finally asked, "How on earth did you get there?"

"I was born in Manchester." He seemed rather proud of it.

"Where were your parents born?"

Marc grinned. He said, "You remind me of the man named Cohen who changed his name to O'Brien and then wanted to change it to Smith, and when the judge asked him why, he said, 'Because people are always wanting to know what my name was before.'" He paused and then told her, "My parents were born in Austria."

"Oh, that explains it," said Erica.

"Explains what?"

"When I first saw you I thought you were Austrian. Why did your parents choose Manchester, of all places?"

"Partly because they didn't want to live in a city, and partly because the Reisers had always been mixed up with lumber in some form or other and my father heard there was a planing mill for sale there. I like it," he said, looking down at her. "I'd far rather spend the rest of my life in Manchester than in Montreal."

"Why?"

"Because in a small town you have a chance to do something. You can be . . ." He broke off, searching for the right word, and went on, "You can be effective. I suppose that's the only criterion of 'success' which isn't somehow associated with the idea of making a lot of money."

"Aren't you interested in making a lot of money?" asked Erica, regarding him curiously.

"Not particularly. I wouldn't know what to do with it." He paused, looking off down the room, and remarked, "I'd like to make enough out of law to be able to have a farm someday, though."

"Why?" asked Erica again.

"Because I like horses. I've always done a lot of riding, and I like living in the country — not out in the middle of nowhere, of course, but near enough to a town so that I could go in to the office every day. You ask an awful lot of questions."

He didn't appear to mind her questions and she said, "It's the only way to get anything out of you. Besides, if you know what a person wants most, you usually have a pretty good idea what he's like."

"What do you want most?"

"Just what every other woman wants," said Erica. "I'm afraid I'm not very original. What else do you dream about besides horses?"

"That sounds rather Freudian," said Marc, grinning, and then answered, "Nothing much. I'd like to be able to buy all the books I want and . . ." He paused for thought and added, "Oh, yes. I want a custom-built radio-phonograph with two loud-speakers and a room full of good records."

"Do you like music too?" asked Erica.

"What do you mean, 'too'?"

"Never mind," said Erica. "I was just wondering where you'd been all these years. What kind of music do you like?"

"Almost everything." He said quickly, "I don't know anything about it; almost every time I go to a concert or turn on the radio I hear something that I haven't heard before. I'm still at the beginning stage."

She told him about her father's custom-built radio-phonograph and his record library and said, "You must come with René some evening and we'll play whatever you like. Charles has everything from Corelli to Shostakovich."

Afterwards she was to remember the way his face lit up, and the way he said, "I'd like to awfully, if your father wouldn't mind."

And the utter confidence with which she had answered, "Charles wouldn't mind at all, once he'd recovered from the shock of meeting someone who was really interested. He doesn't get much encouragement from most of the people we know. Music is all right in its place, of course, but its place is the concert hall, once or twice a month, and Charles has no sense of proportion. He even interrupts bridge games and rushes home from the golf course in order to hear the first North American broadcast of some symphony written by some crazy modern composer, which nobody in their senses would call 'music' in any case. I think a lot of our friends feel that it isn't quite normal, or in very good taste, for a man otherwise as sound in his opinions as C. S. Drake to know so damn much about music and take it so seriously."

She said with amusement, "My father is incapable of being even moderately polite about a bad performance, regardless of how successful it was from a social standpoint."

"What sort of music does he like?"

"Almost everything, except that, in general, he's antiromantic. He has a passion for Bach and the very early composers and for some of the moderns, particularly Mahler."

"Do you always call him 'Charles'?" asked Marc.

"Yes. We have a very odd relationship, I guess. We even lunch together downtown once or twice a week, as if we didn't see enough of each other the rest of the time!"

"How does your mother feel about music?"

"Mother?" said Erica. "Oh, she has far more sense of proportion."

People were beginning to go. Erica got up and crossed the room to say goodbye to someone, and then came back and sat down on the window seat beside Marc again, hoping that no one else would notice her. Their guests were almost all friends of her mother's, with the exception of a few who had been friends of Erica's but who belonged to the period which had come to an end after she went to work on the *Post* and in whom Erica had gradually lost interest. Unlike her mother, who refused to believe it, she knew that the loss of interest was mutual; it was as disconcerting for them to discover that in any discussion involving politics or economics, Erica was likely to be on the side of Labor, as it was for her to realize that they were not. She had tried to explain it to her mother but it was no use. Margaret Drake had invited some of Erica's former friends today because she still felt that Erica was being "left out of things" and remained convinced that the mutual lack of interest was partly the product of Erica's imagination, partly due to a temporary upset in her daughter's sense of values, and partly due to the fact that Erica simply would not make any real effort to see them.

Having done her duty and made the rounds before she had discovered Marc, Erica had no intention of moving again if she could help it, at least until the general exodus got under way. No one else in the still-crowded room showed any sign of being about to leave, and she turned to Marc, who was still leaning with one shoulder against the wall looking down at her, having watched her all the way across the room and back again with an expression which told her nothing except that he was as absorbed and as oblivious to everyone else as she was herself, and asked, "What did you mean a while ago when you said you didn't want to go on living in Montreal indefinitely, because you couldn't be 'effective'?"

"I meant that I didn't want to spend the rest of my life in a place where no matter how bad social conditions are, I can't change anything."

He paused and then said, "I don't know whether I can explain it or not," wondering if she realized that he had never even tried to explain it to anyone else. "It's this feeling of being completely helpless, of having to watch people suffer, through a combination of bigotry and stupidity and sheer backwardness, without ever being able to do anything about it."

His eyes left her face and looking out over the city again, he remarked, "I don't know which is worse, the feeling of not knowing what's going on behind all the barred windows and high walls of these so-called 'welfare' institutions run by the Church, or the feeling that it wouldn't make any difference if you did. You're up against a colossal organization that interferes everywhere, in the life of its own people, but which must never be interfered with — even by its own people. In its treatment of the poor and the sick, of orphans, illegitimate children, juvenile delinquents, adolescent and women prisoners, unmarried mothers, and in fact almost everyone who gets into trouble — it is responsible to no one and nothing but itself. What it chooses to tell you about the way it deals with those people, you are permitted to know; what it does not choose to tell you, is none of your business. And of course, if you're not a Catholic, it's none of your business anyhow."

His oblique, greenish eyes came back to her face and he said, "I suppose it all boils down to the one question of just how you want to live, or what you think you're living *for*. You can make a lot of money in Montreal, you can be a big success, but you can't change anything outside your own little racial category.

You have to adjust your conscience so that it doesn't function, except in relation to people who bear the same label as you do, and then spend most of your life passing by on the other side of the road, minding your own business."

She could not think of any way of telling him that she knew what he was talking about, because he was talking from the same point of view as her own. Instead, she looked up at him and smiled, and then realized that there was no need to tell him. He already knew.

Marc offered her another cigarette, then found he was out of matches and as Erica started up to get them, he said quickly, "No, I'll do it. If you go, someone else will stop you and start telling you the story of his life. Where are they?"

"Over there on that little table at the end of the sofa."

Her eyes followed him as he made his way through the groups of people toward the fireplace, and she said to herself that he would stop to look at the Arlésienne. He did.

When he returned with the matches she asked him where he lived.

"In a rooming house on Sherbrooke Street."

"Is it a nice one?"

"No, it's awful. You don't know where I could get a furnished apartment, more or less central, on a month-to-month lease, do you?"

"Well, there's that new building on Côte des Neiges. I don't know whether it's open yet or not — I think it's called 'The Terrace.'"

"I know, I've been there."

"Didn't they have any vacancies?"

"Yes, they did have then, but the janitor told me they don't take Jews."

He said it so matter-of-factly that Erica almost missed it, and then it was as though it had caught her full in the face. There was an interval during which she was simply taken aback, and then she looked up at him, her expression slowly changing, and found that he had begun to draw away from her, to recede further and further into the back of her mind until finally she no longer saw him at all. He said something else which she did not even hear; she was listening to other voices repeating phrases and statements which she had heard all her life without paying much attention, because they had been said so often before and were so tiresomely unoriginal, but which had abruptly become significant, like a collection of firearms which have been hanging on the wall for years unnoticed, and then are suddenly discovered to be fully loaded.

The voices were talking against a background of signs which she had seen in newspaper advertisements, on hotels, beaches, golf courses, apartment houses, clubs, and the little restaurants for skiers in the Laurentians, an endless stream of signs which, apparently, might just as well have been written in another language, referring to human beings in another country, for until now she had never bothered to read them.

She had met a good many Jews before Marc, but in some way which already seemed to her inexplicable, she had neglected to relate the general situation with any one individual. Evidently some small and yet vital part of the machinery of her thought had failed to work until this moment, or worse still, she might have defeated its efforts to function by taking refuge in the comfortable delusion that even if these prejudices and restrictions were actually in effective operation, they could only be applied against — well, against what is usually designated as "the more undesirable type of Jew." In other words, against people who more or less deserved it.

Now she saw for the first time that it was the label, not the man, that mattered. And even if it had been the man, there was still the good old get-out, "Yes, so-and-so's all right, the very best type of Jew, and we've nothing against him personally, but first thing you know, he'll be wanting to bring in his friends." And so "the best type of Jew" was thereby disposed of.

That human beings, regardless of their own merit, should take upon themselves the right to judge a whole group of men, women, and children, arbitrarily assembled according to a largely meaningless set of definitions, was evil enough; that there should not even be a judgment, was intolerable.

It made no difference what Marc was like; he could still be told by janitors that they didn't take Jews, before the door was slammed in his face.

"Hello," said Marc. He smiled at her, then the smile faded. He stared at her, straightening up so that he was no longer leaning against the window frame, without taking his eyes from her face, and then he said with an undercurrent of desperation in his voice, "You did realize I was Jewish, didn't you?"

"Yes, of course," said Erica, appalled. "Of course I did!"

"I'm sorry, I thought . . ."

"Yes," said Erica. "Well, you thought wrong. If you'll sit down, I'll try and explain it to you."

He sat down beside her on the window seat and after a pause she went on, "You see, the trouble with me is that I'm just like everybody else — I don't realize what something really means until it suddenly walks up and hits me between the eyes. I can be quite convinced intellectually that a situation is wrong, but it's still an academic question which doesn't really affect me personally, until, for some reason or other, it starts coming at me through my emotions as well. It isn't enough to *think*, you have to feel . . ."

"I see," said Marc, as Erica stopped abruptly, somewhat embarrassed. He took her hand without thinking and held it for a moment, then remembered where he was and quickly let it go again, remarking, also embarrassed, "That makes us even."

Erica laughed and said, "You're very tactful, anyhow."

"I wasn't being tactful."

"How long have we known each other?" asked Erica, after a pause.

"What difference does it make?" He glanced at his watch and remarked, "Three quarters of an hour. You're very honest, aren't you?"

"It seems to me my honesty is rather belated. Anyhow," she said, smiling at him, "if I never meet you again, Mr. Reiser, you'll still have done me a lot of good."

"You can't call me Mr. Reiser when I've just been holding your hand. And what makes you think you're not going to see me again? You've already invited me to come and listen to your father's records," he pointed out, and then asked, "What do you do on the *Post*?"

"I'm the Woman's Editor — you know, social stuff, fashions, women's interests, meetings, charities, and now all the rules, regulations, and handouts from the Wartime Prices and Trade Board that have to do with clothes, house furnishings, food, conservation of materials — that sort of thing."

"How many pages?"

"Three or four, usually. Depends on which edition it is. I have an awfully good assistant, a girl named Sylvia Arnold from Ottawa, and an office boy named Weathersby Canning, known as 'Bubbles.'"

"Is he any relation to the stockbroking Cannings?"

"Yes, he's one of their sons — younger brother of the one

who got the D.F.C. in April. Bubbles is waiting to get into the Air Force too; he's got another year to go before he's old enough."

"Do you like your job?"

Erica paused, and said finally, "Yes, I like working on a newspaper because I like people, particularly newspaper people, but I'm not a career woman, if that's what you mean."

She broke off as René appeared, sauntering toward them with a glass in either hand. He asked, "Is there room for me to sit down?" and then remarked, glancing from one to the other, "I see you've met each other. Do I have to give him my drink?" he asked Erica as he lowered himself to the window seat beside her.

"It's about time you did something for him besides leave him alone. I thought you were drinking martinis, René . . ."

"I was," said René.

"Then stick to them," advised Erica, removing the glasses and handing one to Marc. "How do you like Mrs. Oppenheim?"

"I would like her considerably more if she didn't insist on speaking French. She has the most atrocious accent — ça vient du ventre," he explained, gesturing. "She told me I was the first French Canadian she'd met who didn't speak a kind of patois, and with that graceful compliment she passed on to politics. She's a Monarchist."

"My God," said Marc, "another one."

"Well, why not?" said René.

Marc regarded him, evidently amused, and finally inquired: "Just what has Otto of Hapsburg got that the King of England hasn't got?"

"I think he has you there, René," murmured Erica, smiling into her glass, and answered, "The right religion."

"I have nothing against the King of England," protested René.

"No?" said Marc. "But you don't see any reason why our Liberal Government at Ottawa shouldn't go on issuing official pamphlets and placards with 'For King and Country' in the English version and simply 'Pour la Patrie' in the French."

"I haven't your English Canadian passion for England," said René.

"I don't give a damn about England," said Marc impatiently. "It hasn't anything to do with England, as such. It's the British Commonwealth of Nations. We're living in a period where the tendency is toward greater international units, and for us as a country to resign from the Commonwealth is to move in the opposite direction, backwards toward a pure nationalism that's already out of date. I don't see why our Liberal politicians should make such an effort to avoid reminding the people of Quebec that they *are* a part of an organization which, whatever its faults, is still the only concrete example of the kind of international federation which we want to see existing all over the world. What's the use of talking about 'federating Europe' in one breath and unfederating Canada in the next? It doesn't make any sense."

"One of them is a geographical and economic unit and the other isn't," said René mildly. He turned to Erica and said, "And the Hapsburg question hasn't anything to do with religion either. Mrs. Oppenheim appears to be Jewish."

"That just makes it worse," said Marc. He took a drink and added, "Much worse."

"I didn't say that it had anything to do with religion so far as Mrs. Oppenheim is concerned," said Erica.

René smiled back at her, remarking, "I don't know why I put up with you. Speaking of ventres, where's your father?"

"You're about the tenth person that's asked me that. If we ever give another party, which," said Erica, "I must say is unlikely, I'm going to hang a sign in the front hall saying 'Mr. Drake welcomes you all and hopes you will have a good time, but wishes to be left strictly alone.' He's upstairs in the study," she told René.

"Your mother seems to be waving at you," said Marc.

She got up with a sigh, saying, "I'll probably be back sooner or later," and went over to the doorway where her mother was talking to two young Army officers and their wives. Erica smiled at them but kept in the background. As soon as they were on their way down the hall to the front door, her mother said, "I was wondering if you could persuade Charles to come down, at least for long enough to say goodbye to Scotty and the others. I know they're more my friends than his but I don't think Charles realizes that they're on draft and he probably won't have a chance to see them again."

"I'll try," said Erica. "And do talk to Marc Reiser if you get a chance."

"Which one is he?"

"René's refugee friend I was suppose to rescue, only he isn't a refugee, he comes from Ontario. He's over there by the window with René now, and he's awfully nice. You'll like him."

Upstairs, she found her father sitting in the corner of the study with the evening newspaper on the floor at his feet and the ashtray beside him heaped with dead matches. He was very tall and heavily built with dark eyes and black hair streaked with grey, an unusually warm and pleasant voice, and a personality which was both magnetic and charming, so that quite involuntarily he fooled most of the people he met into thinking that he was far more interested in them than he actually was.

The air was full of pipe smoke and the scent of blossoms from the garden next door; her father had his head against the back of the leather-covered chair and his long legs stretched straight out in front of him. He was listening to the short-wave English-language broadcast from Berlin. His custom-built radio-phonograph — with two loudspeakers — was a miracle of construction; the announcer's voice sounded as though it were coming from the next room.

"Hello, Charles."

"Oh, it's you, Erica — come in," he said, beckoning with one hand. He changed his position so that he was sitting instead of half lying in his chair; he was glad it was she, he was always glad it was she, and usually managed to show it in some way.

He never realized that he made more of an effort for his daughter, more of an occasion of her arrivals and departures, than he ever did for anyone else. He knew that Erica was the only human being who really understood him and with whom he did not have to put up a false front of consistency, but that was as far as he got. To go any further would have involved some disloyalty to his wife, and in all the years of his marriage Charles Drake had never been disloyal to her, even in thought.

The growing difference between one side of his character and the other, made Margaret Drake uncomfortable; she was baffled by the way he contradicted himself and was always trying to fuse the two opposing aspects of his nature by sheer force of logic. Since she was more at ease with his conservative side than she was with the other increasingly skeptical and unpredictable part of him, and since he realized that he could not be consistent to both at once and that consistency was what she wanted, with his wife he was tending more and more to be the complete conservative, emotional, prejudiced, and intolerant. In this way Margaret Drake got the worst of him and she knew it, but she had made her choice and did not know how to go back on it. Often when she came into the room where her husband and daughter were talking, there would be a pause, and she would have the very odd feeling that they were both waiting, hoping that she would say the right thing and that she would come in on their level. And sometimes for the first few minutes it was all right, but she could not keep it up. Sooner or later she always returned to her own level of pure logic where the matter of greatest importance was not whether Charles was being consistent in what he was saying now, but whether he was being consistent with what he had said yesterday. From then on, the argument fell into the meaningless pattern of most arguments between Charles Drake and his wife in which she struggled fruitlessly against a rising current of irritation and unreason from her husband, and Erica gradually became silent.

She had accepted the duality of her father's nature; unlike her mother, it seemed to Erica quite possible that an individual could have two opposing opinions on economic, political, and even moral questions and yet be equally sincere in both. It was primarily a conflict between the theories and beliefs on which he had been brought up and which were an integral part of his background and tradition, on the one hand, and the facts, as they presented themselves to him from day to day, on the other. He wanted to go on believing in the continued existence of a world which, although he admitted it only to Erica, he knew had gone for good.

Almost everyone needs at least one person to whom he can talk off the record, and in the case of Charles Drake, that person was his daughter Erica. He had a great many friends, but they were all cut from the same economic and social pattern as himself, and if he sometimes deviated from that pattern, he did not care to have them know it. He neither wanted, nor could he afford to have people going about saying that C. S. Drake had got some rather advanced and unconventional ideas and, worse still, possibly classing him as a "radical." That sort of thing doesn't go down well with your fellow members on the Board of Directors. Erica, however, was safe; he could trust her not to quote him afterwards. He could talk like a Tory one day and like a Socialist the next, without — as often happened with his wife — being informed that he was "hopelessly illogical" and without running the risk of having anything he might say used against him the next time he chose to contradict himself.

As for Erica, her father had fascinated her ever since she could remember. Because she knew when, and still more important, how to disagree with him, he rarely tried to override her opinions and never tried to override her personality. She was the only one of his three children with whom his relationship had so far been entirely successful.

Gesturing toward the radio he said, "Listen to him, Eric. It's too good to miss. He's trying to explain how the R.A.F. got through their 'impregnable' anti-aircraft defences."

Erica lit a cigarette and sat down on the arm of a chair. The broadcast seemed to be almost over, and after making an effort to keep her mind on what the announcer was saying, she gave up and went on thinking about Marc, letting the voice from Berlin drop away from her out of hearing. She was wondering what people meant when they talked about love at first sight, and whether she was already in love with Marc Reiser or simply knew beyond doubt that she was going to fall in love with him.

Her father got to his feet to switch off the radio with the observation, "There don't seem to be any limits to the amount of bilge they think we can swallow."

"Speaking of bilge," said Erica. "That reminds me of our lunch. What happened to it?"

"I had to meet some men at the Club." He sat down heavily,

yawned, and changing his tone he stated, "'The only way to guarantee full employment after the war is by a return to pre-war freedom of enterprise.' What in hell are we supposed to have been doing during the Depression — firing our employees for fun?"

"It must have been a nice lunch."

"Yeah," said her father moodily, then, asserting himself, he said, "Damn it, I don't like the idea of living under a bureaucracy any more than they do. I believe in capitalism," he added firmly, and then remarked with a faintly amused expression in his fine dark eyes, "when it works."

"Yes," said Erica. "Well, in the meantime, Mother thinks you would like to come downstairs and say goodbye to Scotty and the rest of them."

"Does she? Why?"

"They're going overseas, Charles . . ."

"Oh, are they? All right," he said resignedly, but without moving an inch.

Erica wanted to tell him about Marc and was trying to make up her mind how much to tell him and where to begin, when she realized that her father was looking at her intently, as though he also was trying to make up his mind about something.

Finally, he said, "Eric . . ."

"Yes?"

He took up his pipe and began to repack it, asking, "Do you like your job at the *Post*?"

"Yes, why?"

"I was just wondering. Do you really like it or is it just a job?"

"No, I really like it." She waited for him to go on and then asked, "What were you wondering, Charles?"

"About you. You can't go on being a newspaperwoman all

34

your life. It doesn't get you anywhere — you've already gone about as far as you're likely to go, from now on you'll probably just mark time until they fire you because they want a younger woman, or pension you off."

"My, you make it sound attractive," said Erica admiringly.

He grinned, and then, leaning forward and punching the air with his pipe for emphasis, he said, "The same thing would happen to you anywhere else — as a woman you can just go so far, and then you're stuck in a job where you spend your life taking orders from some fathead with half your brains, whose only advantage over you is the fact that he happens to wear trousers. What you need is a job where you can get away from all this sex prejudice and be given a chance to work your way right up to the top if you want to."

"Yes, but . . ."

"I don't know why I didn't see it long ago . . ."

"See what?"

"The answer to the whole thing," said her father impatiently. "Evidently I'm just as narrow-minded as everybody else."

As Erica still did not seem to have a very clear idea of what he was talking about, he said, "Look, I start out with a business, a son, and a daughter . . ."

"Two daughters."

"Miriam doesn't count. She's the kind of girl who gets married . . ."

"Ouch!" said Erica, wincing.

"Well, damn it," Charles exPostulated, "she's already been married once and she's only — how old is Miriam?"

"Twenty-four."

"And how old are you?"

"Twenty-eight."

35

"Besides, Miriam hasn't half your brains," said her father, dismissing Miriam, and asked, "Where was I?"

"Starting a business with a son and a daughter," said Erica. "Though why you have to pick a time when your wife's in the middle of giving a cocktail party . . ."

"Yes," said her father unconcernedly. "Anyhow, the point is that with you and Tony to choose from, I just automatically picked Tony. I don't know why. It isn't even as though Tony had ever particularly liked the idea of going into the firm. He did all right, he was there for five years, but I often had a queer feeling that he was just waiting for something to happen."

"So did I."

"Well, something did happen. I don't know what he's going to do after the war, he's talked a lot about staying in aviation, but at any rate, I might just as well face the fact that he's not going back to Drakes'. After four generations, it looks as though we're finished . . ."

"Wait a minute," said Erica, staring at him. "Are you offering me Tony's job?"

"Not Tony's job — just *a* job. From then on it's up to you."

"No," said Erica involuntarily. "I couldn't. I couldn't possibly."

Ever since her childhood she had had one recurrent nightmare of an interminably long corridor from which there was no turning back and no exit, except the door at the other end toward which she was walking faster and faster, trying to get away from something which threatened to close in on her. Nothing ever happened; the door always remained the same distance ahead of her and whatever it was that threatened her, the same distance behind. The nightmare had neither beginning nor end, and when she woke up, she was still hurrying along the corridor, with a sense of oppression which was so strong that it often stayed with her half the morning.

Sitting on the arm of a chair in her father's study she wondered why the mere suggestion that she should go into the family business had been enough to bring back that unpleasantly familiar sensation of something closing in on her, unless it was simply that, like the corridor, there would be no exit from Drakes' except a door which it would take her forever to reach. The job would be permanent; after all, that was the whole idea. Once there, she would have to stay, and the only way of getting out would be for her to marry someone, and even that possibility would become increasingly remote as time went on. Her father would dominate her life; she would not only be living in his house but working in his office, and at some point, that domination would begin to take effect, probably without her even realizing it. It is all very well to view a situation from a distance and vow to remain detached, but when you are actually in the middle of that situation, detachment is not so easy. Your point of view and your scale of values alter without your being aware of it. Between her father's opposition — and influence — on the one hand, and her own sense of responsibility to him and to her job, on the other, marriage would not stand much of a chance.

"Don't you like the idea, Eric?"

She glanced at him, then got up suddenly from the arm of the chair and went over to the window. There was an apple tree in the sloping garden next door, and as she looked at it, she remembered Marc and felt free again. The tree was in full blossom and half of it was white against the bluish haze of the city below and half of it was gold against the setting sun. The apple tree, the singing and the gold . . .

"You and I have always got along so well together . . ."

She could not bear the sudden drop in his voice and she said quickly, turning back to the room and the dark, heavy figure in the chair in the corner, "It isn't you, darling," remembering that in spite of all his dogged, rather touching efforts — though Tony had never made much effort! — he and his son had never got along well together. "I wouldn't be any good at it, Charles," she said desperately.

"Yes, you would. You're good at everything you really put your mind to." He shifted a little in his chair and added, smiling at her affectionately, "Anyhow, I'm glad it isn't just me."

The smile did not quite hide his disappointment and she said, hoping that if he understood it, he would not mind so much, "There's something too final about going into a family business, particularly when it's been the family business for four generations. Dash it, Charles, I'd have the feeling that I was going to join my ancestors! People are always coming and going on the *Post*, I couldn't be stuck there for the rest of my life even if I wanted to, but Drakes' . . ."

She shook her head and said, "I don't want to end up with rum and molasses instead of a husband and children!"

"Well . . ."

"After all, I'm only twenty-eight!"

"It depends on the husband." He relit his pipe and went on, puffing, "You can be a lot surer that you're not getting married in order to escape from a more or less unsatisfactory set-up, if you've got a really good job that's going to lead somewhere, than if you've got the kind of job that leads nowhere."

She said incredulously, "Do you really imagine that I'd marry anybody for a mealticket?"

"Not anybody," he said, flicking a dead match across the carpet and into a wastebasket standing beside his desk. "And not for a mealticket, but as you've just finished saying yourself, for a husband and children."

"Yes?" said Erica. "Who, for example?"

He blew out a cloud of smoke and as it drifted upwards he said, watching it, "René."

"René! René's not in love with me . . ."

"I've never been wrong yet about any of the men who've been in love with you."

"Well, you can always start."

He said unperturbably, "And I'd prefer rum and molasses to René."

"But he doesn't *want* to marry me!"

"Why not?"

"Why should he?"

"I can think of a lot of reasons besides the fact that he's in love with you . . ."

"Now, look, Charles," said Erica. "René doesn't *approve* of mixed marriages between French and English Canadians, particularly when the English Canadian is Protestant . . ."

"Don't you believe it. He's headed for politics — there's even some talk of his running as Liberal candidate in the provincial by-elections next month . . ."

"Where?"

"In Saint-Cyr down in the Eastern Townships. Apparently his great-grandfather owned a mill there or something."

"He's never said anything about that . . ."

"Hasn't it occurred to you yet that René has a talent for never saying anything about anything — even to you? And he never will, either."

"Really, Charles," said Erica, exasperated.

She sat down on the arm of the chair again. "Have you got a cigarette?"

He tossed her a package and when she had lit one, she said,

"Anyhow, if René's going to be a politician, he won't have much use for a wife who's one of the ultra-Protestant Drakes, will he?"

"That depends on whether he intends to end up in Quebec City or Ottawa. My guess is Ottawa. And if I'm right, then marrying you wouldn't be at all a bad idea."

"I suppose you think René's got all that figured out, too."

"Obviously."

She blew three smoke rings, considered her father for a while with her tongue in her cheek, and finally observed in a detached tone, "You know, Charles, you have a very suspicious mind. No matter who it is, as soon as some poor man shows signs of wanting to invite me out to dinner, you start to think up a set of perfectly hideous motives. Rather unflattering, if you ask me. Who knows? Some day some poor deluded idiot might want to marry me just for the sake of my beaux yeux and then where would you be?"

"I never had any objection to George — George — I've forgotten his last name. Anyhow, I never had any objections to him, did I?"

"No, but you knew damn well that I did." She said reminiscently, "He was always making speeches about how pure he was . . ."

"Now, see here, Erica . . ."

"I know, Charles, I know." She began to laugh and said, "Only really, you can overdo anything, even being pure. And his last name was Strickland."

"Oh, yes, Strickland. Old John Strickland's son. I wonder what's become of him? Must be ten years since I last saw him . . ." He paused, dismissed old John Strickland and back at René again, he said with a sudden change of tone, "I don't want to see you end up as an old maid, Eric, but after what's happened to Miriam's marriage, and God only knows what will happen to Tony's by the time this war's over, I don't want to see you making any mistakes. It's no use my pretending that they mean as much to me as you do. They don't. And if you married someone and then he let you down some way or other, I think I'd probably murder him. So far my children haven't shown much talent for picking the right person."

"Mimi was too young. And give Tony and Madeleine a chance; after all, they were only married two months before Tony went overseas."

"Even when he left, Madeleine didn't really know what Tony was all about. How could she, after spending most of her life in a convent? I don't know what's happening to those boys like Tony in the Air Force, and neither do you or Madeleine or anyone else. They're going to be something new in the way of a Post-war problem. Not that you'd have that to contend with in René, at any rate," he added rather acidly.

"Don't let's get started on René again."

"How in hell can I help it with my only son in the Air Force, making the world safe for René to sit at home playing politics?" he demanded angrily. "Not that René ever says anything about it," he went on sarcastically. "He doesn't even bother to make excuses for himself. He just blandly ignores the whole war except when he's talking all around the subject and then he's so bloody smart when it comes to avoiding issues that you can't even push him into it — apart from the fact that he thinks Tony should have stayed home and played nursemaid to Madeleine, of course, instead of going overseas. It doesn't seem to have dawned on René yet that Tony isn't a French Canadian."

"That's not fair, Charles," she said calmly.

He started to say something else and then let it go. "No, I know it's not fair," he remarked at last, and got up. "Come on,

Eric, I guess it's time we gave your mother some moral support."

As they reached the door leading into the upstairs hall Erica said, "By the way, he's downstairs."

"Who is?" he asked without interest.

"René."

She knew her father and found herself wishing violently that Marc had come with someone else, or at least that they had not got started on René again at this particular time. Her father had always disliked René. She said as casually as she could, "He brought a friend of his, a young lawyer named Reiser . . ."

"Sounds like a Jew."

She said quickly, "But he's the most charming person, Charles, I know you'll like him."

"I don't usually care much for Jewish lawyers," he said coolly. "What firm is he in?"

"Something and Aaronson."

"Then he definitely is a Jew. I didn't know René was so broad-minded. What on earth did he bring him for?"

With steadily rising anxiety she said, "I told you, Charles — because he's thoroughly nice and René wanted him to meet us."

"What are you making all this fuss about?" he asked, eying her curiously.

"I'm not making a fuss!"

He went on, "Anyhow, I'll bet you anything that it wasn't René's idea."

She stopped with her hand on the Post at the top of the stairs and asked, "What do you mean by that?"

"I mean that since we've known René for more than a year and he's never shown much interest in introducing us to his friends before, when he finally turns up with some shyster lawyer, it's more likely to be the shyster lawyer's idea than René's."

The half-sick feeling that she had had when Marc had said so matter-of-factly, "They don't take Jews," came back, only this time it was worse, because instead of some anonymous, ill-educated concierge, it was her father who was saying in effect, "*We* don't take Jews," and because she was already beginning to be frightened. Marc was still downstairs; he would expect to be introduced to her father, and if there was anything wrong with Charles' manner, anything at all, Marc would be certain to notice it.

Her father was on the second step down. She raced out and caught his arm and said, slowly and clearly, "Charles, I've met Marc Reiser and talked to him. I like him. I want you to like him."

He came round slowly and faced her, looking into her eyes which were on a level with his own; his expression altered slightly as he looked at her, and then he said deliberately, "I'm afraid I'm not very interested in whether you like him or not."

They went down the stairs. Erica had made up her mind that she would not introduce Marc to her father; instead, she would get hold of René and tell him to take Marc away at once on any pretext he liked. But it was not to be changed; the pattern had already been designed and laid out, and none of them could change it.

At the foot of the stairs René was standing with Marc, waiting for her, and as Erica and her father reached the last step, he said, "Good afternoon, sir. I'd like to introduce a friend of mine, Marc . . ."

Her father said "Oh, hello, René," cutting him short, then glanced at Marc without pausing and went on.

II

$\mathcal{I}$t was after midnight when Erica got home, having left the house soon after René and Marc. She had spent three hours on the Red Cross story which would ordinarily have taken her less than an hour to write, because she could not keep her mind on what she was doing. From the office she went to the Guild meeting where she heard very little that was said and afterwards was unable to remember who had been there. The Guild was slow in getting organized and every extra person made a difference. She had promised to go, in any case. The meeting broke up late, long after she had finally accepted the fact that nothing could be done about Marc, even supposing her father could be persuaded to do it. It had been quite obvious from the way Marc had said goodbye to her, immediately after Charles had failed to stop at the foot of the stairs, that he did not expect to see her again.

There remained the problem of her father and herself.

He was sitting in his pyjamas and dressing gown with an untouched whisky and soda on the table beside him and from the door of the study Erica said, "Charles, I want to talk to you."

Although he had left the study door open so that, as usual, he would hear her come in, and had in fact been waiting for her ever since dinner, not knowing what to do with himself, he said, barely raising his eyes, "It's rather late, isn't it?"

"I won't take long."

He knew that what she wanted to talk about was his behaviour towards René's Jewish friend, and he not only had no intention of being put in a position where he would have to justify an action which, so far as Charles Drake was concerned, did not require justification, he was still irritated by Erica's rudeness when he had last seen her just before she had left for her office.

As soon as he was certain that René and whatever-his-name-was had taken their departure, he had returned from the drawing-room to find Erica had gone upstairs. His wife said that she had some work to finish downtown and that after that, she was going to some kind of union meeting. He had hung about in the hall trying to avoid getting into conversation with anyone, keeping his eyes on the landing so that he shouldn't miss her. It was not that he wanted to say anything in particular, he just wanted to have a look at his daughter to see if everything was all right, and to let her know that so far as he himself was concerned, there were no hard feelings.

When Erica had finally come running downstairs he could see that she had been crying; he knew that she wouldn't want to stop in the hall among a lot of people, so he had cut across to the front door, getting there just ahead of her, and had opened it for her.

"Have you had any dinner, Eric?"

"No."

"Are you going to get some somewhere?"

She said nothing but simply stood with her hands at her sides and her eyes on some point near the floor at his feet, waiting for him to let her pass.

"You'd better let me pay for your dinner and then I'll be sure you won't forget and go without it."

He took a bill from his pocket and held it out to her but she did not take it, and he asked, "What time do you think you'll be back?"

"I don't know."

"Is something the matter?"

Her eyes moved up to his face, then down again, and she said, "Let me go please, Charles. I'm late enough already."

It was the first time that he could remember Erica ever having gone off without saying what was on her mind and for a while he had been thoroughly upset. He was sensitive to the moods of everyone with whom he lived or worked, particularly where his wife and Erica were concerned, and he had watched his daughter disappear down the long flight of steps which led from their street to the one below, still holding the two-dollar bill in his hand and wondering if he had been right to act on his hunch about the fellow, after all.

Since then, however, he had had four hours in which to think it over, four hours during which he had, in fact, found it impossible to think about anything else. He had intended to spend the evening rearranging and listing fifty or sixty miscellaneous records which were at present scattered through half a dozen big albums so that he could never find anything without searching for it. He had got out all the records and grouped them, according to the composer, on the big, flat-topped desk which he had had brought up from his office for just this sort of thing, and had then lost interest. The listing would have to wait. Having returned the records to their albums in even worse disorder than they had been in to start with, he had then tried to read for a while, and had finally ended up by simply sitting, waiting to hear the front door open and the sound of Erica's footsteps in the hall below.

In the meantime, he had come to certain conclusions. The fact that Erica could be so worried by his behaviour toward a complete stranger that she would first go up to her room and cry, and then refuse even to tell him where she was going to have her dinner or so much as thank him for having offered to pay for it, was clear proof that his hunch had been right. Besides that, even if it had been entirely groundless, what he did in his own house was his own business, and it was not up to Erica either to regard his unwillingness to meet René's singularly ill-chosen friend as an injury to herself, or to take it out on him by refusing to be even civil.

He said, "Whatever you want to talk about can wait till the morning. You'd better go to bed."

Instead of going to bed, she left the door and went over to the windows, asking with her back to him, "Why did you do it, Charles?"

She heard him knocking his pipe against the brass ashtray standing beside his chair and finally his voice saying, "If you'll think back to what I said when you first told me that René had turned up with some Jewish lawyer . . ."

"His name is Marc Reiser." The apple tree in the garden next door had turned to mist and silver; it looked like a ghost in the moonlight. "Anyhow, that isn't enough to explain it."

"I don't think I'm called upon to give explanations."

Erica swung around, so that she was facing him. She was still inwardly raging; like her father, she had had four hours in which to think over his behaviour at the foot of the stairs, but she had come to somewhat different conclusions. Still managing to keep her voice fairly level, however, she said, "It's no use talking like that to me, Charles. It isn't going to work. I've been going around in circles all evening trying to find some way of straightening this thing out. So far as Marc's concerned, there doesn't seem to be any — nothing you or I can say will make the slightest difference, it's done and we can't change it. Every time he remembers what happened to him in our house, it will happen to him all over again . . ."

"I daresay it's happened to him before," said her father dryly.

"Probably," said Erica. "After all, we Canadians don't really disagree fundamentally with the Nazis about the Jews — we just think they go a bit too far."

There was a quick flash of anger in his dark eyes and a momentary tightening of the muscles around his mouth, but he said nothing, and the next minute his face was as impassive as ever. He went on looking at her steadily, almost speculatively, with no indication of what he was thinking showing in his face. It was so unlike him that Erica felt vaguely uneasy, but she added in the same tone, "Anyhow, the fact that other people have kicked him around doesn't mean that Marc has worked up an immunity which more or less lets you out — or that I feel any better because all you did was gang up with the others."

She said, "Apart from your manners, which are usually a good deal better than that, what on earth has become of your sense of justice . . ." and suddenly pulled herself up short. She was on the wrong track. None of them had ever got anywhere with Charles by a discussion of abstract principles — though after thirty-two years of marriage, Margaret Drake was still trying! — the only way to reach him was through his emotions. Her father had never cared what his family thought on any subject, since in most arguments, he did not think himself; he only cared how they felt. Any stand he took with them was likely to be largely emotional, and to counter emotion with logic was useless; the only effective way to deal with him was to take advantage of his intuitive understanding of people and to substitute either your own or someone else's feelings for his own. Once her father started to be sympathetic, he usually defeated himself.

She said, "I don't know when I've met anyone I've liked as much as I liked Marc, or anyone as intelligent and civilized and as easy to talk to. He's the complete opposite of everything you seem to think. He hasn't much self-confidence and he didn't know anybody but René; I think he had an awful time until I came along and rescued him. If you'd even bothered to look at him, you'd have known what kind of person he is because it's all in his face . . ."

Unimpressed and still nowhere near losing his temper, her father broke in at last, "You don't seem to realize that fortunately or unfortunately, the kind of person he is has almost nothing to do with it . . ."

"What matters is the label, is that it?"

"I didn't invent the label, Eric. And I've already told you that I don't intend to sit here and be lectured by one of my children . . ."

"I'm not trying to lecture you," said Erica desperately. "I'm trying to get you to tell me *why* you did it. Along with what you did to Marc, you gave me the worst shock I've ever had — you, of all people! I thought I could count on you to back me up — you always have until now — and instead of that, you let me down. You couldn't have let me down any harder if you'd tried.

And having put me in the most humiliating position — believe it or not, Charles, I'd just finished telling him that you'd like to meet him because both of you are so keen on music; I'd even invited him to come and listen to your records! — you tell me that I'm not even entitled to an explanation."

The reading lamp standing beside his chair was almost in line with Erica and himself, shining into his eyes whenever he looked up at her. She was still standing with her back to the windows, and the pupils of her eyes were so enlarged that her eyes appeared black instead of green. Her pupils had always done that when Erica was either very angry or had gone too long without food.

He swung the lamp out of the way and said at last, "You know as well as I do that among the people we know — your mother's friends, my friends, even your own friends for that matter, or most of them at any rate — a Jewish lawyer sticks out like a sore thumb. He just doesn't fit; from a social point of view, he's unmanageable — makes everybody else feel awkward, and if he's as decent as you seem to think your friend Reiser is, after an intimate acquaintance of half an hour, probably he feels pretty awkward himself."

"He did."

"What's all the argument about, then?"

"Go on, Charles," she said.

He shrugged. "Very well, then, since you asked for it. When you've known as many Jews as I have, particularly young Jewish lawyers who are on the make professionally, you'll realize that when they choose to mix with Gentiles after business hours, it isn't usually because they prefer to spend their free time with Gentiles instead of Jews. It's because they're out to do themselves a bit of good socially. Contacts count, Eric — the more contacts, the better. You never know when they're likely to come in handy . . . particularly a contact with, say, people like us . . ."

"Speak for yourself, Charles."

He gave another shrug of his heavy shoulders and said, "All right — people like me. The point is that once they . . ."

"'They'?" repeated Erica innocently.

He said impatiently, "Jewish lawyers . . ."

"But we're not talking about 'Jewish lawyers,'" said Erica. "We're talking about Marc Reiser."

"I don't give a damn about Marc Reiser!" said her father angrily.

"That was more than obvious," said Erica. "However, you started to say something about the point. What is the point, exactly?"

"The point is that once they get a foot in your door, if you treat them the way you would anyone else, either they deliberately take advantage of it, or simply misunderstand it, and before you know it, they're all the way in and there's no way of getting rid of them."

"So it was in the nature of a prophylactic measure."

"I don't like your tone, Erica."

"Well, I don't like your point of view, so that makes us even," said Erica, unmoved.

He said almost indifferently, "You'll find my point of view is pretty general, whether you like it or not. I've had a great deal more experience of the world than you. I've no objection to Jews, some of the ones I know downtown are very decent fellows, but that doesn't mean I want them in my house any more than they want me in theirs — it works both ways, don't forget that — and I prefer to choose my own friends, and not have René do it for me."

Erica had heard most of that before, particularly the part

about not having any objection to Jews, but, etc., which seemed to be the one that was always used in this connection . . . not by her father, but by people in general. She said mildly, "If René was doing any choosing, it wasn't for you, it was for me."

What her father had said sounded all right, and there was no doubt that he was sincere; the only trouble was that it had nothing to do with Marc, and as the "explanation" of Charles' treatment of Marc, it was totally unsatisfactory. You can't offer a series of vague generalizations referring to the supposed characteristics of approximately sixteen million people scattered over the earth's surface — that was the pre-war figure, of course — as a valid explanation of your attitude toward a given individual. It doesn't make sense. Nor even, narrowing it down somewhat, by referring to the supposed characteristics of "Jewish lawyers." As she herself had just made a futile effort to point out, they were discussing one specific human being, not a category.

She watched her father relighting his pipe and said finally, "If you want to play the heavy father and start telling me whom I'm to know and whom I'm not to know, there's nothing I can do to stop you, at least so far as the people I invite to your house are concerned — presumably whom I see outside your house is my own business." She paused and remarked, "You're starting a bit late, of course," and went on, "however, if you don't pay any more attention to my opinions than you did to Tony's and Miriam's, then you're likely to end up in the same relationship with me as with them . . ."

"It's up to you, Eric."

She said incredulously, "When I ask you particularly to be nice to someone and your answer to that is to refuse even to show him the most ordinary courtesy, how on earth can you say that what happens to us after that is *my* responsibility?"

There was no response, her father did not appear to be listening. After a lifetime of making mountains out of molehills, this time, for some inexplicable reason, he was evidently determined to make a molehill out of a mountain, or determined to try, at any rate. Nothing she had said so far had had any effect; for all she had accomplished, she might just as well have done what he had suggested when she had first told him that she wanted to talk to him, and gone straight to bed.

She sat down in the chair by the radio, regarded her father curiously for a while longer and then asked, "What's back of all this, Charles?"

"I've already explained it once."

"You've only given me half the explanation. The other half is still missing." Strong as they were, she knew that her father's anti-Jewish prejudices and his even more pronounced anti-Jewish lawyer prejudices were still not strong enough to stand alone when they came into conflict with his innate kindness and sense of chivalry. He would blast away at nations, classes, groups, or categories of human beings, but to individuals he was unfailingly considerate, regardless of their category, or always had been, until this afternoon. He had objected violently and at length to a convent-bred French Canadian daughter-in-law, but the moment Anthony had stopped shouting and let all the misery inside him come out, his father's opposition had collapsed. It had collapsed too late to get Tony back, but once rid of the generalization and confronted with the individual, Charles had been so consistently good to Madeleine that, of all the Drakes and outside of Tony himself, Charles was the one Madeleine was fondest of. It was rather unfair, when you came to think of it, for whatever Margaret Drake's opinions had been on the subject, her sense of justice and her determination to respect her children's right to make their own decisions had kept her from expressing them, and now, after she had done her best from the beginning and her husband had done his worst as long as he could, it was her husband who was Madeleine's favourite. As Margaret Drake had once observed ruefully to Erica, Madeleine's devotion to her father-in-law was just another example of Charles Drake's extraordinary talent for having his cake and eating it. People with charm can get away with a lot.

"Do you want a drink?"

"Yes, please."

Her father poured some whisky into a glass and asked, "How much soda?"

"Two thirds of the way up."

He got to his feet and gave her the glass, then began to walk up and down the room, from the flat-topped desk at the one end to the row of bookcases at the other, with his hands in the pockets of his dark blue dressing gown.

As he passed her for the third time, Erica, still searching for the missing half of the explanation, remarked idly, "Of course you knew how much I liked Marc," because in some way or other, her father always knew these things, just as he always knew when someone was lying, and when a member of his immediate family was in serious trouble. His disconcertingly well-developed intuitive processes seemed to be unaffected by the distance between himself and the person concerned; three years before, he had been in New York on a business trip and his wife had been hurt in a motor accident in Montreal, and within half an hour of the accident, Charles Drake had been on the long distance phone, asking in alarm what had happened to her. One night during the Blitz he had had a "feeling" that something was wrong with Miriam in London and had suddenly taken it into his head to cable her: "ARE YOU ALL RIGHT?"

The cable had reached her in the hospital to which she had been taken a few hours before, with a piece of shrapnel embedded in her left shoulder and another one in her thigh.

In 1937, Erica remembered, Miriam had written her mother from Switzerland, mentioning, among other things, that she had met a young Englishman named Peter Kingsley, who was a very good skier, and had a job in a London publishing house and had spent the evening defending British policy in India. "Huh," was Charles' comment. He took an unusual interest in Peter Kingsley from then on, and when Miriam married him two and a half months later, her father was the only person who was not surprised. And four years later, Charles had got the wind up on the strength of nothing whatever but a casual announcement from his son that he, Anthony, had met a girl named Madeleine de Sevigny, at a party the night before, and that he was taking her out to dinner on Thursday.

"Catholic?" asked Charles.

"I suppose so," said Anthony.

"French Canadian?"

"Yes, of course."

"Huh," her father had said for the second time, and then the fireworks had started.

If all he had needed in Miriam's case was a letter containing four facts about one Peter Kingsley, and all he had needed in Anthony's case was a casual statement followed by two facts about Madeleine, then, in telling him about Marc and in saying so desperately, "I like him, I want you to like him," she had certainly provided her father with more than enough to go on.

As he passed her again on his way down the study toward the flat-topped desk, she began, "You know, Charles, you really owe it to the advancement of science to go down to Duke University and offer yourself as a subject for their experiments in extrasensory perception . . ." and came to an abrupt stop.

She had stumbled on the missing half of the explanation. It was precisely because her father had known how much she had liked Marc that he had refused to speak to him. Charles Drake was simply not going to have his favourite daughter, who was also, in some respects, his favourite human being, getting mixed up with a Jewish lawyer.

"Well, I'll be damned," said Erica, viewing her father with amazement. "Of all the nerve . . ."

"What are you talking about?"

"You and your little performance this afternoon. Really, Charles . . ." she said, exasperated, and then as the funny side of it struck her, she began to laugh.

Her father sat down in the corner chair again and finally he said, "Do you mind telling me what in hell you're laughing at?"

"I'm laughing at you. You don't seem to realize that other people just don't behave the way you do. Incidentally," she said, looking at him with interest, "did you say 'Huh' to yourself when I told you about Marc?"

"I don't know what you're talking about!"

"Never mind, it doesn't matter."

"Now what?" he asked a moment later as the amusement died out on her face.

"I just remembered Marc." It wasn't so funny after all. She sat with her head against the back of the chair and her hands on the arms, looking straight ahead of her, remarking idly after a pause, "It seems to me you're being a little previous this time. Besides, your system doesn't make any sense. It's illogical . . ."

"Why?"

"Because if something weren't going to happen, you wouldn't have a premonition about it, so since it is inevitable, what's the use of going to all this trouble to try and stop it? I'm just being academic, by the way," she added, "because judging from the look on his face when he left, Marc Reiser has been stopped quite effectively."

He said impatiently, "It's not the event or whatever you call it that I can see coming — that's pure fatalism. It's just that if you know how people feel, or rather how strongly they feel it, then you can tell whether or not their feelings are likely to lead to a particular course of action . . ."

"That doesn't apply in either Miriam's or Tony's case," Erica interrupted. "You went off the deep end about Madeleine when Tony hardly knew her and didn't 'feel' anything in particular about her . . ."

"I was right, wasn't I?"

"I suppose so."

"As for this afternoon," her father went on, "it was perfectly obvious that Reiser had made a great impression on you. Probably you'd impressed him just as much — it usually works both ways. Anyhow, it seemed to me that it was better for everybody all round to make things quite clear at the very beginning, than to let an impossible situation develop and then have to clear it up later . . ."

"Yes," said Erica. "What you mean is that an ounce of prevention is worth a pound of cure . . ."

"Of course," he said, obviously relieved that she had finally come to see it that way.

". . . and since you've always done exactly what you like, it hasn't even occurred to you to wonder whether it's up to you to prevent it or not." She paused, surveying him, and finally added, "As I remarked a few minutes ago, Charles, you really have a lot of nerve."

III

For three weeks nothing happened. Erica's one contact with Marc Reiser was through René de Sevigny, and the day after the cocktail party, René had gone to Quebec City. His secretary told Erica that she did not know when he would be back, except that it would not be until toward the end of the month. Erica could not get Marc out of her mind, she even tried to persuade her father to write him a note of apology, a suggestion which Charles Drake considered preposterous, and when that failed, she made several unsuccessful attempts to write him herself, but there was no way of either explaining or apologizing for her father's behaviour, and all she could say on her own behalf was that she was sorry, which was hardly enough under the circumstances. There was nothing to do but wait until René came back, and go on hoping that she would run into Marc somewhere by accident. His office was not far from hers, and Erica fell into the habit of looking for him, scanning faces in restaurants and theatres and glancing at everyone who passed her in the street, without even realizing that she was doing it.

On the last Friday in June, Charles and Margaret Drake went away for the weekend, and on Saturday morning Erica's younger sister Miriam telegraphed to say that she was arriving on the train from Quebec City at three o'clock that afternoon. Two months before she had written that she would be sailing "soon" but they had not expected her for at least another week.

The telegram was phoned to the Drakes' house and taken by Mary, the cook, who in turn phoned Erica at her office. Erica had no way of reaching her parents; their fishing cabin was in back of Lachute, separated by five miles of rivers, lakes, and mountains from the nearest village. Letters and telegrams delivered to the village simply stayed there until called for which, in her parents' case, would not be until tomorrow night when they would be on their way home anyhow.

Erica said into the phone, "You'd better make up Miss Miriam's room, Mary . . ."

"Yes, Miss Drake. Will you be asking anyone to dinner tonight?"

"No, I don't think so."

She put down the phone and sat looking at the litter on her desk for a moment, wondering whether Miriam had changed much and whether it would be easy or difficult to get to know her again. Miriam had never been very easy to know, and it was three years since Erica had last seen her, the summer war broke out, when they had had two weeks together in Paris.

There were four other people in Erica's office beside herself — two reporters who had no business to be there, sitting on the bench by the door, one of whom was asleep with his hat on, and his hands folded across his stomach, and the other yawning over the war news; Erica's assistant, Sylvia Arnold, a slim, dark-haired girl with grey eyes, a sense of humor and a clear, balanced intelligence, and finally, a very tall, bony youth of about sixteen whose name was Weathersby Canning, one of the Westmount, stockbroking Cannings, who was usually known as Bubbles. He was a combination copy and messenger boy who was permitted to write up the less important weddings.

Dismissing the subject of Miriam for the time being, Erica read over the page she had just written, which was headed "Sugarless Recipes," and remarked, "For someone who can't cook, this really sounds extraordinarily convincing," then pulled it out of her typewriter and threw it into the cage attached to the side of her desk.

"Who was Wing Commander Howard's wife before she married him last Saturday?" asked Sylvia.

"Margaret Denham," said Weathersby.

"Bubbles knows everything," said Erica.

"For the love of Mike, will you stop calling me 'Bubbles'?"

"Why, what's the matter with it?" asked the reporter who was reading the war news.

"It hasn't any dignity."

"I can't possibly call you Weathersby," Erica pointed out, running a fresh sheet into her typewriter. "It has too much dignity."

"Call him Butch," advised the reporter.

"Butch Canning," repeated Weathersby. "Say, that's not bad. How do you spell 'mousseline de soie'?" he asked, and then as nobody answered and his phone rang, he said, "Social Department, Butch Canning speaking . . ." then to Erica, "Mrs. Wallace Anderson, Mrs. Wallace P. Anderson wants someone from here to cover the A.S.A. meeting this afternoon . . ."

"I can't," said Erica. "My sister's arriving from England. What have you got on for this afternoon?" she asked Sylvia.

"One tea, one art exhibit, and one speech," said Sylvia without looking up from her typewriter.

"Can't you cut the speech?"

Sylvia shook her head. "Some American newspaper woman who's just back from Chungking."

"How about the art exhibit . . .?" She thought a moment and said, "Butch can go."

"I hate art," said Weathersby intensely. "Besides, who's going to answer the phone?"

"You don't have to look at the pictures," said Erica. "And switchboard can answer it. What does the P. stand for?"

"Pritchard." He informed Mrs. Wallace P. Anderson that "a member of the staff" would cover her meeting, and then remarked patiently to the room in general, "I still don't know how to spell '*mousseline de soie.*'"

"'*Mousseline de* what?'" asked the second reporter, waking up. His name was Mike O'Brien; he had an attractive freckled face and red hair.

"*Soie!*" said Weathersby.

"Where's the dope on the Burroughs wedding?" asked Erica, searching through the pile of papers and photographs on her desk.

"Over here — do you want it?" asked Sylvia.

"No, put it with the rest when you've got finished. I suppose I'd better do that Merchant Navy story," she remarked vaguely. "What's the date?"

"The twenty-ninth," someone answered.

Toward the end of the month, René's secretary had said. The twenty-ninth was certainly toward the end of the month.

61

"Mike," said Erica absently, beginning on the Merchant Navy. Mike grunted.

"Tell Butch how to spell *'mousseline de soie,'* only write it out for him."

"What is it?" Mike asked Weathersby.

"How should I know?"

"Well, you work here." Mike pondered, then as the door opened and a middle-aged man in overalls appeared, he asked, "Do you know how to spell *'mousseline de soie'*?"

"Nope," said the stranger, trying the light switch and then attacking it with a screwdriver.

"How in hell would he know?" demanded Weathersby.

"He's probably a French Canadian. Are you a French Canadian?"

"Nope."

"Put something else," Mike advised Weathersby. He got up, yawned, and asked, "Would you like us to lunch together, Eric?"

"Is that your delicate way of suggesting that I should pay for myself or both of us?"

"Both of us."

"I'll just put lace," decided Weathersby.

"No, you don't," said Sylvia. She printed the words "*mousseline de soie*" in block capitals on a pad, muttering, "It beats me how you expect to get into the Air Force when you can't even spell . . ."

"In the Air Force," said Weathersby loftily, "you are not required to spell words like *mousseline de soie.*"

"Lunch?" repeated Mike hopefully from the door.

"Sorry," said Erica, smiling at him.

"How about you?"

"Do you mean me?" asked Sylvia.

"You don't think I'd ask Butch to lunch, do you?"

"That depends on whether or not you thought I could afford it," said Weathersby, typing rapidly with two fingers.

"All right, I'll meet you at Luigi's at one." Mike and the other reporter went out; Sylvia's eyes met Erica's and smiling at her, a little embarrassed, Sylvia said apologetically, "Well, you don't want him, do you, Eric?"

"Mike?" asked Erica, surprised, and shook her head.

"That's good, because I do."

"Women," said Weathersby derisively.

"Bubbles, get me René de Sevigny on the phone and be quick about it," said Erica.

After a pause she heard Weathersby asking, "Est-ce que M. de Sevigny est là, s'il vous plaît? O.K., Eric, he's coming."

Erica picked up her phone. "Hello, René . . ."

"Is that you, Eric? I was just going to call you. I only got back this morning and I'm in an awful rush but I'll be through in half an hour. How about lunch?"

"Love to. Where?"

"Charcot's — in the bar downstairs?"

"Yes. René . . ."

"Yes?"

"How about bringing Marc Reiser with you?" It was out before she had even realized that she was definitely going to say it.

He started to answer, then stopped. "Just a minute, I've got to talk to someone — hold on a minute, will you?"

The silence lasted more than a moment, during which she sat rather nervously, drawing small squares on the back of a photograph of some officers in the Canadian Women's Army Corps. Then René said, "Hello, Eric — did you say you wanted me to ask Marc?"

"Yes," she answered, adding uncertainly, "if you think he'd

like to come."

"Have you heard from him since that day at your house?"

Damn René, she thought, and trying to keep the awkwardness out of her voice, she said, "I wouldn't be asking you to bring him to lunch if I had."

"Well, I don't think he'd like to come."

"René, please listen a moment. I want to . . ."

Weathersby was gesturing violently toward the phone on his desk in the corner or the room; she broke off long enough to say, "Tell whoever it is to go to hell," then heard René's voice again.

"My dear child, I am listening. I'll invite him if you like, but after the kick in the pants that he got from your father, I think you'd better leave Marc alone."

She said desperately, "But don't you see, it's *because* of that . . ."

"Is it, petite?"

"All right," said Erica, giving up. "Forget the whole thing. Lunch à deux, Charcot's, one-thirty. Right?"

"Entendu."

"Well, little man, what now?" she asked Weathersby. "Did you tell him to go to hell?"

"No, I didn't. It's the Managing Editor and he's still there."

"What does he want?"

"He wants to know if you've made up your mind about his niece. Say, Eric, you're not going to let her work here just because she's Pansy's niece, are you?"

"What do you think I joined the Guild for? Don't look so frightened, darling," she said to Sylvia. "Anybody who gets your job gets it over my dead body and that goes for Pansy's relations just like everybody else. Switch him on, Bubbles."

She took up her phone and disposed of Mr. Prescott's niece

as tactfully as she could and for the time being at any rate; finished the Merchant Navy story, did half a column on wartime clothing, sorted out the announcements of next week's meetings and with the Woman's Section of the final edition ready to go to press, she set out to walk to Charcot's.

It was a clear, sunny day with a fresh wind blowing off the river and although she was already a little late, she stopped to buy some corn for the pigeons and to chat with the old *gaspésien* sitting on a stool in the shade of the cathedral. He had been there with his big sack of corn and his pile of little paper bags weighted down with a stone, ever since Erica had gone to work on the *Post*. During the past six years she had bought enough corn from him to fill several wagons and had finally come to understand his French, which was pure Gaspé to start with and further complicated by the fact that the old man had no teeth. From year to year she had watched him grow steadily older, dirtier, poorer, and happier. He was always happy, even when it was twenty below zero and nobody would stop long enough to buy corn, and he had to feed the pigeons himself.

René was waiting for her at Charcot's, having somehow managed to take possession of one of the eight little tables in the crowded little bar downstairs. He was wearing a brown suit and his intelligent face lacked its usual expression of half-amused skepticism; he looked thoroughly tired.

"I'm starved — I've ordered a Manhattan for you, a martini for myself, and lunch for both of us."

She took the cigarette he offered as he sat down opposite her and asked, slightly irritated, "Do you mind telling me what you ordered?"

"Lobster, a green salad, and coffee. You can choose your dessert later."

"Thank you," murmured Erica.

"What for?"

"For allowing me to choose my dessert."

"Don't be American," he said, raising one of his highly arched eyebrows. "You don't lose your feminine prestige merely because I order your lunch without consulting you. Any woman but an American would be more interested in the lobster than in her independence," he stated, and then remarked with a complete change of tone, "You look nice, petite, though your beautiful hair needs combing. Isn't that the suit you insisted on wearing to Philippe's wedding?"

"Do you want me to go and comb my hair?"

He shook his head. "Another martini, please," he said to the waiter who was just setting his first martini in front of him. "How about you?"

"No thanks. Where have you been all this time, René — down in St. Cyr?"

"No, mostly in Quebec City. The Conservatives have decided not to run anyone against me — there's a lot of feeling about wasting money on provincial by-elections in wartime, and besides, St. Cyr has always been a Liberal riding."

"So you're already in," said Erica. She considered him in silence for a moment and then said, "Tell me, René, what's your program? What do you stand for?"

He paused, gazing reflectively at the ceiling, and answered finally, "Let me see — national unity, of course; the preservation of French-Canadian independence and our way of life; compulsory education for Quebec, more and better jobs for French Canadians and a bigger share in the national wealth."

"I see," said Erica. "With a program as revolutionary as that, you'll probably be a sensation."

Some time later, when she was halfway through her lobster, which had turned out to be excellent, she said suddenly, "You're on your way up now, aren't you, René?"

He shrugged and said, "With luck."

"You've always had luck."

"What's that?" he demanded, turning to the waiter.

"The salad dressing, monsieur."

"No, no, no!" said René, closing his eyes. "I told you I wanted to mix the dressing myself. You haven't put any on the salad, have you?"

"Oh no, monsieur." The waiter scrutinized the dressing, remarking at last, "Owing to the war, there is no olive oil. That is what makes it look like that."

"It isn't the way it looks, it's the way it tastes. Bring me some oil, vinegar, salt, pepper, and mustard."

"You forgot the sugar," said Erica.

"Oh, yes, and some sugar. What was I saying when we were interrupted by the outrage?" he asked Erica. "Luck . . . that was it." He paused, his eyes running over her and said, smiling faintly, "Who knows? My luck may be running out."

"You've always got everything you've ever wanted."

"Perhaps I've been careful never to want anything I couldn't have — that is, up till now."

"If, now, you've decided that you want to be Premier of Canada, then you'll be Premier of Canada," said Erica.

René's French dressing was even better than usual, and she had two helpings of salad.

"You are now about to be able to choose your dessert," said René, signaling the waiter.

"I'm sorry I was nasty about the lobster. It was very good."

He bowed to her across the table, and as she looked undecidedly at the tray of French pastries which the waiter was holding for her inspection, he said without thinking, "Take the one with the strawberries," and then said apologetically,

"I didn't mean it, petite. Take whatever you like, the one with the strawberries is probably uneatable."

The waiter looked offended and said, "Pardon, monsieur, but *everything* at Charcot's is eatable."

"Everything but your French dressing."

"Look," said Erica, falling back in her chair and addressing the waiter, "there's really no reason why I should choose my own dessert either. Which pastry would you like me to eat?"

"The one with the strawberries, madame," said the waiter.

"*Mille-feuilles*," said René when the tray came round to his side of the table. "And bring the coffee right away, please. How is your pastry?"

"It's all right so far. If I should wake up with violent pains in the middle of the night, I'll telephone you and you can sue the waiter. How's Madeleine, by the way?"

"I don't know, I haven't been home yet. Haven't you seen her lately?"

"Not since I had dinner with her on Monday night," said Erica, shoving her chair back a little so that she could cross her legs. "Why? Do you think anything's likely to go wrong?"

"I don't know. I only wish Tony were here." He pushed his plate away from him and said unhappily, as she had heard him say so often during the past six months, "I'll be glad when it's all over."

"You haven't told Madeleine what you think about Tony, have you?"

"Of course not," he said almost angrily. "What do you take me for?"

"I'm sorry."

"She knows just as well as I do that the R.C.A.F. wanted him to stay here and instruct, that he was pretty old for a pilot anyhow, and that if he hadn't kicked up such a fuss he wouldn't have been sent overseas just when she was starting to have a baby. It's all in your point of view, Eric," he said, leaning forward with his elbows on the table. "I'm not so enthusiastic about women doctors and lawyers and politicians as Tony is, but I wouldn't desert my wife when she was having her first child if I could help it."

Erica said nothing. The old loyalty to Tony refused to die; she could not discuss him even with her father.

"It isn't just Madeleine," said René. "It's his whole outlook on life. The war seems to have knocked him right off his base."

No, thought Erica, there never was a base, even before the war. Anthony had spent his whole life, not just those five years at Drake's, as her father had said, waiting for something exciting to happen. He was clever, and very good-looking, and he had got by all right; you had to know him very well to realize that he had never found himself, and that he had never done anything but mark time.

Erica had no idea why he had fallen so violently in love with Madeleine de Sevigny; as Charles Drake still observed moodily to his wife and daughter on an average of once a week, Anthony and Madeleine didn't seem to have much in common. As for Erica, she had finally lost contact with her brother sometime toward the end of 1940. Until the war broke out they had been unusually close, partly because there were only two years between them, while the other war had created a gap of almost five between Miriam and herself.

She said mildly, in order to get René off the subject, "You never object to your charwoman or your stenographer earning her own living. You only object to women doing jobs you might like to do yourself."

"Of course," said René. "Trying to stop other people from doing something they like and you don't is a characteristic of Protestants, not Catholics. Who ever heard of a Catholic W.C.T.U.?"

Several of the tables in the little room were already empty, and there were only two people left at the bar, a sailor sitting with his chin in his hands staring fixedly at a bottle of Cointreau and an Air Force officer lounging with his hands in his pockets, apparently waiting for someone. Erica glanced at her watch. It was twenty past two, which gave her another half hour before she would have to leave to meet Miriam at the station. She wanted to talk to René about Marc, but she did not know how René was going to react; he had an implacable streak, and leaving Marc out of it altogether, he himself had been put in a thoroughly awkward position since it was he who had brought Marc to the house and had attempted to introduce him to her father. Erica did not know how to start; she would have preferred to have René bring up the subject first, but they had been sitting here for almost an hour and he had not once referred to either Marc or the cocktail party, even indirectly.

"May I have a cigarette, please?" she asked absently, with her eyes on the familiar small placard reminding readers, "Acheter des certificats d'epargne de guerre," which was hanging among the whisky, wine, and brandy advertisements at the back of the bar. Rather an odd place for it, she thought, and then glanced at René to see if he had heard her.

He was looking at her with such an intensity of feeling in his dark eyes that she forgot all about Marc and everything else in the one overwhelming realization that René was in love with her and that his desire was an agony to him, partly because he could not have her and partly because he knew that if by some chance he did, having her would bring so much unhappiness to both of them.

The look in his eyes began to die away and after a while he remarked flippantly, "For once in my life I wish I were an English Canadian . . ."

"Why?"

"Then I could take you up Mount Royal in a cariole and kiss you for an hour and feel better, instead of infinitely worse."

"René . . ."

"Don't say anything, petite."

She relaxed against the back of her chair, feeling rather weak, and remarked at last, "You seem to have a peculiar impression of English Canadians. Also, you're one of the most race-conscious individuals I've ever met . . ."

"That's what Marc says," he interrupted without thinking. He gave her a cigarette and lit it for her, lit one for himself, sighed, and said resignedly, "Well, there's your opening, Eric. You've been looking for one, haven't you?"

"How did you know?"

He beckoned to the waiter, said, "Bring some more coffee, please," and then asked Erica, "Do you want a brandy?"

"No, thanks."

"Just one brandy, then."

"What did you mean this morning when you said you thought I'd better leave Marc alone?" Erica asked him when the waiter had gone.

He shoved his chair around so that he could sit with his legs crossed and still lean with one elbow on the table, and said, "Marc has enough trouble without your adding to it."

"Why would I add to it?"

"Ask your father." Looking away from her toward the wall he said unwillingly, "Marc liked you just as much as you liked him, I realized that as soon as I saw you together. If he hasn't

71

called you, it's quite deliberate, Eric."

With her eyes following the line of his slightly aquiline profile she asked with difficulty, "René, did he say anything about Charles?"

He turned sharply and asked with a sudden edge on his voice, "You don't really imagine he would, do you?"

"I don't know." She looked down at her hands and said wretchedly, "I suppose it depends on how well you know each other."

There was a pause. He said at last, "The whole thing was my fault," with a curious bitterness in his voice.

"Why?"

"Because I let Marc in for it." His expression changed slightly but he went on looking at the wall. "I'm not usually so naïve as that."

"What's being naïve got to do with it?"

"Isn't it rather naïve to imagine that a man with your father's background and tradition really means what he says?"

"Please look at me! I can't go on talking to the side of your face."

He turned his chair back again and with one hand drumming on the table with a fork, he said, "I've known your father for more than a year, Eric. I know what he thinks about the war, what a violent anti-Nazi he is, how revolted he is by the way the Germans are treating the Jews and the Poles and the Czechs as 'inferior' races either to be exterminated or intellectually sterilized and reduced to the mental and psychological level of robots. I know what a good democrat he is, and that unlike a lot of his friends, he does not imagine that he can have his cake and eat it — or win the war and hang on to his profits and his taxes."

"But he really means it."

"Of course he means it."

"Well?" she asked, after waiting for him to go on.

He looked at her speculatively and said, "I took him a little too literally, that's all. And that was where I was naïve."

"René, don't talk like that!"

He said acidly, "Sorry, I'm just a French Canadian. I don't quite grasp these subtle distinctions. You English Canadians are always preaching at us, but it never seems to occur to you that if you'd once make an effort to practice what you preach, your preaching might have a little more effect."

He took the brandy from the waiter's tray, swallowed it all in one movement, put the empty glass back on the tray and said, "The cheque, please."

"It's there, monsieur."

Having glanced at the total René pulled some bills from his pocket and waved the water away with, "Non, non, c'est correct. More coffee, Eric?"

"Yes, please."

As he was pouring it he said expressionlessly, "So there we were, two representatives of minority groups being entertained by the democratic majority. Don't worry, I know what your father thinks of French Canadians and the Catholic Church."

"I doubt if he thinks as badly of you as you do of us," said Erica wearily. She had realized soon after she had met him that arguing abstract problems with René was useless and that she would never be able to alter his prejudices or change his opinions. He never gave her a fair hearing, because although he probably had more respect for her as a rational being than for most of the women he knew, he was incapable of regarding any woman as primarily rational. They were first and foremost simply women, with reason a long way in the rear.

He dropped two lumps of sugar into her cup and she said, "I

only wanted one."

"Don't stir it then." He raised his eyes to her face and said almost incredulously, "Even people like you don't see how it looks to us."

"It," she thought, "it" is the war, English Canadian domination, English Canada's attitude toward Great Britain and the Empire, English Canada's outlook on the world, English Canada's superiority, hypocrisy, and ineffable Protestant self-righteousness.

"If you want to convince us that you really mean what you say about Nazism, and your 'democratic' ideals, you've got to start at home by smashing the Orange Lodge in Toronto; you've got to stop exploiting French-Canadian labor and let us control our own economic life instead of having you control it for us. And just to make it really impressive, you might take down a few of your 'Gentiles Only' signs."

"As a French Canadian you're hardly in a position to criticize us for being anti-Semitic."

René shrugged. "At least we don't say one thing and do another."

Erica said nothing. She gathered up her gloves and her purse and her handkerchief, which had fallen on the floor, and getting up, René said, "I'm afraid I just smell another racket. Did you ever read about the last war, Eric, and how we were going to see that every nation got the raw materials it needed, how we were going to continue wartime co-operation after the war, and make a better world? You should. It's very instructive."

"I don't want to be instructed that way. You're a Catholic, you ought to know that nothing can be accomplished without faith."

She got up and started toward the door, tired and discouraged for no reason at all, because René was only one person and everyone else she knew had, if not faith, at least a certain amount of hope.

On the pavement outside René put his hand on her arm and asked, "Where are you going?"

"Windsor Station. I told you, my sister's arriving this afternoon."

"I've got to go home and see Madeleine."

There was a syringa bush which was just coming into blossom against the grey stone façade of a house across the street; she would have liked a sprig of it to hold in her hand and sniff at intervals on her way down to the station.

He said involuntarily, "I don't want to leave you like this, Eric!"

Erica glanced up at him quickly and said, "It's all right."

"No, it isn't."

He went on standing there in the middle of the pavement, looking harassed and unhappy. Erica had forgotten how young he was, only thirty-three. He was usually so sure of himself that he seemed much older.

"I hate quarreling with people," said René. "Particularly you. I wish you'd forget everything I said . . ."

"I will if you'll do something for me." She said, "I want a sprig of that syringa . . ."

The notice board in Windsor Station covered a great deal of wall space, and she was standing in front of it, making a bet with herself that the Quebec train would arrive before she had succeeded in finding out when it was due and which track it would be on, when the unforgettable voice of three weeks before said from somewhere behind her, "Hello, Erica."

She caught her breath, then turned and said quite casually, "Hello, Marc, what are you doing here?"

"Meeting the train from Quebec."

"So am I. Is it late?"

He pointed to a smaller board headed "Special" and said, "It's an hour late so far. By the way," he remarked, "you were looking at 'Departures.'"

"Oh, was I?" Evidently he had been watching her for some time before he had spoken to her. He was in uniform, with two pips on his shoulders. As an elderly man in spectacles got between them, he altered his position slightly. He had not really smiled yet; she had no idea whether he was really glad to see her or not.

"Are you expecting someone too?"

"Yes, my sister Miriam. I haven't seen her for three years, she's been living in England."

With his green eyes fixed expressionlessly on her face, as though he was looking through her, he asked, "Where's the rest of your family?"

"They're away for the weekend."

He had his hands in his pockets and went on looking through her in silence, while Erica waited, forcing her eyes back to the long line of chalk figures running down the right-hand column on the notice board. She knew as definitely as if he had told her, that he was trying to make up his mind to go away, and that if he did, she would never see him again, but although she wanted him to stay so much, she would not turn toward him and smile, and try to influence him that way. She would not influence him at all.

To concentrate on something else and keep her eyes away from him was somehow to neutralize the effect of her own personality, and she went on counting the trains marked "Due at . . ." in order to arrive at a total which could, or could not be subtracted from the total marked "On Time."

"Erica," he said at last.

"Hello," said Erica, coming to a full stop at the figures 4:46. "I'm still here."

"Have you got anything to do for the next hour?"

"No. Have you?"

"Yes, but I'm not going to do it. Do you want to go somewhere and have a drink?"

"Well, I've just had lunch . . ."

"Let's go over to Dominion Square then."

As they walked down the concourse he asked, "Where did you get the syringa?"

"It was a peace offering," said Erica, sniffing it.

They crossed the street, passed the line of horses and carriages, the only vehicles except bicycles which were allowed on Mount Royal, and then started over the grass toward Dorchester Street and the broad walk leading to the Boer War Memorial up at the other end of the square.

"I'm sorry I didn't call you, but I've been up to my eyes in work for the past three weeks."

"I know." There were a few pigeons scattered along the walk and Erica threw them some corn from the bag she had bought from the old *gaspésien* at noon and which was still half full. "René told me how busy you are."

A little further on she heard him remark dispassionately, "That excuse sounded even more feeble than I expected."

"You don't have to make excuses," said Erica almost inaudibly.

"I wanted to call you."

They found an empty bench and sat down. For a moment neither of them said anything and then Erica asked, "Who are you meeting from Quebec?"

"My former boss, Mr. Aaronson. He's been there on a case all week."

"What's he like?"

"Mr. Aaronson?" He glanced at her absently, then at the old derelict sitting on the bench opposite them in the sunlight. Further down, on the next bench, there were three New Zealand airmen. If Marc had ever wondered what Mr. Aaronson was like, he had seldom tried to put it into words before, and with his eyes back at the derelict again he said finally, "Well, he's about fifty-five or sixty, quite a lot shorter than I am and three times as big around the middle. He chews cigars all the time except when he's in Court. He's one of the best corporation lawyers in the city."

"Was he born here?"

"No, he was born in a Russian ghetto. His father never got much further than the pushcart stage when his family came over here but he somehow managed to scrape enough money together to send old Aaronson to England for part of his legal training. He's been going back, whenever he could, ever since — sometimes on Privy Council cases and sometimes just on holidays. He's completely nuts on the subject of England; he thinks it's the only really civilized country in the world, and every time we get into a political discussion, it always ends up with Mr. Aaronson making a speech on the subject of the Pax Britannica. He's a complete Imperialist."

Only part of her mind was following what Marc said; most of it was concerned with Marc himself — the warmth of his voice and his unusually fine, rather small hands, and particularly, the startling change in his face when he stopped smiling. It was like a light going out. The indefinable quality of youth which was part of his charm disappeared, and then you saw that he was all of thirty-three, solitary and unsure of himself. There was a lurking bewilderment in his eyes, as though, in spite of all his common sense and most of his experience of living, he still expected things to turn out better than they usually did.

Above all, when that smile went out like a light, his appalling vulnerability became evident, and you began to realize how much strain and effort had gone into the negative and fundamentally uncreative task of sheer resistance — resistance against the general conspiracy among the great majority of the people he met to drive him back into himself, to dam up so many of his natural outlets, to tell him what he was, and finally, to force him to abide by the definition.

". . . so all we have to do is hand it over to England and say, 'Here, you run it.'"

"Run what?"

"The world," said Marc, with a gesture which included the skyscrapers which formed one end and most of one side of the square, the Boer War Memorial on his right, the New Zealand fliers and the old derelict who had settled down full length on the bench with his shoes off and with both his feet and his face covered by newspaper.

"Do you think the English want to run the world?" asked Erica doubtfully, running her fingers through her long fair hair and then shaking it loose so that the sun could get at it.

"It's not me," protested Marc. "It's Mr. Aaronson. Were you listening?"

"Well, some of the time," said Erica apologetically, and before he could go on about Mr. Aaronson or start on another subject, she asked, "Have you got any brothers and sisters?"

"One brother."

"What does he do?"

"He's a bush doctor."

"Where?" asked Erica in surprise.

"Up in the mining country in Ontario." He smiled at her suddenly, to let her know that he was glad she was there, sitting on the bench beside him with the sunlight on her hair. "Give me some corn," he said. "One of those pigeons always gets there late and he looks undernourished."

She poured a stream of corn into his hand and said, "Go on about your brother."

Marc had got up to feed the undernourished pigeon. From a few feet away he said, "Well, he's paid by the local nickel mine because they're required by law to employ a doctor when they employ a certain number of men, but he spends most of his time doctoring the people who live around there — mostly French-Canadian farmers and their families. It's pretty rough country, not much good for farming and only about half cleared; the farms are half rock and half bush and the people are very poor."

"How does he get to them?"

"He rides the freights up and down the line and goes in from there by car or sleigh if somebody meets him, and he just walks or snowshoes if they don't. Sometimes he goes on horseback. There aren't many roads and anyhow, you can't use them except in summer and fall."

"Do you ever see him?"

"Yes, I usually go up to stay with him for part of my holidays and sometimes he comes here for medical meetings or to spend a few days at one of the hospitals. Besides that, he's had to spend his holidays in Montreal since the war started. You see," he explained, sitting down on the bench beside her again, "we each have one thing we like to do outside of our jobs . . ."

"What do you like to do?"

"Fish. Do you fish?" he asked hopefully.

"Well . . ." said Erica, and then the truth prevailed, "No, not much. Somebody else always has to kill them and put the worms on for me."

"Worms," said Marc witheringly, "that's not fishing."

She laughed and asked, "What does your brother like to do?"

"Go to the theatre. Before the war he always spent his holidays in New York — he used to stay two weeks, go to the theatre every night and twice a day when there were matinees, eat enormous dinners in all the best restaurants, and then go back to the bush again for another year. Now the Foreign Exchange Control Board won't let him have anything like enough money for twenty theatre tickets in the third row center, not to mention his dinners and his hotel bill, so he has to stay in Montreal and just go to the movies."

"This is really one of the saddest war stories I've heard. What's your brother's name?"

"David."

"Dr. David Reiser," she repeated. "His name sounds just as nice as he does. Doesn't he ever get homesick?"

"Homesick? What for?"

"For . . . well, after all, he's stuck all by himself off in the middle of nowhere, isn't he?"

"Oh, I see what you mean. No, it's the other way round. He's quite a good surgeon and once, about five years ago, he got a job on the staff of one of the hospitals here, but after three months he was so homesick for his French-Canadian farmers that he quit and went back to the bush again."

Marc lit two cigarettes one after the other, handed her the second, and went on, "He tried to enlist at the beginning of the war but they found out that he was the only doctor for a couple of thousand people and wouldn't take him."

"Does he mind it much?"

"Yes, I think so. His best friend was killed in Burma last spring and he tried to enlist again but it's too tough a life for a doctor over military age and he couldn't get any guarantee that someone else would be sent up there in his place. The doctor the miners had before never left his house and ended up by drinking himself to death." He said matter-of-factly, "Dave really leads a dog's life. He's out at all hours in every kind of weather from thunderstorms to forty below zero, and sometimes he gets paid in potatoes or half a cord of wood, but mostly he never gets paid by the farmers at all. Most doctors couldn't stand it."

Erica had been listening to him with a growing surprise which made her slightly uncomfortable but which she did not wish to analyze for fear of being still more uncomfortable. She kept trying to dismiss the feeling that something about Dr. David Reiser did not seem to fit, and then, suddenly angry at her own evasiveness, she swung around and deliberately faced it. Her surprise was due to the fact that Dr. Reiser did not sound like a Jew.

A Jew describes another Jew simply as a human being; a Gentile describes him, first and foremost, as a Jew. Even if the Gentile doesn't happen to be generalizing at the moment, nevertheless the whole description is given in terms of that one specific frame of reference, at least by implication, so that the finished portrait is, at best, distorted and somewhat less than life size. The highest compliment the average Gentile can pay a Jew, apparently, is to say that he doesn't look or behave like one, so that although it may only be operating in the negative, the frame of reference is still there. All the time Marc had been talking about his brother, she had been trying unconsciously to reduce the individual, David Reiser, to the size of the generalization, and because he simply could not be reduced that far and made to fit, she had been surprised.

Evidently it was not going to be anything like as easy as she had thought; you could not rid yourself of layer upon layer of prejudice and preconceived ideas all in one moment and by one overwhelming effort of will. During the past three weeks she had become conscious of her own reactions, but that was as far as she had got. The reactions themselves remained to be dealt with.

She had counted too much on the fact that her prejudices were relatively mild and her preconceived ideas largely unstated, from an instinctive feeling dating from sometime in 1934, that so long as the Jews of Germany, and after 1938 the Jews of Europe, continued to suffer purely for their Jewishness, then to run down the Jews of Canada was in some way merely to add to that suffering. From 1934 on, whenever the subject of Jews as such had come up to their disfavour, Erica had kept her mouth shut.

Now it occurred to her that her chief problem was not her opinions, which were conscious and had already changed considerably, but the way in which she thought and by which she had arrived at those opinions, which was still largely unconscious. There is nothing in the education of the average non-scientific human being to discourage him from the habit of generalizing from little or no evidence, and worse still and far more important, nothing to discourage him from the habit of starting with a generalization and ending up with the individual, instead of the other way round. That was precisely what she herself had done when she had tried to visualize David Reiser through a miasma of vague impressions associated with the word "Jewish" even though his religion or his race or whatever it was that the adjective actually meant, happened to be entirely irrelevant.

"I'd like you to meet David sometime. You'd like each other."

She had been looking at the pigeons gathered on the walk at their feet, waiting for more corn, but something in the way he said it made her turn her head quickly to glance at him, and she found that he had been watching her and knew what she was thinking. She said, "I might just as well think out loud and be done with it!"

He touched her cheek lightly with one hand, and with his arm lying along the back of the bench again, across the space between them, he said, "We just operate on the same wavelength, that's all."

Erica scattered some corn among the pigeons, and then she said suddenly, letting herself go at last, "The whole world has changed for me since I met you. I'm not being sentimental — I'm not even being particularly personal. It's not that, it's something else." She paused, searching his face, and went on, "It's as though I'd shifted position after twenty-eight years of seeing things mostly from just one standpoint, and I haven't got used to how different everything looks. Do you understand that too?"

"Yes, I think so."

"Maybe it sounds silly, I don't know. I haven't even tried to explain it to anyone else because — well, because there isn't anyone."

She said after a pause, "I got the most awful jolt that day. It was the result of three things, really — first of all, the . . ." she smiled at him quickly and said, "the wavelength, I guess, then what you said about that apartment house, and then Charles — all one right after the other . . ." Her voice trailed off and then she remarked, "You must think I'm awfully stupid."

"You're not stupid." His eyes left her face and looking straight ahead of him he said, "Only you don't know what you're letting yourself in for. It's a lot more comfortable to be on one side or the other than out in the middle where you get it both ways."

"I don't care whether it's comfortable or not."

There was a brief silence and then she heard Marc laugh. "What a weird conversation for two people sitting on a park bench who've only met once before for half an hour! The trouble is that I feel I know you so well that I can't be bothered going through all the preliminaries. I hope you don't mind."

Erica slid down on the seat until her head was resting against the back. Looking up at a patch of blue sky between two trees she said, "No, but I do want to know more about you."

"What, for example?"

"Well . . ." She paused, considering, and then asked, "Is your family very religious?"

"No, not particularly. I doubt if I've been in a synagogue more than half a dozen times since I was confirmed. Why?"

"I think I'm trying to get an idea of the general background."

"The general background in my case is more middle-class and small-town Ontario than particularly Jewish."

He threw away his cigarette and with his hands in his pockets and his eyes following the cars passing by on the other side of the square he said, "It's funny, but for some reason or other it doesn't seem to have occurred to most people that the agnosticism or whatever you call it which has swept over the democratic countries in the past fifty years has hit the Jews in those countries to about the same extent as everyone else. There are still good Orthodox and Reform Jews, of course, but there are still a lot of good Catholics and Protestants too. The chief difference is that the strength of religious feeling among Jews depends to a certain extent on the degree of persecution, so that in general, you might find that even among Canadian Jews, the ones who came originally from Poland and Russia tend to be more devout than those of us who came from Austria, Germany, and Czechoslovakia."

He broke off and said, "By the way, don't ever imagine that

85

I'm giving you 'the Jewish point of view,' will you?"

"Why not?"

"Because there isn't one. You get Jews like Mr. Aaronson who are British Imperialists, Communist Jews who are Russian Imperialists, Jews who are Zionists, Jews who are violently anti-Zionist, Jews like me who are just Canadians or Americans or Englishmen, and if you put them all together and tried to work out a 'Jewish' viewpoint, you wouldn't get very far. There are only two characteristics which most Jews have in common, that I've ever been able to observe anyhow — one of them is a determination to survive, if possible, and the other is a basic sense of insecurity. Yet there's no unanimity on how survival is to be accomplished, and the sense of insecurity takes the form of almost every conceivable kind of behaviour from the extreme of aggressive materialism to the opposite extreme of complete idealism. I have a theory that the ghetto produces a disproportionate number of both and that the effects of the ghetto take two or three generations to wear off, but I may be wrong. It's impossible to prove or disprove it because wherever we go, the ghetto environment still exists to some extent."

He said after a pause, "The only thing to do is to go on being yourself, but in order to do that, you've got to remember when someone's rude to you not to say to yourself that it's because you're a Jew; when you meet people and say, 'How about lunch,' and they turn you down a couple of times, to remember that other people get turned down too and it's probably just because they don't like your face — not to get a chip on your shoulder, not to start looking for insults, not to misinterpret things people say . . ."

He remarked ironically, "Reiser on the subject of the inferiority complex," and then rather abruptly a moment later, "That's enough about me. Have you seen René lately?"

"Yes, I had lunch with him today." There was a group of soldiers a few yards away, reading the inscription on the pedestal of the Boer War Memorial, and as one of them said something which made the others laugh, she remarked, "René seems to think the war is just a racket."

"I know. He says it's just another war for conquest between the Great Powers and the political aspect of it doesn't matter because ideologically, we're immune. Just why he imagines we're more immune to Nazi ideas than anyone else, I don't know. Do you mind if I ask you something?"

"No, what is it?"

"Are you in love with René?"

"No, why?"

"Well, I know how he feels about you and I thought . . ."

He did not go on to explain what he had thought, and she said, "I asked him to bring you to lunch today . . ."

"And René wouldn't."

"Would you have come?"

He smiled at her and said, "No, I don't think so."

"I guess René knew you wouldn't. You know why I wanted you to come, don't you?"

"Yes."

She brought herself back to a straight sitting position and said, "I wanted to explain and tell you that I . . ."

"My dear child, do you imagine that you can possibly tell me anything I don't know already?"

"No," said Erica, "I guess not. But I don't want you to think that Charles makes a habit of that sort of behaviour. He has some Jewish friends downtown and knows quite a lot of refugees . . ."

"That's a little different," said Marc. "I'm sure that if I'd been sixty-five and preferably direct from Europe, he'd have been perfectly charming."

Erica let out a long sigh and then said, slightly embarrassed, "You know too damn much!"

At the end of a brief silence he remarked, "There's a man over there selling popcorn. Do you want some?"

"No thanks."

A middle-aged couple stopped on the walk in front of them, glanced from the sleeping derelict to the New Zealand fliers and then started toward Marc and Erica's bench. They both moved over. After another pause Marc said in a low voice, sitting forward with his elbows on his knees so that all she could see was the back of his head and part of his profile, "But you know, Eric, your father's quite right not to want you to get mixed up with me."

After waiting for her to answer he asked, "Did you hear what I said?"

"Yes, I heard you."

"I don't blame him. I guess he realized what was likely to happen, otherwise he wouldn't have bothered. It's obvious that I don't fit into your particular social set-up. I don't know when I've felt so completely out of place as I did after René walked off and left me and before you came along. It would be silly for me to try and deny it. I was the only Jew in the room, except for a couple of refugees and they don't count. I'd probably just go on being the only Jew in the room so far as your family and most of your family's friends are concerned, which isn't awfully pleasant for either them or me."

He had stopped again, evidently still expecting her to say something, even though it was again obvious that if he agreed with Charles, then nothing she could say would make any difference.

She continued to sit motionless and silent beside him, feeling completely cut off from him, as though he had suddenly closed the door in her face without warning, leaving her standing on the mat outside. It had happened so fast that to the people passing by and glancing casually in their direction, she thought they must already look as though they were as unrelated and as irrelevant to one another as they themselves were to the middle-aged couple at the other end of the bench.

Anything would have been better than to find that Marc was, in effect, taking the same side as her father. Where does that leave me? Exactly nowhere. That was probably what Marc had meant when he had made that remark about how uncomfortable it was to be stranded somewhere in the middle. Uncomfortable is not the word for it, thought Erica, and with her eyes following a shabby, very young girl who was wheeling a carriage down the walk away from them, she asked indifferently, "Have you any other reasons for thinking he's right?"

"Didn't you listen to what I was saying a while ago?"

"Yes, of course I was listening."

His voice was pitched so low that it was almost inaudible, and she could still see nothing more than the back of his head and part of his profile. "Do you think I usually talk about myself that way?"

"I don't know." She went on mechanically after a pause, "I suppose I thought you wanted me to understand as much as I could so that I . . ." So that what? So that nothing. Understanding doesn't get you anywhere; you are not permitted to make use of it. It is of no practical advantage, since the issues have been decided long ago and both sides have agreed that it is too bad, really most unfortunate, but human nature being what it is, nothing can be done about it. We'll stay on our side of the fence and you stay on yours, and that way, there won't be any complications and nobody will get into trouble.

"Did you ever see *The Insect Play?*" asked Erica.

"No."

"The last act is the battle between the Black and the Red Ants for the space between two blades of grass. If there's anyone on Mars at the moment, I guess that's about the way we look to him . . ."

He did not let her go on. He said, not patiently, but as though he had been scarcely listening, "I was trying to give you the other side of your father's case, Eric."

"My father's case is already quite complete, you needn't have bothered. Anyhow, I didn't take it that way. I thought it was the case for the defence."

"No, it wasn't. With things as they are, you haven't any case and neither have I, and if I'd had any sense, I'd have said, 'Hello, how are you,' and left you standing by the notice board trying to find the train from Quebec under 'Departures.'"

That was as much as Erica could stand.

She said, "Well, better luck next time. You came pretty close to it, anyhow," and got up, adding over her shoulder as she started away from the bench, "I guess we'd better be getting back."

He caught up with her after a few steps, but she said nothing to him all the way back down the square, across Dorchester Street, past the line of carriages, through the arched stone entrance of the station and along the concourse to Track 5, where Miriam's and Mr. Aaronson's train was already in sight, far down at the other end of the long shed.

He was standing beside her in the crowd behind the rope barrier by the gate when he said suddenly, "I meant to buy you some flowers."

For one appalling moment Erica thought she was going to cry. She blinked, swallowed, kept her eyes fixed on a sergeant of the Provost Corps who was standing just inside the gate talking to a railway policeman, and when the danger had passed, she asked stonily, "What for? As a sort of going-away present?"

"Don't be a bloody fool!" said Marc, exasperated.

Then suddenly it was all over. She said, "You can't call me a bloody fool the second time we meet, it isn't polite." She let out her breath in a long sigh of relief and then asked with interest, "What kind of flowers would you have bought me?"

"I don't know. What kind do you like?"

She glanced down at her beige suit, observing tentatively, "Everything seems to go with it . . ." and, after another pause, "I think I would have liked dark red carnations."

"Supposing there weren't any?"

"Then I would have liked white carnations."

"I object to this persistent use of the past conditional," said Marc. "I'm asking you for purposes of future reference so the least you can do is put it in the indicative. Do you always insist on carnations?"

"No," said Erica faintly, "just get whatever you like."

The train had stopped and as the first passengers began to appear on the long platform stretching away from the gate, he asked, "Could we have dinner together some night next week?"

She turned suddenly so that she was facing him and said quickly, looking up into his oblique, greenish eyes, "Are you sure you want to?"

"I told you I haven't any sense," he said under his breath. "Wednesday?"

"I'd love to."

"I'll call for you about seven. There's Mr. Aaronson."

"Which one is he?" asked Erica.

"The fat man with the briefcase and the cigar, just in front of those two sailors. Do you see your sister anywhere?"

"It's much too early for Miriam to put in an appearance. She's always the last one off." She drew back a little as Mr. Aaronson came through the gate and said, "You'd better go, hadn't you?"

"Yes, I guess so. Goodbye, Eric, see you Wednesday."

"Goodbye, Marc."

The long concrete platform was empty except for a few straggling passengers, some porters and a noisy little motor pulling half a dozen clattering freight wagons toward the baggage room when she caught sight of Miriam at last, stepping down from a car near the other end.

She was wearing a black suit with a foam of white at her throat, carrying her hat in her hand and walking rapidly with that extraordinary grace which characterized all her movements. She was perfectly proportioned, tall, slender and yet fully developed, what the French call *fausse mince*, with her father's dark eyes and dark hair, and her own almost flawless features, the only really beautiful woman Erica had ever known who seemed to take her own beauty for granted. She seldom made use of it and when she did, it was always with her tongue in her cheek and usually in order to manoeuvre her way out of a ticket for speeding, or past a gateman. People in general did not interest her, and she could rarely be bothered to go out of her way for anyone. Most of the men who fell in love with her bored her; she would put up with their efforts to make an impression for just so long and then, because they always turned out to want just one thing, and worse still, were apparently incapable of believing that she herself could really be interested in anything else, still wholly unimpressed, Miriam would proceed to get rid of them. In spite of her appearance, she had a pronounced intellectual streak which was generally ignored by all unattached men under sixty, and she had grown thoroughly tired of always discussing the same subject. She had told Erica when they had been together in Paris three years before, that it was like being expected to subsist entirely on a diet of cake, adding with an abrupt change of expression that it was not as though cake had ever agreed with her very well either.

She had always been uncommunicative, and that remark in Paris was one of the most revealing that Erica had ever heard from Miriam.

As soon as she saw Erica standing by the barrier, Miriam began to run, lifting her shoulders and half turning her body like a dancer to get past the few remaining people at the gate.

"Eric!"

"Hello, darling," said Erica with a catch in her throat. She kissed her sister somewhere near her ear, then drew back and looked up into the glowing dark eyes a little above her own. "How are you? Is everything all right? We've been scared to death ever since we got your letter about coming back. What kind of crossing did you have?"

"Just a minute," said Miriam. "Where are Mother and Dad?"

"They're up in the mountains for the weekend, I couldn't reach them. If you'd only had enough sense to wire from Halifax . . ."

"When will they be back?"

"Tomorrow night."

"How are they?"

"Oh, fine, although Mother still doesn't know how to say 'No' when people ask her to take on still more war-work. Three years are too long if you're that conscientious, and not so young as you once were; she's practically worn out and so are most of her friends."

"And how about you?" asked Miriam as they started after the porter who was trundling Miriam's luggage toward the station entrance.

"I'm still on the *Post*," said Erica.

"My God."

Erica did not know what she meant by that exactly. She asked, "How's Tony?"

"Having the time of his life. You knew he'd been promoted, didn't you?"

"Yes."

In the cab Erica said, "You'll have to go and see Madeleine tonight, or sometime tomorrow anyhow . . ."

"Why the rush?"

"Because she'll be dying to hear about Tony, of course. How long is it since you've seen him?"

"About three weeks."

"Well, it's almost six months since Madeleine's seen him." There was evidently still a lot about people which Miriam didn't grasp until it was explained to her. "How's Peter?" asked Erica idly.

"He's been missing since Hong Kong," said Miriam in the same tone in which she would have said that her ex-husband was lunching at his club. They had gone three blocks when she suddenly added, "I spent his last leave with him in London. It was the one thing he seemed to want and I . . ." She broke off and then observed, "I guess there are times when it means a lot less to you to do something than not doing it means to someone else. There must be quite a few women in the world who have gone to bed with motives which, in almost any other form of human conduct, would be regarded as thoroughly unselfish," she remarked in the quizzical tone which characterized most of Miriam's more serious utterances. "Still, we'd been divorced for over a year by that time, so perhaps you'd better not mention it to the family."

"I wasn't thinking of mentioning it," said Erica absently, suddenly struck by the change in her sister's face. Something had happened to her sister since Erica had last seen her; she had lost the rather guarded and slightly inscrutable expression she had had as long as Erica could remember. She was leaning forward, looking out the open windows of the cab on first one side and then the other; her dark hair was blown back and along with her eagerness to see everything that there was to be seen along the way from the station to the home which she had left six years before, there was another quality, an inner light reflected softly in her face which made her more beautiful than ever.

They were winding their way up through Westmount, past the big houses set in their own gardens which sloped steeply down to the retaining wall running along the inner edge of the pavement. A little more of Montreal became visible with each hairpin turn in the road until at last they reached the street where the Drakes lived and the whole city lay spread out in the sunlight.

Erica had forgotten her key and had to ring the doorbell. "Hello, Mary," she said, when their plump, grey-haired cook appeared. "This is my sister, Miss Miriam."

As the taxi driver carried Miriam's luggage into the hall, Erica saw Mary glance at Miriam from time to time, as though, like so many people, she would not believe at first that Miriam was quite real. Or that she could be my sister, though Erica, feeling discouraged. Nobody had ever looked at her like that.

When the three of them had carried the bags up from the hall and into Miriam's pale-green and beige bedroom, Mary paused in the doorway, still plainly beglamoured, and asked, "Is there anything you'd like, Miss Miriam?"

"Yes," said Miriam, throwing her hat on the bed. "I want

some oranges, lots and lots of oranges."

She went over to the windows which faced the mountain and said whistling, "My gosh, look at that garden," her eyes traveling slowly up from the retaining wall across the street, past flowering shrubs, a fountain, some dwarf cedars, and innumerable flower beds to the summer house at the top. "If it was England, it would be full of carrots."

"Come on," said Erica, "let's unpack and get it over with."

Sometime later, as she was on her way to the cupboard with an armful of shoes, Erica asked, "Mimi, why did you come back? You wouldn't leave during the Blitz . . ."

"I know, but we weren't being blitzed any more." She paused and said with her back to Erica, "I came because someone else did."

"Did he come with you?"

"No. He's been over here for about a month."

"Whereabouts?"

"I don't know exactly — Washington and Ottawa, I guess. He's on the Purchasing Commission."

"English?"

Miriam straightened up, having put the last of her underwear into the chest of drawers, and glancing at her three suitcases lying open and now almost empty in a row on the window seat, she said, "No, one of those Americans who has lived all over the place and might be almost anything. Sit down, Eric, I'll finish up. There isn't much left."

"Are you going to marry him?" asked Erica after a brief silence.

"Not at the moment anyhow. He's already got a wife somewhere in California. They've been separated for five years."

"Do you think . . ."

"I don't think," said Miriam with her back to Erica again.

"I just hope."

"How old is he?"

"Forty-two."

"Here are your oranges, Miss Miriam," said Mary from the door.

"Put them over there by the bed, will you, please?"

On her way out again Mary said, "I'll take your bags up to the storeroom if you're ready with them, Miss Miriam."

"Thanks, Mary."

Erica helped her move the bags as far as the hall, closed the door again and went over to the chaise longue in the corner. She lit a cigarette and smoked in silence while Miriam changed into a flowered housecoat, and sitting cross-legged in the center of her bed, began peeling an orange. Finally Erica asked, "Why are you so much in love with him, Mimi?" thinking that anyone who had known Miriam before had only to look at her now to realize how much that was.

It was a silly question to ask anyone, particularly Miriam, who had always disliked personal questions even when she knew the answer, and Erica was startled to hear her say rather slowly a moment later, "You don't know how much he's done for me, Eric. He's given me something that I've never had before. I didn't think I ever would have it. Some women manage to be philosophical about it — they even manage to go on being married and make up for what they're missing by raising a family and having 'outside interests.' I don't know how they do it. I couldn't."

She ate two slices of orange and said, "The worst of it was that I didn't look the part, and I got so sick of having men make passes at me that by the time I met Max, I'd reacted so violently against the whole business that what I really needed was a psychiatrist."

97

"Or Max," said Erica.

"Yes," said Miriam, half smiling to herself. "Or Max. Are you shocked?"

"What about?" asked Erica, bewildered. "What kind of person do you think I am?"

"You?" Miriam scrutinized her in silence and said finally, "You're the best of the three of us, you're the one everybody depends on. Tony and I just do what we want, but you spend your life doing what other people want. You're the sucker. They say there's one in every family," she added.

"Thanks," said Erica.

There was a bird singing in the tree outside the bedroom windows and they could hear the fountain splashing in the garden across the street. Downstairs the telephone began to ring and Miriam turned her head toward the door to listen, then as Mary's footsteps retreated into the kitchen again she said, relaxing, "I guess it must have been for Mother or Dad."

"Do you think he'll call you today?"

"I don't know. I sent him a wire to the Mount Royal because he expected to be in Ottawa this week and said he'd be here for the weekend but he may not have been able to make it."

"Why don't you phone and find out?"

"If he's here he'll call me."

"What's his last name?"

"Eliot."

"Throw me an orange, will you?" asked Erica. She caught it and began peeling. "What did you mean when you said I was a sucker?"

"I don't know. You've never even thought of getting out and living somewhere else, have you?"

"Why should I?"

"Because you're the sort of person who ought to be married, not staying home and keeping your parents company year after year."

Miriam lit a cigarette, looked about for an ashtray and failing to see any but the one Erica was using on the other side of the room, she rolled over and reached out for the wastebasket. The wastebasket was some distance away and anyone else, thought Erica, watching her fascinated, would have fallen off the bed. But not Miriam. She stretched out, half her body apparently supported by nothing, picked up the basket and deposited it beside her, then rolled over and back all in one movement until she was lying down with her head against the pillows again.

"I suppose you realize that there's never going to be anyone Charles will let you marry."

"Why not?"

"You're too important to him. Sometimes I think he could get along without Mother better than he could without you, at least in some ways. It isn't just that he adores you. It's more complicated than that."

Miriam paused, frowning at the wall above Erica's head. Finally she went on, "I remember when he and Mother were in London last time he was always saying how interested you would have been in some speech or other and cutting things out of the papers to send to you. More or less radical ideas that should have shocked him, didn't seem to shock him at all . . ."

"Charles is a lot more radical than most people think," interrupted Erica. "He just doesn't want to be labeled, that's all. I don't know exactly where he stands, but it's certainly somewhere to the left of center . . ."

"Because of you," said Miriam.

"It's not because of me," Erica said impatiently. "He's too much aware of things and has too much heart to belong to the Right."

"Maybe, but he's pretty deeply rooted in the past too." Miriam paused again, watching the smoke from her cigarette drifting toward the window, and finally she remarked, "I don't think you or I can begin to realize how completely cockeyed everything must seem to people who are so aware of events and at the same time so conditioned by pre-Depression ideas on almost every subject as Charles. If he could fool himself like his friends he'd be all right, but he can't. He knows he'll never be rich again . . ."

"That isn't what matters," said Erica. Fundamentally, Charles isn't really awfully interested in money."

"I know. What does matter, though, is the fact that every-thing looks so horribly unsettled. He doesn't know where he's at now, and still less where he's going to be ten years from now. All he knows is that whatever is coming, it won't be his kind of world, and he's scared, or he would be if it weren't for you. He has a lot of respect for you — you know the way he's always saying that 'Erica's got her head screwed on straight.' And besides, you know how to talk to him without putting his back up . . ."

"It's perfectly simple . . ." began Erica.

"It may be simple for you but it isn't for the rest of us! Anyhow, the point is that Charles will listen to you. You're about the only person who isn't hopelessly committed to the past that he *will* listen to. So far as he's concerned, you're about his only bridge between the past and the future because you can translate ideas into terms he can understand and because, when you say something, it makes sense. He's going to hang on to you as long as he possibly can, and I'm willing to bet you anything you like that no matter whom you pick, Charles will try to stop you from marrying him."

"There's no way he can stop me," said Erica. "This is 1942, not 1867 . . ."

Looking at her rather oddly, Erica thought, Miriam interrupted, "And as a situation, it's been so overdone and it's so out of date that it just couldn't happen to you, could it?"

"What do you expect Charles to do? Lock me up in my room and feed me on bread and water until I come to my senses?"

"He doesn't have to do that, Eric — so long as you're living here, he can work on you without your ever even realizing it."

"Look," said Erica patiently. "You got married when Charles thought you were far too young and Tony married someone he didn't approve of at all — even if Charles doesn't want to let me go, if you two could get away with it, why can't I?"

"He didn't care half as much about us." She said rather deliberately, "And we didn't care half as much about him either."

"And you forget one thing," said Erica. "I have far more influence on Charles than you ever had."

"You'll probably need it."

A door slammed somewhere downstairs and Miriam started, then said lightly, "If you're determined to stick around until someone decides to come and rescue you from your overly devoted father, at least pick a man who's got all the necessary qualifications and a couple of extra ones for good measure, so that Charles won't have any valid grounds for objecting. He'll object anyhow, but you might just as well make it as tough for him as you can . . ."

"I wish you'd shut up," said Erica with sudden violence.

Miriam glanced at her quickly and after a pause she said,

"I'm sorry, Eric."

"It's all right. Do you want this orange? It's all peeled."

"Don't you want it?"

"No." She got up and gave it to Miriam, then went over to the window and sat down on the seat with her hands in the pockets of her jacket. She said, looking down at the toe of her shoe, "I have picked someone, only he hasn't got the necessary qualifications — he came to a cocktail party here with René, and Charles refused to meet him."

"My God, what was he?" asked Miriam in amazement.

"A Jewish lawyer."

"Oh." She said as though she were reading aloud to herself. "Mr. and Mrs. Charles Sickert Drake announce the engagement of their daughter, Erica Elizabeth, to a Jewish lawyer . . ." She broke off and said, "Well, never mind, Eric, you can count on me anyhow. What's he like?"

"He's about six feet, with brown hair and eyes about the same color as mine, but they slant . . ."

"Upwards or downwards?" inquired Miriam with interest.

"Upwards, you ass!"

"That's good. Otherwise I should think he'd have rather a droopy look — you know, like a bloodhound. Is he good-looking?"

"Not particularly, he's just attractive. Nice shoulders and no hips. His skin is dark enough so that he won't look as though he's come out from under a stone the first time he goes swimming — you know, that sort of golden skin that's very smooth . . ."

"How many times have you met this guy?"

"Just twice."

"I must say you notice a lot," said Miriam admiringly. "And what sort of person is René?"

"Thirty-four, dark, aquiline, slightly satirical, very intelligent, and very Catholic."

"Very Quebec Catholic?"

"I don't know. We usually try to stay off the subject. I somehow can't see René with twelve children, but you never can tell. We might even invite ourselves there for dinner tomorrow night. Mary's going to be out."

"For heaven's sake let's get ourselves invited somewhere, then."

"You'd better leave out the part about Tony 'having the time of his life' when you're talking to Madeleine and René. Madeleine still has too many illusions about Tony and René hasn't enough. I suppose there's someone else in the picture?" she asked.

"Well, there was for a while anyhow. I don't know whether it's still going on or not, and if it is, how much it means to Tony or how far it goes. She was certainly nuts about him, at any rate. I ran into them together a couple of times."

"So here's Madeleine," said Erica, "having a baby in August and saying, 'Of course Tony always hated writing letters, and anyhow he's so busy, and besides there are so many sinkings that we're not getting half the English mails . . .'" She said furiously, "I could break his bloody neck!"

Miriam said calmly, "You can't imagine the sort of life he leads now, Eric. These are extraordinary circumstances . . ." she began and stopped, confused by the sheer inanity of her own remark. "Anyhow, Madeleine doesn't need to know anything about it," she added at last.

They were silent for a while and then Erica said idly, "John Gardiner's been phoning practically every day for the last month to see if you'd got here yet . . ."

"Good Old Faithful," said Miriam. "Is he still strong and silent and full of ideals?"

"I guess so," said Erica, uncomfortably. The description,

while recognizable, did not strike her as quite just, although there was no doubt that so far as his attitude toward Miriam was concerned, John was certainly too full of ideals for his own good. Erica had had to spend a good many evenings off and on during the past eight years listening to John on the subject of Miriam, and half the time he had sounded as though he were talking about someone else. Or so she had thought, but now Erica was beginning to wonder. It was possible that he had not been so far off the track after all. Unlike the rest of them, he had never regarded Miriam as impervious; unlike Charles and Margaret Drake he had never believed that Miriam had divorced Peter Kingsley "for no really good reason"; John had said over and over again that Miriam was altogether too vulnerable, that her emotions were likely to run away with her, that her ex-husband had given her a "raw deal" — Erica did not know exactly how John had worked that out for himself — and that what Miriam needed was someone to look after her. All of which, Erica reflected, might turn out to be true after all.

"How is he?" asked Miriam, turning her head toward the door again as the telephone rang.

"He's still mad about being sent back from England just because he's bilingual. Apparently they're short of bilingual officers."

Miriam finished her second orange and then asked suddenly, "Why don't you tell him what I'm really like, Eric? He still thinks I'm some kind of superfatted angel. After all this time, he deserves a break."

"Maybe he knows," said Erica.

There was a knock on the door and Mary said, "The telephone's for you, Miss Miriam — a Mr. Eliot. I called you but I guess you didn't hear me . . ."

Miriam was off the bed and out the door before Mary had

finished her sentence.

From the window Erica said resignedly, "I'll be alone for dinner after all, Mary."

"Yes, Miss Drake," she said, and then added vaguely, "but it's only a quarter past six and maybe something will turn up."

"At a quarter past six?" asked Erica. "Well, maybe." She got up from the window seat, wandered about for a while after Mary had gone, then decided she would kill the next half hour by taking a bath.

When the telephone rang again she did not hear it; she was cold-creaming her face in her bathroom with both taps running.

"Miss Drake . . ."

"Yes, Mary?"

"You're wanted on the phone." As Erica opened the door Mary said happily, "It's a gentleman, Miss Drake. I told you something would turn up."

Erica went off down the hall to her mother's room to answer. By the time she got there, she had succeeded in convincing herself that it could not possibly be Marc, and that it was probably someone from the *Post*. Thus fortified against the inevitable letdown, she picked up the phone, sat down on the edge of her mother's bed and said, "Hello?"

"Hello, this is Marc Reiser — you know, the guy you only managed to get rid of three hours ago."

"Yes, hello," said Erica, taking a firmer grip on the phone.

"I'm in my office."

He did not seem to know where to go from there so she said, "What are you doing in your office at this hour?"

"I don't seem to be doing anything much but sit here wondering why in hell I asked you out to dinner next Wednesday when it's still . . ." He paused, evidently counting, and went on, ". . . almost five days off. Look," he said hurriedly, "I know it's awfully late notice but . . . Oh, Good Lord!"

"Now what?" Erica wanted to know.

"I forgot about your sister."

"My sister has already forgotten about me," said Erica, "so that makes us even."

"Do you mean you can have dinner with me tonight?"

"I'd love to."

"There's some kind of ghastly affair at the mess and I'm supposed to put in an appearance — do you mind if we drop in for a while later on?"

"I don't mind a bit."

"We don't have to stay long. Is it all right if I pick you up about seven-thirty?"

"Yes, that's fine," said Erica in a tone which was admirably matter-of-fact, she thought, under the circumstances.

"Goodbye, Eric."

"Goodbye."

She put down the phone and went on sitting on the edge of her mother's bed for a while, looking up at a watercolour of some calla lilies on the opposite wall. Instead of next Wednesday, she would be seeing Marc again in less than an hour.

Downstairs Miriam called out something which she did not hear, then a door slammed, and some minutes later Erica became slowly aware of a clock ticking somewhere in the house. She listened to it for a while, still half dreaming, and wondering idly where it came from, and then finally she recognized the sound. It was the clock in her father's study.

IV

~

At breakfast the following Wednesday morning Erica remarked to her mother, "By the way, I'm going to be out to dinner tonight."

Her father put down his cup with an abrupt movement which spilled some of his coffee over the edge of the saucer onto the cloth, and looking directly at Erica around the corner of the table on his right he asked, "Are you going out with René?"

It was obvious from his expression that he already knew who it was without asking, but she said matter-of-factly, "No, with Marc Reiser."

His eyes left her face and returned to his newspaper. He said nothing.

"More coffee, Eric?" asked her mother.

"Yes, please."

Miriam was not down yet. Erica held out her cup, returned it quickly to her place as she noticed that her hand was shaking slightly, put in some cream and sugar, and then said into the silence, "I ran into Marc at the station when I was meeting Miriam and had dinner with him on Saturday night . . ."

"Do you mean to say that you left Miriam to have dinner here alone on her first night home?" interrupted her mother.

"No, she'd already arranged to go out with a friend of hers from England — some American on the Purchasing Commission."

Her father was still reading his newspaper but he could not avoid hearing her. In order to get it over with, once and for all, Erica went on as casually as she could, "I saw Marc again on Sunday. We went swimming at Oka."

"You could hardly wait for your mother and me to get out of town, could you?" said her father without glancing up from his paper.

"After twenty-eight years I'm not likely to start doing things behind your back, Charles," said Erica calmly. She had no intention of allowing herself to be sidetracked by losing her temper if she could help it; she had seen Anthony and Miriam make that mistake too often.

"You must have known that we wouldn't like it, Erica," said her mother.

"How was I supposed to know? You've never objected to any of my friends before."

There was another silence and finally Erica said, "I think we'd better get this thing settled now. So far as I'm concerned, I like Marc and I respect him, and I intend to go on seeing him . . ."

"Regardless of our opinions on the subject?" asked her mother.

"You can't have 'opinions' on the subject of someone you've

scarcely met and Charles has never met at all . . ."

Her father put down his paper and said, interrupting, "We've already been over all this, Eric. If some Jewish lawyer nobody's ever heard of is more important to you than we are, and as you say, you intend to go on seeing him in spite of knowing perfectly well the way we feel about him, then I'm afraid you'll have to do your seeing somewhere else."

"Do you mean that I can't even bring him to the house?" Her father did not answer and turning to her mother, she said incredulously, "You're not going to be as unfair as Charles, are you?"

"It's not a question of being fair or unfair, Eric. It's simply a question of facing facts. There's no sense in going out of your way to create a situation which might turn out to be very awkward for everyone, when you can so easily avoid it. You scarcely know the man yourself, and he can't possibly mean anything to you."

"And you, Brutus," said Erica.

Her father said angrily, "You have no reason to feel so sorry for yourself, Erica."

"The persecution complex seems to be catching," observed Margaret Drake. With a gesture which had become almost automatic, she straightened the skirt of her pale blue linen dress to keep it from crushing, and then shoved her chair away from the table in order to change her sitting position. Although it was so early in the day, her back had already begun to ache again. She said, "I've never known you to behave like this before. You're usually so reasonable. And apart from everything else, since he is the only person we've ever objected to, why can't you just . . ."

"You wouldn't expect me to sacrifice someone I like for a set of objections I don't agree with, would you?"

She was appealing to that sense of justice which was one of her mother's strongest characteristics and after considering it, her eyes raised toward the light flowing through the windows of the dining room, her mother said at last, "No, I wouldn't, but I would expect you to give us a fair hearing."

"But the only thing you've got against Marc is the fact that he's Jewish."

"No," said her father. "What I've got against him is the fact that he's obviously making use of my daughter."

"How? By taking me out to dinner on Saturday and swimming on Sunday?"

"A man who makes three engagements in five days with a girl he hardly knows is obviously out for something, isn't he? You're not exactly high school age, either of you."

"Out for what?"

"Well," said Charles shrugging, "say he seems just a little too eager."

"And just why should you say a thing like that about a friend of mine? Or does the fact that you're my father automatically give you the right to say anything you choose?"

"I'm not going to quarrel with you, Erica," he said, unmoved. He lit a cigarette, observing through the smoke, "I got your friend Reiser's number the moment I heard he'd turned up here with René."

"That was remarkably psychic even for you, considering the fact that you were still upstairs and had to form your opinion of Marc's character through a hardwood floor."

"What's the matter with you, Erica?" demanded her mother who had been watching her with increasing anxiety and surprise. "I've never seen you like this before. You're not yourself at all."

"I don't think Charles is either." Looking down at her empty coffee cup, Erica went on without raising her voice, "I told you that one of these days some guy was going to fall for me just for the sake of my beaux yeux. I'm not so bad, Charles — he doesn't necessarily have to have ulterior motives."

"Why doesn't he pick up a Jewish girl then?"

"That's not supposed to be necessary in this country," said Erica after a pause.

"Erica, what *is* the matter with you?" said her mother desperately. "There's no need to go on about it, is there?"

"Why don't you ask Charles?" Without taking her eyes from his face she said, "Charles knows everything. The only thing he doesn't seem to know is that what with the war and various other developments, the Drake connection isn't quite as important as it used to be, even to a Jewish lawyer. So far as Marc Reiser is concerned, you might just as well be a couple of people named Smith, except that if you were, you wouldn't be quite so likely to assume that he was 'out for something,'" she added with a slight change of tone. "He's in the Army, he's going overseas in a few months, maybe sooner, and he's got something else to think about besides how to do himself a bit of good by getting to know the Drakes and running after the Drakes' daughter in order to improve his social, and indirectly his professional standing."

She paused again and then asked, "That's about it, isn't it, Charles?"

"No, that is *not* it!" her mother burst out before Charles, still as impassive as ever, had a chance to answer. She did not know what to make of Erica; she was not only badly hurt, but utterly at a loss to understand her daughter's behaviour. As she had so often said to her friends in the past, in all her life Erica had never given either of her parents a moment of unhappiness or even a moment of worry.

Grasping the arms of her chair and almost in tears, Margaret

Drake said, "It doesn't even seem to have occurred to you that all we're trying to do is protect you against yourself. I thought your father was wrong to take this man so seriously. I told him I thought he was simply being melodramatic when he said he knew that something like this was going to happen. I couldn't imagine you losing your head over anyone, particularly a man you hardly know, who obviously isn't your kind of person at all, and who can't possibly really matter to you."

She broke off, her eyes searching Erica's face for some kind of change and then she said hopelessly, "I don't understand you, Eric. It isn't as though we'd ever tried to interfere with you before, and surely you can see why we don't want you to get involved with him for your own sake."

"But Mother, I am involved with him," said Erica steadily.

At that moment Miriam entered the dining room. She was wearing her flowered housecoat and had a red ribbon in her dark hair. She glanced from her parents to Erica, then slipped into her chair murmuring, "Good morning, everybody."

Neither her mother nor father answered; they did not even appear to have noticed her.

"Hello, darling," said Erica mechanically.

Her father asked her at last, "And what do you mean by that, exactly?"

"I don't know, except that I can't just stop seeing him." It was no use trying to explain to them how she felt about Marc; so far as her mother and father were concerned, you could not feel deeply about someone you had only met three times, and that was all there was to it. As her mother had already pointed out, Marc Reiser could not possibly really matter to her, and anything else she might say to the contrary would simply be taken as a further proof that she had "lost her head" and was "simply not herself."

Looking aimlessly at the breakfast table in front of her, Erica said, "I realize that it's awkward for everyone, but at least it's nothing like as awkward now as it will be if you go on refusing to have anything to do with him . . ."

"In other words, you're not interested in our opinions. We're just to shut up and do what we're told." He said, "Well, that's clear enough. You're not only deliberately walking into God knows what kind of mess, but you expect your mother and me to go along with you and back you up . . ."

"Not necessarily," said Miriam, helping herself to a piece of toast. "Why not just give the guy an even break and reserve judgment? Who knows? He may not turn out to be so bad after all."

"Mind your own business, Miriam!"

"Yes, please, darling," said Erica, as her self-control suddenly began to give way. The worst her father had been able to say had somehow been far easier to take than that one casual remark from Miriam.

"No," said Margaret Drake from the head of the table. "That's not the point." She sipped some cold coffee and went on more matter-of-factly, still determined not to allow herself to break down although she was so tired and so upset, "You can't pretend with people, Miriam. It isn't a question of giving him an even break, it's a question of being honest with him. It's no use our having him here and pretending that he's on the same basis as Erica's other friends, as though we were actually encouraging him in fact. You can't go just so far with people and then suddenly stop. It's not fair."

"You sound as though I were already engaged to him," said Erica under her breath.

His face more set than ever, her father said, "You probably will be next week at this rate."

"Charles!" Gasped his wife.

"We might as well face it, Margaret." He paused and then remarked, "Mr. Reiser seems to have done pretty well up to now. Erica would hardly be making all this fuss if he hadn't. Would you?" he asked, turning to Erica.

"No."

"And you're going to go on seeing him, aren't you?"

"Yes," said Erica.

There was a complete silence and then Erica said suddenly, "Charles, I want to know why."

"Why?" he repeated, looking at her. "All right, I'll tell you why. I don't want my daughter to go through life neither flesh, fowl, nor good red herring, living in a kind of no man's land where half the people you know will never accept him, and half the people he knows will never accept you. I don't want a son-in-law who can't be put up at my club and who can't go with us to places where we've gone all our lives. I don't want a son-in-law whom I'll have to apologize for, and explain, and have to hear insulted indirectly unless I can remember to warn people off first."

"In fact," said Miriam coolly, "you don't want a son-in-law. Or not if it's Erica who's married to him at any rate."

"Don't be ridiculous," said her mother. "Charles has never objected to anyone else."

"Erica has never showed any signs of wanting to marry anyone else."

Her father was paying no attention. Still looking at Erica, he observed, "If Reiser is anything like you say he is, he deserves something better than that . . ."

"We want you to marry someone — someone like us. Someone who'll fit in and whom we can . . ." Margaret Drake caught her breath, then managed to say, ". . . can all be proud of," and suddenly shoving back her chair, she got up and left the room. With one final glance at Erica, Charles followed his wife out the door.

"Mother was crying," said Erica, and then began to cry herself, with her face in her hands and the tears running through her fingers.

"Have you got a handkerchief?" inquired Miriam after a while.

Erica shook her head.

"Take mine, then." She gave Erica the handkerchief across the table, bit into her piece of toast, put it down on her plate again and asked at last, "Do you remember what I said, Eric?"

"No," said Erica, blowing her nose. "What did you say?"

"I said they wouldn't have to lock you up in your room and feed you on bread and water."

Her father never asked Erica again who was taking her out or where she was going; sometime during the day following the scene at the breakfast table, he had apparently decided to show no further interest in Marc Reiser, nor for the time being at any rate, even in Erica herself. When she came home at ten-thirty that night, having cut short her evening with Marc in order to try once more to talk to her father and work out some compromise which would make it possible for them to go on living as they had before, she found that his attitude toward her had changed completely. Instead of the anger, which she had expected, she was faced with a wall of indifference. He did not refuse to discuss the subject; he simply went on reading his paper and did not bother to listen.

To his wife and Miriam he was the same as ever, but from then on into the first week of August, whenever Erica tried speaking to him directly, no matter what she said, his expression would begin to set at the first sound of her voice, and by the time he had swung round to look at her, he had walled himself up again. Erica did not know what to do; he was treating her rather like a guest who had overstayed her welcome, and it was so unlike him and such a startling reversal of their former relationship, that in the beginning she somehow managed to ignore it and to go on as though nothing had happened. At the end of a week, however, the most bewildering and miserable week she had had for years, her father remained as remote and as unapproachable as ever, and she gradually lost hope and stopped trying. She began to avoid him as much as she could, and hardly ever said anything to him without including either her mother or Miriam. On the evenings when both of them were out, Erica either stayed out herself or went to bed almost immediately after dinner, in order not to be left alone with him.

The whole atmosphere of the house had changed with the change in the relationship between Charles and Erica, but Margaret Drake could do nothing. It had only taken her a few hours to regret her loss of self-control at the breakfast table; and early in the afternoon, just after the final edition had gone to press — nothing short of disaster could have induced her to disturb Erica before then; she had too much respect for her daughter and her daughter's working hours — she had phoned from Red Cross Headquarters where she had been working full-time, eight hours a day, ever since September 1939, to apologize. She told Erica that her opinions remained unaltered, but that on thinking it over, she could not see that either her own or Charles' behaviour had been in any way justified. If, on her side, Erica would make a genuine effort to see things from their point of view and to realize that their one desire was to protect her as far as possible, she herself would do her best to persuade Charles to adopt a more rational and less emotional viewpoint.

But her best was not good enough. Night after night, some-times until very late, Erica could hear their voices in the study. It was like the year before, when Margaret Drake had stayed up till all hours attempting to persuade her husband to adopt a more rational viewpoint toward his son's French Canadian and devoutly Catholic fiancée. She had not got anywhere then either. Now, she needed sleep more than ever; for three years everything which did not come under the heading of war work had been crammed into the hours before nine in the morning and after five, and the only way Margaret Drake had been able to keep it up was by going to bed each night at ten. Instead of that, she was once more talking until eleven, twelve, and occasionally even one, dragging herself out of bed again at seven in the morning, having slept only in the intervals when the argument stopped turning round and round in her head and let her alone for a while. If she had appealed to Erica at that time, Erica would have given in for her mother's sake, not for the sake of her father who, apart from the fact that he was obvi-ously lonely without Erica, seemed comfortable enough behind his wall of indifference. For reasons of her own, however, Margaret Drake preferred to wait, to go on struggling with her husband until she was finally convinced that it was hopeless, and then only appeal to Erica as a last resort and not because she felt that Erica was chiefly to blame. By then it was too late.

Charles did not budge an inch. He told his wife that his position was clear and his decision final; he would not have Reiser in the house, and so long as Erica continued to ignore her parents and show so little concern for their peace of mind that she could go on seeing a cheap Jewish lawyer two and three times a week outside the house, he, Charles, would have noth-ing to say to her.

As an explanation of his own attitude toward the whole

affair, it was fairly good as far as it went, and since Margaret Drake had always had a tendency to oversimplify her husband's character and motives, largely because her own character and motives were so eminently simple and straightforward that she could not conceive of his as being anything else, she accepted his explanation for what it was worth, and failed to realize that even for Charles Drake, it did not go far enough.

Putting it like that, it implied that Erica was the cause of his behaviour, which was only partly true, and that he himself really believed that she was oblivious to his own feelings and those of his wife, which was not true at all.

He knew exactly how unoblivious Erica was, and how much she cared about her parents' peace of mind, and in actual fact, whether he was entirely aware of it or not, half his behaviour was put on in the instinctive effort to wear down Erica's resistance. The effort might have been successful if it had not been for one fact which he had overlooked. Erica's concern for her mother and father and their evident unhappiness was slowly becoming outbalanced by her resentment at their treatment of Marc.

That resentment was steadily growing, having taken root on Wednesday afternoon, the day everything had started, when she had had to telephone Marc from her office to ask him not to call for her that night. It had not occurred to her until the lull after the final edition went to press and she at last had had time to think, that if Marc were to call for her that night, there was no way of making certain that he and Charles would not run into each other again. At that hour, just before or during dinner, her father was likely to be almost anywhere on the ground floor. She could not instruct Mary to leave Mr. Reiser standing on the front steps with the door closed; the only thing to do was to keep him away from the house altogether.

Keeping Marc away from the house without telling him why, which would have made him feel worse than ever, turned out to be even more difficult than she had expected. For that first evening, she had invented an appointment downtown which would keep her so late that it would not be worthwhile to go home before dinner. The second time, it was gas rationing and the distance up to the top of Westmount. Marc had been well brought up, and he appeared to be definitely unreceptive to the idea that when you invite a girl to dine at a restaurant, you do not necessarily have to call for her. The third time, as his car happened to be laid up for repairs, he told Erica that he would take a tram to the boulevard, and walk up from there. After all, he pointed out, there were steps and other people used them. Unable to think up a fresh excuse on such short notice, Erica had fallen back on the one about having a late appointment downtown.

So then, at last, he got it. There was no fourth time, he never suggested calling for her again.

Compared to the problem as a whole, whether he called for her or not was relatively unimportant, but Marc happened to be one of those people to whom good manners are second nature, and he could not get used to letting Erica find her own way to wherever it was that they were to meet, while he simply sat and waited for her.

One Sunday afternoon when they were walking on Mount Royal, along one of the roads which always reminded Erica of Europe, there were so many people on bicycles, on foot, or riding by in carriages since no cars were allowed on the mountain, he said suddenly, "Remember Hans Castorp, Eric? 'Life consists of getting used to not getting used to it.'" A moment later he added moodily, "Well, at least I can still take you home."

Only as far as the front door, however. He would probably just have to get used to not getting used to that too.

Sometimes Erica found herself thinking that it was as though Charles and Margaret Drake were determined to put Marc down on the level on which they apparently thought he belonged, to force him to be as they imagined him to be, and not as he actually was. Each time that Erica set out to meet him at a restaurant, a bar, a hotel lobby, and once or twice even on a street corner, and each time that she left him at the front door and watched him turn back, down the walk to his car or along the street leading to the steps which were a shortcut to the street below, back to his own world again, she could feel her resentment growing and the gulf between herself and her mother and father steadily widening.

The gulf was worse than the resentment. To be really good at resentment, you have to have had considerable practice, and until the Wednesday afternoon when she had heard herself telling her first lie to Marc, over the telephone, Erica could not remember ever having resented anything in her life. The moment her parents showed signs of coming round, she knew that her resentment would be over and done with, but the gulf was a different matter. The most vital part of her life was lived with Marc, away from home, and in spite of herself, she was coming to regard the house in Westmount merely as a place to eat and sleep. In a desperate effort to bridge the gulf, at least to some extent, and to bring the two separate halves of her life closer together, she had tried to talk to her mother and father about Marc, literally forcing herself to refer to him or quote something that he had said just as though he were — well, just as though he were anybody else. But she found herself talking into a vacuum; the moment she mentioned him, or even looked as though she were about to mention him — Erica was no actress, and the effort it required in order to sound natural was probably fairly obvious — her mother and father stopped listening. And the gulf went on widening.

The night before Margaret Drake finally appealed to Erica, Max Eliot, Miriam's American on the Purchasing Committee, had come to dinner and the gulf suddenly widened still further.

He had turned out to be quite presentable, of medium height, rather heavily built, very well-dressed and very good-looking, but everything about him seemed to Erica to stop just short of too much. Another few pounds and he would have been overweight, his clothes were such that John Gardiner summed him up a few weeks later as "something out of *Esquire*," and his profile was so good that it made you wonder whether he was conscious of it or not. With Max Eliot, you could not be sure. All his various qualities and characteristics added up to a personality which just missed being both slick and a little caddish; he was neither slick nor caddish, as it happened, but it was too close a miss for either Charles, his wife, or Erica to feel entirely at ease with him.

Apart from the fact that he was obviously very intelligent, he had almost nothing to recommend him, since with everything else, there was even a Mrs. Eliot in California; he was in almost every respect Marc Reiser's inferior, and his one advantage over Marc was purely negative. But negative or not, it made all the difference. He could call for Miriam when he was taking her out; he could have a drink with Charles in the drawing-room while he was waiting for her, because Miriam was always late, and he could come for dinner.

Erica spent the evening observing Mr. Eliot from the sidelines, saying almost nothing, and trying to figure out the system by which one negative advantage counted for more than any number of positive ones. Whatever it was, it had nothing to do with ordinary human values, or with even the most elementary justice, although you had to know Marc Reiser as Erica knew him by this time, really to appreciate how unjust it was.

The following day her mother came into Erica's room as she was dressing to go out to dinner with Marc and after talking disjointedly for a while about people and things which interested neither of them at the moment, she said at last, "I can't do anything with Charles; I've tried and tried, but it's hopeless. I guess from now on, it's up to you, Eric."

"You don't imagine he'll listen to me, do you?"

"No."

Erica was sitting at her dressing table taking the cold cream off her face; she had her back to her mother who was standing by the chest of drawers on the other side of the room but in direct line with the dressing table mirror which reflected her straight, slender figure like a full-length portrait. After waiting for her to say something else, Erica asked expressionlessly, although she knew the answer already, "What do you want me to do then?"

"I want you to stop seeing him." She went on without pausing, "You've got to, Erica! We can't go on like this, our whole life seems to be falling apart. Marc Reiser can't possibly mean as much to you as you mean to us, and the damage you're doing is out of all proportion to the very most you can hope to get out of an infatuation which can't conceivably last or lead anywhere. It isn't worth it, Eric!"

"It is to me," said Erica. "I wouldn't be doing it if it weren't. You know me well enough to know that."

Her mother said despairingly, "I don't know you at all any more! You've changed so much . . . sometimes I think . . ."

"Yes, what?"

She said, her mouth trembling, "Sometimes I wonder if Marc

Reiser has any idea what he's done to you — what he's doing to all of us. I don't suppose he'd care anyhow."

A moment later she burst out, "You think you're in love with him, but real love doesn't make you turn into someone else overnight — it doesn't make you hate everyone else because of it. You couldn't be in love with him anyhow, you haven't known him long enough and he isn't the sort of person you could . . ."

"How can you tell what sort of person he is?"

"I can tell easily enough and so can your father, just from the way he's behaving. If he were genuinely in love with you, instead of just out for what he can get, apparently, he wouldn't be rushing you off your feet and doing his best to make you fall in love with him, when he's old enough and certainly experienced enough to be fully aware of the fact that there's no real future in it for either of you, and you're the one who's going to have to pay for it. He must realize how we feel about it, of course, although obviously our opinions don't matter in the least so far as Marc Reiser is concerned, but that's beside the point. If he were really in love with you, he'd care far more about your happiness and far less about himself."

There was no point in arguing; the system of ready-made definitions and generalities by which Margaret Drake arrived at her moral judgments was infallible. All you had to do was to compare the behaviour and reactions of a given individual with the standard set of measurements which had long ago been laid down for all time, and you could even tell whether he or she was "genuinely" in love or not. It was as simple as that. Erica had been brought up on the system, but she had never been able to make it work, although she realized that it had worked well enough for her mother and father and for a great many others of their generation, enabling them to go through life with fewer misgivings, less uncertainty, and probably a good deal less muddle in the long run than she herself had any reason to expect.

She said, "I don't think you're being fair to either of us," and let it go at that.

"Do you imagine you're being fair to us?"

She left the chest of drawers and sat down on the chair by Erica's desk with her back to the windows. She was wearing her pale blue linen dress and the late afternoon light fell on her shoulders and her soft brown hair, and was kind to her tired face. She said, "You don't understand, Eric. You seem to expect us just to sit back and do nothing and let you make a mess of your life without even trying to stop you. That's not what we're for. That's not what any parents are for, just to sit back and say nothing . . ."

"But most of what you say about Marc simply doesn't make any sense. You always sound as though you're talking about a couple of other people."

Her mother said impatiently, "I'm talking about a general situation which you know exists as well as I do! There is no use your trying to pretend that it doesn't exist . . ."

"I'm not," said Erica, switching on the light by her dressing table mirror in order to put on some makeup. "And I don't, but what I do have to do is balance Marc, and what he's worth to me, against the general situation and decide for myself whether I'm going to gain more than I lose. Nobody else can decide that for me. I haven't lived your sort of life, you were born in 1890 and I was born in 1914, and obviously what matters most to me isn't what matters most to you. Our whole scale of values is different. What would 'ruin' your life wouldn't necessarily ruin mine, and anyhow, I don't think it's a question of ruining my life at the moment, so much as a question of who's going to run it. Obviously, if I were to stop seeing Marc purely because you wanted me to and for a set of reasons which I don't agree with, then it would be you and Charles who were running it, not I."

"You know perfectly well your father and I haven't the faintest desire to run your life. If we had, we'd have started long ago." Her mother paused, looked at Erica, one hand absently turning a pencil by hitting first one end and then the other against the desk and sliding it through her fingers.

She was on the point of saying something else when Erica broke in suddenly, "Mother . . ."

"Yes?"

"Do you remember what Miriam said about Charles not wanting a son-in-law at all if it was a question of my getting married?"

"A lot of what Miriam says is pure nonsense."

"Is it?" She herself had not taken the idea very seriously until now, but she had been listening to her mother for the past few minutes with a growing feeling that something was wrong somewhere, for while her father was as prejudiced as her mother on the subject of Jews, at the same time, he was a great deal less conventional. He could not possibly be as concerned with the purely social aspect of the problem, since he was such a thorough going individualist, so that, strictly speaking, he actually had fewer reasons for objecting — unless there was another motive still unaccounted for.

Erica said at last, "I'm not so sure that Charles doesn't want to run my life, and I'm beginning to wonder if he ever will want me to marry anyone."

To Erica's surprise, her mother answered calmly, "I doubt if Charles will ever think anyone is really good enough for you, if that's what you mean, but Marc Reiser is hardly a fair example. After all, what matters most to your father is your happiness, and no one in his senses could possibly imagine that you and

Marc have even a reasonable chance of being happy. There's too much against you." She glanced at Erica and then went on in a different tone, "There'll be someone else, Eric — someone who'll really belong and who'll mean far more to you than Marc Reiser ever could and who wouldn't put you into an impossible situation simply by marrying you."

"Marc has never said anything about marrying me. He's never even said anything about being in love with me." Although she knew it was useless, because her mother's theories on the subject of Marc Reiser were so wildly at variance with the facts that they were literally discussing two different people, one real and one imaginary, she added, "You keep forgetting that the person who's going to take the most convincing is Marc, not me — or you and Charles."

"Then just what does Mr. Reiser think he's doing at the moment?" inquired her mother.

"Maybe, like Miriam, he doesn't think, he just hopes."

"Really, Erica," said her mother, exasperated.

Erica picked up her lipstick and said as she unscrewed the cap, "As for there being 'someone else,' the only answer to that is that I'm in love with Marc."

Her mother said nothing but went on silently turning the pencil through her fingers.

"I can understand why you and Charles feel the way you do and why it would be hell for either of you to be married to a Jew, in the world in which you've lived, but I'm not you and your world isn't the same as mine, and what I simply cannot see is how you can expect me to feel the same way. One of the things that seems to appall Charles most is the fact that if I married Marc, my husband could not be admitted to his club. *I* don't care about clubs!"

She got up, took the green and white print dress which was

lying on her bed and as she pulled it over her head, Erica asked suddenly, "What did you mean when you said that you couldn't do anything with Charles? You agree with him, don't you?"

"Yes, so far as your marrying Marc Reiser is concerned. Yes, I know," she said impatiently as Erica's head appeared and she saw that her daughter was about to protest again, "but neither of us has ever seen you so worked up about anyone else, you're obviously not yourself and there's no telling what may happen or what you're likely to do in this state," she added, her face drawn with anxiety. "You're in love with him, or you think you are, and you've said absolutely nothing to give us any grounds for thinking that you wouldn't marry him, or that you even realize what you'd be letting yourself in for."

"Listen, Mother," said Erica, staring at her. "The first night I ever went out with Marc, he asked me where I wanted to go and I suggested a restaurant over on the Back River. It's quite a long drive to the Back River, and when we finally got there, there was a sign on the gate saying 'Select Clientele.'"

In a voice of sheer despair her mother said, "And you expect us to help you and treat Marc Reiser as though he were anybody else, when all he has to offer you is that sort of thing for the rest of your life!"

"I only told you that to make you see that I do know what I'd be letting myself in for, and so does Marc. The second time I saw him he said it was better to be on one side or the other than out in the middle where you get it both ways . . ."

"Then why doesn't he leave you *alone* . . ."

"I don't want to be left alone," said Erica after a moment's silence. She realized now that to have expected her mother and father to treat Marc as though he were anyone else was to have expected them not only to change character but to alter *their* scale of values, which was obviously out of the question and far more than she herself was capable of doing, even supposing she had been willing to try. They were not to be blamed for doing everything in their power to shield their daughter against even the possibility of a lifetime out in the middle and for acting in what, in all sincerity, they conceived to be her best interests.

It was a complete deadlock.

Her mother went on at last with a visible effort, "What I don't agree with is the way Charles is going about it. This is your home, and although I can't imagine your father and me and Marc Reiser having much to say to each other," she observed with a slightly different expression, "whether we happen to care for him or not, he is a friend of yours and you should be able to invite him here. You might just as well be living in a boarding house . . ." she said, and broke off, remembering that she had said it before in another connection altogether. Then, because Margaret Drake was nothing if not honest, she made herself go on. She said wearily, "Well, it's true, and certainly that part of it is not your fault."

Erica was standing by the window, so that her mother had to turn her head toward the light in order to look at her. The long rays of the sun drove straight into her mother's face, and for the first time, Erica could see how tired she was. She was tired out.

In spite of everything Margaret Drake had been saying, Erica knew that left to herself, she would have followed a different course. She would have said what she thought, but having done that, she would not only have invited Marc to the house but she would have done her utmost to regard him objectively and to be fair to both Marc and her daughter.

Erica said suddenly, "It's Charles who's behind all this! It's our fault, not yours. Why should you have to be dragged into it?" she asked desperately. "You can't do anything, you're just caught . . ."

"I can't stop unless you do, darling," said her mother, smiling faintly. "I can't help being dragged into something that concerns both my husband and my daughter. You're such a baby in some ways, Eric."

A moment later she remarked, "I always wondered what would happen if you and Charles came up against each other. I don't understand you as well as he does, and I don't understand him the way you do, but I couldn't just sit by and watch you killing the best in each of you, even if I weren't involved in it myself. Your relationship with your father was a very fine thing, Eric," she said, glancing at Erica and then back to the window again. "There's one side of him which you've been able to bring out, but which I've scarcely been able to touch since we were first married."

Her eyes came back into the room, to the poster of Carcassonne which Erica had brought back from her last trip to France, just before the war, and she said, "Because it was you and not me is no reason for me to let that side of Charles disappear again without a struggle. I don't know what he'd do without you. If he should lose you, he'll lose an outlet that he needs and that he's never been able to find in anyone else."

She said quietly, "I want him to keep his outlet," and got up, adding on her way to the door, "As for you, I just want what every mother wants — I want you to be happy, to marry the right person, and not the wrong one."

"Mother," said Erica.

"Yes?"

"Won't you meet Marc? Couldn't we have lunch together some day, just the three of us?"

"Why?" she asked, pausing with her hand on the doorknob. "What difference would it make?"

"I don't know," said Erica, dropping her eyes. "I just thought that you wouldn't be so worried if you really knew him. I'm sure you'd like him . . ."

"Liking him would just make everything that much more complicated, wouldn't it? The situation is awkward enough as it is. I don't think I particularly care about meeting him now in any case. After all, he must have some idea of the damage he's doing by this time."

"You don't know how hard I work to keep him from finding out!" said Erica involuntarily.

"What do you mean?" asked her mother, staring at her. As Erica did not answer she said, "How hard you work to keep him from finding out the truth, is that it?"

"I told you Marc was the one who really needed to be convinced," said Erica after a pause.

"I don't know what you're talking about."

Her mother opened the door and Erica said, "You will meet him sometime, won't you?"

"I don't see how I can manage lunch very well. You know I always stay at the Red Cross, it takes too much time if I go out."

"All right," said Erica. "No harm in asking."

She realized that it was still Charles, and not her mother, but she was crying when Miriam wandered in through the communicating door between her bedroom and Erica's.

Miriam was in slacks and a white shirt, carrying a glass of rye in one hand and a hairbrush and another glass of rye in the other. She put the first glass down in front of Erica on the dressing table and retired to the window seat, remarking, "Private stock. If this goes on, we're all bound to take to drink sooner or later anyhow, and I thought it might just as well be sooner. How are things?" she inquired conversationally.

"Lousy, thank you," said Erica, drying her eyes.

"So I gathered. Is that a new dress? It looks nice, darling — I'll say this for Marc Reiser, at least he's got you out of suits."

She scrutinized Erica in silence for a while, absently brushing her dark hair, and then asked suddenly, "Would it make any difference if I came along some night? After all, I'm family — sort of," she added, qualifying it.

"Thanks, Mimi!"

"You don't have to start crying all over again. Have a drink instead. And how about a cigarette?" She tossed one to Erica, lit one for herself, and observed, "I suppose you've heard the latest . . ."

"No, what?"

"The latest is that Mother and Charles are not going to take any holidays this summer because they're so worried about you that they wouldn't get any real rest anyhow, and they might just as well stay in town and go on working."

She inhaled deeply, blew out a long, thin stream of smoke and added, shrugging, "Well, it's probably true, but it's still blackmail. This whole business is so damn silly, all they do is stay at home brooding over a man they don't even know."

"It isn't just that," said Erica. "Even if they knew him and liked him, he'd still be impossible."

"Yes, but not so impossible as he is now. People are funny," said Miriam, gazing thoughtfully into space. "You'd think one problem would be enough, without going out of your way to invent a couple of extra ones. Most of what Charles says about Marc comes under the heading of pure invention, doesn't it?"

"I guess so."

"He reminds me of someone erecting an ogre to frighten himself with."

A moment later she said idly, "Do you know what I'd do if I were you?"

Erica was sitting on the edge of her bed, completely discouraged, with her head and her shoulders down, and as she raised her eyes inquiringly but without much interest, Miriam said, "If I were you I'd get out."

"Why?" asked Erica, startled.

"Not for your own sake, but for Marc's. I don't know much about him, and maybe he's so tough he can go on taking it, but there are other ways of knocking a man down than just hauling off and socking him!"

"What are you getting at?"

"Every time he meets you somewhere and every time he brings you home and leaves you on the doorstep, it must get him down that much further, whether he realizes it or not. I think that is what Charles is counting on," she went on reflectively. "He's banking on the probability that some day, Marc will get so far down that he'll just quit."

"How did you know that?" demanded Erica.

"Oh," said Miriam, raising her eyebrows. "So I'm not the only one."

"I didn't mean about Charles. He can't be doing it deliberately . . ."

"Why can't he?"

"He thinks Marc is the aggressive type with a skin six inches thick."

"Oh, nuts," said Miriam.

"But Mimi, he doesn't know what Marc is like. You've heard him on the subject of Marc often enough."

"A lot of that is eyewash put on for your benefit. Charles doesn't really believe it; he did in the beginning but he doesn't now. The only person who does is Mother. You see, Eric, the great thing about being temperamental, like Charles, is that when ninety-nine times in a row your outbursts against someone are genuine, nobody is likely to spot the hundredth as partly faked. I don't mean that Charles isn't sincere — just say that he's letting himself be carried away by his own arguments. He may end up where he started by believing that Marc is just a 'cheap Jewish lawyer,' as he so charmingly expresses it, but he doesn't at the moment."

"Why not?"

"He's been making a few judicial inquiries about Marc downtown and over at Divisional Headquarters . . ."

"But, Mimi, that makes all the difference," said Erica eagerly.

"Does it?"

"Of course it does. Good heavens, it means that . . ."

Miriam interrupted. She said flatly, "It means nothing. What good does it do Charles to hear Marc described as quite exceptional — for a Jewish lawyer? Or first-rate — for a Jewish officer? You don't imagine any of them left out the word 'Jew,' do you? Nobody ever does."

Erica sank back again. She said listlessly, "I suppose that was what Mother meant."

"Mother doesn't know even that much. He hasn't told her."

"Why?"

Miriam regarded her quizzically for a moment and said finally, "What's the use of getting Mother all confused?"

She smoked for a while in silence and then remarked, "However, that's not the point. If you think this atmosphere of concentrated disapproval is all you're going to have to contend with, you're crazy. Charles hasn't finished with you yet, he hasn't even started, and he'll put up the fight of his life before he'll hand you over to a Jewish lawyer — even if he is exceptional.

And though you may be able to stand it, some of it is bound to get through to Marc sooner or later. Since he must have been getting it in one form or another all his life, my advice to you is to make up your mind whether you want Marc or Charles, because Charles isn't going to allow you to have both of them, and if it's Marc, then clear out where Charles can't get at him and where you don't have to leave him standing on the doorstep."

Miriam drank some rye, lit a cigarette and as Erica glanced at her clock and got up, Miriam said, "I guess I sound pretty hardboiled but compared to Charles, I'm not even coddled."

"He's only trying to do what he thinks is best for me," said Erica, running a comb through her hair and then taking her bag and gloves from the dressing table.

"Nobody can really tell what's 'best' for anyone else." Looking up at Erica who had paused in the center of the room on her way to the door, she said, "If you don't clear out, what are you going to do?"

"Nothing. I'm just going to hang on. Charles can't break this thing up if I don't let him, and provided I just hang on long enough, he'll come around sooner or later."

"I hope you're right," said Miriam.

Marc was waiting for Erica in the main dining room at Charcot's, sitting at a table in the back of the room underneath a great golden cock painted on the smooth light wall over his head. He did not notice Erica until she was within a few feet of him; he was looking fixedly at the big menu in front of him. The menu was actually just a trick, a form of protection against his own nerves and the glances of the people around him, for he hated waiting alone in a crowd. Usually he bought a paper and took refuge behind the war news, but today he must have forgotten.

"Hello, Marc . . ."

"Eric!" He got up so quickly that he almost upset the table. When he first caught sight of her, his face always lit up as though he had not seen her for weeks.

"Have you been waiting long?"

"No, only about five minutes."

"I'm sorry," said Erica, smiling at him.

They sat side by side on the white leather banquette facing down the room, Erica in a green and white print dress and Marc in uniform.

"What's ris de veau à la bonne femme?" Marc wanted to know.

"Haven't you read *Young Man of Caracas*?"

"I've just started it."

"Well, when you get a little further you'll find out that it means 'Laugh of the sheep at the good woman.'"

"Really," said Marc. "It sounded more like an hors d'oeuvre than an entrée."

"What else is there?" asked Erica, looking at the menu over his shoulder.

"Poulet, filet mignon, escaloppe de veau, filet de sole à la something and something grenouilles. Why do they always have to write these menus in purple ink?" He paused and then asked, "What does that remind me of, Eric?"

"*This Above All*?"

"Right. Cultured, aren't we? Well, which do you want?"

"Let's have poulet."

"Poulet frit, poulet grillé, or poulet rôti?"

"Grillé. They do it well here."

"Poulet grillé, s'il vous plaît," he said to the waiter. "Des hors d'oeuvres — do you want soup?" Erica shook her head.

"Moi non plus. Fish?"

"No, thanks."

"Pas de poisson. We'll choose our dessert later. How about a cocktail?"

"Yes, Manhattan, please."

"Two Manhattans — non, je prendrai un martini."

"Un Manhattan, un martini," said the waiter.

"Merci." He turned to Erica and said, "You look beautiful tonight, darling. Don't ever cut your hair, will you?"

He remembered that it was the combination of fine, almost delicate features and that look of emotional strength which came through from underneath, which had so struck him the first time he had met her. It was not only in her face but in the lines of her slender, almost boneless body, a blending of sensitivity and passion which disturbed him so profoundly whenever he was with her, close to her, that afterwards he forgot what they talked about and almost forgot where they had gone — what remained chiefly in his mind was his own sense of strain at always holding back, sitting on the opposite side of a table or if they were in a restaurant like this with seats along the wall, of keeping a foot of space between them, and when they were driving, staying on his own side of the car.

Erica was something that had never happened to him before. With all the others, an essential part of him had remained detached and isolated from the rest of his consciousness, out of reach of everyone, including himself. He could do nothing about it but try to confine it and fight it off as long as possible. His detachment had set a time limit to all his relationships, and since he was always aware of it, he had never been able to fool himself into believing that any of them would be permanent. Sooner or later and against his will, because he had no liking for short-lived affairs and wanted permanence, the old withdrawal process would begin again, until eventually he would find himself back where he had started, having completed another circle and got nowhere.

Then Erica had come along and for the first time in his life, he had found himself wholly involved. He did not know how or why it had happened, or, more importantly, since under the circumstances a lot of people were going to take a lot of convincing, how to explain to anyone else that, this time, he knew he was not going to get over it. So far he had only tried explaining it to one person, his brother David, having run into him accidentally at the Rosenbergs' when both of them had been in Toronto on business the week before, and David had remained quite unconvinced. Apparently the more you talk about being in love, the more you sound like a dime novel. At one point he had even heard himself protesting that this time it was different and that he and Erica belonged together!

They had been sitting in some ghastly Toronto beer parlor, having left the Rosenbergs' with an hour still to spare before both of them had to catch their trains. He would probably not have mentioned Erica to his brother if he had not been thoroughly depressed, partially by things in general and partly by the Rosenbergs. Betty Rosenberg was not Jewish, and she was a Montrealer with much the same background as Erica. In order to get away from the apparently inevitable family complications, when they had been married two years they had moved to Toronto where Max had had to start all over again. They had two children, there was another due soon, and Marc had been heartsick at the way in which life was obviously wearing them down. He had not known Betty Rosenberg before her marriage, but she was fair-haired, and he supposed that she had once looked like Erica.

"Is that what happens?" he had asked David as they were

walking away from the house.

His brother was shorter than Marc, with black hair and dark eyes; he glanced up sideways at Marc and said briefly, "I guess all married couples have their off nights."

He had forgotten what they had talked about after that, until they were sitting at a corner table in the beer parlor and his brother had asked suddenly, "What's the matter with you?"

"I don't know," he answered after a pause. "I guess it was just the Rosenberg atmosphere."

"Why? Are you thinking of doing what Max did?" After waiting for a while, David said resignedly, "You might just as well tell me all about it, laddie. You will sooner or later anyhow. What's her name?"

"Erica Drake."

His brother finished his beer and then asked, "What's she like?"

He tried to tell David what Erica was like but that came out all wrong too. The more he said, the less it sounded like Erica. Finally his brother cut him short with, "All right, all right . . . so you think you're in love with her."

"I don't just think so."

"It wouldn't be the first time if you did."

"I know," said Marc impatiently, "but this time it's different."

"Not really."

"I can't remember ever having wanted to marry anyone before."

His brother was sitting hunched over his glass with his pipe between his teeth. He removed the pipe, glanced at Marc and with his eyes back on the table again he said, "You haven't shown much talent for sticking so far, and if you're really serious about marrying her, you'll need a lot. I wouldn't make it too tough for myself if I were you."

"I'm not worried about myself. I'm really in love with her; I've never felt this way about anyone before in my life. We just belong together, that's all. Oh, hell," he said, exasperated, grinding out his cigarette. "You can't explain these things."

There was a brief silence and then Marc asked, "Are you just against it on principle?"

"No," said David. "I haven't got any of those particular principles. How long have you known her?"

"About a month. It hasn't anything to do with that. I knew Eric better after I'd been talking to her for half an hour than I know René de Sevigny after ten years."

"That's not what I'm talking about." David glanced at his watch, signaled the waiter for their bill and got up. Looking down at Marc, he said, "The trouble with you is, laddie, you've never really grown up. You haven't found yourself yet. I'm sorry if I sound like a copybook but I can't think of any other way of putting it. And until you have, and really know what you want, you'd better stay clear of complicated situations. After all, it isn't just a question of messing up your own life."

You haven't found yourself yet.

He still did not know exactly what his brother had meant by that. And he certainly did not want to mess up Erica's life, or even run the risk of hurting her. It was because he was afraid for her and for himself, but particularly for Erica, that he had sat on the opposite side of the car and kept on driving, or had gone from one public place to another, for what had once begun in the car or on the mountain or in a park — the only places in which they were ever alone — would inevitably end in a hotel in the Laurentians for a weekend. The idea of leaving Erica to pick up the pieces in Montreal when he himself went overseas, after one or several weekends in the Laurentians, did not appeal to Marc particularly.

And along with everything else, he had himself to cope with.

The cocktails had arrived. He drank his all at once, then said to Erica who was staring at the cherry in the bottom of her glass, "Spear it with a match."

"I wonder what's become of the toothpick?"

"It's probably a war measure."

"What were you thinking about?"

"You," he said. "Us."

His life had been run largely by his intelligence so far; his emotions had never threatened to run away with him until now — the only thing which could be said ever to have run away with him was his lack of emotion. He had never got either himself or anyone else into trouble through feeling too much, only through his having felt too little.

And now, Erica. She was wearing some kind of green and white summer dress, sitting beside him with her fair hair almost down to her shoulders, spearing the cherry at the bottom of her glass with a match.

"Don't look like that!" said Marc.

Erica raised her head and asked, startled, "Like what?"

But he did not know what he wanted her to look like, except that it would have been a help if she had looked less like herself. He moved a few inches away from her and ordered another cocktail.

There was a radio playing out in the hall. Erica ate the cherry and listened above the murmur of voices and the soft clatter of dishes, and asked finally, "What is it?"

"Schubert No. 5. I think he stole most of the last movement from Mozart."

Charles would have liked that, even if he had considered that Marc was slandering Schubert. The utterly lunatic part of it was that there was nothing about Marc that either Charles or her mother would *not* have liked.

"What did you say?" she asked a moment later.

"I said, you should have had a martini too."

"Why?"

"Because all I've got in my room is half a bottle of gin."

"Are we going to your room?" Erica asked, looking at a woman out in the middle of the long, light room who was wearing a very large black hat and eating lobster.

"Don't you think it's about time you learned something about my background?"

She felt that he was smiling at her, but the next moment the amusement died out of his oblique, greenish eyes. He took her hand suddenly for the first time, and held it with a pressure which went on steadily increasing until the waiter appeared on the other side of the table with his wagon of hors d'oeuvres, and he released it.

"Everything except onions, beets, herring, and that pink stuff," said Erica, after the waiter had waited patiently for one of them to pay some attention to him. "What's your room like?" she asked Marc.

"Depressing."

Some time later, as she was struggling with her chicken, Erica remarked, "When I eat hors d'oeuvres I never have any appetite left for the rest of the meal."

"You never have any appetite anyhow."

He was watching her with an anxious expression and an angry look in the tight muscles around his mouth. "What was it today?" he demanded without warning. "More trouble?"

Erica glanced at him quickly and then answered matter-of-factly, "No, of course not. I'm just not hungry."

He picked up the basket of bread and when she shook her head, he put a slice on her plate anyhow. "You've got to eat,

Eric." He gave her some butter and then asked, "Do you really think I'm worth it?"

"Yes," said Erica under her breath. Her eyes met his, and she said involuntarily, "Darling, don't look at me like that!"

"I can't help it. I've behaved very well so far but I don't think it's going to last much longer. In the meantime, you'd better go on eating. No woman looks romantic with her mouth full."

"Do I have to eat all of it?"

"There isn't much, Eric, it's mostly bones."

He was talking about something else and she thought that once again she had succeeded in heading him off, when he asked suddenly, as they were waiting for their dessert, "Do they go on at you about me all the time, or is it just intermittent?"

Evidently some of it had got through to him anyhow, in spite of the way she had worked to keep him from finding out, having realized from the beginning that the most dangerous aspect of the whole situation was not her father's attitude toward Marc but Marc's reaction to that attitude once he became fully aware of it. He would take it as final, because it was confirmed by so much in his own experience if for no other reason, when in fact it was not. Erica's conviction that sooner or later Charles Drake would come round was not based on hope so much as on a fairly complete knowledge of Charles Drake. If, at some future date, he should be faced with the choice of accepting Marc Reiser or losing his daughter, then Miriam to the contrary, Charles would accept Marc Reiser, but whether she could succeed in convincing Marc of that fact was a different matter. Marc did not know her father. And in any case, to ask Marc simply to wait and put up with the attitude until her father was forced into a position where he had to change it, and with nothing to look forward to, so far as Marc could see, but a grudging "acceptance" under due pressure, was to ask altogether too much of anyone with as much pride as Marc Reiser. He could not be expected to realize that the word "acceptance" had a different meaning for her father than it had for most people. You had actually to have seen Charles Drake do one of his *voltes-faces* before you could believe it was possible. He did not put his prejudices behind him and go on from there; he went back to the beginning and started all over again.

If only Marc had known her father — if only her father had known Marc. But neither of them did, and all she could do was to go on playing for time, trying to keep Marc from finding out what her family really thought of him, until, after a while, they thought a little better.

She said, "They don't 'go on' about you, darling; you're hardly ever mentioned."

After dinner they drove through the grey streets lined with trees, every shade and depth of green in the evening light, out of the city, through a village and across the canal, then on the straight new highway for a while and finally off to the left down a series of narrow country roads until they came to the river, and the primitive cable ferry which sailed back and forth on the current between Ile de Montreal and Ile Bizard. They found the old ferryman sitting as usual on a kitchen chair at one end of his barge, puffing on his pipe. There was no sound but the movement of the water in the long grasses by the bank, and some bells ringing in the monastery across the river. The old man stood up, beckoning them to drive onto the barge, then he cast off, and barge, car, and kitchen chair started for Ile Bizard. Of all the islands near the island of Montreal, Bizard was the one Erica loved best.

"How can anyone make a living out of ferrying people across here?" asked Erica. "Nobody ever goes to Ile Bizard but us, I mean not on this thing. Everybody else uses the bridge. Which river is this anyhow?"

"The Back River."

Erica sighed. "I'm always hoping it will turn out to be the Ottawa or the St. Lawrence but it never does."

The top of the car was down and looking up at the sky she remarked, "By the way, Vic and Barbara Wells are having a cocktail party on Friday. Do you want to go?"

"Was I invited?"

"Yes, Barbie asked if I'd bring you. She's going to phone you herself tomorrow."

"I don't have to be brought."

It sounded more like an observation than an objection.

So far so good, thought Erica, and said, "May I have a cigarette, please?"

He lit one for her and then one for himself and said at last, "I've known Vic ever since my first year at law school; he was a year ahead of me and he went into his father's firm as soon as he graduated. I've had lunch with him a couple of times since but that's about all — strictly business. So why the sudden interest?"

Farther up, the river was dotted with heavily wooded islands and there were a few villages hidden among the trees along the shore, although all you could see of them was an occasional roof or a church spire. Erica had been born and brought up in Montreal but she had never managed to get the geography of the region completely straightened out; it remained a green and watery tangle of islands, rivers, lakes, and villages all named after saints, the more obscure and improbable, the better. Just who, for example, was St. Polycarp de Crabtree Mills?

The sudden interest was due to the fact that she had had lunch with Barbara Wells the day before and since she knew Barbara very well, she had asked, "You wouldn't like to invite a friend of mine too, would you? His name is Marc Reiser, he's a Jewish lawyer and Charles won't have him in the house."

"Good Lord," said Barbara. After a moment she remarked, "If he's a lawyer, Vic probably knows him."

"That's more than can be said for Charles," said Erica. "He's one of those people who can judge the quality of the contents by the label on the can."

"Your father's not the only one. Vic can be pretty stuffy when he wants to be, particularly about the Jewish legal fraternity — he was well away on some frightful story about a firm of Jewish lawyers last night before he remembered that the Oppenheims are Jews and they were sitting on the opposite side of the table. Of course they're Austrians and you'd never guess . . ."

"Yes, dear," Erica interrupted patiently. "Well, Marc's parents are Austrian too, if that's any help." She could not imagine anyone who knew Marc not liking him and she said, "Anyhow, ask Vic what he thinks."

Later in the afternoon Barbara had phoned to say that Vic had said by all means, bring him along, and that was that, except for the fact that there was something in the tone in which Marc had asked about the sudden interest which made Erica suspect that he had no intention of going.

She did not care particularly whether he went or not, but she knew that this business of always being alone together was bad for them both and sooner or later, something would definitely have to be done about it. As things were, they were simply playing the parts Charles Drake had assigned them — the parts of a couple of outcasts. With the exception of one or two friends of Marc's who, like himself, were waiting to go overseas, most of his other friends having gone long since, and an occasional friend of Erica's, they had kept to themselves. The longer they went on keeping to themselves, without even trying to behave like ordinary people with a place in the society which surrounded them, the easier it was for Charles. If, on the other hand, enough people outside the family got to the point where they took Marc and herself for granted, the situation would begin to be thoroughly awkward for her parents. The Drakes could not go on indefinitely refusing to meet someone whom a steadily increasing number of other people they knew had met and accepted, without appearing rather silly. Vic and Barbara Wells combined an unassailable social position — which meant that their approval would automatically carry some weight with her father and mother, since the social aspect of the problem seemed to be one of their chief worries — with intelligence and, in spite of Vic's temporary lapse in the presence of the Oppenheims, a general lack of stuffiness, so their cocktail party looked to Erica like a good place to start.

The ringing of the monastery bells had died away. They heard the long whistle of a distant railway train, then a faint shout from somewhere on the shore behind them, and then there was silence again except for the splashing of the swift current, driving at an angle against the barge, and the noise the pulleys made as they creaked along the cable up in the air.

"I think I'd rather not go," said Marc.

"Why?" Before he could answer Erica said, "You know what cocktail parties are like, Marc — a lot of people bring their friends without even asking."

"Did *you* ask, Eric?"

"No."

His right arm was lying on the back of the seat behind her, and all he had to do was let it down to her shoulders in order to bring her around so that she was facing him. "Say it again."

"All right then," said Erica defiantly, "I did ask her. Good heavens, I've asked dozens of people if I could bring someone to their parties. Look at the one we gave in June — we started out with thirty people and ended up with over fifty."

"I know, I was one of them," said Marc noncommittally.

He took his arm away from her shoulders and turned so that he was sitting under the wheel again, looking past the bent figure of the old ferryman who was standing on the bow staring upriver, to the tumbledown landing stage on the green shore in front of him.

"You said that once . . ."

"Go on."

"You said it was important not to start imagining things."

"I'm not imagining anything, darling. You don't realize what the legal profession is like. It isn't the same as being a Jewish doctor, or professor, or even a Jewish businessman. You've got Vic on the spot, and the only thing for me to do is not to turn up. He knows he's never made any effort to see me outside of business hours since we were at law school — I tried once or twice after we graduated but he was always busy or something — and I know it, and he knows I know it. So now when you come along and finally get me invited to his house after twelve years — what does it all add up to?"

"It adds up to everybody going on forever playing this idiotic game according to the rules and never getting anywhere!" She said miserably, "You're just helping to make it work."

"Well, if I didn't, I'd only be accused of pushing in where I'm not wanted."

The barge slid into place against the beach and with her eyes on the old French Canadian who was adjusting the two planks which served as runways, she asked after a pause, "Are you going to feel like this about everyone?"

"No, of course not. You just happened to pick the wrong people."

They drove past the monastery, then into a village by a steepled church, around one side of the green square where a few old men were playing bowls, and out the other side among the fields and scattered farmhouses painted white and with the softly curving bell-cast roofs of Quebec, and the great barns of faded yellow and blue and red. There was a shrine by the side of the road and a few people grouped around it, old men and women and children and the village curé, and later on they came to a herd of cows and had to follow along behind with the car in low gear until the cows turned in at a gate.

This is Quebec, where you were born and brought up, and these are some of the things you would remember if you had to go away and live somewhere else — wayside shrines and fields of cornflowers, the view from the top of Mount Oka where you can look down on the roofs of the great Trappist monastery and out over the valleys of the Ottawa and the St. Lawrence, green islands and green shores, blue water with a white sail here and there and the blue mountains in the distance. You would remember a village with a white church steeple at the end of a Laurentian valley, a farmer driving a high-wheeled buggy down a dark country road at night, singing on his way home; seagulls flying over the rocky coast of Gaspé, sailing-boats and villages and the long narrow farms running down to the St. Lawrence, and everywhere over cities, towns, villages, and the green countryside, over mountains and valleys, rivers and lakes, the sound of bells tolling for mass and the dark, anonymous figures of priests, nuns, and monks. You would remember the jangle of sleighbells in winter, the sharp, pointed outlines of pine trees black against the snow, the flat white expanse of frozen lakes crossed and recrossed with ski tracks, and the skiers themselves pouring down the cold mountainside at dusk, toward the train waiting down below in the valley.

And you would remember Montreal, the incredible tropical green of this northern city in summer, the old grey squares, the Serpentine at Lafontaine Park with little overhanging casinos and packed with little boats; the harbour, the river; the formalized black-and-white figures of the nuns taking the air just at dusk among the trees around the Mother House of the Congregation de Notre Dame, the narrow grey streets of downtown Montreal like the streets of an old French provincial town, the figure of the Blessed Virgin keeping watch over the harbour from her place high up on Bonsecours, the sailors' church; the steep terraced gardens of Westmount, and the endless narrow balconies of endless walled convents and monasteries, where nobody ever walks.

Erica said reflectively as they passed an old stone farmhouse on one side of the road with a grove of pines on the other, "When they go on about preserving the French-Canadian way of life, sometimes I think I know what they're talking about."

"Yes," said Marc, adding after a pause, "Only their way of life is rather a luxury at the moment and somebody has to pay for it. I don't feel the way you do about Quebec. I feel that way about Ontario."

He slowed down, looking warily at a dog which was standing undecidedly in the middle of the narrow, winding dirt road just ahead of them, and then finally came to a dead stop. "Well, make up your mind," he said patiently. "We're not in a hurry, just take your time about it." The dog regarded him without interest, and eventually started toward a nearby gate, waving his tail in the air.

"It doesn't matter so much where it is, though, provided it's Canada. I'm hopelessly provincial, Eric. I've been in Europe and the States of course, but though I had a marvellous time, it was always a relief to come home again. I just belong here, that's all. I couldn't imagine living anywhere else. How long can you see the shore after you leave Halifax?"

"Only for a short while."

"That's good. The shorter the better. I don't want to stand around for hours watching Canada fade into the distance."

He drove on in silence for a while, looking straight ahead of him, and then said suddenly, "Gosh, it will be great to come back again, though, won't it, Eric?"

"Yes, darling."

"How about something on the radio?" He turned past several dance orchestras and an announcer saying, "Ainsi se termine, chers auditeurs, un autre concert symphonique ..." and another one beginning, "Nous vous presentons maintenant quelques bulletins de guerre ..." and finally he left it at a symphony orchestra playing a Strauss waltz.

A hay wagon was lumbering toward them and as he slowed down again in order to go off the road and give it room to pass, he said, "They told me at Headquarters today that it probably wouldn't be much more than a month now."

"And then what?"

"Petawawa or Borden for a while, and then overseas."

"I hope it's Petawawa," said Erica under her breath. Camp Borden was four hundred miles away.

He stopped the car in an open space under some evergreens at the edge of a small wood and turned off the radio which had changed from Strauss to advertising, so that they were caught up in the silence all around them. The moon was rising over an orchard, and the lamps were already lit in the small farmhouse up the road. Nearer at hand there was a wayside cross partly outlined against the dying light of the west.

Marc took the cigarette from her hand and threw it out on the road and then his arm was around her, drawing them together. He kissed her throat and then her mouth and she had no will at all until at last memory came back. She slipped one arm up behind his head and clung to him, trying to forget the time when she would have to let him go, probably not much more than a month from now.

V

In the first week of August, Charles Drake suddenly changed tactics. His conduct from the Wednesday morning in mid-July when they had had that scene at the breakfast table, through to the end, sometime in September, represented three different and distinctive methods of attack, from the negative, in which he had withdrawn in apparent indifference and simply waited, through the positive but indirect, in which he attempted to break down Erica's resistance by abandoning all efforts to conceal what he felt while never actually referring to his feelings, and at the same time by letting loose a continuous stream of broad statements, anecdotes, and even rather pointless jokes on the subject of Jews in general, to the third and last stage, in which he swung around and made use of every weapon he could lay his hands on.

For reasons of her own, Margaret Drake went along with him. Although so far as her surface behaviour was concerned, she seemed to take her cue from her husband, her attitude was fundamentally different. She believed that all mésalliances are the result of infatuation, and therefore from start to finish, she consistently underestimated Erica's love for Marc. In fact, she did not regard it as love, in the proper sense of the word. She lacked her husband's ability to understand emotion as such, particularly an emotion which lay outside the field of her own experience. The sexual element did not exist for her except in a derogatory sense; in her conception of a valid and lasting relationship between a man and a woman, that element was removed. She did not discount it; she simply left it out altogether. The ingredients of a successful marriage, she had often said, were community of tastes, interests, and a similarity of viewpoint and background. All these were blended together by an emotion called "love" of course, but a love which was to her a composite of other kinds of love, rather than a separate entity with a basic character of its own. She was devoted to her husband; he was her best friend, her father and counselor, her child, her brother — in fact he was the sum total of all her other relationships and because that was so much, it had never occurred to her, consciously at any rate, that he could have been anything more.

Surveying Erica's relationship to Marc from the standpoint of community of tastes and interests and similarity of viewpoint and background — above all, similarity of background, since it is the background which gives rise to the viewpoint — and convinced as she was that you cannot be "genuinely" in love with a man whom you have only known for a period of weeks, rather than months, Margaret Drake could not bring herself to regard it as anything but an infatuation.

Charles Drake was under no such delusions, and in this respect, his conduct was considerably less justifiable than that of his wife. If he had regarded it as an infatuation, he would have let it run its course, and trusted Erica to come to her senses in time to prevent her from taking any final step on the strength of it, but as a matter of fact, he knew Erica too well to imagine that she was capable of being infatuated with anyone.

It was precisely because he realized how much Marc meant to her that he did everything in his power to get rid of him. In the end, unlike his wife, he could not plead ignorance; he could not say as Margaret Drake was to say in sheer despair, after Marc had finally gone home, "Erica, I didn't know — I didn't know!"

Charles Drake had known, as he generally did, from the very beginning. His only excuse was self-defence, for in trying to defend Erica, he was defending not her interests, but his conception of her interests.

The change in tactics came without warning so far as Erica was concerned, except for Miriam's statement that her parents had decided to stay in town because they were too worried to derive any benefit from their much-needed holiday.

The morning after Marc and Erica had crossed the river to Ile Bizard by the cable ferry, her father asked Erica suddenly if she was going to be in to dinner the following night.

"No, I don't think so," said Erica.

"Who are you going out with? René?"

Once before he had asked her if she were going out with René when he already knew she was not.

"I haven't seen him for weeks."

"So even René is getting the short end of it. Do you mind telling me who you are going out with?"

"Yes, Marc Reiser."

"Weren't you out with him last night, Erica?" asked her mother.

"Rather overdoing it, isn't he?" asked Charles.

"He isn't going to be here much longer ..."

"Oh, I don't know," interrupted her father. "We've been at war three years and he seems to have managed pretty well so far."

"You don't know anything about it, Charles," said Erica expressionlessly. She had reached the stage where nothing he said about Marc could make her angry, which, she thought, was simply so much the worse for them both. "It isn't his fault that he was posted to a reinforcement unit and just told to mark time at Divisional Headquarters until ..." Erica stopped. Neither of them, as usual, appeared to be listening; her father's eyes were back on his newspaper and her mother was pouring a second cup of coffee for Miriam, who opened her mouth to say something, glanced at Erica, and then subsided, muttering resignedly, "O.K., darling, have it your own way."

Erica said at last, looking down at her plate, "I thought you wanted to know why Marc and I are seeing so much of each other."

"We already know that without being told." Her father made an effort to read a little further, obviously thoroughly depressed, then with an exclamation he suddenly put down his paper, got up, and left the room.

From then on, any direct or indirect reference to Marc always produced the same result. It wasn't what they said, for they rarely said anything, but the way they looked. Whenever they knew that Erica was on her way to meet Marc somewhere or had just come back from meeting him, the moment she entered the room, that look would settle down over their faces. It was apparently necessary that she should not go out the front door under any illusion that they would be enjoying themselves while she was with Marc, and when she returned home, it was equally necessary that she should realize that it was they who were paying for any happiness she might have had from her dinner, or her drive or whatever it was. The look was not in any way put on; it was a matter of simple fact that they did not and could not enjoy themselves when they knew Erica was with Marc, and that her happiness, such as it was, was purchased at their expense, and they made no effort to conceal it, that was all.

Erica lived with that look from the beginning of August until the middle of September when Marc went home, back to his own people, and she finally broke down. She never got used to it, and up to the very end, it still required an effort of will before she could force herself to enter a room and face it.

The indirect attack on Marc started a few nights later at dinner. It did not amount to much; Charles Drake had lunched that day with a dollar-a-year man on the Wartime Prices and Trading Board who had told him that the most persistent violators of the price ceiling were the Jews, particularly the Jewish clothing firms who were so universally determined to beat the Government that there would have been no particular risk involved in arresting every Jewish clothier first and taking the chance of being able to secure enough evidence for the conviction of each of them individually, afterwards. "The Jews" had no sense of responsibility and regarding themselves as outside the community, for some reason or other, you simply could not make them realize that what affected the community as a whole would ultimately affect them to the same extent as everyone else.

Since she had heard it all before from various other people, and had grown up in a society in which almost everyone threw off derogatory remarks about "The Jews," often from sheer force of habit, Erica would probably not have attached any particular significance to her father's remarks if he had not rather gone out of his way to avoid all unflattering references to Jews, as such, until now. He was too imaginative ever to be accidentally tactless and since he himself bracketed Marc with Jews in general, until now he had preferred to stay off the subject altogether.

Erica was out the following night. The night after that it was something about "The Jews" safeguarding themselves against the inflation for which their own conduct would be partly responsible, by buying up all the available real estate.

At breakfast a day or so later, it was the old story of fire insurance; in a slightly different form, however. The previous night he had been playing bridge at his club with the president of an insurance company who had remarked in the course of a discussion about the Jews that Jews and fires always went together, and that if you wanted to find the Jewish districts in any given city, all you had to do was look at the nearest insurance company map for the heaviest concentration of fires. In fact they were such a bad risk that a good many companies preferred not to sell them fire insurance, with the result that a group of Jews who were angered by the discrimination against them had got together and started an insurance company of their own, only to go broke in short order. The richest part of it was that these same Jews would now sell fire insurance only to Gentiles.

The maps were something new so far as Erica was concerned, but the Jewish company which refused to insure other Jews against fire was not. She had often wondered if it really existed.

There was a curious, very faint deliberateness in the way her father went about it, a barely perceptible change of expression and a barely audible change in his voice, so that she always knew when he was going to start, and tried to steel herself against what was coming. She had an odd feeling that to allow herself to be hurt by it would be to fall into the same fundamental error as her father — the error of identifying the characteristics of the individual with the usually misinterpreted characteristics of the group.

It was not until his observations on the subject of "The Jews" began to be interspersed with anti-Jewish anecdotes and rather unfunny jokes which Charles Drake had usually heard from "a man downtown" — well, he undoubtedly had; Erica knew from her own experience that there were a large number of people with that particular kind of sense of humor — that Erica realized what was happening to him.

The faint air of deliberateness had gone; having set out to convince his daughter, Charles Drake was in danger of convincing himself. He had already forgotten what he had been told about Marc downtown and over at Divisional Headquarters. After a very brief appearance, the individual had once more been obliterated by the generalization.

Some time very lately he must have begun to associate the interminable gossip about Jews which he heard "downtown" directly with Marc, to assume more and more that this endless stream of astronomical generalizations which tossed sixteen million human beings, scattered all over the pre-war world, into one heap and covered the lot of them, must inevitably apply at least to some extent to the man his daughter was in love with and probably intended to marry. From then on, every chance remark that other people made, either to him or simply in his hearing, must have struck home, until the idea that someone about whom such things could be said might also in the future be referred to as Erica's husband and C. S. Drake's son-in-law became finally too much for him.

It was an indication of how far Charles Drake had degenerated in the past two months that he could tell a pointless and sordid story of "Jewish" behaviour during the Blitz, for example, and insult both Erica and himself by suggesting, even indirectly, that it reflected on Marc. All his life he had been unusually free of malice and in spite of his explosive prejudices, he had had a certain largeness of mind and generosity of spirit which had prevented him from gibing at individuals for characteristics beyond their control. That he should have lost so much of what had been the best in him in such a short time was also an indication of the way he was suffering.

He no longer seemed to care what methods he had to use in order to get through to Erica, provided she could be made to face facts. There was no reason why she should be protected and encouraged to go on living in a world of illusions, among a handful of friends who apparently believed that one war could change the whole structure of human society. Married to a Jewish lawyer whose parents had been ordinary immigrants, life would be no easier for Erica in 1945 than in 1910.

He had no idea what she would do with Marc Reiser; he had no idea what any of them would do with him. He could not be made to fit in, one Jew among a lot of Drakes. Wherever they took him, to the houses of their relatives or their friends, he would stick out like a sore thumb.

That was not all. Later on there would be children, Erica's children who would be half Jewish by race and probably brought up in the Jewish religion — Jews and Catholics could always be counted on to look out for their own interests — so that his grandchildren would be wholly Jewish by faith.

And what on earth would they do with Marc Reiser's family,

since presumably he had a family? When your son or daughter marries, you cannot pretend that the relatives of your daughter-in-law or son-in-law simply do not exist.

Charles Drake could not imagine what Marc Reiser's family would be like. The fact that their son was presentable enough on the surface proved nothing, since there was often an extraordinary difference between the first and the second generation. He remembered what a shock he had had when the parents of a Jewish importer whom he had known for years and had always regarded as quite exceptional, the very best type of Jew ... what a shock he had had when the fellow's parents had turned out to be pure ghetto. The old man wore a black skull cap, both he and his wife kept dropping into Yiddish, and what English they knew sounded as though they had learned it on New York's East Side. Their accent had reminded Charles Drake of the old days of vaudeville and the inevitable cheap Jewish comic who had elected to make a living by holding up his own people to ridicule. There always seemed to be one on every program and either he or his straight man was usually called "Ikey." To this day Erica's father did not know what had possessed their son when he had suddenly invited C. S. Drake to his home for "supper" on Saturday night; it was one of the most uncomfortable evenings Charles Drake had ever had.

Uncomfortable or not, however, at least he had been able to escape at the end of the evening. From the elder Reisers there would be no escape, and no end, from the day on which he would find himself standing beside his wife and a couple of middle-aged immigrant Jews from some small town in Ontario, attempting to introduce his son-in-law's parents to Montreal society.

It is no good thinking of life in terms of vague and idealistic principles; life is not made up of common sense, logic, or even elementary justice. It is made up of the way people think, feel, and behave, with or without due cause, and when they have felt and thought that way for two thousand years, one war and a fresh outburst of lofty generalities about a better world are not going to make much difference. Even supposing by some miracle or other the Reisers should turn out to be moderately well-bred, from a social point of view they would still be unmanageable.

Charles Drake was almost beside himself.

At breakfast, at dinner, and in the evenings when Erica was at home, he would suddenly start in on the Jews again and go on talking, talking, talking; he said anything that came into his head without fully realizing what he was saying, except that he was careful never to refer to Marc directly. It was as though everything he had ever heard against the Jews, back to his earliest childhood, was coming out all in a period of a few weeks, five, ten, or fifteen minutes at a time, during which he would keep his eyes fixed on Erica, searching her face to see if at last he had succeeded in making an impression.

He did not succeed; he failed altogether. Erica had lost the faculty of thinking in reverse, she was no longer even capable of applying the generalization to the individual. She knew Marc, she was in possession of the evidence, of the actual facts concerning Marc Reiser, and between those facts and her father's statements about Jews, there was simply no connection. He was still talking about someone else.

She would sit and listen to him in silence, or at any rate she appeared to be listening. His voice only reached her at intervals, becoming audible and then fading away again, according to the rise and fall in the level of her consciousness.

What he was saying was of no importance in itself, it had all been said before so many times, repeated parrot-like but with an air of acute perception and originality by one person after another, in one country after another, all the way down through history. After all, even Hitler was unable to think up anything really new on the subject of the Jews; he merely said what everybody else had been saying, only of course he said it louder and oftener, and put it a bit more strongly.

The importance lay, first, in the fact that it was Charles who was saying it, and second, in the fact that if he believed what he said, if he believed that even half of what he was saying applied to Marc, then, whether or not her father ultimately came round, it would make no real difference. He might put up with Marc, he might endure him for her sake, but he would never like him. He would never even get near enough to Marc to find out whether he was likable or not.

You might just as well try to see a man through a brick wall as try to see him through a mass of preconceived ideas.

In the intervals when she was really listening, Erica sometimes tried to visualize Marc as he must appear to her father. He always came out as a nightmare figure, a crazy conglomerate of a shyster lawyer, quick, insinuating, and tricky; a fat clothing merchant with a cigar in his mouth, employing sweated labor with one hand and contriving to outsmart both his competitors and the government with the other; a loud-voiced, flashy young man pushing his way up to the head of the queue; a skullcapped figure muttering incantations in a synagogue; a furtive, greasy individual setting fire to his own house or his own shop in order to collect the insurance . . . all this not only combined in one individual, but an individual who was determined not to be assimilated but to remain an outsider, and who was perpetually turning up where he was not wanted, overrunning hotels, beaches, clubs, and practically every place he was permitted to enter.

It might have been funny, only it wasn't. Coming from her father — not Charles, her Charles, the individual on the left with whom she was never in contact any more except when they were listening to music — as the creature of his imagination and set beside Marc Reiser who, in this house, lived only in her mind and in her heart, it was not funny at all. Neither was the spectacle of her father, apparently powerless in the grip of a steadily mounting obsession — he had told his wife and his wife had told Erica that there was not one moment of the day when Erica was really out of his mind — nor the spectacle of her mother, appalled at what might happen to Erica and what was already happening to her husband, nor Erica herself. Beneath her silence and her expressionless face, she was beginning to break up, and she knew it.

Only Miriam remained detached and objective, partly because she was Miriam, not Charles or Margaret Drake, and Erica was her sister, not her daughter, and partly because she knew Marc.

VI
❧

*M*iriam had met Marc in the last week of August. The four of them, Erica, Marc, Max Eliot, and herself were to have had dinner together, but that morning Max Eliot had left unexpectedly for England, and Miriam brought John Gardiner instead. John was the complete opposite of Max in almost every respect — blond, towering, physically hard and innately kind — and he and Marc took an immediate liking to each other. They were both in uniform, John with a red First Division patch on his sleeve. As soon as Marc had finished ordering, they began to talk about various men they both knew among the officers of the First Battalion of the Gatineau Rifles, who had been stationed near John's unit on the south coast of England for almost a year.

They were well away, and Erica said to Miriam, "Where's Max?"

"He's gone."

"Where?"

"England. He left on a bomber this morning."

"When is he coming back?"

Miriam was looking at the wall behind John's fair head, her dark eyes wide and her face unnaturally stiff. She said at last, as though she had had to wait in order to be sure that she would say it casually, "I haven't the remotest idea. I got the air last night."

A little later when she had finished her cocktail and Marc had ordered another one for her, she observed to Erica as the two men went on talking, "I guess I always knew it was going to happen. I had such a strong feeling about it that I even tried to plan the whole thing in advance, so that if or when it did happen, I wouldn't make any fuss."

"And did you, darling?"

"No," she said under her breath. "No fuss." She glanced at Erica and went on in the same even tone, "I can't let go because if I do, I'll probably just go to pieces. I hate crying, it always makes everything so much worse. What shall we do after dinner?"

"We might go somewhere and dance."

"You should have seen me getting the air at two o'clock this morning. I was really terrific, Eric. Not that it makes any difference. An exit is just an exit, whether you mess it up or not."

"You should have stayed home, darling," said Erica, watching her.

"Not on your life. I'm going to get good and drunk."

"How do you like Marc?" asked Erica after a pause.

Miriam looked at him and said, "He isn't exactly what I expected."

"What *did* you expect?"

"He looks marvellous in uniform," remarked Miriam irrele-vantly, and then answered, "Somebody you could probably do pretty much what you liked with . . . up to a point, that is."

"Oh, dear no," said Erica, shaking her head.

"No," said Miriam, "evidently not." Since she was the first member of Erica's family that Marc had really met, she realized now that what she had chiefly expected was that Marc would try to make some kind of an impression. Not an obvious effort, of course, but still, an effort. She had supposed that he would put himself out at least to some extent. Instead of that, and although she had never seen him before, she was certain that he was simply being himself, and nothing more. Of the four of them, he seemed to Miriam to be the one in control, as though it were John and herself who were up for inspection, so to speak, and not the other way round, and finding that it helped her to keep her mind off Max, she went on watching Marc as he sat across the table with his head turned toward John, twist-ing the stem of a cocktail glass through his fingers and not talking much himself, wondering how he did it. It occurred to her that there was something in his oddly set eyes and his sensitive face which was rather disconcerting — a latent quality, both hard and resistant, like a metal which will be hot on the surface and cold in the center and which, try as you will, you cannot heat all the way through.

She thought with sudden astonishment, Marc Reiser is just as tough as Charles and probably still harder to handle. She said again to Erica, sitting on the banquette beside her because it was more comfortable than the two straight-backed chairs occupied by Marc and John across the table, "No, he definitely isn't what I expected," and suddenly found herself back at Max again. This small restaurant with old-fashioned wallpaper, white-clothed tables, and dark woodwork, in a converted house on a side street, had been Max Eliot's favourite place to dine when he was in Montreal. She had often been here with him, and had even sat at this very table one Saturday night when all the tables for two were already taken.

She said, gripping the edge of the banquette with both hands, "May I have another drink?"

She had already drunk two cocktails and John asked, "Why don't you wait for a while, Mimi?"

"Mind your own business," said Miriam in French, and then added in English, "I've got a headache."

John looked relieved, and then almost immediately concerned again. "Wouldn't you like some aspirin?" he asked.

"I would like another cocktail," said Miriam patiently. She smiled faintly as she saw a flicker of amusement in Marc's face. He turned to give the order to a passing waiter and then started talking to John again. They were discussing the problem of Germany, and she tried to focus her mind on what they were saying for a while but it was no use, and she lapsed back into herself again.

It was not only Max and the fact that she was not going to see him again, never again; there was something else which she could not afford to think about until she was back on solid ground and had really got hold of herself again. It was the old game of keeping your balance by looking straight ahead and not allowing yourself to look down. When they were children, they had sometimes gone for walks along the railway up in the Laurentians, and she had always been able to balance on the rail long after Tony and Eric had got bored and were down in the ditch or racing along the path. Erica had never been any good at it, though she was almost five years older than Miriam; she had always looked down and then fallen off. Through all these unpredictable years leading up to the present, with Tony flying a bomber over Europe, Erica close to a final break with their mother and father because she was in love with a Jew, and herself . . . well, anyhow, she could still hear Tony yelling at the fair-haired, tottering little figure on the rail, "Don't look down, Eric! Look straight ahead . . ."

Don't look down, Miriam, look straight ahead. Straight ahead at what? That was the trouble, instead of a curve of a railway track, a white farmhouse and the plowed fields running halfway up the mountain to the edge of the pine forest, there was nothing to look at, absolutely nothing.

She realized now that although consciously she had known that she could not hold Max indefinitely, unconsciously she had gone on hoping that not only would he not leave her, but that by some miracle he would want her enough to go through all the bother of a divorce so that he could marry her.

She said suddenly to Erica, "Damn it, I thought I'd be a better sport than this!" Eric did not answer, she was listening to Marc and John. She would not have known what Miriam was talking about anyhow, for no one, not even Erica, knew how much Max had done for her. When someone does as much as that for you, the least you can do is not feel sorry for yourself all over the place because he didn't do more!

"Putting the whole blame on the German nation isn't going to get us anywhere," said Marc. "It's like treating a case of smallpox by cutting off a man's leg because there happen to be more spots on his leg than anywhere else."

"You're Jewish, aren't you?"

What was John asking that for? She had told him the whole story of Marc, Erica, and her parents when she and John had been pub crawling one night the week before. Somewhere between the Mount Royal bar and the Colony Club, she had observed that John was about to start telling her how much he loved her all over again. Miriam always knew when he was about to start, because whatever he was feeling found its way to his face before he could get hold of the right words, and in order to stop him, she had hurriedly taken refuge in Erica and Marc and the behaviour of her parents. She could not remember what she had said, exactly, but she had certainly told John that Marc was a Jew. After all, that was the whole point.

"Yes, of course," said Marc.

"Most of the Jews I know would like to see the entire German nation at the bottom of the Atlantic."

"Oh?" Marc looked briefly at Erica's plate, remarked, "There's no excuse for your leaving half your steak, darling, it hasn't any bones in it," and then back at John again, he said mildly, "I'm not giving you a racial opinion of the Germans, if there is such a thing. I'm just giving you my own opinion, though as a matter of fact, every Jew ought to know by this time that Nazism isn't a German monopoly. Given complete power over every possible source of public information, I'm inclined to think that you could make any nation believe anything in six months."

"I don't agree with you," said John.

"Have you ever met anyone who's actually lived under the Nazis?"

"Well, a lot of refugees."

"I don't mean refugees, particularly Jews. I mean ordinary Germans. I met a lot of them coming back from Europe on the boat in 1937. They were just out on business and expected to be back in Germany in a few months. Anyhow, arguing with them was like arguing with someone in a nightmare, or arguing geography with a man who's been brought up to believe that the earth is square. They'd been so consistently misinformed on every subject for so long that there was no common ground for discussion at all. It was hopeless. Every time you produced a fact, they produced a contrary fact, and neither of you could advance an inch."

"It's a lot easier to convince the Germans that the earth is square than it is most people," said John.

Miriam saw Marc glance at him with a skeptical expression but he said nothing. Then she heard Erica remark, "It probably depends on whether the particular nation wants to be convinced or not."

"And what makes them want to be convinced?"

"I suppose a combination of certain historical, economic, and environmental factors."

Miriam began to lose track again. Her mind was like a badly functioning radio transmitter; for a while the voices would come over quite clearly, then they would begin to fade, and finally there would be another interval of silence.

Some time later John's voice reached her, asking if anyone minded if he smoked a pipe. He never smoked until he had finished a meal and Miriam glanced at him in surprise, then down at her own plate. Somebody, she remembered, had said something about steak, but all she herself had been aware of eating was a shrimp cocktail. On her plate, however, was half a French pastry.

"Just as a matter of interest, Eric," she said, "what entrée did I have?"

"Chicken."

"Well, well. I must be going nuts." Here, she added peremptorily to herself, pull yourself together. Hoping that they were still on the same subject, she said almost briskly, "There seem to be two theories about this war. One that it's all the fault of the Germans and the other that it's part of a — of a . . ."

She looked helplessly at Marc who said ". . . a historical process?"

"Yes, thanks."

He said to John, "We've got to a point where we recognize that the basis of government is the individual, but the individual is not yet the basis of the economic system, and until we produce primarily for consumption and not primarily for profits, democracy as a purely political system with almost no economic application is not going to work. We'll just have another war if we blame it all on the Germans and try to revert to the status quo ante. That's what you mean, isn't it?" he asked, turning to Miriam.

"Er . . . yes," said Miriam.

"What are you two?" asked John, glancing from Marc to Erica across the table. "Socialists?"

"Must we be labelled?" asked Erica, making a face. She grinned at Marc and said, "I'm allergic to labels."

A cloud of smoke from John's pipe floated over to an elderly woman at the next table who turned slowly and deliberately in her chair, directed a long look in John's direction, and slowly resumed her former position.

John put down his pipe and said resignedly, "Give me a cigarette, somebody."

He took one from Marc's case and Miriam asked him rather curiously, "What do *you* think we're fighting for?"

He said slowly after a pause, "I can tell you what the men in the Army don't think they're fighting for, if that's any help. They're not fighting for the kind of life they've been leading for the past ten or twelve years." He paused again, frowning, and went on at last, "The trouble is that so far, even after three years of war, their only definite ideas seem to be negative ones — they know they've got to beat Hitler, of course, but they seem to be fairly cynical about the Post-war world. It's not their fault; the people who do all the talking haven't really said anything yet."

"Do you think the people who are in a position to do all the talking really know?" asked Erica.

"Maybe a few of them do, but all we seem to have got so far is a kind of mass consciousness of the way things are changing, or ought to change, if we're really going to get anywhere after the war. At least the English masses seem to be getting the hang of things, and I guess we are too, though naturally not to the same extent yet, because we haven't taken anything like the beating they have. I don't know about the Americans, though I'd be willing to bet that when capitalism is a dead duck in the rest of the world, the Americans will be the last nation to admit it."

"Why?" asked Erica.

"Because their attitude towards government seems to be fundamentally different from ours. The further you get from unrestricted capitalism the more government you have to have. So far as the war is concerned, for example, the Americans apparently get production in spite of their government, half the time, and not because of it. It's their individual industrial geniuses who work the miracles, not Washington. They still believe in rugged individualism and don't believe in 'govern-ment interference,' so rugged individualism works and government doesn't. Most of the Americans I know talk about their government as though it was on one side of the fence and they were on the other. Good old-fashioned capitalism is the only economic system that suits that point of view."

He said, "That's not the point though. I can't describe what I mean by a mass consciousness, exactly. A few people up top seem to know what it's all about, like Vice-President Wallace and Sumner Welles and their opposite numbers in England. They have to put into words what the masses just sort of feel. But it's all vague, and the worst of it is that the people with most of the power have everything tied up in the status quo, so we're back where we started again, with the big interests fighting for one kind of world and the masses fighting for something else."

Miriam had been staring at him with growing amazement. Now she asked, "How long has this been going on, for goodness' sake?"

"How long has what been going on?"

Failing to think of any way of saying it which wouldn't sound rude, she answered finally with a hopeless gesture, "You've come such a long way from the bond house!"

"Thanks," said John. "When you've been in the Army for three years, you're bound to start wondering why you're there, some time or other."

"And do you know now?" inquired Miriam.

"Yes, or at least I'm beginning to get a general idea. I joined up more or less at the start in '39 because my sort always does," he said matter-of-factly, as though he were discussing someone else. "Not because I was particularly anxious to pull up stakes and go out and die for my country, but just because I come from a certain type of background — a good school, university, do your job and don't leave it to the other fellow — that sort of thing. Fine in 1900, but not enough to get you through this kind of war. I don't like England much, it gives me claustrophobia, and I was stuck in a holding unit down on the south coast, homesick as the devil for a country big enough so that if you went walking at night you wouldn't be running the risk of falling off the edge, and half the time I had nothing to do but play chess with the local vicar and think."

"So you thought," said Miriam.

"Shut up," he said good-humoredly, but he was embarrassed. He ran one hand over his fair hair, glanced at Miriam with that expression at the back of his blue eyes which gave him away every time he looked at her, and asked, "What shall we do now? Has anybody got any good ideas?"

"I want to go somewhere and dance," said Miriam.

On the way to the door she asked John how he liked Marc. "First rate," said John. "Your father must be crazy."

"Oh, no," said Miriam. "He just thinks we're fighting the other kind of war — you know, the one for the status quo."

Later, as she was dancing with Marc, Miriam asked suddenly, "Don't you think it would be a good idea if Eric got a place of her own to live?"

"Why?"

He was watching a couple who were dancing on the floor somewhere behind her and she said, "Eric thinks Charles is going to change his mind, but he isn't. Not . . ." She stopped herself just in time, having been on the point of adding without thinking, "Not until it's too late," and said instead, "Not until he's just about worn her ragged."

"She doesn't eat enough," said Marc noncommittally.

"Well, no," said Miriam, rather at a loss. Marc was too close for her to see him properly and find out whether he minded her going on or not. She decided to take a chance on his not minding and said, "He never leaves her alone, that's the trouble. He doesn't say anything about you directly, of course, but he does manage to get in a devil of a lot indirectly, and when he's not doing that, he and Mother just sit and look blue, as though Erica's the only thing they ever think about."

He surprised her by saying in the same expressionless tone, "Maybe she is." Still looking over Miriam's shoulder, he added, "I didn't know they still objected to me so much. I thought they were probably getting used to it by now."

She did not know how he could possibly have thought

that when Erica must have told him that her parents were not making the slightest effort to get used to it — on the contrary!

The music stopped, then started again, and she said, "Tell me, Mr. Reiser, do you do everything as well as you dance?"

"Practically everything," said Marc, grinning. "By the way, I like your friend Major Gardiner."

"He likes you too." Like Erica, she found it difficult to imagine anyone with a grain of sense not liking Marc. It was not only that he was attractive and intelligent, with charm and good manners and a marvellous smile, but he had another quality, still more important. He was completely straight. After talking to him for even a short time, you knew that he would never lie nor take an advantage, and after a little longer, you also knew that he was incapable of consciously going out of his way to make an impression no matter who it was, and that he would be the same person in court or at a social affair as he was with Erica, John, his own family, or his Chinese laundryman.

"You have a Chinese laundryman, haven't you?" asked Miriam.

"I think he has me. He always comes when I'm out and takes whatever he thinks needs washing. It doesn't make any difference whether I think so or not, unless I take the trouble to hide it somewhere so he won't find it." He sighed and said reminiscently, "My secretary used to be like that too. She even had my lunch sent up to the office whenever she could, so that she could make certain I had a properly balanced meal."

He went on talking about his secretary, whose name was Miss Carruthers, who was wonderful, and who had promised to come back as soon as he got out of the Army and started practicing law again.

Miriam was only half listening, she was far more interested in Marc himself than in his former secretary.

Without realizing it, she had assumed that the chief problem in Erica's apparently hopeless situation was her father . . . as though Marc were more or less in the position of someone hanging around the door waiting to be let in. Now that she had met him and he had turned out to be so subtly different from what she had expected, that bland assumption, which she supposed was shared by her father, already struck her as fantastic.

"There's no sense your starting to worry about it," said Marc suddenly.

She had been following him automatically with her left hand twisting the upper of the two pips on his shoulder. She moved her hand nearer his collar and said, "I can't help worrying. I care more about Eric than I do about anyone else. If she weren't so damned decent, none of this would have happened to her. Mother used to be fond of saying that Erica had never given either her or Charles a moment's worry — well, you'd think that since she's never done anything they didn't want her to do until now, they'd take her seriously and show some respect for her. But it doesn't work that way at all — they're so used to Erica never doing anything they don't want that they're damn well not going to allow her to start at the age of twenty-eight."

"That's a rather brutal way of putting it, isn't it?"

"Isn't that really what Charles means when he says this is the first time Erica has ever let them down, and that he's not going to let her ruin her life if he can help it? Whose life is it, for God's sake? Charles' or Erica's?"

He said nothing. He only smiled at her and looked away again.

She remarked a moment later, "It's amazing the way people can assume that they know what's 'best' for someone else — that they know better than the individual concerned what is going to make him or her happy or unhappy. Really, when you come to think of it, it is the most stupefying arrogance. I'm not talking about children, of course, but grown-up people who are obviously old enough to make up their own minds."

The music stopped again and in the pause he said, watching the band leader who was talking to one of the saxophone players, gesturing as though he were angry about something, "It's not always as simple as that. Their assumptions may simply be based on what they know happened to everybody who tried breaking the rules because they thought they were exceptions too."

"But surely there are exceptions, aren't there?"

He said wearily, "For every individual who really is exceptional there are about fifty thousand who just imagine they are — until it's too late, and they find out they aren't after all."

She was too disturbed to notice that the other couples had left the floor and after looking at him blankly for a moment she said, "Let's go to the bar. I feel like a drink and we can't talk very well at the table with John and Eric."

The bar was all blue and silver, dimly lit by pinpricks of light scattered over the low, dark blue ceiling. There were a few people sitting here and there, talking in low voices against the sound of the orchestra from the next room. Miriam and Marc sat down at a table in the corner beside a large, stylized plant which appeared to be made of some kind of metal.

It was another place where she had often been with Max, even oftener than at the little restaurant in which the four of them had had dinner. For some reason or other he had taken a liking to the blue atmosphere and the deep, comfortable leather-covered chairs, and there was an interval just after they sat down and before she or Marc said anything, when the past obliterated the present, like one picture dissolving into another on a screen. The room blurred, then slowly came into focus again, only it was very slightly changed, with the chairs and tables not where they were now but a few inches to the left or right, where they had been last time, Tuesday night of the week before. Miriam had reason to remember that it was Tuesday in particular.

Max was sitting beside her in a dark suit, his legs straight out under the table and his head against the back of the low chair, running his fingers lightly over the inside of his wrist. His profile was outlined against the light drifting through the door down the wall. She had been talking about herself and Peter and the deep-rooted conviction of her own inadequacy with which she had had to go on living after her divorce. She was wondering why it was so easy to talk to Max when it had been so difficult to talk to anyone else, and she had turned her head toward that profile, on the point of asking him, when she saw that for the first time since they had known each other, she was boring him. She had told him too much.

She had forgotten that there are people who are born superficial, whose superficiality is usually related to ideas, to their attitude toward politics, economics, art, literature, and the objective world, but also occasionally to their attitude toward other people. They prefer not to have to deal with more than a limited number of oversimplified ideas — they prefer the book reviews to the books, the headlines and the leading paragraph to the full report, the generalization to the facts, and the negative to the positive. For these people, more than a little knowledge is a burden; they don't know what to do with it. They put down a book or a newspaper, turn off the radio, change the subject or break off a love affair, simply for fear of knowing too much and getting in too deep.

That was what had happened with Max. He had found

himself getting in too deep. The basis of their relationship had been almost entirely physical and in her mistaken effort to broaden that basis, she had overlooked the fact that Max simply did not want it broadened. It suited him far better as it was. In telling him a lot of things about herself which, she realized now that it was too late, he did not in the least desire to know, she had given herself away for the first time in her life, and to the wrong person. Not knowing what to do with her, he had taken a week to think it over and had then, in effect, handed her back to Miriam Drake again.

She became aware of Marc's greenish eyes watching her with an expression which was oddly incurious and understanding. She had no idea how long they had been sitting here, it probably wasn't more than a few minutes but even so, if Marc had been John, he would have been all over her with bewilderment and sympathy by this time. She found herself thinking that she might still marry John sometime in the future, if she could get over her fear of his inexperience and if, in the meantime, someone would just tell her how you can manage to get through life with a man who has to have all but the most elementary emotions explained to him in words of one syllable.

"There's your drink, Miriam," said Marc at last. "Would you rather go back?"

"No, I'm all right." She raised her glass, then put it down again, remarking, "I thought I was one of the exceptions, that's all — one of your fifty thousand who think they're smart enough to figure out what's going to happen in advance so that it won't hurt so much when the time comes. You know, a realist. Are you a realist?"

"I'm a superrealist," said Marc, grinning. "I know that no matter how bad I think something's going to be, it will undoubtedly turn out to be a lot worse."

"Optimistic, aren't you? Why don't you marry Eric before you go?" she asked abruptly.

"And leave her to cope with the whole thing alone?"

She knew that she had had no right to ask such a question and was surprised at his giving her even that much of an answer. He had been definitely uncommunicative up till now.

A moment later he surprised her still more. He said, "Anyhow, I may not come back, and I've complicated Erica's life enough already without going on doing it after I'm dead. Some day she might want to marry someone else and I'd rather it was the first time for her, not the second. If I were going to be here another six months it might be different."

After a pause he went on, looking down at his glass, "And apart from everything else, we've got to win the war first. I know that's what a lot of people say but in our case it happens to be true. So long as there's even one chance in ten that we don't win, I couldn't afford to take it, because naturally I couldn't involve her in what would happen if we lost."

"Wouldn't she be involved anyhow?"

"Not quite to the same extent," said Marc rather dryly. "I don't know whether I have any right to involve her if we win the war and then lose the peace."

"What do you mean?"

"I mean if we get rid of the Nazis only to end up with the status quo ante. You know, a lot of the mud that Hitler slung at us from '33 to '39 is still sticking. Even when he didn't succeed in stirring up active anti-Semitism, he managed to make almost everybody thoroughly Jew-conscious, even over here and in the States."

"Do you think things are worse here than they were before 1933?"

"Oh, yes. Much worse." He paused and said, "Erica doesn't

really know what she's walking into. I do." His face lost some of its expression and he said, "Evidently your father does too."

"How do you know Eric doesn't?"

"Because she can't."

"Well," said Miriam into her glass. "At least Eric's beginning to learn."

For the second time she was realizing that there was something inside Marc Reiser which you couldn't change, and which, perhaps, he couldn't even change himself. He had been born skeptical, and under ideal conditions, he might simply have gone on with the same degree of passive skepticism or it might even have been gradually reduced and eradicated finally, if not in his children, then in his grandchildren. But the conditions were not ideal; you might almost say that they were specially designed to work on that skepticism, to confirm it and enlarge it and ultimately to transform it into an active influence.

She had grown up in a country where Jews were Jews, and with a few exceptions — musicians, one or two painters, occasionally a university professor, scientist, or doctor — that was all there was to it. You leave us alone and we'll leave you alone. Thus having been brought up to view "The Jews" from a safe distance, she had thought of them as a category rather than as individuals, and therefore, without being aware of it and more or less in spite of herself, all this time she had been waiting for Marc to do something which would relate him directly to the category — in short, to do or say something "Jewish."

Now, she thought, this is it, this skepticism, this "superrealism" which consists of reminding yourself that no matter how bad you think things are going to be, they usually turn out to be worse; this basic sense of insecurity, this profound discouragement which was all the more baffling because it was so matter of fact.

She said at last, "You can't tell whether or not it would be worth it to Erica. Nobody can. Nobody can tell which things matter and which don't, or how much they matter one way or the other — to anyone but himself. You can't tell what price anyone else can afford to pay for what they want most, because their price is their whole system of values, and their system of values is the result of everything which has ever happened to them — the way they have come to think and feel and the sum total of all their experience. You'd have to know all that about Eric, and you don't. You can't." She broke off for a moment, staring at him, and then said half to herself, "That's what I simply can't forgive Charles for. He presumes to know everything about Eric, far better, of course, than she knows herself."

"Let's leave your father out of it."

"Sorry."

"He isn't the main problem anyhow."

She raised her eyes to his face again and said, "I'm beginning to realize that, but to do Charles justice, he helps!"

"He certainly helps," said Marc, smiling at her. "I suppose you know you're beginning to get drunk?"

"Yes," said Miriam. She glanced around the small blue and silver bar and then remarked, "Everything seems nice and distant. I'm even getting away from myself."

He signaled the waiter and ordered another drink for her and then said, "After that we'd better go back."

"Cigarette, please."

Leaning forward to light it for her he observed, "You're quite right, I don't know enough about Erica, but she doesn't know enough about what she would have to deal with either. It's not just marrying into a set of social restrictions — like not being able to go to some beach to swim or to some hotel in the Laurentians to ski, unless she goes without me and carefully explains that although her name is Reiser, she herself isn't Jewish. It isn't even knowing that there are certain things I can't do, like going on the bench or the board of directors of a bank or something. The big restrictions aren't so important, there aren't an awful lot of them, and they're not what gets you down. What does get you down, particularly when it's not you but someone you're fond of, are the intangibles — the negatives, the endless little problems in human relationships which you never think of until you come up against them and which are so small that you hardly notice them until they start to pile up and eventually amount to a staggering total."

"Don't be so vague," said Miriam. "I'm a little too drunk to follow you except when you're specific."

"All right, then. Erica was born on top. She's been on top all her life. She's part of a complicated social system where she has a place, where she can go anywhere and do anything on a basis of complete equality with anyone, and it's simply up to her. If she marries me, she'll lose all that overnight. Where there was certainty, there'll be doubt — nothing definite, just doubt. She'll lose some of her friends who simply won't take to the idea of always having to invite a Jew along with Erica; she'll keep others. Maybe she'll keep most of the others, but she'll never again be sure. She'll never be sure of anyone the first time she meets him. She won't even be sure of people she's known all her life until she's had a chance to re-examine every last one of them and find out where they stand. She's never before had to pick her friends on the basis of whether they liked Jews or not, Miriam."

"And what about you?" asked Miriam. "Would you be willing to go through life waiting for the verdict of one person after another?"

"I have to anyhow," he said quietly.

That was a rather extraordinary remark when you came to think of it. "I really think it's about time we tried that new system." She put her elbows on the table, gazed at him dreamily and then asked, "What do they call it? You know the one I mean — the one that begins with a D. Oh, yes, democracy, that's it. Have you heard about it?"

"Everything is relative," said Marc.

"You mean, you don't mind being kicked out of hotels and most of the better Montreal homes when you think of Nazi Germany . . ."

"You bet I don't!"

"I suppose that's the reason nothing's ever done about it here," said Miriam reflectively. "Whenever a good Canadian begins to have doubts, he says, 'Oh, well, look at the Nazis,' and figures he's so superior, he's practically perfect."

"But he is."

"Oh, nuts," said Miriam. "Has it occurred to you that you might have a lot less trouble if you moved away from Montreal?"

"Why?"

"To get rid of your wife's family and most of your wife's friends. Or are you wedded to Mr. what's-his-name?"

"Aaronson?"

Miriam nodded.

"Not that I know of. But I don't think that would help much."

"It might," said Miriam, sliding down in her chair until her dark head was resting against the back. She closed her eyes and said sleepily, "They say it's much better out west, for example."

"I doubt it."

"You doubt everything, damn it! You're a nice person, in fact you're one of the nicest people I've ever met but you . . ." She yawned unexpectedly, opening her dark eyes and said with renewed decision, "You're too bloody fatalistic. What you need is a little simple faith in your fellow men, a dash of optimism, a couple of illusions and a lot more self-confidence. You've got everything else, and if someone like you can't break it down, then no one can. At least you can try — God damn it," said Miriam, exasperated, "it's your *duty* to try!"

She found that he was regarding her with a certain amusement and she said, "I know. It's easy for me to talk. All the same, if you just stay away instead of facing up to it and jolly well making people take a good look at you . . . if you don't have a shot at it, no one else will." She was no longer quite clear what she was driving at, but it sounded as though she was suggesting that he should put himself permanently on exhibition. Life must be almost intolerable when, like Marc, you know that you will always have to turn up in person, to pass the inspection, in order to get a break. Never to be taken for granted but always to bear the burden of proof. The burden of proof, she repeated to herself, trying to imagine what it would be like to be Marc Reiser. She could not imagine it; her mind was too tired and too muddled, and anyhow, she herself was a Drake, and had been taken for granted ever since she could remember.

Marc was back on the subject of Erica. His voice seemed to be coming from some point a lot farther away than the other side of the rather small table in front of her, and by the time her mind had veered round again, he was saying, "Put it this way. I don't know what price she can afford to pay and Erica doesn't know what she's buying."

"Couldn't you get together and pool your information?"

"My God," said Marc in amazement. "What do you think we do all the time?"

At a table on the edge of the dance floor opposite the orchestra, Erica was building a house out of matches and once again listening to John on the subject of Miriam. He was feeling discouraged and was sitting with his heavy shoulders against the frail back of the chair, drawing a series of squares and rectangles on the white cloth with the pointed handle of a fork.

"What odds would you give on our ever getting married?"

"Five to one," said Erica.

"The last time I asked you that you said five to one against."

"I know, but you've improved a lot. If you could manage to be as bright about Miriam as you are about most things now, I'd even give you ten to one."

"Why?"

"Because Miriam's on the rebound. Max walked out on her for good this morning and went to England on a bomber."

"But she didn't really care about him, Eric . . ."

"Didn't she? Why not?"

"Eliot wasn't her type."

He seemed so sure of that anyhow that Erica asked, "And what is Miriam's type?"

"Well, whatever it is, it's not something straight out of *Esquire*!" he said impatiently.

"Well, maybe not," said Erica, "but even if he wasn't her type, Miriam is now getting good and drunk out in the bar."

"Miriam doesn't get drunk." He frowned at her, looking less certain, and finally asked, "Are you serious, Eric?"

"Mm," said Erica, carefully placing another match.

"We'd better go and get her then."

"Marc will look after her," said Erica without moving. Her eyes had been following one line, from the pile of matches on the table before her to the door which led to the bar, from the door back to the matches, the matches back to the door again for what already seemed like several hours, but although every minute without Marc dragged interminably, what mattered most to her at the moment was not Marc and herself, but Marc and Miriam. She wanted them to have a chance to get to know each other.

It did not even occur to her that while Marc and her sister were getting to know each other, Marc might also be getting to know a good deal about her parents as well. He asked no direct questions; he was simply letting Miriam talk. In telling him her attitude toward the whole situation, she was giving him a fairly clear idea of the situation itself, without being aware of what she was doing. She never realized that in part of one evening, Marc had found out more from her than he had been able to find out from Erica in two months. By the time he left the bar and returned with Miriam, his former guesswork and suspicion had turned into actual knowledge. He was not yet ready to admit that he was beaten; it was simply that the future had become much darker and he was no longer able to see clearly beyond the next few weeks. The rest was obscurity. His point of view had not changed, it had merely shortened and covered only the period between the present and the day on which he would leave for overseas.

John was still looking unsettled, and Erica said, "Besides, Miriam never gets drunk enough for it to be noticeable."

"That was rather unnecessary, wasn't it?"

"What was?"

"I wasn't worrying whether it would be 'noticeable' or not."

"Oh, hell," said Erica as her house of matches collapsed. "I meant that since there's no danger of her making an ass of herself, it'll probably do her good. And for heaven's sake, Johnny, don't be *stuffy*."

"Sorry, Eric. You've had an awful lot to put up with, haven't you? I don't know why you didn't tell me to damn well pack up my troubles and take them somewhere else long ago. Do you think Miriam's really upset about that fellow?" he asked incredulously.

"More upset than I've ever seen her before, anyhow."

"Why on earth did she come out with us then?"

"Haven't you ever tried to postpone thinking about something until you've had a chance to get used to the idea a little at a time?"

His handsome face stiffened, only instead of looking years older as Marc always did, unhappiness made him much younger, as young as he had been when Erica had first known him, eight years before.

At that time, all his thoughts had been orderly, catalogued and arranged under the proper headings. He had just graduated from McGill and started work in the family bond house. Until he had been sent back from England after two years overseas, because there was such a shortage of bilingual officers, Erica could not remember ever having heard John say anything which had not been said before. He had been quite unoriginal; his life had been unoriginal, conforming completely to the given pattern for his age, class, and country, so that looking first at John Gardiner and then at his father and his father's friends, you could see quite clearly the direction he was taking and where he would undoubtedly end up.

Erica could remember the way he had thought, if you could call it thinking. At university he had done the required reading and no more. In a bond house, no reading is required, so at the age of twenty-one, and apart from the sports and finance sections of the morning and evening papers, a few magazines, and still fewer bestsellers, John had found himself relieved of the necessity for doing any reading at all. He played a very good game of bridge, golf, and tennis; he was an officer in the Reserve Army of peacetime, he had no interest whatever in any of the arts or in ideas, as such; he was unshakably decent, honest, hard-working, and unimaginative. He was a typical Canadian. From 1930 until far too late, he had assumed that the Depression would right itself; he had hung on to the illusion that the Depression would right itself long after Charles Drake had abandoned it, and had resigned his Reserve commission because his regiment showed no signs of being mobilized, for the time being at any rate, in order to enlist for Active Service in September, 1939, because, as he had said at dinner, his sort always does.

He was, however, one of the few men Erica knew whom the war had turned right-side up, instead of temporarily upside down. When you've been in the Army for three years, as John had pointed out himself, sooner or later you're bound to start wondering why you're there.

His face stiffer, younger, and more uncomprehending than ever, he said, "Did Miriam think she was going to marry him, Eric?"

"No," said Erica.

"Then what's it all about?"

Erica regarded him helplessly for a moment and then said, "Don't you think you'd better ask Miriam instead of me?"

"Did she *want* to marry him?"

"She may have," said Erica vaguely.

"Why?"

Having finally found an answer which she thought would do, she said, "Well, you know they say that when divorced people remarry, they usually go to the opposite extreme."

"Really," said John. "I've never heard that before."

Neither had Erica, but it was as good an explanation of Max

Eliot's attraction for Miriam as any Erica could think of as well as a partial explanation of Miriam's continuing inability to fall in love with John, she realized a moment later. In one respect, John and Peter Kingsley, Miriam's ex-husband, were too much alike, or at least Miriam thought they were, and it was impossible to talk her out of it. The worst mistake John had made was when he had told Miriam in London, just when she had been on the point of falling in love with him at last, that he had never looked at anyone else since he had met her, adding, rather embarrassed, that of course that meant he had never looked at anyone else at all. If he had not been embarrassed, Miriam might not have known what he was talking about, or rather that what he was saying was to be taken literally; as it was, she did know, even before he went on still more embarrassed, to add something about having kept himself for her.

Even without the embarrassment, it would have sounded like Peter all over again, and that was enough for Miriam. Out of every ten idealists, nine are likely to be more or less neurotic and only one entirely genuine, and having been tricked once, Miriam was not going to run the risk of being tricked a second time. And genuine or not, she did not want the burden of John's idealism and above all, she wanted no more embarrassment and no more speeches. Instead of being moved by what he said, because John happened to be a thoroughly genuine human being genuinely in love with her, Miriam froze up. From then on she had scarcely allowed him to touch her. In some very deep sense, she was afraid of him, and because he was so decent and hadn't the faintest idea what was wrong, he let her get away with it, thereby following up his worst mistake with another which was almost as bad for both of them.

Erica had no idea what it would be like for him when he found out, as he must inevitably find out sometime, that during this past year and in fact up until last night, while he had been denying his own desire for Miriam's sake and his, and for the sake of their future, as he thought, she had been the mistress of a man for whom he had so little use that he had just described him as something out of *Esquire*. John hadn't much vanity, but even if he had had none at all, he could not fail to realize that he was worth a great deal more according to anybody's standards, except those of the one person who mattered most to him, than Max Eliot. And leaving out everything else, that would hurt. It would hurt like hell.

As though he had guessed a little of what she was thinking he said, "I didn't know I'd been playing second fiddle again, Eric."

He was looking down at the table, the orchestra was making a great deal of noise and his voice was pitched so low that Erica could hardly make out what he said. She missed the next few words altogether and then, "I ought to have got it through my head by this time that there always is someone else."

"Always?"

"Yes, there was another one she was in love with after Kingsley and before she met Eliot — while I was still in England."

The whole romantic room with the long windows at one end through which you could see a cluster of lighted buildings against the night sky, the orchestra in its fantastic white shell, and the people dancing or talking at their tables — all of it had dropped away from him. He had forgotten where he was and went on sitting half-turned away from her, a tall, fair-haired man in an officer's uniform whose blue eyes were fixed on some point near the door leading to the bar.

"Eric."

"Yes?"

"Remember that nursery rhyme, 'The Farmer Takes a Wife'

and the wife takes somebody else who takes somebody else? Even when I was a kid I always hated that rhyme."

The next moment Miriam and Marc were skirting the edge of the dance floor on their way back again, Marc with his hands in his trouser pockets and Miriam walking with her head up, her movements as light and full of grace as ever. Except for her burning dark eyes and a slight flush, there was no outward sign that she had eaten almost nothing for the past twenty-four hours and had drunk far too much in the last three and a half.

"Hello," said Marc, smiling down at Erica. He touched her fair hair lightly with one hand and then added, "Come and dance, darling."

She was the right height for him, in fact everything about her was right and he held her close, wishing that they would play a waltz and turn the lights down so that he could kiss her. There was always an interval like this after he came back to her, when everything that had been confused, remote, and difficult to understand seemed to be rearranging itself in order, and all he could feel for the first few minutes was relief and happiness and a kind of amazement which usually took a while to wear off. He was in love with her, and it seemed to him that if only Erica and he could stay together, then sooner or later he would know what it was all about. But they could not stay together; all they had left was a handful of days scattered over a month or possibly six weeks at the most, although Erica did not know it yet.

"Do you love me?"

Her arm moved up a little on his shoulder and with her mouth brushing his ear she murmured, "I adore you."

His grip tightened for a moment, then loosened a little and he said, "Don't, darling."

"Don't what?"

"Don't melt in public, it's not done."

"You started it, I didn't."

"Damn it," said Marc, "why don't they play a waltz?" and swerved just in time to avoid an overstuffed colonel who was sailing back and forth across the floor, four sheets to the wind, with a rather bewildered redheaded girl in tow.

"I thought you didn't like waltzes," said Erica.

"I don't. It's what goes with them. By the way, your sister is definitely drunk. I wouldn't mention it, but she's bound to tell you herself sooner or later."

"You liked her, didn't you?" asked Erica anxiously.

"Yes, darling, of course. I never saw a woman who could drink so much and show it so little."

"This is one of her off nights," said Erica apologetically.

"Extremely off, I should say. What I liked most about her is the fact that she likes you. By the way, she asked me if I didn't think it might be better for you to leave home and get a place of your own to live."

Erica missed a step, said mechanically, "I'm sorry," and then answered matter-of-factly, "She thinks I'm going to develop into one of those spinsters who devote their lives to their parents. It's just one of her ideas."

"Yes," said Marc.

"What else did she say?" asked Erica over his shoulder.

"Nothing much. My God," said Marc, "he's back again." The only way to make certain of avoiding him was to dance in a circle around the outside of the dance floor, for the colonel always tacked several feet from the edge.

It took them several minutes to get past the orchestra where Marc could talk again without shouting into her ear. He said, "Don't look so worried, Eric."

"I'm not, only . . ."

"Only what?"

"Miriam often makes things sound much worse than they really are."

"I haven't the remotest idea what you're talking about. If you think your sister was giving me a blow-by-blow account of your home life . . ."

"That's a nice way of putting it!"

"I was speaking figuratively," said Marc with dignity. "Anyhow, the conversation was entirely general, mostly on the subject of relative values, only just as I was beginning to be really profound, she said she felt sleepy."

The music stopped and they waited, hand in hand, and then the lights went down. "Thank God. Where do you think we're least likely to be noticed?"

"Out in the middle," said Erica, "but you don't waltz that badly."

He took her in his arms without answering, steered her out to the middle, kissed her quickly and holding her very close again, he said with his lips against her cheek, "We're too tall. I don't suppose it's ever occurred to you that there are distinct advantages in being a dwarf?"

"Well, no, it hadn't," Erica admitted, "but I see what you mean."

They danced for a while in silence. She could feel his mood changing, and at last he said abruptly, "Eric . . ."

"Yes?"

He paused and then said, "I've got something to tell you."

"Something — unpleasant?"

"Yes, darling."

She drew away from him so that she could look up into his face, his dark, sensitive, intelligent face which she loved so much. The orchestra was playing a waltz left over from the last war; she had been trying to think of its name and for some idiotic reason, she went on trying to think of its name although it did not matter in the least, and she already knew from his expression what was coming. She said, "All right, I'm ready."

"I'm on draft."

"Yes," said Erica. A young naval officer knocked against her left shoulder as he danced by and she said, "I'm sorry," again, without thinking, and asked, "When, Marc?"

"Some time around the last week in September."

About a month from now.

She said suddenly, "It's the 'Missouri Waltz.'"

"I know. There are only two waltzes I really like, except the Viennese waltzes, of course, and that's one of them."

"What's the other?"

"'Moonlight Madonna.' It always reminds me of your — I mean, your hair isn't really gold, it's . . ."

He stopped, and she said, "That means you're going to camp again, doesn't it?"

"Yes, next Monday."

It was Wednesday already.

The Gatineau Rifles had gone over to Dieppe a few days before; time and again she had heard Marc say, "Reinforcements for the First Battalion overseas," but it had sounded like something which would materialize with the opening of the Second Front some time next year, and not — next Monday.

'The Missouri Waltz' went on and the colonel passed them again, this time with a brunette in tow. She found herself thinking that he must go through his partners a lot faster than most people, and hoped that he had come well provided, like a racing car equipped with several extra sets of spark plugs.

"Marc, you are going to Petawawa, aren't you?"

"Yes, darling."

He could feel the breath going out of her with relief and he said, "I'm sorry, Eric. I should have told you that right away."

"I was so afraid it would be Camp Borden, and you'd be too far for me to see you."

It was better to figure things out so that you knew exactly where you stood, like collecting all your bills and adding them up when you were broke, in order to see just how broke you were. He would get one forty-eight hour leave, so what it amounted to was five days between now and Monday, then forty-eight hours, and finally a week or ten days' embarkation leave — probably a week, because they were obviously rushing it now — most of which Marc would have to spend with his parents five hundred miles away. They had already discussed that. Five days, forty-eight hours, say two days of his embarkation leave to be on the safe side, and finally a last dinner together when he was on his way through to Halifax. They could be more broke, this being August, 1942, though not much.

"It makes nine days altogether," said Marc. "That is counting from now to next Monday too, of course."

He paused and then went on hurriedly, evidently afraid that if he stopped to think how this thing ought to be said, he might not be able to say it at all, "They told me at Headquarters that I could go as soon as I'd got everything cleaned up there. I don't think it will take more than one day — tomorrow and maybe part of Friday. If you could get off, then we'd have almost three days together. Sylvia wouldn't mind, would she? I can get to Petawawa any time before midnight on Monday and . . ."

It seemed to him that he had been talking a long time without getting anywhere except back to Petawawa again. The music stopped and he stood facing her, his hands at his sides, and said, "I'm asking you to go away with me, Eric."

"Yes," said Erica. "Yes. Darling, you didn't have to ask!"

VII

❧

Through the open windows of the bedroom they could hear the church clock striking in the village down at the other end of the lake, and Erica said wonderingly, "It's three o'clock." So five hours had flowed by them uncounted, into the past, for she remembered that the clock had been striking ten as they opened the door of Marc's room. Before that, there had only been one brief interval since they had left Montreal when she had known what time it was. They had gone for a swim as soon as they arrived at the hotel, drifted for a while in a canoe, and then spent what was left of the afternoon lying in their bathing suits on the float anchored off-shore. Someone had called to them from the beach, "It's half past seven and the dining room closes at eight; if you want any dinner, you'd better hurry."

The lake was in a valley with the Laurentian mountains

rising steeply all around the edge, except at the other end where the rise began farther back, leaving enough more or less level ground for the village. The hillsides were green, and across the lake there were a lot of small houses up and down on different levels, like brightly painted toys.

Above them as they lay on the float, up a path like a stairway with broad, grassy steps, was the hotel, a long half-timbered building from which you could look down on the lake or out over the mountains, north, west, and south. The hotel stood with its back to the east, and the road wound its way through the Laurentians and then down a steep slope to the back door, so that you came into a small lobby on the second floor and went downstairs to get to the front door facing the lake, and the path to the beach.

There was a stone-paved terrace with small tables under orange and yellow umbrellas where they had sat for a while after dinner drinking coffee and then a brandy, watching the sunset and the slowly moving, slowly changing reflections in the water. The lights had come on one by one in the little houses across the lake, but before the moon rose they had come upstairs. Erica had heard the village clock striking the first of the ten notes as Marc opened the door, and the last sound to reach her from the outside world was a whippoorwill calling from the bush somewhere behind the hotel. After that there was silence and she was in his arms at last.

As she lay beside him later, individuality began to return and take form; she could feel the outlines growing clearer and more firm but it was a new mould, subtly different from the old one. She wondered if you got a new one each time and was on the point of asking Marc, but it was all rather involved and diffi-cult to explain, and instead she went to sleep.

"Hello," said Marc.

"Hello. Have I been asleep long?"

"I don't know."

"Have you?"

He drew his arm out from under her and sat up, rubbing it, "No, I've just been looking at you."

Erica also sat up, asking anxiously, "Have you got a cramp?"

He shook his head. "Just stiff."

"Why didn't you shove me off?"

"Because I didn't want to." He paused, listening, and remarked, "Romeo and Juliet had a nightingale but all we get is a whippoorwill. Persistent, isn't he?"

"Maybe it's a different one."

"I don't think so. He always goes flat on the second note."

"He may have a slight cold," said Erica. "I remember thinking he probably had when we first came up, so I guess it must be the same one." She settled back on the pillow again while Marc took two cigarettes from the table beside the bed and lit them, and finally Erica said candidly, "I don't see how even a whippoorwill can expect to get anywhere with a voice like that. He might just as well give up and go home. Incidentally, it was a lark, not a nightingale — remember?"

She repeated softly,

"'It is the lark that sings so out of tune,
Straining harsh discords and unpleasing sharps.'"

"Go on," said Marc.

"What with?"

"Shakespeare."

She thought a moment, looking up at the ceiling, and then said,

"'O fortune, fortune! All men call thee fickle;
If thou art fickle what dost thou with him
That is renowned for faith? Be fickle, fortune;
For then, I hope, you wilt not keep him long . . ."

"I don't think I particularly care for that bit after all," said Erica after a moment's silence.

"I wasn't listening to the words," said Marc. "It's your voice. Did I ever tell you what a lovely voice you have?"

"No, I don't think so. You may tell me now if you like."

"Some other time." He kissed her shoulder and the hollow at the base of her throat and then lifting his head to listen again he said, "Everything is sort of suspended. It's so quiet, Eric . . . even our whippoorwill seems to have gone off the air for the time being."

He pulled the pillows up behind his head and turned so that he could see her better. "Are you sleepy?"

"No, are you?"

He shook his head.

"When *do* we sleep?" asked Erica without much interest.

"Later," he said vaguely, paused, and then added, "Probably much later."

Erica moved over so that she was lying with her head on his shoulder and observed in a detached tone, "You know, you're going to be in a shocking condition when you arrive at camp Monday."

"They must be used to it by this time."

After another brief silence she asked suddenly, "What were you like when you were a little boy?"

"Why?"

"You've told me a lot, but there are still too many gaps. It's like a jigsaw puzzle with half the pieces missing; I want a whole picture, not one full of holes."

"Where shall I start?"

"Well . . ." She thought, and then asked, "Have you always lived in the same house?" He nodded. "What's it like?"

"It's just a house, with a big veranda in front and a lot of trees around it, and a garden at the back that slopes slightly down toward the garage, so in winter when the snow is melting, the water in front of the garage is about a foot deep. David and I used to get hold of some planks every year and paddle around on them till we fell off. It was wonderful," he said reminiscently. "The water was good and muddy."

Erica wanted to know about the inside of the house and after struggling, Marc finally produced the information that the sitting room contained some ferns or something in brass pots, and a canary named Mike that never sang.

"How long have you had Mike?"

"Oh, years. He must be pretty old by now."

After trying to visualize the sitting room furnished with brass pots and one aging canary, Erica gave up. "What about your room?"

He was much more satisfactory on the subject of his own room. He even told her that there was a large spot on one corner of the carpet where years ago, the afternoon plane on the Moscow-Zagreb line running above his desk had come down too low, picked up a bottle of ink and deposited it somewhere in Transylvania.

"Of course that was around 1922 when the airplane industry was still pretty young and almost anything was like to happen."

Erica laughed and then asked, "How did the planes work?"

"On wires. They had hooks on the nose and tail so you could

attach them to the wire on one side of the room and they'd shoot down the slope to the landingfield on the other. I kept building more planes and rigging more wires and our maid kept complaining to Mother that whenever she tried to get in there to clean, the wires either caught in her hair or tripped her up. Mother was sympathetic but that was about as far as she was willing to go. For the first time in my life I seemed to be learning geography, accidentally, of course, but she'd realized by then that accidentally was the only way I was ever likely to learn any. Then David came home from his first year at medical school and I lost interest in airplanes and began dissecting frogs all over the house and filling my room with bottles containing various forms of animal life, more or less preserved in alcohol."

"What happened to the less preserved ones?"

"Mother used to go into my room and remove them when I was out," he said, sighing. "I remember being particularly annoyed about a small mud puppy which vanished when I was out fishing. Mud puppies are pretty rare and it had taken me weeks of digging around in swamps and streams before I finally found one. I felt that its scarcity value should have outweighed its smell. Mother didn't."

He said thoughtfully, "You know, I've always wondered what Mother did with those things. Do you suppose a young mud puppy, slightly overripe, would burn easily?"

"I shouldn't think so."

"I must ask her some time."

"What's her name?"

"Maria," he said, giving it the German pronunciation. "How are the gaps?"

"Filling up nicely, thank you."

"Mine aren't," Marc pointed out.

Erica was more interested in her own gaps than in his, and she asked, "When did you first decide you wanted to be a lawyer?"

"I don't know. I must have been pretty small anyhow. I used to sit on the back fence and look at the Algoma Hills and dream of being a judge. I don't know what gave me the idea of going on the Bench either, it must have been something I'd read."

There it was again, she thought, as the stone wall which had appeared for the first time that day back in June when Marc had said, "They don't take Jews," suddenly turned up again in front of her. She knew by now that there was no way of getting through it, over it or around it, but she had not yet learned to take it for granted. Whenever she was confronted with it she always stopped and stared for a moment, while the conversation went on without her.

Marc, however, having been brought up with it, barely gave it a glance. He said, "By the time I got cured of that idea it was too late to change my mind," and then asked immediately, reverting to his own gaps again, "What did you want to do when you grew up?"

"I wanted to be a conductor."

"On a tram?"

"Certainly not," said Erica indignantly. "I wanted to conduct an orchestra."

"And what happened?"

"Nothing, that was the trouble. I took theory and harmony and tried awfully hard, but no matter how hard I tried, I always ended up at the top of the class in English and at the bottom in music, so finally I got discouraged."

"Did you collect anything?"

"Yes. Later on I collected rocks."

"What kind of rocks?"

"Any kind of rocks. After giving up music, I'd decided I wanted to be a geologist."

"And what happened that time?"

Erica sighed, leaned over to reach the ashtray on the side table beside him, then back on the pillows again she remarked sadly, "Nothing happened then either. I took various courses at McGill and tried awfully hard, but I still ended up at the head of my year in English and the bottom in geology, so then I . . ."

"You decided to be a journalist."

"No, I decided to get married."

He looked at her, rather startled, and then said, his face clearing, "Oh, yes, I remember. You told me you were engaged to someone who was killed in a motor accident. That must have been pretty tough . . . How old were you?"

"Twenty-one. We were supposed to be married in June after I'd graduated. Well, I did graduate, but he was killed two weeks before the wedding."

"Do you want to talk about it?"

"Yes," said Erica.

At the end she remarked, "It seems now as though it had all happened to someone else, because I'm not the same person now that I was then. My whole life would have been different if I'd married him. I like it better the way it is, not just because it is this way, but because I've had to develop more and work harder and adapt myself to life, rather than arrange things so that it would more or less adapt itself to me. You see, he had quite a lot of money, and I don't know what would have happened to us, but we would probably have been much too comfortable for our own good."

"How old was he?"

"Twenty-six."

"What was his name?"

"Eric Gardiner."

"Any relation to John?"

"Yes, his older brother. That was the way John got to know Miriam, though we'd always vaguely known each other." Leaning across him toward the bedside table again, she said, "You might put that ashtray where I can reach it, darling."

This time he caught and held her against him, murmuring into her hair, "Why should I? It's much nicer this way."

When he finally let her go he said reflectively, "You know, Eric, this is one of the best things in life . . ."

"What is?"

"Just talking. Maybe it's the only time when it's really easy to talk, because you're so mixed up with someone else that you're not sure which of you is which, and it's like talking to yourself."

"Is it always like this?"

"No, of course it isn't. Why?"

"Because I don't mind the idea of your having made love to other women before you met me — at least, not much — but I would object to your having got mixed up with them so you didn't know which was you and which was several other people. I mean it sounds sort of collective."

"Yes, it does, doesn't it? It sounds awful. I think I'm insulted, as a matter of fact, or I would be if there were any truth in it."

"Isn't there any?" asked Erica hopefully.

"Not an atom of truth. I've never been mixed up with anyone but you."

"How do you like it?"

His expression changed as he looked at her and he said under his breath, "You know how much I like it, darling."

"Yes," said Erica faintly, and putting both her arms around

him she said, "Well, kiss me, for heaven's sake."

After a while he said, looking up at the ceiling, "I wasn't just talking, when I told you that you'd never happened to me before and I know nothing like you will ever happen to me again. Life is pretty average, on the whole, and even when you fall in love, you feel the way most everybody else has felt at some time or other. You only hit perfection by accident. It's like a sweepstake, trying doesn't get you anywhere and the odds are a million to one against the accident taking place. Have you ever been absolutely happy?" he asked suddenly. "I mean as though the whole world were an orchestra and instead of playing more or less off key, for once in your life you managed to be in complete harmony and for one day or just maybe for a couple of hours, everything was exactly right?"

"Yes, once," said Erica.

"Once for me too."

"Tell me about yours first."

He said, "It was four years ago, in October 1938, when I was staying with David on a fishing trip. At least I was fishing but he wasn't. Morning after morning we'd start out together and then someone would fall off a horse or decide to have a baby or something and I'd end up going alone. Finally, the second to last day I was there, by some sort of coincidence nobody needed a doctor for once and off we went. It was early October, one of those autumn days when everything seems to be standing still, holding its breath and waiting . . ."

He broke off, trying to remember, with his eyes fixed on the mirror over the chest of drawers. The mirror dissolved into a window through which he could see, not the soft rise and fall of the Laurentians all around them, but the high, clear-cut barrier of the Algoma mountains, guarding the North. He said, "I've got it. Listen:

'Along the line of smoky hills
*   The crimson forest stands*
And all the day the bluejay calls
*   Throughout the autumn lands.*

Now by the brook the maple leans
*   With all his glory spread*
And all the sumachs on the hills
*   Have turned their green to red.'*

"It was like that. We walked through the bush and fished for a while and then had lunch and fished some more. We came out by a small lake just at sunset, and then we went home. That was all."

His eyes left the mirror and came back to her face and he said, "What about your day?"

"It wasn't a day, it was an evening in Paris the last time I was there, when Mimi and I were walking down Champs Elysées all the way from the Arc de Triomphe to Place de la Concorde. Every time a car went by it lit up the lower branches of the trees and then it was dark with just the street lamps and the moon again. Mimi was as happy as I was. We couldn't even talk."

"Paris will never look like that again, Eric . . ."

"It wasn't just Paris, it was the whole world."

". . . or the woods back of David's place in October 1938." A moment later he said, looking straight ahead of him, "Or anyone else after you."

Days later, when she was trying to locate the exact moment at which she had received the first warning, the moment which marked the beginning of the final stage in their relationship, she was to remember the way he had said, "Or anyone else after you." There was no hope in his voice at that moment, either for a future with Erica or a future without her, only the first indication of his acceptance of a world in which the chances were still a million to one against his ever managing to be in complete harmony again.

The moment went by unnoticed at the time, for immediately after he said, "October 1938," in a different tone, and after another pause he repeated it a third time, as though the words were the key to another memory of which all he could recall so far was its purely evil associations.

Not October, Erica thought. He was a month out.

She said, "May I have a cigarette, please?" He handed her the package and she took one, and after waiting a little, she asked for a match.

He said absently, "I'm sorry," and gave her the packet of matches.

"Our whippoorwill's back again." There was another pause and she asked, "Who wrote that poem?"

"Wilfrid Campbell."

It was no use. You could not hope to keep it out, even out of a hotel in the Laurentians at three o'clock in the morning, by talking about whippoorwills and poetry and asking for cigarettes and matches, and at last she said, "I know what you're thinking of. You've got the wrong date; it wasn't October, it was November 1938."

"Yes," said Marc. "Yes, of course it was."

He put the ashtray down on the bed between them and remarked, "I'm glad it wasn't October, that would have been carrying escapism too far. Besides, I'd hate to have my pet memory go sour on me." He turned his head and smiled at her and said, "I don't know what I'm talking about."

"You hadn't any relatives in Germany, had you?"

"Yes, some of my mother's family, particularly my first

cousin. He was about my age, and when I was over there in 1932 I stayed with them and he and I went on a hiking trip in Switzerland together. We were both students then. Afterwards he took a degree in science and another one in law and got a job working on patents in one of the big chemical firms. He was pretty brilliant and I guess the Nazis just decided to overlook him — anyhow, he and his family managed to get along somehow or another until November '38."

He said aimlessly, "I was always arguing with them about getting out but they wouldn't, of course, because even in 1932 there were fewer restrictions in Germany than here. I mean, they were a part of things."

"What happened to him?"

"I don't know. They said he'd been 'shot trying to escape' from a concentration camp. My uncle was arrested at the same time and last year my aunt and Hedy, the daughter, were sent to Poland. They were the only ones left."

As soon as she had heard him say "October 1938" the second time, she had known that there was something more than the fact that November 1938 had been a black month, by far the blackest until much later, but she had not known that there was a family with whom he had lived and a cousin about his own age with whom he had gone hiking in Switzerland.

He was lying on his back looking up at the ceiling, and she could feel him drawing steadily farther and farther away from her until he seemed to be wholly detached. There began to be something strange and unfamiliar about him, and she was seized with panic, wondering what she was doing here beside him where she so obviously did not belong. His isolation was so complete that it was as though he had entirely finished with her. In despair, and overwhelmed by the one impulse to cover herself with something beside the sheet which covered both of them, in a single movement she caught up her nightdress which had been thrown across the foot of the bed and slipped it over her shoulders.

"What are you doing that for?"

She was so startled by the sound of his voice that she stopped, transfixed, with her arms over her head. "Because — because you — Oh!" said Erica helplessly. "The damn thing's got twisted. Help me on with it and don't ask silly questions."

"Not until you tell me why."

"I feel indecent."

She got her head out at last and their eyes met. They looked at each other in silence until Marc said, "I'm sorry, Eric."

"It's all right."

"No," he said, shaking his head. Still looking at her he said, "You certainly do get it both ways, don't you?" and a moment later he suddenly pulled her down beside him and said again with his face against hers, "I'm sorry, darling, I'm an awful fool. I didn't mean to desert you like that . . ."

"Particularly with nothing on," she said in a muffled voice. She clung to him until it was really all right again, and then raising her head so that she could look into his eyes she said, "I want to tell you something, Marc. I'm not afraid of other people, nothing they say or do can get inside me where it really hurts if I don't let it. I'm only afraid of one thing . . ."

"Yes, go on."

"I'm afraid of being shut out." She sat up, holding his hand tightly in both hers and said, "Please start by assuming that I can understand and not that I can't. It's terribly important, I think it's more important to me than anything else. If you say or even let yourself think that I can't understand something simply because I'm not Jewish, then you put me in a position where

I'm utterly helpless. It's like . . ." She stopped and then said, "It's like tying me to a chair and then blaming me because I can't get up and walk. I've got quite a lot of imagination and I don't think I'm stupid or insensitive . . ."

Her grip on his hand tightened still more and she said, "Give me a chance to understand and if I let you down, then — well, *then* you can shut me out. I guess I'll have deserved it. It's not my fault that I'm not Jewish and I can't do anything about it, but surely . . ." She stopped again, and with her eyes and her voice full of tears she said, "Surely the fact that I love you so much makes up for it!"

He had not once taken his eyes from her face. He said roughly, "Eric, for God's sake!" and took her in his arms again.

She said at last, "Darling, you've got a grip like a steel trap and you're hurting me."

He relaxed a little, smoothed back a strand of fair hair which had fallen over her forehead and smiled down at her. He was still somewhat unnerved. "Are you all right?"

Erica nodded. "Are you?"

"Well, almost," said Marc. "You have an awful effect on me, Eric. Whenever you say that you love me, I feel as though I'm being turned inside out, only this time it was worse because of the build up. Do you know what we need?"

"No, what?"

"Some kind of insulation."

"Why?"

"I mean just to protect ourselves when we're together so we won't feel so much."

"I don't think I want to be insulated," said Erica, after considering it. "Probably it all goes together, so that if . . ."

"You have the most irritating habit of starting to say something interesting and then stopping in the middle. However, I see what you mean." He kissed her and then asked, "Do you still feel indecent?"

"No."

"All right, take that thing off again then."

He got up and went over to the window. "It's a marvellous night, Eric," he said, his eyes following the course of the Milky Way through the sky until the stream of stars disappeared over the dark shoulder of the mountain across the lake. The lake itself was full of moonlight and there was a light breeze which had turned the water in the path of the moon to frozen silver.

He came back and stood looking down at her face and her hair spread out on the pillow.

"You belong to a museum," said Erica, for there was such perfection of line and form in the moulding of his body that he seemed unreal in the dimly lit room, like a figure out of Greece two thousand years before. "Except for your face," she added. "Your face doesn't go with the rest of you. One of your ancestors must have got mixed up with a good Austrian peasant . . ."

Her voice died away in the stillness of the room as he went on standing there, and then suddenly took the top of the sheet with one hand and pulled it down to her feet. "I want to remember the way you look," he said, his voice so low that she could hardly hear it.

She lay motionless under his eyes and then turned over on her face and began to cry again. He dropped down on the bed beside her and put his arm around her and said, his voice shaking, "Don't, Eric, please, my dearest, please don't. You can't cry now, it's only Friday."

But it was not because there was so little time left that she was crying, although that was part of it. There was something else which she did not know how to explain, even to herself, except that in this one night she seemed to have lost what little had remained of her detachment; she had taken on his vulnerability without his endurance, and she was crying for herself as well as for Marc.

She put both her arms around him and went on crying until there were no more tears left, and after a while both of them had forgotten how it had started or what it was all about. When the church clock struck five in the village at the other end of the lake, neither of them heard it.

VIII

❧

"Our government is really wonderful," remarked Sylvia as the telephone rang on Erica's desk at half past eleven on Monday morning.

"You take it, Bubbles," said Erica. The train from Ottawa where she had spent Sunday night with Marc had been late arriving in Montreal; the first edition had gone to press ten minutes after she had reached her office and she was still struggling to catch up. "I won't talk to anybody."

"The Consumer's Division of the Department of Agriculture," continued Sylvia, although no one seemed to be listening, "has just produced another masterpiece in the form of a cake which takes no butter, no eggs, and no sugar. Now why not just no cake, and be done with it?"

"You might write and ask them," said Erica absently.

"It's for you, Eric," said Weathersby, adding as Erica was about to protest, "I know, but it's someone who claims she's your sister. You'd better investigate."

"Tell her to hold on a minute," said Erica, still typing. "Bubbles . . ."

"Yeah?"

"Have you got my cigarettes again?"

"What do you mean, 'again'?" he demanded, looking injured.

"Never mind. Hand them over."

"It probably is her sister," Sylvia pointed out to him as he passed her desk bearing Erica's cigarettes. "At your age, you've no reason to be so suspicious. You ought to be in a good school somewhere," she added vaguely, "learning about cricket, instead of learning about life in a newspaper office. Where are those wedding pictures, Bubbles?"

"On Eric's desk. And I already know all about cricket, I finished school last year. Eric . . ."

"Mm?"

"Do you want me to do the stuff on wartime canning?"

"I suppose you know all about canning too?" inquired Sylvia.

"I'll bet I know just as much about it as you do. Don't I, Eric?

"Don't you what?"

"Don't I know as much about canning as Sylvia does?"

"Leave me out of it," said Erica. "I'm busy."

Weathersby returned to his desk, regarding Sylvia thoughtfully for a while, and asked finally, "Now supposing you wanted to make jelly . . . how would you go about it?"

"What kind of jelly?"

"Any kind."

"Couldn't we start with jam and work up to it gradually?"

"We did," said Weathersby patiently. "We did the jam yesterday. Today, we are going to make jelly. So what would be the first step?"

"The first step would be to read the government bulletin on wartime canning, just like you," she added pointedly. "If you can understand it, presumably anyone can. Give," she said, holding out her hand.

"I haven't read it yet," said Weathersby without moving.

"Oh? How did you get to be such an authority on making jelly, then?"

"Because I've watched my mother. The trick is to get it to set so it doesn't come out all runny."

"Not really," said Sylvia. "Did you figure all that out for yourself?"

"And just how would *you* get it to set?"

"I'll bite," said Sylvia. "How would I?"

"Well, if you knew anything about canning, which you obviously don't, you'd mix it with wax."

"I beg your pardon?"

"You'd mix the fruit with melted wax — after you'd strained it, of course."

"I see," said Sylvia. She regarded the long stringy figure of Weathersby Canning with some admiration and then said at last, "Bubbles, how would you like to have a column of your own? We could call it . . ." She paused, her chin on her hand, and then suggested, "We could call it 'Canning on Canning.' If you were given a sufficiently free hand, the results ought to be genuinely interesting."

"I don't know," said Weathersby doubtfully. "I don't think I know enough about it to keep it up indefinitely." He picked up the government bulletin, glanced through a few pages and said, "Well, can I do it, Eric?"

"Ask Sylvia."

"What is it?" said Sylvia. "A press release?"

Weathersby nodded.

"O.K., go ahead and rehash it but stick to what it says there and don't put in any of your mother's bright ideas. We don't want all our readers to be poisoned."

"Why not?" said Weathersby. "They wouldn't be poisoned all at once; a lot of them wouldn't get around to eating the stuff till sometime next spring. I mean, it would be so gradual that no one would notice."

"No one but the circulation department and they'd start noticing in a couple of days. The circulation department is unusually sensitive."

"What's the matter with you two?" asked Erica, finally ripping the sheet from her typewriter with one hand and reaching for her phone with the other.

"I wouldn't know about Weathersby," said Sylvia dreamily, "but I'm getting married."

Erica's hand dropped from the phone and she said, "Mike?" Sylvia nodded. "Oh, darling, I'm so glad!"

"Thanks, Eric. I still feel sort of dizzy," she remarked apologetically. "We're going to be married a week from Saturday. We're only inviting a few people — just you and Marc and one or two others. Do you think Marc will be able to make it?"

Erica shook her head. "He won't get any leave till the week after. I'll come, though. That doesn't mean you've given up your job, does it?"

"No such luck. Mike's joined the Army. We'll have a week together somewhere and then he's going to camp."

"He'll be here for months yet, anyhow," said Erica, her face changing. "You're lucky."

"After all," said Weathersby, talking to himself out loud.

"What difference does it make? She's probably died of old age by this time, so why bother?"

"Why bother what? Who are you talking about?" asked Erica.

"Why bother answering your telephone."

"Good heavens," said Erica, and grabbed her phone. "Hello, Mimi . . . are you still there?"

"Hello, Eric. This seems to be a lousy time to call you . . ."

"No, it's all right. I was finishing up a job and then Sylvia suddenly announced that she was getting married."

"Who to?"

"Mike O'Brien, one of the reporters."

"Wish her luck for me," said Miriam. "How are you, Eric?"

Erica looked blankly at Weathersby who was sitting with his feet on his desk in the corner, engrossed in the government bulletin on wartime canning, and she said, "I guess I'm all right."

"When did you get in?"

"On the ten-thirty from Ottawa, only it was late. Marc's train left just after mine so I didn't have to . . ." She stopped, and asked, "What do you want, Mimi?"

"I wanted you to lunch with me."

"All right. I'll meet you at that Italian restaurant round the corner from the cathedral at one. It's just off Place d'Armes . . ."

"I know where it is," said Miriam. "Thanks, Eric."

Erica rang off, sat for a moment, then straightened up, drawing in her breath, and asked, "Where's the stuff on the Wrens?"

"On your desk underneath that pile of pictures," said Weathersby. "Are you feeling all right, Eric?"

She stared at him and then said suddenly, "Shut up."

"O.K.," said Weathersby. "O.K." He glanced at Sylvia, raised one eyebrow and demanded, "Why Mike, for God's sake?"

"And what's the matter with Mike?"

"He's got red hair. If I were a woman, I wouldn't marry a guy with red hair who can't even afford to pay for his own lunch. Well, anyhow," said Weathersby kindly, "congratulations. I hope you'll be happy on relief."

"Thank you, Weathersby," said Sylvia. "Just for that, I'll allow you to write up my wedding. Eric . . ."

"Yes?"

"I'll do the Wren story for you."

"No, thanks, I'll do it. What's this?" she asked, referring to a pile of photographs. "Don't tell me we had that many weddings left over!"

Erica started to work again. When the final edition was ready to go to press, she began to line up her material for Tuesday's first edition. The thing was to go on working and not to look up, for fear you might see him standing there and hear the sound of his voice and feel the touch of his hands, not to stop for a moment for fear you would be caught. The thing to do was to go on working and not to think of the future which contained forty-eight hours, one weekend, and probably nothing more. Some women were lucky; they say goodbye and knew exactly what they're up against — the simple, straightforward, uncomplicated all-or-nothing alternative of life or death. If he lives, he comes back; if he's killed, he doesn't. But Marc may live or he may not, and if he lives he may come back, or he may not.

Later, put it off until later. Get your mind on something else.

She looked down at the typewritten page in front of her which was headed "Women's War Group Extends Work," and a moment later she heard her own voice call out, "Sylvia!"

"Yes," said Sylvia, starting. "Yes, what is it?"

"I . . . I don't . . ." She put one hand to her forehead, wondering what it was she had meant to say. Sylvia was looking at her in alarm, and it was necessary to say something, so she asked, "Where's the syndicate stuff?"

"On your desk, Eric." She got up, crossed the room and standing in front of Erica she said, "Are you sure you're feeling all right?"

"Yes, I'm sorry."

She said, "He hasn't gone yet, Eric. Besides, they get postponements — my brother was home three times after his embarkation leave."

"Was he?" Erica looked up at her for a moment, and then said, "It isn't that."

"Why don't you go and get some lunch."

"What time is it?"

"Five past one. Weren't you supposed to meet Miriam at one?"

Erica remembered Miriam then, and she said, "My gosh, I must be going nuts."

She found Miriam sitting at a small table by the wall which was decorated with a large colored photograph of the Bay of Naples. She was wearing a white dress, and in spite of the heat which swept into the half-shuttered restaurant from the blazing street outside whenever the door was opened, and seeped through cracks when it was closed, her face was chalky and she looked cold.

She cut short Erica's apologies for once more keeping her waiting, with, "Let's order and get it over with." When the waitress had come and gone and Erica asked if there was something wrong, instead of answering she asked, "How was your weekend, Eric?"

"It was almost perfect."

Her eyes left Miriam's face, followed a waiter as he made his way down the stuffy little room and disappeared through the swing door leading to the kitchen, and finally came to rest at a bad oil painting of Venice hanging on the back wall. There was nothing, no typewriter, no story of the Wrens, no weddings or meetings, not even two familiar voices discussing the best method of making jelly on the other side of the room — nothing to hold her to the present and keep her from slipping back into the past. She gave up trying and let herself go, back to the mountain lake, the little brightly painted houses like toys on the hillside opposite the hotel, the terrace with orange and yellow umbrellas, the light panelled bedroom with homespun curtains and a small lamp on the bedside table which cast a long oval shadow across the ceiling. Everywhere she looked she saw Marc again, lying on the float beside her, sitting in the stern of a red canoe watching the water dripping off the blade of his paddle, stretched out on a deck chair in a pair of dark red bathing trunks, grinning because some woman had just remarked very audibly to her companion that he ought to be in the Army. "What does she want me to do — wear my uniform in swimming?"

"Why 'almost'?" asked Miriam.

Her eyes left the painting of Venice on the back wall and returned to Miriam and she said, "Because I'm not going to win after all, Mimi. I'm going to lose."

"Why?"

"I don't know why," said Erica, having failed to think of any way of explaining it so that it made sense. Sometime during the past three days she had realized that Marc was tired out, that was all, but added to everything else, sooner or later that tiredness would prove to be fatal. He had been up against it for seventeen years, ever since he had left home, and he had already had more than enough; he was simply not fit to take on another and far worse struggle involving another person, when he needed his resources for himself. He was due to go overseas in a few weeks, and although he had somehow contrived to get through his officer's training, one of a total of seven out of a class of five hundred to finish with a Q-I rating, and by the same willpower he would somehow contrive to get through the war just as creditably, at the same time it was not going to be easy. Of all the men Erica had ever known, he was by nature the least adapted to military life. There are limits to the number of demands you can make on anyone's endurance, and to expect Marc to take on his family, his wife's family and most of his own friends as well as hers, at this time of all times, was really to expect too much.

"Did he say anything in particular?" asked Miriam.

"No. It wasn't anything he said or did, it was just something I . . ." she paused and then said hopelessly, "something I could feel."

"You're not imagining, are you?"

Erica shook her head.

"Then how much longer do you give it?"

"Until he goes home for the last half of his embarkation leave."

"It's too bad it's not the other way round," said Miriam. "I'd rather you had the last half."

"It wouldn't make any difference," said Erica, looking down at the plate of food which had appeared in front of her. "I guess I'm just hopelessly outnumbered."

"You think his family is going to work on him, is that it?"

"I don't think it, I know it. They'll say everything he knows my family has been saying for the past three months, only they'll have to pack it all into three days."

He had often talked to her about his home and his own people, but she could not remember his ever having said anything to suggest that they would not go to work on him, and in her confused, exhausted mind, there was only the growing fear that his family and his environment would be as inimical to her as hers were to him, and this new realization that he was too tired, too discouraged, and too ridden with other problems not to give in, particularly when he knew that he might never see his parents again. Like Erica, he was greatly attached to his father and mother, but unlike Erica, who had believed and who had never for a moment ceased to believe, that her parents were wrong, his whole experience of life would lay him open to the conviction that the Reisers were right. His parents even had the Drakes on their side. They might not know it at the beginning, but they would find out sooner or later, and Erica could imagine what they would make of it when they did find out.

She said, "I wonder who's going to take the case for the defence . . . I can't very well take my own case when I'm five hundred miles away. Anyhow, it would have to be someone who's Jewish. Nobody but a Jew can help me now."

She picked up some coleslaw on her fork and then put it down again. She laughed and said, "That's funny, isn't it, Mimi?"

"Not particularly," said Miriam, looking at her. "Eat some lunch."

After a brief silence she said, "I suppose it hasn't even occurred to you that there just might be someone who's Jewish and who would back you up?"

"Don't be silly."

A moment later she said suddenly, "Mimi, I'm going to tell you something. Everybody else is wrong and I'm right. To the day I die, I'll know that we should have got married and that our not marrying each other was the worst mistake we ever made."

She laughed again and said, "Do me a favour, Mimi. When I'm dead, see that they put on my tombstone, 'Everybody was out of step but our Erica.' It's all right, I'm not getting hysterical."

"I wish you'd eat something," said Miriam miserably.

"It's a sort of drawing-room version of *Abie's Irish Rose*, without the comedy relief, isn't it? Very high class, of course, and brought up to date with the background of World War II."

There was a fat man drinking soup a few tables away with a napkin tucked under his chin and Erica watched him for a while. Then she said to Miriam, "You know, all the way up the mountains in the car, I kept wondering if the hotel people knew Marc was a Jew when they made the reservations. I guess they usually go by the names, but 'Reiser' doesn't sound Jewish, necessarily, and I didn't know if Marc had remembered to volunteer the information. I looked up the hotel advertisement in the paper but they didn't say whether their clientele was selected or not and I didn't like to ask him about it so I just sat and worried. To be thrown out of a hotel on arrival seemed a rather grim way of starting a weekend. It was all right, though, so I guess he had remembered. Incidentally, how do you suppose it's done?"

"What?"

"I mean how do they manage to work it in gracefully? Do they say, 'I should like to reserve two rooms and a bath for three days beginning Friday, the 27th, provided you have no objection to Jews,' or do they just write an ordinary letter and stick 'By the way, I'm Jewish' in a postscript?"

"Eric, for heaven's sake!"

"Sorry," said Erica. "But it all goes together, doesn't it?"

She tried to eat some coleslaw and then some cold salmon, but it was too difficult to swallow and she pushed her plate away from her. After a while she said suddenly in complete despair, "I never knew anyone who seemed to be so alone — even with me, and I know I'm closer to him than anyone else has ever been. But there's still something — something I can't get through, except for a little while, and then he's on the other side of it again, with — whatever it is — between us. He's so alone, that I can't bear to think of it. I used to lie awake at night after he'd gone to sleep and look at him, and just cry."

"Eric . . ."

"But Mimi, I want to know *why*. Marc's never done anything to anybody . . ."

"It's going to get *better*, darling!" said Miriam in agony.

"Oh, sure. Sure, we're going to win the war so we can go on hanging out our own 'Gentiles Only' signs instead of having the Nazis do it for us. After all, that's what's known as democracy, isn't it?"

"You don't mean that, Eric." It seemed to Miriam that the most intolerable aspect of this intolerable situation was what it was doing to Erica and as her eyes filled with tears, she said, "Don't talk like that. You mustn't change, Eric, you've got to go on being the same person you've always been. You've got to, Eric . . ."

"Have I?" said Erica. "Why?" As Miriam did not seem to be able to think of a reason she remarked, "You just want me to go on being a sucker. Remember, you said there was one in every family."

"No," said Miriam almost inaudibly. "No, that's not what I mean." She took a mouthful of food, then sipped some water and went on more steadily, "If you don't pull yourself together, Eric, you'll go to pieces."

"Not for a while," said Erica matter of factly. "Not till Marc says, 'Well, so long, Eric, see you after the war.'" She paused and then observed, "What a relief that will be to Charles and Mother. If Marc goes overseas by the end of September, they might even still have time for a holiday." As she saw Miriam's expression, she said, "They bought their share, Mimi, and provided I can arrange not to go to pieces in front of them, they're not even going to have to pay for it. So stop worrying. What are you crying for?"

"Oh, shut up," said Miriam. She found a handkerchief in her bag, a very fine linen handkerchief with the initial "M" worked into an intricate embroidered design in one corner and she glanced at it, remarking, "Max gave me that," and dried her eyes. Looking first at Erica's plate and then at her own, she said, "Since neither of us seems to be much good at eating today, we might have a drink."

"Yes, we might."

"What do you want?" asked Miriam, beckoning to the waitress.

"Rye and water."

"Two rye and water, please," Miriam said.

There was a family of Italians, mother, father, and three children, all eating spaghetti at the next table. Erica said, looking at them, "You've got to put it behind you and forget about it." A moment later she was surprised to hear herself adding suddenly, "And you've got to marry John."

Miriam shook her head smiling, her face stiff, and said, "It's going to be a bit too much this time, Eric, even for John."

At that moment the waitress appeared with two glasses on a tray, explaining that they were out of rye and that she had brought Scotch, which cost ten cents more. "That's all right," said Erica. When the waitress had gone she asked, still rather surprised, "Do you want to marry him, Mimi?"

"I don't know," she said helplessly. "I'm so muddled, I don't know anything any more. What difference does it make? It's too late anyhow."

"Well," said Erica. She straightened up and said, "Well, here's to you, darling. Keep your chin up."

René had taken his sister to the hospital at noon and shortly before midnight, Madeleine's son was born, the first Catholic Drake since the time of Charles the Second.

"We might just as well never have bothered to leave England," observed Madeleine's father-in-law somewhat gloomily when the excitement had worn off, Madeleine was reported to be already peacefully asleep, and the four Protestant Drakes were on their way upstairs to bed. "The Holy Roman Church always catches up with you again, sooner or later, even if it takes them three hundred years. When can we see Madeleine and the baby?" he asked his wife.

"They might let you look at the baby through the nursery door — it's made of glass," she added hastily, "but you won't be able to see Madeleine for a few days."

"Why not?" demanded Charles.

"Don't be silly, Charles. Even if she is unusually well, they won't let her have visitors for the first week."

"A week!" said Charles, exploding. "I'm not a visitor, damn it!" He thought, and then asked suddenly, "They wouldn't make her father wait a week, would they? Or her mother?"

"You're not her father and mother," Miriam pointed out.

"No? Well, I'm all the father she's got, and if the rest of you are willing to let a bunch of bureaucratic nurses keep you hanging around the outside of Madeleine's room for a week trying to see her through a glass door . . ."

"It's the nursery that has a glass door, Charles," interrupted his wife patiently.

". . . while they unwind a lot of unnecessary and ridiculous red tape," continued Charles obliviously, "I'm not. And that goes for the baby too."

"Charles, do be sensible for once! It's not red tape, it's a question of taking the most ordinary precautions . . ."

"Precautions against what?"

"Against infection, of course."

"I'm not infectious." He thought some more and finally admitted grudgingly, "Well, maybe you're right about the baby. If I have to look at my grandson through a glass door, then I'll look at him through a glass door, but I'm not going to have Madeleine lying there for a week seeing nobody but that ass René and a lot of sour-faced nurses, and that's final. *Final*," he repeated, giving it a bit more emphasis. "She's probably lonely, lonely as the devil, with Tony . . ." He left the sentence unfinished, shaking his head, and then announced, "I'll go and see her on my way home from the office tomorrow."

"Don't you think someone should warn Royal Victoria Hospital that Charles is impending?" Miriam asked her mother as Charles disappeared into his study.

"What difference would it make?" asked Margaret Drake wearily. "He'll get in anyhow, he always does."

His wife was right. Charles arrived at the hospital next day with a long box of flowers, a bottle of his best brandy "for emergencies," two baskets of fruit, his portable radio, and a rather startling bright pink marabou bedjacket which he had noticed in a shop at noonhour, when he was on his way back to the office after lunching at his club. For the baby he had brought a large pale blue teddy bear. In the corridor he passed a room which was evidently a nursery, came to a dead stop and discovered that a newcomer labelled "Drake" had been placed most conveniently a few feet away on the other side of the glass door. He shifted some of his packages and stood for a while, admiring what he could see of the first Catholic Drake since the time of Charles the Second, which wasn't much, and then advanced down the corridor to the door of Madeleine's room where he knocked gently with one foot, informed the nurse that he was Mr. Drake and would be staying ten minutes, and walked straight in.

That afternoon Erica had withdrawn all her savings from the bank and two of her three Victory bonds, having interviewed the doctor whose name had been given her by Sylvia, who had got it from Mike, who had got it from someone else. As she had said to Miriam, people who work on newspapers know practically everything, and what they don't know they can usually find out. To her astonishment, it was the name of a doctor who was fairly well known and the larger part of whose practice was perfectly legitimate, so that up to the last moment, Erica was sure that someone had blundered and that she had got into the wrong office. The doctor seemed to understand her well enough, however, in spite of her stammering and evasions, told her the price and made an appointment for "her friend" for ten o'clock the following morning, which meant that for most of the day, and except for Mary who would be busy downstairs, Miriam and she would have the house to themselves.

It was not as bad as it might have been if she had not been able to pay such a price, but it was still bad enough. It was worse than anything Erica had imagined; she was appalled at the responsibility she had taken on herself, although she knew that it was the only way out, and for three days her mind rocked back and forth between her fear for Miriam on the one hand and her fear for her mother and father on the other, if by some ill chance or through her father's unpredictable intuitive processes, they should fail to believe Miriam's story that she was simply feeling under the weather, when they returned home at dinnertime on Wednesday to find her in bed.

Except for a brief interval on Wednesday night after Charles and Margaret Drake had gone to bed, having noticed nothing out of the ordinary, when all in one moment of overwhelming relief, Erica realized that it was over and done with and between the two of them, they had got away with it, from beginning to end, she had almost no sense of reality. It had started as a nightmare, it continued as a nightmare, and it finished as a nightmare from which she gradually awoke over a period of days. By the weekend, if it had not been for the effect on Miriam, Erica would almost have been prepared to deny, even to herself, that it had ever happened.

On Monday night she had dinner with René in the flat which he had been sharing with his sister again since Anthony had been overseas. Until late in the evening she found it difficult to keep her mind on what he was saying; she was too tired, too lonely for Marc and too uneasy about Miriam, who was looking as though the bottom had dropped out of her world and as though she were feeling her way along, trying to find something solid to put her feet on.

It was about eleven when René elected to tell her almost casually that he was in love with her and still hoped to marry her, as he simply could not believe that she would ever marry Marc. His reasons for not believing it seemed to be much like those of Charles Drake and almost everyone else, so she found herself once more in the position of having to listen to the same arguments all over again. It never seemed to occur to anyone that you might be deathly tired of simply listening.

She interrupted him at last and tried to give him some idea of what was actually going on. Toward the end she said, "I can't do anything. I can't convince Marc unless I can convince my family first, and nothing's going to convince them. Marc won't be the cause of a final break between us. He just won't, that's all, partly because he wouldn't do that to anyone's father and mother, and partly because he thinks that if marrying him means that I have to give up my parents along with — well, whatever it is you have to give up when you marry a Jewish lawyer, and for whatever it's worth, I don't know — then it's too much altogether."

She leaned over to put her cigarette in the ashtray on the coffee table beside her, and then lying back on the sofa again with her head resting on the arm, she said, "Marc knows perfectly well what's going on at home. I guess, like Mother and Charles and the effect they have on me, it isn't what I say when I'm with him, it's the way I look. I'm not much of an actress, and I'm so scared and miserable most of the time nowadays that I guess I can't help showing it, and of course when I do, Marc thinks he's responsible for it, that if it weren't for him, my life would still be just like a duckpond, and he gets just that much more discouraged."

She stopped again, wondering why she was saying all this to René, whose point of view was essentially the same as her parents' only more so, because he wanted to marry her himself. She smiled at him apologetically, and said finally, "So you see, René, my family hold all the cards. Provided they just go on doing nothing, they can't lose, and I guess they know it. And if you put your money on the Drakes, probably in the long run, you won't lose either."

When she got home shortly after one, Erica found a letter from Marc saying that he would probably have his forty-eight hour leave the following weekend and asking her to meet him in Ottawa on Saturday morning, and a note from her father on the hall table, telling her to call Operator 14 at Farnham, regardless of how late it was.

Anyone using the phone in the downstairs hall could be heard all over the house. Her father always slept with his bedroom door open, and she went into the kitchen and dialed long distance, wondering what it was all about. She knew no one in Farnham.

Operator 14 said, "Is that Miss Drake? It's a personal call."

"Miss Drake speaking."

"Just a moment, please. I'll connect you."

She sat on the edge of the white-topped kitchen table listening to a faint voice repeating, "Hello, New York — New York, please — hello, New York . . ." and then suddenly a man's voice said in her ear, "47 Garrison, Captain Henderson speaking."

"On your call to Miss Drake in Montreal, Miss Drake is ready. Go ahead please."

"Hello," said Erica.

"Hello, Miss Drake, this is Jim Henderson speaking. Sorry to bother you so late but I've been trying to get in touch with you ever since around ten. I don't know whether you remember me or not but I met you at the Ritz a couple of weeks ago . . ."

She could not remember meeting anyone named Henderson at the Ritz, but she said, "Yes, though I'm afraid I . . ."

"I'm a friend of Major Gardiner's. As a matter of fact, it's about him that I'm phoning you . . ."

"About John?"

"Yes, you see he . . ."

Erica interrupted. "I'm afraid you've got the wrong Miss Drake . . ."

"Oh. I was hoping you might have some idea where he

is," said Captain Henderson, his voice dropping with disappointment.

Erica said, completely at sea, "Well, I know he has a flat here — I can give you the number if you like. And you can usually get him through Headquarters during the day . . ."

"Yes, Miss Drake," he said patiently, "I know that. But what I don't know is where he is now. He's supposed to be here. He came down on Monday, went up to Headquarters on Saturday afternoon, and hasn't been heard of since."

"Do you mean John is missing?" said Erica incredulously.

"If it were anyone else, I'd say 'missing' isn't the word for it!"

She said, "Just a minute, please. I'll get my sister."

"I beg your pardon?"

"I've been trying to tell you, you've got the wrong Miss Drake. John is a friend of my sister Miriam. If you'll hold on a minute, I'll go and wake her and find out if she knows anything . . ."

"I'd like to talk to her myself, if you don't mind."

"No, certainly."

Erica ran up the back stairs, down the hall and into Miriam's room where she shook her by one shoulder saying quietly, "Wake up, Mimi — wake up, darling!"

"I'm awake." She turned over, opened her dark eyes and asked, "What's the matter?"

"John's missing. He's been missing for two days, apparently. Someone's just called from Farnham — someone named Captain Henderson. He got me by mistake. I guess he must have called the first time, after you went to bed and Charles didn't think of asking whether he meant you or not."

She stared at Erica, fully awake now, then suddenly got up. "Which phone is it?"

"The kitchen. I didn't want to make a noise."

"Come down with me, Eric."

She did not stop to put on shoes or a dressing gown but rushed ahead of Erica down the back stairs.

Into the phone Erica heard her say, "This is Miriam Drake speaking . . . Yes, Captain Henderson, I remember. What's this about John? No, not since Saturday night, but wasn't he supposed to have leave over the weekend? Oh, I see. What!" She put out one hand, feeling for the edge of the table so that she could lean on it, and said dully, "I'm afraid not. I don't know where he's likely to be, except the usual places. You know all those. Yes," she said, her voice so heavy that Erica looked at her in alarm, "yes, I think he had. All right. As soon as you hear anything, would you let me know, please?"

She hung up and sat down on the table in her nightgown. Finally she said, "He didn't go back on Saturday night, Eric."

"Why not?"

"I guess because of me," she answered after a pause.

"What do you mean?"

"Just what I said. Because of me."

Erica sat down on the edge of the cupboard facing her and asked, "Just how much did you tell him?"

"Everything."

She added after another pause, "I told him everything for the last six years."

"Miriam, you fool," said Erica softly, "you damn fool."

She said desperately, "Don't you see, Eric, I had to! I had to give it to him straight. There wasn't any other way of doing it. Where do you suppose he is?"

"Down at some joint on St. Antoine Street, though if he is, I don't know why the M.P.s haven't picked him up by this time."

"John?" asked Miriam, horrified.

"Yes, John," repeated Erica impatiently.

"But people don't do that sort of thing, Eric!"

"People like John do. He probably started drinking and then eventually passed out, and when he came to, the only thing he could think of was you, so he got drunk all over again. Where do you suppose he is?"

"I don't know," said Miriam frantically.

"You'd better go back to bed or you'll catch cold."

"Come and talk to me, Eric. Please."

They went back upstairs and Erica undressed, and with a satin negligee which Marc had given her thrown over her shoulders, she went into Miriam's room and sat down beside her on the bed. "What did Captain Henderson say?"

"Just that he hadn't turned up when he was supposed to, on Saturday night. He asked me if I knew whether John had had some kind of shock. What will they do to him, Eric?"

"I don't know." She remembered that Miriam had been looking worse since Saturday, instead of better, and she asked, "Why didn't you tell me, Mimi?"

"I couldn't. I didn't realize how much he meant to me until I saw him walk out for good. I knew he was going to, of course. I knew it all along."

"What did you tell him exactly?"

"I didn't make it any worse than it was — rather difficult anyhow," she added, smiling faintly in spite of the tears in her eyes. "I told him about Peter; I told him that the reason he himself had never had a chance was because he reminded me of Peter . . ."

"That was a nice touch," commented Erica. "Did you tell him why he reminded you of Peter?" Miriam nodded and Erica said, "A still nicer touch. You couldn't have done much better than that if you'd tried."

She said quietly, "I did try. I thought I might just as well let

235

him know the whole truth while I was at it."

"Well, go on," asked Erica, after waiting for a while.

"Then he got up and walked out."

"Out of where?"

"Here — downstairs, in the drawing-room."

She sat up with a jerk a moment later, saying wildly, "We've got to go and look for him, Eric! We can't just sit here . . ."

"Where do you suggest we start looking?" inquired Erica without moving.

"He must be somewhere — he might even be in his flat and not answering the door or the phone because he was still . . ."

"They'll have looked in his flat long ago."

Again Miriam asked despairingly, "What will they do to him?"

"I don't know," said Erica hopelessly.

IX
∾

On Friday night when Erica had already started to pack, in order to catch the early train to Ottawa next day, Marc telephoned her long distance to tell her that his forty-eight hour leave had been cancelled, and that a week from the following Monday, on September 14th, he was to start his embarkation leave.

Erica had taken the call in her mother's room. She was alone on the second floor; the rest of the family were downstairs having coffee in the drawing-room, and in the intervals when neither Marc nor she was talking, she could hear the clock ticking in her father's study. She was sitting on the edge of her mother's bed, looking up unseeingly at the watercolour of some calla lilies on the opposite wall. Everything was the same as it had been the first time he had called her, the night Miriam had come home; she was even wearing the same grey flannel suit. But now it was September, instead of early in July; the summer was over, and Marc was to start his embarkation leave a week from the following Monday.

"How long have you got, Marc?"

"We're due in Halifax on the twenty-fourth."

"What day is the twenty-fourth?"

"Thursday. The Halifax train doesn't leave till seven-thirty at night so I'll have most of Wednesday in Montreal. I can report any time up till midnight."

"When are you going to Algoma?"

"If I leave on Friday I'll be there Saturday night, and that will give me three days at home. Can you be at the hotel on Monday night, Eric?"

"Yes, don't worry, I'll be there."

"That means we'll have three days together too — a bit more as a matter of fact, and then I'll be seeing you again on Wednesday on my way through." He paused and then asked, "What is the *Post* going to say, Eric? Do you think they'll mind?"

She had no idea what the *Post* would say and did not care whether they minded or not, but before she could answer, her mother called her from downstairs.

"Just a minute, Mother, I'm telephoning."

"Your coffee's getting cold."

"I'll be right down."

"Are you still there?" asked Marc.

"Yes, darling."

"There won't be any hitches, will there, Eric?" he asked anxiously.

"No, darling. I told you, you're not to worry." Monday, September 14th was ten days and two weekends off, and she

asked, "Isn't there any chance of — of anything — in the meantime, Marc?"

"It doesn't look like it."

There was another flat silence. He said finally, "Well, I guess
that's about all, Eric."

"I guess so," said Erica, after making sure of her voice. She
did not want to start crying again.

"Somebody else wants the phone, darling. I'd better hang
up."

Erica went downstairs, took her cup of coffee from the tray
and carried it over to the window seat. Her mother and father
were sitting at either end of the sofa facing the empty fireplace,
with Miriam curled up in a nearby chair. He father was reading
the evening paper.

One of them asked, "What's the matter, Eric?"

"Nothing," said Erica.

There was a blue haze over the city and the lights were
already lit in some of the buildings. Off to the right, just above
where the Adirondacks ought to be, Erica thought, a new moon
was rising and one star was faintly visible. Sometimes you could
see the Adirondacks when the atmosphere was very clear.

Miriam came over and sat down beside her. She had been
looking a little better since Captain Henderson had reported
that John had turned up at Headquarters, somewhat the worse
for wear, on Tuesday morning. He told Miriam that there was
nothing to be alarmed about; John's record was too good for
anything very drastic to happen to him just because he had gone
"temporarily nuts." As a matter of fact, his c.o. had covered up
for him by simply giving him three days' leave, beginning the
previous Saturday. "That's the reason we were raising heaven
and earth to find him before it was too late and the c.o. would
have to think up something else."

Miriam glanced at the new moon and the first star and said, "I'm going to wish on them both."

"Have you heard from John yet?"

Miriam shook her head. "That's what I'm wishing about."

"You'll get your wish, darling. He's sure to call you sooner or later."

"Is he?" asked Miriam. "Why?"

Erica did not know why she was so sure that he would call her. She said at last, "I guess just because he's John."

"Was that Marc?" asked Miriam after a pause.

"Yes."

She waited for Erica to say something else, but nothing came. Her sister was looking out the window and Miriam said, "Why don't you wish on it too?"

"I can't think of anything I want."

"Erica," said her mother from the sofa.

"Yes, Mother."

"Your father thinks he may be able to get away for a holiday after all, though probably only for about ten days starting next Saturday — I think it's the 19th. If we go up to the cabin is there any chance of your being able to come with us?"

Why that week for their long overdue holiday? Why that week of all weeks, unless there had been a special fate appointed to make certain that everything which affected Marc and her should always go wrong?

She said, "I'm sorry, Mother. I can't manage it then."

"When are you going to take your holidays?" asked her father.

"It's not that." She waited a moment, gripping the edge of the window seat with both hands, and then said, "I'm going to the Laurentians for a few days week after next . . ."

"Why?"

"Marc's going to be on embarkation leave. He starts on

Monday but he has to go to Algoma on Friday to spend the last three days with his family."

There was the usual silence, only this time it was more complete, if possible, and lasted longer. Finally her father remarked, "Evidently your friend's family matters slightly more to him than yours does to you."

Miriam glanced at Erica quickly and then said rather acidly, "It's not quite the same thing, is it, Charles?"

"This is the only holiday your father is going to have this year, Miriam," said her mother.

"It's the only embarkation leave Marc is going to have too," said Miriam.

"I think you'd better mind your own business, Miriam," said her father.

"Erica's business is my business." She glanced at Erica again and then said with sudden fury, "You leave her alone for once! All she's got left is three days, you've seen to that. She's not going to marry Marc Reiser, she's not going to have the rest of her life with him . . ."

"Mimi," said Erica.

Her father had said something angrily which Miriam had not heard, but at the sound of Erica's voice she stopped and said, "Yes, darling . . ."

"I don't want to have a row."

"It seems to be Miriam who's having it," said her mother. She turned to Miriam, too worn and discouraged even to raise her voice, and said, "Naturally your father and I don't expect Erica to alter any of her plans on our account. We've given up expecting that. So far as Erica is concerned, this isn't her home any longer . . ."

"Meeting Marc on streetcorners wasn't Erica's idea, Mother."

"So long as your mother and I are living here, Miriam, I think we're entitled to say who comes into our home and who doesn't. And I don't think either of us is particularly interested in your opinions on the subject."

"No," said Miriam more reasonably, "I guess there's no reason why you should be."

Erica was still motionless beside her, with her shoulders down, and her eyes fixed on some point out in the middle of the light broadloom rug which ran the full length of the room. With her long fair hair and slender figure, she looked like a child waiting in a railway station for someone to come and take her away.

Miriam gritted her teeth, her eyes following the bookcases down the opposite wall, around the corner to the Arlésienne over the fireplace and then finally back to her father and mother at either end of the sofa. Evidently neither of them had anything further to say, and at last she asked, "Couldn't you go without her?"

"We could, but we wouldn't get much fun out of it if we did," said her mother.

"You overestimate us," said Charles.

"What?" He did not answer and she said, "I'm sorry, Charles, but what has overestimating you got to do with it?"

"Well, you can hardly expect your mother and me to go off on a holiday while Erica is having a holiday of her own with . . ."

Miriam thought, if he uses that word "friend" just once more I'm going to lose my temper again. But he said, ". . . with Mr. Reiser," after another pause, and added, "We're not quite that detached, though doubtless we should be by this time."

"I see," said Miriam.

"We should take a few lessons in detachment from Erica. She seems to manage a great deal better than we do."

"Oh, leave her alone, Charles! You've got everything you wanted, except for three days week after next. Why don't you take your winnings — they're big enough! — and be sporting enough to call quits?"

"I don't want to have a row, Mimi," said Erica for the second time.

"As Mother has already pointed out, it's not your row, it's mine."

She got up suddenly, leaving Erica by herself on the window seat, crossed the room, and standing in front of her mother and father with her back to the fireplace, as though she wished to indicate that the row was to be confined to the area immediately around the sofa and did not include Erica, she said, "You brought us up to stick together — you always said to Tony and Eric and me that we should stand up for each other. I've listened to you going after Erica, Charles, and I've kept out of it because she wanted me to . . ." Miriam paused and then added deliberately, "I assure you that it was only because she wanted me to, and *not* because I agreed with you, but it's gone too far altogether and I can't keep out of it any longer."

She began, "I told Erica at the very beginning . . ." and then broke off, her eyes following Erica as her sister got up from the window seat and ran out of the room. She stared at the empty door through which Erica had disappeared, listening to her footsteps on the stairs, and then turning to her father she said, "I told her at the beginning that she was going to have to choose between you and Marc because you would make it impossible for her to do anything else. She wouldn't believe me. She said that sooner or later you'd come round; if only she were quiet and didn't say anything so there wouldn't be any rows, then she was sure you'd come round. She was wrong about that, but I was wrong too — I didn't realize how much you mattered to Marc. There was no choice; so far as Marc was con-cerned it was either both of you, or he was out of the picture."

"Evidently he has a few more scruples than we gave him credit for," said her father.

"He has a lot more of what it takes to make a first-rate human being than you've ever given him credit for, I know that!"

Her father shifted his position on the sofa, and with his steady dark eyes fixed on her face and his expression still unchanged, he said, "What you mean is that there was never any choice so far as Erica was concerned either — she had chosen Mr. Reiser at the very start of this infatuation of hers, and her mother and I could simply take it or leave it, that was all. The way we felt about it was of course completely unimportant."

Miriam surveyed him in silence for a moment, and said finally, "Listen to me, Charles. Erica is in love with Marc. She's not infatuated with him, she loves him. Her whole life is going to be different because of what you've done. But it can't be undone now, and I'm not going to argue about it. I'm only trying to warn you."

"Warn us?" repeated her mother, staring at her.

"In less than three weeks you're going to be rid of Marc Reiser for good. That's enough, isn't it?" she asked both of them. "Surely you don't want to be rid of Erica too . . ."

"Miriam!" gasped her mother.

"I know the way you feel about things," said Miriam, look-ing down at the floor, "but you can't stop Eric from going away with Marc week after next. If you try, she'll go anyhow, but she won't come back again." She raised her eyes, looking from one to the other, and said desperately, "Don't you see, if you try to stop her, you'll put her in a position where she has to choose between you and Marc. She can't come back again, after you've told her not to go, and particularly after the kind of row you'll have if you do. She's just about at the end of her rope and she knows it. That's the reason she keeps saying 'I don't want any rows, I don't want any rows.' You simply must not make an issue of it."

"Do you realize what you're suggesting?" asked her father when at last he had found his voice.

"It's a question of what matters most to you, Charles." She could not bring herself even to glance at her mother, and with her eyes back at the floor in front of her, she said, "I'm sorry for you, but I'm not half as sorry for you as I am for Erica."

"That's quite obvious." She heard him draw in his breath, and then he said, his voice shaking. "I suppose you'd go with her."

"You suppose wrong."

"Why?"

"Never mind me. There's no reason I can think of why a daughter should have to explain to her mother and father why she is not going to walk out on them, anyhow. It's a silly question," she said dispassionately, "and you know the answer as well as I do."

She said, her face strained, "Maybe I shouldn't have let you go on, maybe I shouldn't have kept out of it, I don't know. I've never got on with you as well as she has, and I haven't been awfully successful in running my own life. I don't suppose you would have paid any attention to what I thought. I've made the damnedest mistakes about people," she added as though she were talking to herself, "so I couldn't really expect you to be very interested in my opinion of Marc Reiser."

"Do you know him, Miriam?" asked her mother, looking straight ahead at the empty fireplace.

"Yes, of course I know him."

"So you were encouraging her behind our backs," said her father.

She said immediately, "If you choose to turn your back, Charles, you can hardly complain about what goes on behind it!"

"Miriam . . ." said her mother.

"Yes, darling?"

"I am interested in your opinion of Marc Reiser." All the life seemed to have gone from her face, and her husband might just as well not have been in the room. Still looking straight ahead of her, she said, "I want to know what he's like, Miriam."

She knew that at last her mother was in a mood to listen and to believe what she was told, and Miriam said quietly, "He's the opposite of everything you thought. If he weren't you wouldn't have been able to get rid of him so easily, because he really cares about Eric. Maybe you have to know him to realize what a difference it would have made if you'd only been willing to give him a break, not for his sake, but for Erica's . . ."

"I wish I had known him."

"Margaret . . ."

She glanced at her husband without really seeing him and then said to Miriam, "Go on, please."

"I can't tell you what Marc's like, except that he's the same kind of person as Erica, he's the other side of the same medal. They just seem to belong together, that's all. I guess if you didn't know he was Jewish, or if that didn't matter so much, you'd say that there couldn't be anyone better for Erica than Marc."

Her mother went on staring at her for just a moment after Miriam had finished, then turning away, she began to cry in her corner of the sofa with her face hidden in her arms.

No one had ever seen Margaret Drake cry like that before.

Watching her, Miriam found herself thinking dully that whatever Charles Drake did or said from now on, her mother was through. Miriam made a sudden movement toward her, then drew back again. She said, "Well, it wasn't really your fault anyhow, darling . . ."

"My fault!" she repeated, gasping.

"Margaret, for heaven's sake . . ."

She did not even hear him. With her face still hidden she said, "Of course it's my fault! All the excuse I've got is that I didn't know him and I didn't realize how much he means to her, and what kind of an excuse is that?"

She could not stop crying, she had to wait again before she could make herself intelligible, and then she said, "Mothers have no *right* not to know. It isn't as though Erica hadn't tried to tell me, she tried over and over again — she even asked me to lunch with her and Marc and all I . . . I . . ." she said incredulously, "all I, her own mother, could think of to say was that I was too busy!"

"Margaret, stop that!"

"I can't stop." As she felt his hands she pushed him away, saying despairingly, "Leave me alone, Charles. I don't blame you, I blame myself."

He was thoroughly frightened and he did not know what to do; he watched her helplessly for a while, his face working, and then he suddenly rounded on Miriam. He said, raging, "Well, you wanted your row, and now you've finished, I'd like to know exactly what you think you've accomplished . . ."

Miriam did not answer. At that moment she had remembered a remark that Erica had made to her weeks before when they were walking on the mountain where Erica and Charles had once walked every Sunday afternoon after the Philharmonic broadcast from New York. They had stopped to watch the model yachts sailing back and forth on Beaver Pond, and out of nothing, except perhaps that the place itself was so associated with her father in her mind, Erica had said suddenly, "Charles doesn't want to go on this way, but he got started on the wrong track at the very beginning and he can't stop, he just has to keep on going."

It was in order to stop him before it was too late that Miriam, who detested rows, had deliberately created this one, but as her father turned away from her, back to his wife again, she knew that so far as Charles Drake was concerned she had accomplished nothing. He had already gone so far that no one else could stop him either.

X

The managing editor of the Montreal *Post* was a slight, grey-haired man in his early forties, with small, unusually white hands, a soft voice, and a fondness for light grey suits, grey ties, and suede shoes. Nobody liked him, but he was recognized as exceptionally capable, and by and large, Erica reflected as she sat facing him across his desk, waiting for the verdict, and compared to the other *Post* employees of whom it was generally said that they learned more in less time and were fired faster than the employees of any other paper in the country, she herself had had a fairly easy time of it, chiefly because she was a Drake and Mr. Prescott was a snob.

This morning, however, Mr. Prescott was in one of his subtle moods. He had said nothing so far, he had merely regarded her rather curiously across the desk, listened to what she had to say, and then swung around so that he could look out the window and watch some pigeons on a nearby roof. She realized that she might have approached him more tactfully, instead of having come straight to the point, but during the past three years of war she had been gradually losing interest in the Woman's Section of the *Post*, and during the past six years, she had become thoroughly tired of being tactful with Mr. Prescott, who demanded the utmost tact from his staff, and then invariably walked all over them anyway.

He said at last, "You'd be away three days in the middle of next week, then, wouldn't you?" and then remarked vaguely, "By the way, one or two of the boys seem to think you're a member of the Guild . . ."

"Yes," said Erica. She had joined the Guild on the 20th of June, and unless Mr. Prescott was slipping badly, he had found out within something more like three hours than three months. Evidently he was leading up to something.

"We're not much in favour of it, of course."

There was another pause, and finally Erica suggested that the three days be counted as part of her holidays.

"Yes, we might do that," he said, and then added, "I'll just ask Miss Munroe to come in and give Miss Arnold a hand while you're gone."

So it was Miss Munroe again. "I beg your pardon?" said Erica innocently. "I'm afraid I don't quite remember who . . ."

"My niece," said Mr. Prescott coldly.

"Oh, yes, you said something about her in July, didn't you? It seems hardly worthwhile to bring your niece in for just three days, though . . ."

"No, it doesn't, does it?"

Erica said nothing. They had been over all this before, but she knew that Mr. Prescott could not manoeuvre his niece into

Sylvia's job without her consent, and Mr. Prescott knew that she knew it. Although the managing editor of the *Post* went in for hiring relatives, the owner of the *Post* did not, and furthermore, the owner of the *Post* was a friend of Charles Drake's. Although Erica had never yet made use of that friendship, still it might come in handy as a last resort. Mr. Prescott knew that too.

On the other hand, Erica thought, if she did go directly to the owner of the paper in order to out-manoeuvre Mr. Prescott, the managing editor would think up some reason for firing her in fairly short order, and the Guild could do nothing about it, because most of the men on the *Post*, which was supposed to be pro-Labour in its editorial policy, were too frightened to join. But what difference does it make? Erica asked herself wearily. She was not only tired of being tactful with Mr. Prescott, she was tired of Mr. Prescott.

"There's a certain amount of give-and-take in any job," said Mr. Prescott, in the same tone in which he reminded his staff from time to time that they should regard themselves simply as one big happy family. "Have you any particular reason for wanting to go away next week?"

"Yes. My fiancé is going overseas."

"I see."

After waiting for him to say something else, Erica got up. She said coolly, "As I have no intention of resigning from the Guild or of permitting Miss Arnold to be fired in order to make room for Miss Munroe, I think the simplest thing for me to do is to resign from my own job. Then Miss Arnold can take over from me, your niece can take over from Miss Arnold — and I'll have my three days' holiday."

It was the first time that she had ever seen the managing editor really startled. He looked up at her, obviously taken aback, and then finally recovering himself, he said, "A rather expensive holiday, isn't it?"

"I don't think so."

Mr. Prescott was strong on clichés. Presumably in order to be able to make the speech about watching her future career with considerable interest, he asked, "Have you any other job in mind?"

"Not at the moment," said Erica, and then discovered when she was halfway to the door that all the time she had been wondering how she was going to manage after Marc left, she had had another job in mind without fully realizing it. Now that she was finished with the *Post*, there was nothing to stop her from joining up. In the Army, they don't give you time to think, or at least not during the basic training period anyhow, and by the time that was over, she would have had a chance to get used to things.

Back in her office again, she sat down at her desk by the window and opening the top drawer in which she had left a package of cigarettes, she announced to Sylvia and Weathersby, "I've resigned."

"Congratulations," said Weathersby.

Sylvia stopped typing in the middle of a word and asked, "Are you serious, Eric?"

"Yes, I'm leaving on Monday."

"But why?"

"I didn't feel like making a deal with Mr. Prescott." Opening another drawer in which she was certain that she had not left her package of cigarettes, she added, "It was sort of suggested that one good turn deserves another, and that if I wanted three days off in the middle of the week, I ought to be more reasonable on the subject of Mr. Prescott's niece."

"Her again," said Weathersby, groaning. "Have you ever seen her, Eric?"

"No, what's she like?"

"Dumb," said Weathersby. "They don't come any dumber."

"Does that mean that she's coming in here?" asked Sylvia incredulously.

"It means that she gets your job and you get mine."

"And what about you?"

"Oh, me," said Erica, abandoning the search through her desk drawers and starting to look among the litter on her desk. "I'm going to join the Canadian Women's Army Corps. Bubbles, have you taken my cigarettes again?"

"They were going stale," said Weathersby defensively.

"I've only been gone a quarter of an hour. They couldn't go stale that fast. Here, hand them over."

He recovered the package from underneath his typewriter and tossed it across to her. It missed her desk and as she stooped over to pick it up from the floor, she muttered resentfully, "And out of my desk drawer too. You never used to snitch them unless they were lying on top. It's about time I resigned, I can't afford to keep us both in cigarettes. Have we got any matches, Sylvia?"

"No, but your lighter's working. I got it filled yesterday."

"Thanks, darling."

"Eric," said Sylvia after a pause.

"Yes?"

"What do they do about leaves if you're married to someone in the Army?"

"Who?"

"The CWAC."

"I think they arrange it so that you have your leaves together. Don't they, Bubbles?"

Weathersby grunted.

"I suppose he means yes," said Erica, "and Bubbles knows everything, even if he has no manners, and is under the peculiar delusion that it is his duty to smoke other peoples' cigarettes in order to keep them from going stale."

"Do you mind if I join up with you?"

"Mind!" repeated Erica in amazement. "Darling, would you?"

She had had one week of marriage which had ended three days before when Mike had gone off to camp; they had been the longest and emptiest three days that Sylvia had ever lived through, and she said, "Yes," adding more definitely, "Yes, I would."

There was a kind of explosion from Weathersby who demanded, as soon as he could talk again, "And who gets out the Woman's Section of the *Post*, may I ask?"

"You do," said Erica and Sylvia together.

"You and Mr. Prescott's niece," said Sylvia.

"Are you really serious, Sylvia?" asked Erica.

"Why not?" She looked across at Erica and said, "I'd have joined up long ago, I guess, if it hadn't been for leaving Mike. Besides, I didn't much like the idea of doing it alone, but now he's left me and I won't be doing it alone — so why not?" she asked again, shrugging. "We're sort of used to each other and we get along awfully well . . ."

"My gosh, yes," said Erica.

"Then let's stick together."

"Leaving me holding the bag with Mr. Prescott's niece," said Weathersby, brooding. "But I'll catch up with you," he said, pointing a finger at them. "Six months and I'll be old enough for the Air Force. Did I ever tell you that my brother got the D.F.C. and bar?"

"You've told us about the D.F.C. several times," said Sylvia, "but I don't think you've ever mentioned the bar. Has he ever mentioned the bar, Eric?"

"I don't think so," said Erica, after due reflection.

"You may now tell us about the bar, Bubbles," said Sylvia.

"Oh, shut up," said Weathersby. "Women," he said resentfully. "Women. I've had enough women around here to last me the rest of my life."

"Speaking of women," remarked Sylvia, returning to work. "How's your mother's jelly?"

"She still sets it with wax!" said Weathersby hotly.

Erica and Sylvia started to laugh. They went on laughing for a while and finally Erica said, "Well, it's almost over, Sylvia, but we've had an awful lot of fun."

"Yes," said Sylvia. Glancing first at Erica, who was rolling a fresh sheet of copy paper into her typewriter, with a light from the window behind her falling on her long fair hair and around her tired, sensitive face, and then at Weathersby in his corner, growling as he embarked on still another account of a wedding, she said again, "Yes, we've had a lot of fun."

Back at work herself, she asked absently after a pause, "What was the bride wearing this time, Bubbles?"

"*Mousseline de soie*," said Weathersby. "If I'm ever dope enough to get married, my wife is going to be 'radiant in her grandmother's bathing suit,' God damn it. Anything for a little variety."

XI

~

*F*rom the Friday evening when Erica had told her parents
that she was going to spend the first half of Marc's embarkation
leave with him in the Laurentians until a week from the following Monday, less than two hours before her train was due
to leave, Charles Drake did not mention the subject again.
During those ten days he scarcely spoke to her at all; even the
indirect references to Marc which had acted to some extent as
escape valves had abruptly come to an end, and he said nothing
in Erica's hearing which could possibly be related to Marc by
even the most roundabout route.

Shortly after three o'clock on Monday afternoon, Erica went
up to her bedroom to pack, and a few minutes later she returned
from her bathroom with a handful of toilet articles to find her
father standing against the closed door leading to the hall.

Erica had not heard him come in and on first sight of him she started, dropping one of her cosmetic jars on the soft carpet, although she had known all along, and in spite of his silence, that some kind of ultimatum was inevitable. He was simply not going to allow her to walk out, on her way to spend three days with Marc, without making any effort to stop her.

She picked up the jar and asked calmly, "What are you doing home at this hour, Charles?"

"I wasn't getting any work done. I couldn't keep my mind on it." He watched her for a moment in silence, while Erica went on with her packing, and then said jerkily, "I came — to ask you — not to go."

"Why?"

"You know why."

He moved out of the shadow by the door into the light, a big, dark-haired man with hands clenched at his sides, and said, "That other weekend you were away was bad enough but I didn't know definitely . . ."

"There's nothing more to know now than there was then."

He went on as though he had not heard her, "I didn't know for certain that he was going to be there, or whether you — whether you were definitely . . ."

His voice trailed off; he left the sentence unfinished and fumbled in his pocket with one hand, taking out his cigar case and a bunch of keys, then putting them back again. He looked almost ill; the flesh around his fine dark eyes was puffed and discoloured and in the strong light from the windows his skin had a yellowish tinge. He said, trying to keep his voice level, "You can't expect your mother and me to sit here for three days, from now till Thursday night, while you — while you . . ."

He swallowed, and then said with sudden violence, "We can't stand it. I tell you, Erica, we can't stand it! We're too old;

if you go through with this thing, you'll leave a mark on us that will last the rest of our lives."

"You sound as though I was going to commit murder."

She took two pairs of shoes from the cupboard, then sat down on her bed with the shoes in her lap, remarking aimlessly, "It's a bit late, isn't it? Marc left Petawawa two hours ago and it's less than two hours till my train goes. Why didn't you get all this over with last night or even this morning? You went off downtown after breakfast without saying a word."

"I wasn't going to say anything. Your mother didn't . . ." He stopped again.

"What made you change your mind?"

With his eyes fixed on her face, he tried to say something, but nothing came. At last he answered only, "I told you, I can't go through with it."

"I don't know what you want, Charles, except that you seem to want everything."

"All I want you to do is to stay at home and behave like any decent girl who values her own self-respect!"

"You don't know what this is all about." She put one pair of shoes into the suitcase lying on the bed beside her, and looking down at the other pair in her lap, she said hopelessly, "Apparently you play the game on the principle of 'Heads I win, tails you lose.' You haven't the remotest idea what this is all about because you've never given me a chance to tell you. Ever since the beginning, whenever I tried to tell you, *you told me*. You knew. You knew without being told, just as you knew exactly what Marc was like without ever having met him."

He said, staring at her, "I'll admit it hadn't even occurred to me that you might try to justify yourself by putting the blame on me . . ."

"I'm not trying to justify myself! I don't give a damn about justifying myself."

She began wrapping the second pair of shoes in tissue paper with her hands shaking. She had no idea where this was going to end, but she knew that if she lost her temper, it could only end in disaster. She had kept her feelings dammed up for too long.

"Do you know what I've been doing for the past two months, Charles?" she asked without looking at him. "I've been trying to out-balance thirty-three years. It's been quite a job with only two months to do it in, and now when all I've got left is three days, you . . ."

He said, cutting her short, "You've got the rest of your life!"

". . . I've got to prove . . ." She stopped, glanced at him, and said, "No, I haven't got the rest of my life. It isn't even a question of whether he comes back or not, but whether I'll ever see him again if he does."

Evidently he did have at least a vague idea of what it was all about, for he said, "Isn't it possible that instead of all these subtle reasons you keep looking for, it may simply be that he's not really in love with you?"

"Otherwise it would be a case of all for love and the world well lost, is that it? I thought that was one of the notions you get over when you grow up." She turned suddenly and said, facing him, "And supposing he isn't in love with me, or not enough in love with me — then why?"

"Why what?"

"Why isn't he?"

He fumbled for his cigar case again, still standing in the middle of the room a few feet from the foot of her bed, and answered finally through a cloud of smoke, "You wouldn't be the first girl to find out that respect is what matters most in the long run."

"Doesn't that depend somewhat on the individual?"

"No, it's just human nature."

"There's a generalization to take care of everything, isn't there?" asked Erica, starting toward the chest of drawers behind him.

He said angrily, "Generalizations only exist because they represent the accumulated experience of the human race right down through history!"

"And so whenever we find someone who doesn't fit, we go to work on him and by the time we're finished, we've damn well made him fit! Like Procrustes and his bed — all you have to do is stretch him or chop him down to the right size."

He scrutinized her in silence for a moment as she stood with her back to the chest of drawers, and at last he said, "You haven't any idea how much you've changed in the past three months . . ."

"It doesn't do to lose all your illusions at once, does it?"

"Eric, for heaven's sake!"

She could feel the anger mounting higher and higher inside her, but it had not yet broken loose and she said almost conversationally, "You know, Charles, I had illusions about practically everything. About you and Mother and this precious country of ours, and the kind of world we're supposed to be fighting for — I was so full of illusions that really, I must have been quite a spectacle."

"I liked you better that way, Eric," he said under his breath.

"I liked you better too."

It was as though she had struck him. She took note of his reaction, without reacting herself in any way. He might just as well have been someone else, not her father.

He said, his voice trembling, "Listen, Eric. I don't know what's already happened between you and Reiser, and neither your mother nor I want to know . . ."

"Is Mother included in this?"

"No. She doesn't even know I'm home." He paused, and forcing himself to speak more matter of factly, he said, "We'll forget about it — that's fair enough, isn't it?"

"Go on," said Erica, watching him.

"Anyhow, we didn't ask you not to go last time, and it isn't as though you went in spite of everything we could do to stop you. But this time, we *are* asking you . . ."

"Yes?" said Erica. "What right have you to ask me not to go?"

"What did you say?"

"Are you and Mother the only ones who have any rights?"

"I don't think I have to answer that."

"As you like," said Erica, shrugging. "Go on. I'd still like to know what you're getting at."

"I told you. I don't want you to go. If you do go, you'll go deliberately this time, knowing exactly how we feel about it and the price we're paying for your three days of happiness or whatever you call it, and as long as you live, you'll never be able to forget what you did to us and to yourself, and neither will we. You'll never be quite the same to us again."

"You don't mean that," she asked incredulously.

"I do mean it." He looked straight at her. His face had become quite colourless, and he said, "We'll go to our graves knowing that when it came to a choice between your mother and father and a rotten . . ."

"Don't say anything about Marc," said Erica warningly.

"I'll say anything I like!" he burst out angrily.

"I don't think you'd better. I've had about enough from you on the subject, Charles. I don't intend to listen to any more."

"If you'd listened to me in the first place, none of this would have happened! I told you Reiser was just out for what he could get. I told you that, didn't I? Well, he's got it evidently, and I was only wrong about one thing — I'll admit I was wrong about that. I thought he really intended to marry you."

Erica stared at him in silence and finally she said, her heart pounding, "Charles, get out. Go away . . . please go away, because I — I . . ."

"No," said her father.

"All right," she said faintly. "I guess I can't make you." It was twenty minutes to four and her train left at five, but she did not move. Still standing with her back against the chest of drawers she said, "What you want me to do is wire Marc to meet me at the drug store on the corner of Peel and St. Catherine. That's your idea of a suitable way for Marc to spend his last leave, isn't it? Meeting me on street corners, going from Charcot's to the Ritz bar and from the Ritz bar to a bench in Dominion Square, looking for a place to sit down because his car's in storage and we can't sit in it any more. Well, why not, you're probably asking yourself. He must be used to it by this time." She took a step forward and looking up at him she said, "I'll tell you why not, Charles. He's had enough of that. For me to ask him to come here and do just what we've been doing ever since we met, would be like saying, 'This is all you get — this is all you're ever going to get if you stick with me,' when the one thing I've been trying to get into his head from the very beginning is that this is *not* all he's ever going to get. Heaven help me, I even promised him that you would not only change your mind but that you'd like him and be really nice to him. You don't realize what a difference it would have made if you'd given us a break . . ."

"Oh, yes I do," he said before he could stop himself.

"Yes," said Erica. "Yes, of course you realize. I forgot. And now you want us to stay in town for your sake."

"Eric . . ."

Turning away from him she said, "You're just wasting your breath." She went back to the chest of drawers and gathering up a few articles of clothing, she carried them over to the bed and put them in her suitcase. When she glanced at him again, she found that her father's expression had changed, and she regarded him without interest, waiting for whatever was coming next. She had an odd idea that it was something which he had been holding in reserve until now, intended to be used only as a last resort. Finally he said with a visible effort, stumbling over the words, "Erica — if your mother and I — if we agreed to have him here, the way you said . . ."

"Good God!"

For a moment she could only gape at him in amazement. Then she thought that she must have misunderstood him, for it could not be true, it was so utterly outrageous that it could not possibly be true. She said, "Wait a minute — I don't think I quite get it. You're not suggesting that you're willing to make some kind of deal, are you?"

He said despairingly, "I guess I'm willing to make almost any kind of a deal to keep you from going."

"Why?"

"*Why?*" Almost beside himself he said, "Good God, don't you realize that after what he's done to me, having him in the house is really more than I can stomach? The idea of you, my daughter, and that . . ."

"I see," said Erica, for now at last she did see all of it, including the motive which had been largely hidden by all the other motives and had remained unaccounted for. It was not what he was saying, or even the rasping tone of his voice, but the way he looked.

Her father managed to get hold of himself again, for the time being at any rate, and went on with a little less emotion, "You wanted us to treat him like anyone else. That's what you said, isn't it? That's what you've said all along. Well, he isn't 'anybody else,' now less than ever," he said between his teeth. "But don't worry, we'll manage some way or other. You needn't worry about that."

"I'm not worrying about that." She was lost now, and she knew it. She was going down for the last time, but before she went down, she was going to do the talking for once, she was going to make up for all the times she had sat and simply listened, in order not to have a row. She was finally going to tell her father what she thought of him.

She said, "Not for the sake of my soul or even out of common decency and kindness, but for the sake of my virtue which you regard as your private property, you're going to start treating Marc 'as though he were anyone else.' You needn't look like that, Charles. You gave yourself away when you said, 'After what he's done to me.' It would have sounded nicer if you'd at least said 'After what he's done to you.' Better still if you'd said, 'After what *I've* done to you.'"

"So it's all my fault."

"Yes, it's your fault. Nobody has any right to be as stupid as you, and no one can afford to be so muddled. Nothing matters to you compared to *your* prejudices, *your* opinions and *your* theories as to what's 'best' for other people and you'd see us all dead before you'd give them up and admit you're wrong. You don't care what happens to me, you've proved that over and over again. If you had cared, you would have stopped all this long ago."

He was angry but not as angry as Erica. She moved a little nearer to him, seeing his lips move but deaf to what he was trying to say and went on, raging, "My, how cozy it would be, Charles — how frightfully cozy, with just the four of us together on Marc's last leave, you and Mother and Marc and me. I can't think of a more agreeable way for Marc to spend his three days than sitting in the living room downstairs listening to you and Mother desperately making conversation in order to keep us from going out and misbehaving ourselves. What would you talk about, Charles? How would you keep him interested? Or hadn't you thought of that? And are you so insane that you think all you have to do is crook your little finger at Marc and he'll come running? What do you think he's been doing for the past three months — skulking around your door waiting for you to condescend to let him in?"

"I know what Mr. Reiser has been doing," he said at last between his teeth. "All I have to do is look at you and I know what Mr. Reiser has been doing for the past three months."

"You ought to be grateful to him."

"Grateful!" he said hoarsely. "Grateful for taking my daughter away from me and turning you into what you are now."

"Oh, no. For what I am now you can be grateful to yourself. You've got something else to be grateful to Marc for — after all, it was very thoughtful of him to turn out to be even more of a swine than you expected — to settle for a couple of weekends instead of marriage. He would have been so much harder to get rid of then, if we'd actually got married, and if I'd held out for a license and made sure of his 'respect' instead of selling myself cheap."

"Erica, for God's sake, stop it!"

"You got what you wanted," she said, paying no attention. "He isn't going to marry a Drake. You fixed it." She went a little closer to him and asked, "Would you like to know how you fixed it, Charles?"

"Erica, I warn you I'm not going to stand for much more of this . . ."

"Oh, now look," said Erica, "be reasonable. For almost three months you've been saying exactly what you liked and writing it all off under the heading of Father Knows Best. I'm not going to take three months, I'll probably be finished in less than three minutes. That's fair enough, isn't it?"

He said, catching his breath, "Erica, you don't know what you're saying!"

"Then there's more excuse for me than there ever was for you, because you always knew, right from the start." She paused and then said softly, "I'll tell you how you fixed it, Charles. You did precisely what Marc expected you to do, right from the beginning. Remember, you said once that you'd got his number as soon as you heard he was downstairs with René? Well, you hadn't. You never said one thing about him which was true. But he had your number — yours and everybody else's."

She stopped. It sounded like someone else, someone else using her voice, and after a moment she heard that person saying, "Listen to me, Charles. Listen to me very carefully so that after I'm gone, you'll know at last just how it all happened. Every time I told Marc he was wrong, wrong about you and wrong about everyone else, you, my father, my ex-best friend — you made a liar out of me."

He said, peering at her, his voice hardly more than a whisper, "You are going, Eric?"

"Yes, I'm going," said Erica. "And I'm not coming back again."

XII

༄

There was a clearing near the top of the mountain from which you could look out over a semicircle of valley with scattered lakes and villages, and over fold upon fold of heavily wooded mountains growing more indefinitely blue toward the northern horizon. The clearing was almost level, fenced in on three sides by evergreens and a thick mass of undergrowth, and open in front where the mountain shelved steeply away from the edge in a small cliff. Below the cliff was a stretch of sloping forest giving way suddenly to the hilly pastures and fields on the uneven floor of the valley.

Marc and Erica had ridden up the steep trail under a blazing sun, and after tethering their horses to a fallen pine at the back of the clearing they had eaten their lunch in the shade, and then moved out into the sun again.

Erica was lying with her head on one arm and her face turned toward Marc, sitting with his back against a boulder overgrown with moss, so that he could see out. It was Wednesday afternoon, two of their last three days together already lay behind them, and neither of them had as yet said anything that really mattered. They had simply stood still, letting time rush by them, each of them apparently waiting for the other to speak first. Something had gone wrong and they knew it; they had felt it the moment Erica had arrived from Montreal an hour after Marc from Ottawa, and first on Monday and again on Tuesday, they had said goodnight at the door of Erica's room. They were both haunted, Marc by a sense of failure and Erica by the recollection of the scene with her father on Monday afternoon, and whatever affected the one affected the other, so that together each of them carried a double burden.

Against the background of evergreens which were like a dark robe thrown over the hills, there was an occasional splash of yellow and crimson; the wind blowing lazily from the northwest was cool and dry, and the sky was too deep a blue for summer.

"It's going to be a marvellous autumn, Eric. It's going to be the best autumn for years. Write me about it, will you?"

"Yes, darling," she said under her breath.

"Tell me how everything looks. You might even send me a maple leaf, the reddest you can find. It wouldn't wither by the time it got there, would it?"

He leaned forward, reaching into the back pocket of his riding breeches for cigarettes, and as he lit first one and then the other, she asked, "What are you going to do after the war — go back to Maresch and Aaronson?"

"Probably for a while, I don't know. I'd rather like to practice in a small town in Ontario. When I was taking my C.O.T.C.

at Brockville I got to know the country around there pretty well, and I wouldn't mind spending the rest of my life in one of those old towns along the river or out on Presqu'Ile. Have you ever been to Presqu'Ile?"

"No, what's it like?"

"It's lovely country — rolling and green, and old and rich. The farmhouses are great big old places with enormous barns. You know I've always wanted to own a farm . . ."

"Yes, I remember," said Erica. "It was one of the first things you ever said to me. If you go back to Ontario you'll have to write your exams all over again before you can practice there, won't you?"

"Yes, but it doesn't matter. How would you like living in a small town?" he asked lightly.

"I don't mind where I live," said Erica, turning her head suddenly so that she was looking the other way, toward the two horses standing together under the pines.

There was another silence, just like so many others during the past few days, only this one was broken by Marc saying at last, "I think it's about time we got started, don't you? We can't go on like this, or rather we can't — we can't leave, like this, tomorrow . . ." He paused and said, "You start, Eric. You're going to have to tell me sooner or later anyhow."

"Tell you what?"

"Whatever it is that's been making you look the way you have ever since you arrived — or like someone trying awfully hard not to look like that."

As she did not answer but kept her head turned away from him, he said, "I finally got you into a real mess, didn't I?" as though he already knew what had happened on Monday afternoon.

She had realized as soon as it was over, that the break with her father would react on Marc to almost the same degree as it had reacted on Charles and herself, unless she could somehow manage to keep Marc from finding out about it. She had tried, she had not for a moment stopped trying except when she was safely in her room at the hotel, and although it had been rather like attempting to hide an object twice as big as herself by standing in front of it, still she had thought that she was getting away with it.

And all she had actually succeeded in doing was to look like someone trying awfully hard not to look like that.

She said, "I had a row with Charles."

"About me," he said.

"Yes."

He was watching a bird circling in and out of the sun toward the west and he said, "All your rows are about me, aren't they? You never had any till I came along."

"It was just by accident that we didn't. I never happened to want to do anything that Charles and Mother disapproved of until now, that's all. They knew I didn't agree with them about a lot of things, of course, but they didn't seem to mind, and it's taken me all this time to discover that the only reason they didn't mind was because they thought it was just so much talk and so naturally it didn't matter. The moment they realized that it wasn't just so much talk, then all hell broke loose. They were bound to realize it sooner or later."

He said after a long pause, "I wish it hadn't been me."

Erica sat up, as though the ground on which she had been lying had, in fact, begun to slip out from under her, and moving back so that she was sitting cross-legged facing him, she said desperately, "Darling, it *isn't* just you. Can't you get that into your head? It was you who started it, but if it hadn't been you, it would have been something else, and if I never saw you again after today, it wouldn't make any difference to Charles and me." With her voice rigidly controlled she said almost matter-of-factly, "We both know where we stand now, and we'll never get back to where we both thought we stood before."

"All your father wants is to get rid of me."

"What my father wants is unconditional surrender to a set of prejudices and a bunch of filthy conventions which are hopelessly out of date!"

The bird flew down, out of the path of the sun and disappeared among the trees edging the trail, and as his eyes came back to her face he said quietly, "They're not out of date, Eric. The moment you'd married me, you'd find that out. The prejudices are still there, working overtime as a result of war conditions," he added a little ironically.

"Not with us . . ."

"Us?" he repeated. "You mean people of our generation? Don't be silly. I live and eat and sleep with people of our generation; I happen to be the only Jewish officer in our particular outfit at the moment, and although most of my brother officers are thoroughly decent and do their damnedest to make me feel as though I belong, they have to make an effort, and I know they have to make it, and I think it's probably just as difficult for them to get used to the idea of always having a Jew in the room as it was for their fathers in the last war. Even when people don't dislike you, even when they really like you, you still make them feel slightly self-conscious, I don't know why. Maybe it's just because they've been brought up to regard Jews as 'different.' Do you want a biscuit?"

"Yes, please," said Erica. "One of the chocolate ones."

He handed her two chocolate biscuits and said, "Except for a very few people, so few they hardly count, that self-consciousness so far as I'm concerned would be about the best you could hope for. What you could actually expect, as opposed to just hoping, is usually something a lot worse."

He said, "You've *got* to see it, Eric."

"Yes," said Erica. "Well, go on. We might just as well get it over with."

"It's not your father and your friends, it's not even just us and what we can take — if we were married, it would be our children — your children — who'd have to take it. First, you'd suffer through me and then you'd start getting it through them, only what came to you through them would hit you far harder because I'm grown up and more or less used to it, and anyhow you didn't bring me into the world, you're not responsible for me. But to have to watch your children go through school tagged as 'Jews,' as outsiders — that's not so easy."

He broke off, and then remarked, looking out over the mountains again, "I'll never forget the way my mother looked the first time I came running home from school bawling my eyes out with a bunch of kids after me, pelting me with snowballs and yelling, 'Marc's a dirty kike.' It wasn't the snowballs that scared me," he added hastily. "It was the word 'kike.' I'd never heard it before and I didn't know what it meant — I don't suppose the kids who were yelling it did either," he added. "It just sounded awful. It sounded even worse to my mother and she's Jewish herself."

"But that was twenty-five years ago," protested Erica.

"Yes," said Marc. "That was twenty-five years ago and Hitler was just a corporal in the German Army. It will probably take us another twenty-five years to get back to where we were in 1915." He said incredulously, "You think after ten years of Nazism that things are easier for us now than they were then?"

"I don't know," said Erica miserably.

"Well, I do," said Marc. "The outlook, my darling, is not very bright, and just why you should be dragged into it when you don't have to be, I can't quite see."

"Can't you? I should think it would be fairly obvious." Before he could say anything she asked, "Isn't it easier for children who are half-Jewish?"

"No. Most Gentiles regard half-Jews as Jews — look at the refugees! — particularly if the father's Jewish, regardless of whether they've been brought up as Christians or not, and if they have, then the Jews won't accept them, so they end up by not really belonging anywhere."

"Would you want our children to be brought up as Jews?"

"Yes, of course."

"Why?" asked Erica in amazement.

"Why?" he repeated, looking surprised. "Well, apart from the fact that I'm Jewish, simply because it's easier for them in the long run. It's much easier to grow up knowing you're Jewish from the time you're old enough to know anything, than to have it suddenly thrown in your face when you're twenty or twenty-five. That was what happened to G d knows how many people in Austria and Germany who' gone through life under the impression that they were Catholics or Protestants who'd been 'assimilated.' Assimilated," he said derisively, "I wonder who invented that word."

"I don't see what Germany and Austria have to do with it. Naturally, the Nazis . . ."

"Do you mean to say you've never heard a good Canadian Gentile say about some refugee or other, 'Yes, I know he's supposed to be a Catholic but he's really Jewish . . .'"

She could not deny it; she had heard plenty of good Canadian Gentiles say that, sometimes even about refugees who were racially, or whatever you could call it, even less than half Jewish.

Erica opened her mouth to say something else, and then

thought better of it. She knew now that unless there were a miracle, she would never marry Marc, but sometimes miracles happened and there was still one day left.

"Aren't you going to argue about it?" asked Marc, looking still more surprised.

"No," said Erica. The idea that if they were married, their children would be brought up as Jews had come as a shock, the worst shock Marc had given her so far, she realized. At the moment it did not seem to her to make much sense, and it was certainly going to take some getting used to, but to argue about it now struck her as just about as futile as stopping a film in the middle and proceeding to quarrel over what took place in the part neither of them had yet seen.

She said suddenly a moment later, "These children of ours would be brought up as both anyhow."

"Why?"

"Because, darling," she said patiently, "whether we like it or not, *we're* both."

"Oh," said Marc. He grinned, remarking, "I guess that stops me."

"Temporarily," said Erica, carefully putting out her cigarette.

He glanced at her but she said nothing more. At the end of another silence he asked, "What did you mean when you said that you and your father were never going to get back to where you were before?"

"The whole basis of our relationship has gone. When I think of the way Charles and I used to be, it seems to me we were like those characters in cartoon comedies who run off a cliff and keep on running until they happen to look down and discover that the cliff isn't there any more, and then start to fall."

With her eyes on a sumac flaming against the dark green of two young pines on the other side of the clearing, she said,

"Well, we had a good run for our money, Charles and I. It took us longer than most people to find out that there wasn't anything underneath us."

He was staring straight ahead of him with the rather bleak look which she had seen in his face at odd times ever since she had known him, only lately it had become much more frequent. It made him look older, not younger like his smile.

"My God, Eric, what a mess I've made of your life! I've taken you away from your family — I've even taken you away from your job."

"Oh, damn my job," said Erica. "I was sick to death of it anyway."

"What are you going to do?"

"Join the Army, just like you."

"Oh," said Marc again. She knew that he still disliked the idea of women in uniform, and that he must dislike the idea of Erica in uniform still more, but all he said was, "Are you sure you want to?"

She nodded. He was silent a moment and then he said, "They'll cut your hair, darling."

"I know," she said, amused, because she had been so certain that Marc's first comment would be something about her hair.

"Is there any chance of your getting overseas?"

"I'm late for that. They take you in the order of enlistment . . ."

"When are you going to enlist?"

He was due to leave for Halifax at seven-thirty on Wednesday night and she said, "Thursday morning."

"Is Miriam joining up too?"

"No, Sylvia is. Miriam's too busy trying to talk John into believing that she really cares about him."

"I hope she succeeds," said Marc. "Your father has always

liked John, hasn't he?"

A flock of crows flew by, down toward the ragged autumn fields below, and they listened to the cawing as it grew steadily fainter in the distance, looking out over the valley and the mountains which were slowly changing colour in the afternoon light.

She knew that Marc was still thinking about her mother and father, although all she had told him so far was that there had been a row, and he still had no idea how bad things actually were.

"Eric, if I thought . . ."

"If you thought what?" she asked him after waiting for him to go on.

"If I thought there was going to be someone else — someone like John, someone who'd mean as much to you as I do . . ." He stopped again, his face very strained, and then made himself finish the sentence. ". . . I guess I'd call quits for good and never see you again. Life isn't a bed of roses anyhow, without adding a lot of extra complications that you can so easily avoid . . ."

". . . by not marrying you," said Erica.

"Yes," he said hopelessly. "Just by not marrying me."

She was beginning to realize that nothing she could say would make any real difference now, but for the sake of that one chance, that miracle which might still happen sometime between now and tomorrow night, she answered, "Maybe there will be someone else, I don't know. All I do know is that it will be different, and I won't feel like this again. When I'm with you, I feel — I feel safe. I feel safe all the way through. I know that whatever you do, you'll never hurt me, and all the little things that are so deep down and so vulnerable — they're safe too."

She smiled at him, although her throat and eyes were too dry and it was hard to talk. "I know lots of people who are comfortably married, with nothing much to worry about, no really serious problems of their own, but they sit on opposite sides of the living room at night and they might just as well be sitting on opposite sides of the Atlantic, because they're not two halves of a whole, they're two separate wholes, two separate individuals who give you the feeling that they got married by accident and might just as well have married — someone else," she said, looking at him. "They're not fundamentally interested in each other — they're interested in other things, in their children, their house, their friends, and what keeps them together comes from outside, rather than from any inner necessity."

She broke off and then said with difficulty, "That's something I've always been afraid of. What matters most to me is not being lonely, and what scares me most is not being poor, or ending up on the wrong side of the local prejudices or even the local conventions, but ending up . . ."

". . . on the wrong side of the living room."

She said, her eyes searching his face, "I wish you'd believe me."

"I do believe you, darling."

"No," said Erica, "not quite."

After that there was another silence, and at last he said, "I keep thinking of all the people who've started feeling the way you do now, and then realized when it was too late, that one person couldn't make up for so many disadvantages — no matter how hard that person tried, no matter how hard they both tried — particularly when it was only that one person who stood in the way."

She said again, "It depends on what matters most to you," wondering how often, just how many times she had said that before, first to her father and then to Marc. Ultimately every argument involving the ability of any individual to make a valid choice comes down to that one question of relative values. And your relative values depend on your experience of living, which in turn forms the basis for your outlook on life as a whole.

She herself belonged to the generation born during the last war, who were still too young to be greatly influenced either by the disillusionment of the immediate post-war years or by the blind optimism of the late twenties. She had come to full consciousness when political security had begun to go and economic security had already gone. Change was to Erica the only permanent condition of life; she had no idea what tomorrow would be like, except that it would be different from yesterday and today. The more you could learn to do without, the safer you were; security consisted in traveling light and staking your happiness on a few fundamentals of a non-material nature which could not, or at least were unlikely to be taken away from you.

Looking back now, she realized that long before Marc, this point of view had shaped her existence; among other things, it had prevented her from marrying any one of several different men who had been in love with her in the past. She had recognized the fact that any individual looks quite different when he is viewed in terms of a specific and familiar social and economic structure from when he is viewed as an isolated human being, solely in terms of his own inherent qualities. You might be reasonably happy living with someone in Montreal and with that social and economic structure to absorb the inevitable stresses and strains, only to find that life on a desert island with that same person was quite unendurable.

For Erica, the desert island was always more or less imminent, or if not imminent, it was at least a possibility which loomed too large to be ignored. Marc was the only man she had ever known with whom she was willing to risk it, and so far as her own values were concerned, what she would be giving up in marrying him was a handful of social, and if the worst came to the worst, economic nonessentials which were not important to her and in whose continued existence she did not put much faith in any case. She had been born in 1914, so that the first twenty-eight years of her life had begun with one world war and ended with another; she had earned her living on a newspaper for the past six years, and she knew beyond doubt that what mattered most to Erica Drake was Marc Reiser.

Marc, however, did not know it, and even if he had, the problem would still have been only half solved. It was not enough for him to believe in her; he had also to believe in himself.

His eyes met hers and he said, "You should have known me ten years ago when I was still full of illusions."

"And still trying," said Erica, looking away from him. "Instead of just sitting around — or rather just lying around, you're too supine to be described as 'sitting'! — agreeing with everybody." She jabbed the burned match which she was still holding in her hand as far as it would go into the earth which was covered with a thin carpet of pine needles, then bringing her eyes back to his face she said in a different tone, "Most people are born into a fixed social pattern and just travel along their particular groove until they get to the other end and die, but once in a while, somebody gets a chance to climb out of his groove and give the whole thing a push from behind. Well, they either take that chance or they don't. I know a couple of people who have and so do you. Look at Max Rosenberg and Betty Innes . . ."

"Yes," said Marc. "Look at them — or rather look at their families. Their families kicked up such a row that Max and Betty ended up by moving to Toronto, flat broke and starting all over again."

"Well, Toronto's better."

"Is it?"

"You know it is!" said Erica, exasperated.

"Go on about the groove, darling," he said, looking amused. "Most people haven't got the Rosenbergs' guts. They just climb out for a while, take a good look around, get scared and decide it's too tough and climb down again. They play safe. But the people who play safe don't change anything — they just sit tight and wait for someone else to change it. Do you think that's what you and I are for — just to play safe and wait?"

"I don't know," he said, looking down at the long cloud of smoke which the afternoon train from Montreal had left behind on its way through the valley a few minutes before. The smoke was drifting upwards against the background of evergreens, so slowly that he knew the wind must have dropped. He glanced upwards at the motionless trees overhead and said hopelessly again, "I don't know, Eric. I wouldn't want you to look the way Betty Rosenberg does now, anyhow."

"Why?"

"She looks as though she's washed too many dishes and scrubbed too many floors and stayed awake too many nights worrying because they can't afford to send the kids to a private school, where the fact that they're Jews maybe wouldn't matter so much. She's even beginning to look as though she's not sure now whether it was worth it or not."

"I don't believe you," said Erica involuntarily.

He shrugged and said, "Well, perhaps she just happened to look like that the evening I was there."

They were silent for a while, and then he asked without warning, "Did your father object to your coming up here?"

"Yes," said Erica after a pause. "I didn't think he'd make an issue of it now, particularly when he only has to stand it a few more days."

For a moment Marc seemed merely surprised, then he said, "But you are here. How did you manage it?"

"I just came."

"You couldn't 'just come.' You must have walked out."

She turned her head quickly to look at him and then asked with sudden terror, "What do you think I should have done?"

"I can't answer that, Eric."

"Would you have come to Montreal?"

"I'm not sure," he said almost inaudibly.

She began to cry and he put his arm around her and drew her head down on his shoulder without saying anything. She knew that he was still looking straight ahead of him with that bleak look, and she went on crying with her face partly hidden against his shirt.

Finally he said, "This must be about the last straw so far as your family is concerned." He took out his handkerchief and dried her eyes and put the handkerchief away again. Then he asked, "Exactly what did happen on Monday?"

"Charles came into my room when I was packing and said that I was not to go."

"Didn't you tell him beforehand that you were going?"

"Yes, I told them the night you phoned."

"Then why didn't he . . ."

"I guess it was because of Mother. She tried to make Charles promise not to try to stop me from going, and when it was all over and she found out what was happening, she came running down the hall and she kept saying, 'I told you, Charles, I *told* you,' and she was so upset that she was nearly out of her head. So was Charles, only he was angry too. I've never seen him so angry. He just went into his study and shut the door. I told Mother I'd behaved awfully badly and that it was just as much my fault as it was his, only he'd put me in a position where either I had to stay home, or if I went, then he made it clear that I'd be doing something so wrong that there wouldn't be enough left for us to go on with afterwards. He said I'd never be the same to them again."

At least she could leave Marc a few shreds of self-respect; there was no unfairness to her father in leaving out the part in which he had offered to have Marc to the house. It did not put Charles Drake in any better light.

She went on, as Marc had said nothing, "I guess Mother knew what would happen. She's just as uncompromising as Charles is, she was brought up in the same way and she feels the same way about things, and it was just as hard for her as it was for Charles, but she cares far more for justice, and she has a terrible sense of moral responsibility for this whole situation. She said that it was mostly her fault because she's my mother, and that they'd both let me down so badly that they no longer had any right to interfere. I wouldn't have gone then if she'd asked me not to, but she wouldn't. She said she wouldn't even ask me to come back, because it was up to Charles now."

After a pause Erica added, trying to steady her voice, "It wasn't her fault. That's what is so rotten about it."

"Yes," said Marc.

A little later she said, "You've got to understand why I could-n't give in to Charles. It's not facts that hurt people, it's their attitude toward facts. I'm not responsible for Charles' attitude toward you and toward something that only concerns us. I can't make you pay for it, because it's not fair. I can't help his attitude, I can't change it. He invents half his own suffering, and I can't make you suffer instead, simply because my father chooses to think that . . ."

"I know what he thinks I am."

She turned to him and put her arms around him and said with tears running down her face again, "Marc, I love you so much!"

"Don't cry, darling. It doesn't help."

She knew now that there was no longer any chance, even for a miracle, and she said, "I wanted these last three days to be perfect, so that when you went away, you'd remember what it was like at the end, and maybe the rest of it wouldn't be so important . . ."

"But you see, Eric, this is just the end of the rest of it."

He took out his handkerchief and wiped away her tears and smiled at her. Then the smile faded from his oblique, greenish eyes and he asked, "What else did you want, darling?"

"I wanted you to *believe* — to believe in us. I wanted you to go overseas believing in us. I don't care how long I have to wait, that isn't what matters."

Her throat was aching intolerably but she was no longer crying. She managed to say quite evenly, "I don't think I matter much either. What does matter is you. I can't bear the idea of your going overseas with nothing to come back to at the end of it but a world in which there is no place for you and me."

He said despairingly, "Eric, I can't . . . I can't . . ."

"It's all right, darling," she said quietly. "I know you can't." When they got back to the hotel, the church clock in the village down at the other end of the lake was striking six. A telegram had come for Erica some hours before; it was from her father and contained only the four words, "Anthony is reported missing."

XIII

~

The town of Manchester lies sprawled along the shore of a
lake and faces over a few scattered granite islands toward an
empty western horizon. At the back of the town is a stretch of
open country cleared and farmed by French-Canadian families,
with fields and pastures which become steadily poorer and
rougher as they approach the bush. The bush is a stony, tangled
wilderness of trees and undergrowth cut by a few roads,
spotted with little blue lakes and crossed and recrossed by innumerable small streams. Behind the bush are the Algoma Hills,
rising high, strong, and magnificently coloured against the clear
northern sky. This is the edge of the mining country; this is the
beginning of Canada's North.

Manchester itself is a tribute to the Canadian talent for
choosing a remarkably fine natural setting for a town, and then

proceeding to ruin it as far as possible. There is an interminably long, straight main street running parallel with the shore, flanked by the inevitable collection of two- and three-storey office buildings, shops, gas stations, beauty parlors, Chinese laundries, pool rooms, soda fountains, cheap restaurants, movie houses, and the usual Protestant and Catholic churches, apparently dedicated, like most of the buildings in English Canada, to the Puritan proposition that even in architecture, beauty is unnecessary and possibly even dangerous. Below the main street are warehouses, rundown dwellings, a few factories, great piles of lumber, a sawmill, and the docks. The whole region smells slightly of stagnant water and rotting wood. Above the main street is the residential district, a series of tree-shaded streets intersecting at right angles, with houses set well back and surrounded by lawns, bushes, and scattered flower beds.

In Austria the Reisers had been timber merchants for some generations, and when Leopold Reiser came out to Canada in 1907, he bought a small planing mill in Manchester and settled there with his wife and four-year-old son, David. Marc was born two years later in the house in which his parents were still living when he went home on his last leave in September, 1942.

It was a comfortable house painted white with green shutters and a wide front porch screened on three sides by lilac bushes. In the living room there was an upright piano which nobody ever played, some glassed-in bookcases containing, among other works, a complete set of Schiller which nobody ever read, a chesterfield suite upholstered in dark blue plush but fortunately covered with chintz of an inoffensive pattern during the summer months, a canary named Mike which never sang, and half a dozen ferns in polished brass pots. Behind the living room was the dining room which was fairly large, but still not quite large enough to do justice to the fine, old, highly polished and somewhat massive furniture which had been brought from Austria. The kitchen had windows on two sides and took up most of the remaining space on the ground floor except for cupboards and a sort of drawing-room opposite the living room, which nobody ever used. Up the wide oak staircases there were four bedrooms, a bathroom and sunroom, and on the top floor, one room well furnished for the general servant of the moment, and three others full of trunks, hockey sticks, skates, schoolbooks, fishing tackle, and everything else which Maria Reiser could not bear to throw out.

The town was about two thirds Protestant and one third Catholic, with only a few Jewish families who were too small a community to afford the upkeep of a temple or synagogue. For the two most important festivals of the year, they were accustomed to hire the public hall down on the main street, and one of the older German or Polish Jews would conduct the services. The hall was a long, narrow building facing almost due north, so that the small congregation had to sit at right angles to the platform at the other end, and with an expanse of bare floor on either side of them, in order that the Ark might stand against the east wall.

In the third year of the war, the services of Yom Kippur were taken by a young student rabbi who had arrived in Manchester a week before to visit his cousins, the Rabinovitches, who owned the clothing store. Neither Orthodox nor especially devout, the Reisers had come to Kol Nidre on the eve of the Day of Atonement and then did not return until early the following afternoon. It was Monday, September 21st, of the Jewish year 5703.

Although the rows of hard wooden chairs were divided by an

aisle down the middle, with most of the women on the left and the men on the right, the Reisers were sitting together near the back, first Leopold Reiser, then Marc and his mother. The opening of the service made no impression on Marc; after four days at home he was still unable to stop thinking of Erica, and he got up and sat down as the rest of the congregation got up and sat down, his eyes wandering from the little pulpit to the high reading stand and the tired face of the young student rabbi, and then to the Ark with the two seven-branched candlesticks on either side, fourteen points of light flickering in the rather dusty air of the hall, and finally back to the student rabbi again. His leave was almost up; by Tuesday night he would be on the train for Montreal, where he would see Erica again for a few hours, and then take the seven-thirty train to Halifax. Except for those few hours he might never see her again, and he had not only failed her completely, he had also failed himself. He did not know how it had happened or when it had begun to happen, but he did know that it was he himself who had got off the track, and that if he hadn't, in spite of Charles Drake and everyone else, it would not have turned out like this.

A thick-set, middle-aged man had been summoned to the high reading stand and through some kind of break in his thoughts Marc became conscious of the new voice, less fine and resonant, but fresher and stronger than the voice of the tired young rabbi. He missed the first few sentences and then heard the words,

So the shipmaster came and said unto him, What meanest thou, O Sleeper? Arise, call upon thy God, if so be that God will think upon us that we perish not.

What meanest thou, O Sleeper?

If he could find out what he, Marc Reiser, actually meant,

then he would know what to do, if it were still possible to do anything, when all the time he had left was the time between two trains. For some reason or other he had expected the problem to clarify itself once he was home and back in his own environment, but after four days he was still living in two worlds and the world in which he had grown up was less real than the world he had left on Wednesday night, after going with Erica as far as the front door of the house up in Westmount and then returning to the station to catch the westbound train for Manchester, on the transcontinental line. He was not, in fact, back in his own environment in any but a purely physical sense, and with only one more day to go, his own existence was as meaningless as ever.

Someone coughed, and one of the women in the front row on the left was wearing a taffeta blouse which rustled every time she moved, but the profound silence, which was heightened by the steady voice of the reader, continued unbroken and undisturbed by the faint noises from the street outside. You would not have thought that forty people could be so still and make so little sound, when many of them were old enough to be stiff with fatigue from twenty hours of fasting and many hours of prayer, and some of them were very young. The dusty, commonplace, smalltown public hall was pervaded with a spirit of unity and faith which went back to the remote beginnings of this people in a country far away, and then returned, steadily broadening out until it had encompassed the world and made these men and women and children one with those who had died long ago, and with those who had died only yesterday and those who were dying today, and with those who would die tomorrow. There was no past and no present; the interminable, timeless stream ebbed and flowed and from synagogues and temples, houses and hired halls, barracks, concentration camps, prisons, torture chambers, and pitiful, futile barricades, the Jews of the world were drawn together across time and space on this Day of Atonement and were made one with God.

Then said they unto him, Tell us, we pray thee, for whose cause this evil is upon us; what is thine occupation and whence comest thou? what is thy country and of what people art thou? and he said unto them: I am an Hebrew. . . .

Once a barrister and now a soldier about to go overseas, born and bred in Canada, a Canadian of Jewish origin.

What is a Jew?

Now, if ever, with his eyes fixed on a seven-branched candlestick and the words of the Yom Kippur service in his ears, surrounded by his own people and only by his own people, he should be able to find the answer to that riddle once and for all, and he waited, but the answer did not come.

He realized that his sense of identity with the men and women around him was more of race, of race suffering and race achievement, than of religion, for his religious convictions involved only a simple belief in one God, one God for everyone regardless of sect and regardless of the form or worship. Nothing is so timeless as the atmosphere of a synagogue, and whenever he had gone into one of the great synagogues of Montreal or Toronto or London, his immediate reaction had been one of an almost overwhelming sense of history and tradition so ancient and so powerful that even if he had wanted to escape, it would have bound him indissolubly and forever to his own people.

Yet even the word "race" was misleading, for even supposing there had been such a thing as a specifically Jewish race, the racial force was not by itself strong enough to survive and, from a sociological, much less from an anthropological point of view, to identify a Jew whose family had lived for centuries in

England or Austria with a Jew whose family had lived as long or longer in Poland. The English, Austrian and Polish environments were too dissimilar.

Having been forced to rule out both race and religion on a logical basis, he was still a Jew, however, and he could not conceive of being anything else. He could feel his own Jewishness in his very bones and he was proud to be what he was, partly because of that long, unbroken continuity of history and tradition, that unending record of faith and sheer guts, and partly because, in spite of everything which the so-called Christian nations had done to them, his own people had continued to give the world such a disproportionately large number of great men to whom humanity would be eternally indebted. As a Canadian and a Jew, he had to admit that eleven million Canadians had so far failed to produce one individual as outstanding as uncounted living Jews, out of a total world population before Hitler of approximately sixteen million — let alone the innumerable Jewish scientists, philosophers, and artists no longer living.

Have mercy upon Zion for it is the home of our life.

He knew that his mother was looking at him again with that expression of uncertainty and concern that he had seen so often in her face during the past two days before she had caught his eyes and quickly looked away again. She was worried about him. So was his father, who was staring straight ahead with his prayer book open at the wrong page. What were they worried about? What did they think he could do between trains? The danger had been averted; they were safe now, the Drakes were safe, everybody was safe except Erica and himself, and since they were bound to get over it sooner or later, no one doubted that for a moment, then presumably sooner or later he and Erica would be safe too.

So what does it all add up to? Apart from safety, of course. It adds up to everybody going on forever playing the game according to the rules, each on his own side of the fence. It adds up to precisely nothing.

Blessed art thou, O Lord, the Shield of David.

The young student rabbi left the high reading stand and went to the Ark. One of the readers pulled a cord and the doors of the Ark rolled back, revealing the sacred Scrolls. And from one of them the rabbi read:

Let them praise the Name of the Lord; for his name alone is exalted.

Then from the congregation Marc heard a low murmur of voices, and he glanced hurriedly down at his mother's prayer book. She put her fingers on the place to show him where they were, and he repeated with the others:

His glory is above the earth and heaven. He also hath lifted up the horn of his people, the praise of all his saints, even the children of Israel, a people near unto him.

A people near unto him — in this year, 5703; in this year, 1942. Yet the unbroken and unbreakable faith contained in those five words had finally caught him up and carried him along with the others, through the psalm, "The earth is the Lord's and the fullness thereof," and the replacing of the Scroll. The doors of the Ark were closed again and the rabbi said:

O Lord open thou my lips and my mouth shall declare thy praise.

Blessed art thou, O Lord our God and God of our fathers, God of Abraham, God of Isaac and God of Jacob.

Soon after that his mind began to cloud over and he lost track again. He found himself watching the people in the rows in front of him, thinking that although Erica understood so much, she could never really understand his feeling of having deserted them, in some way, by marrying her. It would be like going over to the other side, or like deliberately creating a breach in their own defences — if not in his own mind, then in the minds of the other Jews. Now more than ever before, the ranks must be closed to all outsiders.

His father had said something like that to him when he had told him about Erica on Sunday night. Although he had arrived late on Thursday, he had said nothing about her to either of his parents until he had been home for three days. He had slept late on Friday morning, exhausted from the strain of being with her for two days and yet not feeling as though he were with her at all, then taking her back to Montreal after that telegram about her brother, and finally, the interminable aching hours in the train.

When he had come downstairs on Friday morning, his father had already left for the mill on the edge of town, but his mother was still sitting in the dining room waiting for him. They had talked for almost two hours. She had asked him questions about himself and the Army and going overseas, and had given him news of various people, sitting at the head of the big mahogany table with the sun coming through the windows of the dining room and lighting up her dark, greying hair and her lovely dark eyes. She was almost sixty, but she looked younger, and unlike his father, had never put on weight, in spite of the fact that she was naturally serene and rather passive, while his father was nervous and extremely active.

He had thought that she had noticed nothing; it was just like all the other long and leisurely breakfasts on his first morning home, until she asked suddenly as she was getting up, "Marc, what's the matter?"

"Nothing." As she went on looking down at him, he added,

"I'll tell you some other time. It's nothing to worry about."

It was characteristic of her that she had let it go at that, and left it to him to bring up the subject again in his own time. It was characteristic of both his parents. He had been brought up in a family of four very different individuals who respected each other and would argue passionately and at length on impersonal issues, but who said only what was necessary and then usually only when they were asked for an opinion on questions which affected any one of them directly.

On Sunday night, after they'd got home from Kol Nidre, it had taken his father less than a quarter of an hour to say all that he had to say about Erica.

He had spent most of those three days wandering about the town where the first seventeen years of his life lay spread out like the pieces in a puzzle, simply waiting to be put together. Three blocks away from the house was the public school where he had started in kindergarten. There were some Jewish children in the upper classes and later a few behind him, but he had gone through the next six years on his own. He didn't mind it; small towns are more democratic than big cities, and apart from a few peltings with snowballs and a couple of fights with an Irish Catholic whose parents had become violently anti-Semitic after their badly run tailoring establishment had failed owing to competition with the new and well-run firm of Rabinovitch and Son, he was never singled out because he was Jewish. Protestants, Catholics, and Marc Reiser skated together in winter, played baseball and went fishing in the spring, fished, swam, and played more baseball in the summer, and switched to football, rabbit hunting, hiking, and corn roasts in the autumn. Marc was popular, good at games, liked fishing and football best of all, and didn't particularly like to work.

Surveying his own thoroughly undistinguished record from the age of six to the age of twenty-one, he was inclined to agree that a high proportion of Jewish brilliance is due to compensatory motivation. Once, at the collegiate, he had headed his class, but only because his father had bribed him with the offer of a small sailboat. Having got his sailboat, he had promptly subsided to somewhere around eighth or tenth place again.

At seventeen he had been ready for university and had started out for the city two hundred miles away full of hope and illusions. Two weeks later he was back in Manchester again, with some of the hope and most of the illusions gone for good. For all but strictly academic purposes, the university was divided into Gentiles and Jews; there was only a handful of Jews registered for his course, and he had spent his first two weeks away from home either alone in the great crowd, eating alone in restaurants, or sitting alone in his room in the rooming house, to which, it turned out on the thirteenth day, he had only been admitted because the landlady had failed to realize that he was Jewish.

Home again on the fourteenth day, he had told his mother and father everything that had happened, and after waiting for his mother to say something instead of just looking at the wall, he had turned to his father and asked, "Do I have to go back?"

"No," said his father. "But you have to go somewhere. Why don't you try a small-town university? Then when you're ready for law school, you'll be older and you'll have had a chance to get used to it gradually."

So he had lived for another four years in a small town. At the university he had averaged around tenth in his course, played football, and spent a good many weekends and holidays fishing and canoeing up in the Gatineau country. He had made a lot of friends, some Gentile as well as Jewish, though it was a lot tougher going than it had been at public school and collegiate. Still, as his father had said, he was having a chance to get used to it gradually, and had almost forgotten the two weeks in that other university and everything he had been up against there, when, at the very end of his fourth year, he had gone into the Senior Common Room and found that someone had written in block capitals on the notice board: "WE GAVE YOU BACK JERUSALEM; LEAVE US THE SENIOR COMMON ROOM." There were two or three men from his class over by the windows; he knew that they were watching him. He turned round and walked out. It was the day before graduation.

He discovered, too late, that there was an unofficial Jewish quota for students entering the law school, and with his thoroughly undistinguished record, he almost failed to make it. He had wanted to be a lawyer for as long as he could remember, and he had come so close to not being admitted that it gave him a bad fright. The fright did it; for the first time in his life, he really began to work. He headed his course all three years and working got to be a habit. If the other students occasionally wondered why Reiser was always at the top, they probably decided that being a Jew, he was just naturally clever.

And thou has given us in love, O Lord our God, this Day of Atonement, for pardon, forgiveness and atonement, that we may obtain pardon thereon for all our iniquities; a holy convocation, a memorial of the departure from Egypt.

He was suddenly aware of the rabbi's chant, of the slowly changing atmosphere of the hall and the growing tension, as the service drew nearer the long confession in which they would confess and make supplication not only for themselves but for the whole House of Israel and for all Jews, living and dead. He glanced at the faces around him and was struck by their simplicity and the exaltation which had washed away all the marks of ordinary, everyday living and left them transfigured. And the wave which was mounting steadily higher toward the climax of the service caught him up for the second time.

Holy, holy, holy is the Lord of hosts.

The past is not and the present is not; the House of Israel stands apart from time and from place, one people, one brotherhood, one God.

The whole earth is full of his glory.

He had been dreading the interminable list of sins which covered every conceivable and sometimes inconceivable individual and collective act and which were repeated phrase by phrase by the rabbi and repeated back phrase by phrase by the congregation. Now he was unaware of the minutes passing by.

We have trespassed, we have dealt treacherously, we have robbed, we have spoken slander, we have acted perversely and we have wrought wickedness.

The minutes stretched out in a gradually lengthening path behind these forty people gathered together in the public hall of Manchester, Ontario.

As it is written by the hand of thy prophet, "Who is a God like unto thee, that pardoneth iniquity and passeth by the transgression of the remnant of his heritage?" He retaineth not his anger forever because he delighteth in mercy. He will turn again and have compassion upon us. . . .

The wave carried him off to one side and left him there, going on without him, and he found himself alone again, wishing violently that he had not come, that like David, he had been honest enough to stay home. He had come partly to please his mother and father and partly because it was the last complete day of his last leave. Now it seemed to him that he was like a man going to the bank in which he had left a small deposit twenty years before, expecting to find himself rich. Since he had put almost nothing into his religion at any time during his life, there was no real reason why he should have expected, suddenly in an emergency, to get something out of it.

He remembered having said once to Erica that marriage to a Jew would mean living in a kind of no man's land, an undefined area out in the middle distance somewhere between the majority from which she had come and the minority on the other side who would never admit her. He could tell her more about that now, for he was apparently drifting toward no man's land himself, unable to become one even with his own people and at this crucial moment.

It was his father who was looking at him this time, still worried.

Sunday, the day he had finally told them about Erica, he had spent picking up the last pieces of the puzzle, a series of individual portraits, each with a segment of background, until the first seventeen years of his life were complete. There was old George Brophy, still fishing off the end of the long dock by the warehouse, who had taught him how to cast; Mac Tyrrel who had stored Marc's boat for him each winter; old Isadore Rabinovitch who had made him his first pair of long pants and stayed in his shop till midnight two days later mending a tear eight inches long which Marc had got fishing back up the river. The mend was so well done that his parents had never found out about it. They had issued strict orders that he was not to wear his new trousers fishing.

Two blocks away from Rabinovitch and Son was O'Reilly's, where they sold tobacco, candy, newspapers, magazines, and soft drinks in front, with a pool room and beer parlour behind. O'Reilly still had a vast assortment of highly coloured candies sold by the cent. Marc remembered particularly some big round ones which you could get in either bright pink, orange, purple, or green, five for a cent, and which had been his favourites for years. He did not know what they were made of; having been offered a couple on Sunday afternoon for old time's sake, he still did not know what they were made of.

The beer parlour behind had had no part in his past; he had never liked beer and had been singularly free of the adolescent urge to do something because the crowd is doing it. He had been just as immune to influence where girls were concerned, until his third year in college when he had fallen in love with a girl named Helen. It had lasted until they both graduated and she went back to her home in Ottawa and he went on to law school. His family had known about her; for a while they had been afraid that he might marry her, and when he was home for his holidays, they had talked all round the subject, letting him know what they thought of his marrying a Gentile without actually saying it. That was fourteen years ago, however, and he had forgotten all about it, until Sunday night when they were in the living room, his father sitting in one of the big chairs and his mother and himself at opposite ends of the sofa, and he had told them about Erica.

"You're not thinking of marrying her, are you?" his father had asked.

"I don't know."

There was a pause and then his father said, "That's the second time, isn't it?"

"What do you mean?"

"That other girl — the one you knew in college — she wasn't Jewish either." He knocked his pipe against the heavy brass ashtray standing beside his chair and asked, "What's her family like?"

"They're — well, they're the Drakes, that's all. They're pretty well known."

"What do they think of you?"

He had known that he was going to be asked that question, he had known it ever since he had realized that he was going to have to talk to his mother and father about Erica. He said, "I've never met them."

"You . . ." his father began incredulously, and stopped.

His mother glanced at him quickly and said nothing at all.

He waited for a moment and then burst out, "I wish you could meet her! You'd both like her, I know you would. She's so straight. She even knows how to think straight. She knows exactly what matters . . ."

"Does she?" asked his father.

His mother said quietly, "Then she must know that her family matters, Marc."

"Yes," said Marc hopelessly. "I guess she does."

In his cage in the corner, Mike, the canary that never sang, shifted restlessly on his perch and then chirruped faintly.

"Hello, Mike," said Marc.

"He wants his cover on so that he can go to bed," said his mother.

"Where is it?"

"Over there on top of the piano."

He got up and put the cover around the cage and then went to the mantelpiece for a cigarette. With his back to the empty fireplace, he said, looking down at the worn spot in the middle of the carpet, "Nobody else has ever meant as much to me as she does. I can't explain it."

"You aren't going to do her any good by marrying her," said his father.

"But she feels just the same about me . . ."

"Maybe she does now."

His father's rather heavy face was out of range of the

light from the lamp on the table behind the sofa, but even in the dimness and from the fireplace some distance away, Marc could see his expression. His father was not going to change his mind. Nothing would make him change his mind. He said, "It won't work."

"Why can't we make it work?"

"Because you're too different, and because other people won't let you."

He turned to his mother and said, "You'd let us, wouldn't you?"

Her face changed and she said unhappily, "I don't know, Marc."

Then his father's voice cut across the room saying grimly, "We wouldn't behave like the Drakes, if that's what you mean!"

He glanced at his wife and sank heavily back into his chair again, muttering, "All right, Maria, all right," and then said in a different tone, "You're a Jew, Marc. You ought to know we can't afford to lose anyone we don't have to lose. There aren't so many of us now as there were before Hitler and his friends got going on us."

"I'm not going to stop being a Jew."

"You wouldn't be able to help it. You'd be neither one thing nor the other, and that goes for your wife and children too, particularly your children. You'd just be . . ." he spread out his hands and said, ". . . nothing. It's like mixing oil and water. You can't do it, it doesn't work."

He paused again, looking up at Marc, and then with his voice still pitched low but speaking with profound conviction, as though this were a summing up of his sixty-five years of living experience, he went on, "You think you could compromise and somehow you'd manage, but sooner or later you'd find out

that you can go just so far and no farther. You'd get sick of compromising, and so would she, and some day you'd wake up and
realize that it wasn't a question of compromising on little things
any more, but of compromising yourself. And you couldn't
do it, neither of you could do it. Nobody can do it. You've got
to be yourself, otherwise you're better off dead." He said with
a sudden undercurrent of violence, "For God's sake, Marc,
you're a Jew. You ought to know that!"

The violence died away again and he said, "It isn't just a
question of conventions; it's five thousand years which have
made you and her hopelessly different. You don't know how
different you are yet."

"I've had a pretty good chance to find out, since I left home
sixteen years ago!"

"Find out," he repeated. "You haven't even begun to find
out. Getting yourself kicked out of a hotel is the worst thing
that's ever happened to you! You've had a pretty easy time of it,
don't fool yourself. It would probably be better for you if you
hadn't. You don't yet know how Jewish you are, otherwise you
wouldn't be talking about marrying a Gentile; you'd realize that
no matter how much you have in common, it doesn't make up
for that one fundamental difference between you. Nothing can
make up for that. What counts in the long run isn't whether or
not you and your wife like the same books or like to do the
same things — it's whether or not, down underneath, you're the
same kind of person. Whether you have the same attitude
toward things, the same outlook on life — the same background, and heredity, and the same traditions."

He paused again and then finished it. He said, "And if there's
one thing that's dead certain, it is that no Jew and no Gentile
that ever lived have the same outlook on life."

That was all his father had had to say.

Our Father, Our King, remember thy mercy and suppress thine anger, and remove pestilence, sword and famine, destruction, captivity, iniquity and plague, all evil occurrences, and every disease, every stumbling block and contention, every kind of punishment, every evil decree and all causeless enmity, from us and from all the children of thy covenant. . . .

In this year Five Thousand, Seven Hundred and Three, in this year of causeless enmity, One Thousand Nine Hundred and Forty-Two, remember thy mercy.

One voice merged with another; it seemed to him that for weeks he had had nothing to say for himself, even to Marc Reiser. He had only listened:

To Erica saying, "Most people just travel along their particular groove till they get to the end of it and die." And his father, "You aren't going to do her any good by marrying her." And Erica again, "They just climb out for a while, take a good look around, get scared, and climb down again."

That was what he had done. First of all, before he had gone away to college, he had been unaware of a groove, he didn't know he was in one. Or maybe the groove was wider in those days, so wide that it didn't matter. Anyhow, for the next four years he had been aware of it, but had succeeded pretty well in ignoring it, up to the day before graduation when it had abruptly narrowed down to a point where it was no use even trying to ignore it. He had just put up with it and had more or less come to accept it as a permanent condition of life when he had heard that voice for the fist time. From just behind him she was saying, "Hello, I'm Erica, one of the invisible Drakes."

Invisible was right, as it had turned out.

So then he had climbed out and stayed there on top for three months, taking a good look around.

You can't do it, it doesn't work. You're a Jew, and you ought to know that. But the people who play safe don't change anything, they just sit tight and wait for someone else to change it. And that's not what you and I are for, just to play safe and wait.

To wait — the whole history of our race is the history of a people whose faith has never run out, whose faith has never wavered, and who are never done with waiting.

He who maketh peace in his high places, may he make peace for us and for all Israel, and say ye, Amen. . . .

Peace for us and for all Israel — it was nothing but words, words patiently repeated year after year, century after century, for a thousand, two thousand years and all the way back to Jeremiah crying, Peace, peace, when there is no peace.

He remembered that on Sunday night, or rather early Monday morning, his mother had come into his room. He was lying in bed, still awake, watching the shadows of the elm leaves on his ceiling. There was a street lamp below the tree by his window, and ever since he could remember those shadows had been there overhead for him to look at when he was awake at night — the faint outlines of bare branches in winter, slowly thickening and spreading out as spring drew into summer, until the whole ceiling was covered with an intricate pattern which was seldom still and usually in continuous flickering motion.

He saw the door opening and the widening strip of light on the carpet which finally stopped at the large bluish spot in the corner where the afternoon plane on the Moscow-Zagreb line had crashed somewhere in Transylvania.

"Marc, are you awake?"

"Yes, Mother. Come in and sit down."

"I'll sit here," she said, motioning toward the chair by the dresser. She was wearing a wrapper of some kind of printed material, and her hair was hanging over her shoulders in two thick braids. She did not turn on the light, but closed the door and sat down in the chair, with the dresser behind her. The moon was full, shining in an oblique line across his carpet. He could see her quite clearly.

"I wanted to talk to you."

"Yes, I thought you would," he said, for downstairs she had let his father do almost all the talking. She had obviously agreed with him, but he had sensed a faint inner reservation which was still unaccounted for.

She looked at the old battered desk across the room, then at the map above it, which showed the world as it had been in 1922, and finally at the bookcase in the corner, and remarked, "It's hard for me to realize that you're grown up when I come in here, or that David is either. Mothers are so silly — Good heavens, David's almost forty!"

A moment later she added, "And you're going overseas." After another pause, looking down at her hands lying loosely on her lap, she said, "I'm proud of you, Marc — not because you're going overseas, though that's part of it, but mostly just because you're a fine person. So is David. I've been lucky, both my sons have turned out to be fine people. I'm glad about your Captaincy too, darling."

"That doesn't mean anything, Mum. It's just a formality. Lieutenants of my age aren't allowed to go overseas any more."

"I know, but still . . ."

He took a cigarette from the table beside his bed and she said, "You smoke too much."

"I know."

"So does David. That pipe of his reminds me of those awful things you used to keep in bottles!"

"That reminds me," said Marc with sudden interest, "what became of my mud puppy? I've always meant to ask you."

"I buried it."

"Oh, that explains it then," he said, adding without think-ing, "Eric was sure it wouldn't burn."

She stared at him, her expression changing completely, and suddenly she said, her voice trembling, "Marc, I want you to be happy! I don't care about anything else."

"I know you don't, Mother."

"I wish I could see that girl of yours. You're thirty-three, and you've never really been in love with anyone else. I'm sure she must be fine too, because you wouldn't be in love with her if she wasn't. And though everything your father said tonight was true, there's no getting around it, still I kept thinking all the time he was talking that she should have been there to speak for herself."

"You're the first person who's thought that. I don't know whether even I have, really . . ."

He stopped and she said, letting out her breath in a long sigh, "Of course she doesn't know what it's like." In a different tone she added after a pause, "And you don't really, either."

"Yes, I do."

"No."

She was still sitting in the same position but her hands were clasped tightly together now, and her whole body had stiffened. She said, "You don't know what happens to people when they live together year after year. They get angry sometimes, and they say things that they couldn't have imagined themselves say-ing before they were married, and that they wouldn't dream of saying to anyone else. That's what I'm afraid of, and I simply couldn't bear to have it happen to you."

"What are you afraid of?" he asked, after waiting for her to go on.

She had begun to rock in a slight back and forth movement.

He never forgot the way she looked or the tone of her voice as she said despairingly, "I'm afraid that sometime when she was very angry, she would round on you and blame you for being a Jew."

Tell us, we pray thee, for whose cause this evil is upon us, and he said unto them, I am an Hebrew.

The afternoon service for Yom Kippur was almost over. The scene in his bedroom faded from his mind and he glanced at the congregation ahead of him; then beside him, his mother touched his arm and turned her head slightly, gesturing toward the back of the hall. His brother David had come after all and was standing by the door, a short, almost stocky figure in baggy grey flannels and an old leather windbreaker. He had very thick black hair, a black mustache, a rather pronounced nose which must have been a throwback to some fairly remote ancestor, for none of the recent Reisers or Mendals, Maria Reiser's family, were particularly Semitic in appearance; black eyes which gave you the feeling that he never missed anything, and a manner which was so offhand that it was frequently mistaken for rudeness. He was almost seven years older than Marc; his mind had been conditioned by twenty years of scientific training and his range of interests lay almost entirely outside himself. He had few personal problems; he lived a hard life as a bush doctor attached to a nickel mine some distance north, and he lived it to the best of his ability, indifferent to his own comfort and absorbed in his work. He was passionately fond of poetry and occasionally wrote good verse himself.

As he caught Marc's eye he waved casually with one hand but stayed where he was, leaning against the back wall by the door.

They had come to the final Kaddish in the Afternoon Service.

May the prayers and supplications of the whole house of Israel be accepted in the presence of their Father who is in heaven; and say ye, Amen.

May there be abundant peace from heaven, and life for us and for all Israel, and say ye, Amen.

May he who maketh peace in his high places, make peace for us and for all Israel, and say ye, Amen.

The tired congregation stirred a little, but there was still another service before the Day of Atonement would end.

Marc turned to his mother and asked, "Do you mind if I go? Dave seems to have something on his mind."

"No, go along, I'll see you back at the house."

Outside in the street David said to Marc, "Let's go for a walk before dinner. I want to talk to you."

"And you, Brutus," said Marc wearily.

"Sorry. If you're hungry, I'll buy you a sandwich and a cup of coffee first, though. That Greek joint is just up the street."

"All right," said Marc indifferently. He was wondering just how his mother and father had managed to tell David about Erica, when his brother had only arrived late the night before, had gone to bed when he himself had gone, and had come downstairs for breakfast at approximately the same moment. It could only have been while he, Marc, had been taking a bath later on in the morning. His parents had certainly made the most of that bath, for it was obvious that David knew all about it.

Whatever it was he had to say on the subject, however, he said nothing while they were in the Greek restaurant or when they were walking through the town toward the road which led back through the strip of rough farm country to the bush, and eventually into the Algoma Hills. When they had passed the last rundown cottage on the outskirts of town, he was still talking about Father LaFleur, the new priest in his district, who was a great improvement on the old one, younger, more adaptable, and far less fatalistic in his attitude toward the wretched living conditions in his parish. He was already talking about co-operatives, and on top of all of his other qualifications, he could even play a good game of chess.

"We usually manage to get together for a game every week or so," David remarked, his black eyes following a flock of crows which flew up from a haystack near the road, high into the blue autumn air and off toward the town behind them. "You have no idea what a difference a good priest can make to the local doctor. I had a devil of a time with the other one; he was as hard as nails, he'd put off calling me till the last moment, and sometimes I used to wonder if he didn't actually prefer to have his parishioners enter the Kingdom of Heaven right away, rather than have their entry postponed by a Jewish doctor butting in and interfering with the Will of God. He was very strong on the Will of God."

"Does the new priest object to your being Jewish?"

"Well, he put out a few feelers when he first came, on the off chance of converting me, but I told him that my attitude toward religion in general, Judaism, Catholicism, or any other, was chiefly scientific, and after that he gave up. On the spiritual side, we have a strictly live and let live attitude toward each other. Got a cigarette?"

They stopped in the middle of the road, and shielding a match with his hands, David lit Marc's cigarette and his own, blew out the match and said, "I've got a couple of things to tell you."

"You and everybody else," said Marc, starting to walk up the road again. Straight ahead of them were the Algoma Hills, strung out like sentinels guarding the deep mining country beyond; below the hills was the bush, heavily splashed with colour, and somewhere in there off to the left was a certain maple tree overhanging some falls, a long narrow shaft of water pouring down past the maple into an almost circular pond edged with evergreens, poplars, white birch trees, and sumac. The effect at this time of year was always extraordinary, a kind of annual miracle, for the maple turned to pure scarlet, the water of the pool to cobalt blue, and the trees were a tangled mass of colour ranging from deep bluish green through rust and orange to a clear, translucent yellow. He wished violently, so violently he felt almost sick, that Erica was with him, that it was early morning and they were starting back toward the hills with the whole day ahead of them, and instead of that, it was late afternoon, the hills had a darkening, purplish cast, and he was with David, about to listen to still another voice saying the same things all over again, and about to answer a lot of silly questions, with Erica five hundred miles away.

Eric, what are we doing? How are we going to live, you without me and I without you?

"Would you like to know what I think?" asked David suddenly beside him.

He started and then answered shortly, "Not if it's what everybody else thinks."

"It isn't. At least it's not what Mother and Dad seem to think. I told them that if you decided you wanted to marry Erica Drake, I was going to back you up."

"You're going to back *me* up?" he said incredulously.

"Well," said David shrugging, "Erica anyhow. I don't know about you yet, I want to hear your side of it first." He paused and then remarked, "I gather the chief objection to her is the fact that she's not Jewish."

"Obviously. There aren't any other objections."

His brother glanced at him briefly and said, "I didn't realize that you were so particular."

"It's not me, for God's sake," said Marc irritably. "I don't give a damn whether she's Jewish or not. It's what will happen to her — what has already happened to her, in less than three months. You don't know how much she's changed. She's been getting it from every direction because of me — because just by being what I am, I lay her open to it. And I can't help it, I can't even do anything to make it easier for her. I just go on making it harder."

He said, "I keep seeing her the way she was when I met her . . ." and broke off, as the picture of Erica in his mind divided into two impressions, one three months old and the other less than a week old, two portraits labeled "Before" and "After," before and after Marc Reiser, only reversing the usual order because After was always supposed to be a great improvement over Before, instead of the other way round.

Two portraits side by side, of Erica as she had been the day he had met her, with that look of having come to terms with life, and Erica as she had been up at the clearing near the top of the mountain the day he had left her, bewildered and beaten.

He said to the short, stocky figure marching along beside him, "You haven't any idea how much she's changed — My God, how much she's changed! She doesn't even look really young any more. If I'd deliberately set out to see how much damage I could do, I couldn't have made a better job of it. What kind of case have we got? I haven't given her anything compared to what I've already taken away from her."

Not for years and perhaps never again would he walk this road as he had walked it so many times with a fishing rod and a basket slung over his shoulder, this road which led back through the fields and the bush to the hills, standing like sentinels against the sky, but he had forgotten where he was; he might just as well have been walking down a city street, he who had always loved Algoma and the bush and had always hated cities.

He said to David, who was having a hard time keeping up with him, his legs were so much shorter than Marc's, "The first weekend we went away, she had a copy of *The Shropshire Lad* with her, and when I picked it up it fell open at those lines that begin:

> '*Be still, my soul, be still; the arms you bear are brittle . . .*
> *Earth and high heaven are fixed of old and founded strong.'*"

"It's no use going on like that, Marc."

"Do you remember the rest of it?"

His brother did not answer.

Still walking blindly up the road, toward the bush which began abruptly at the edge of the last stony field just ahead of them, Marc said,

> "*'Think rather — call to thought if you now grieve a little,*
> *The days when we had rest, O soul, for they were long.'*"

"All right," said David, exasperated. "You don't need to go on, I know every word of it. So that's your idea of Erica now. All you have to do is be noble, make your exit, and Erica will promptly forget all the horror and scorn and fear and indignation and go back to sleep again. Is that it?"

"I suppose so."

"She must be a nice, simple soul."

He glanced at Marc again and asked, "By the way, just what did you think was going to happen while you were home this weekend?"

The road had entered the bush and narrowed down to a rough track which looked as though it might end at every turn, but which actually continued for miles, winding its way through the trees and undergrowth and bracken and then through the hills and on into the heart of the mining country. Staring at a flaming sumac a few yards ahead, Marc said, "I suppose I thought there would be something that she couldn't . . ."

"Something you belonged to and she didn't?"

"Yes."

"And was there?"

Marc shook his head. "It was the opposite. Because she wasn't with me, I felt as though I didn't belong either. I kept wishing she was here, so I could take her around and show her things. I even felt that way about the service this afternoon — how interested she would have been, and how much it would have impressed her, because it is impressive, and how much more it would have meant to me if she'd been beside me." He stopped, embarrassed, and remarked, "I guess it sounds pretty silly, doesn't it? After all, nothing could be much more exclusively Jewish than the Day of Atonement."

"I don't see what that has to do with it. Does it sound silly to you?"

"No, but it probably would to everybody else."

"Oh? And what have they got to do with it?"

There was a bridge crossing a small, clear stream just ahead, and they left the road and sat down beside the bridge at a place where the light came filtering down through the trees from the west and shone on the clean sand underneath the water.

As he felt through the pockets of his windbreaker for one
of the several pipes he always carried about with him, David
asked, "Has Erica ever said anything at all, to justify this
theory of yours that you'd do less damage in the long run, by
just walking out on her?"

"No, but . . ."

"Isn't that something she's entitled to decide for herself?
Or isn't Erica entitled to decide anything for herself? I don't
wonder she's changed so much in the last three months, but I
wouldn't blame it all on her father if I were you."

"What do you mean?"

"You're enough to drive anybody nuts."

"Do you mean to say that you think it's all my fault?" asked
Marc incredulously.

He shrugged and said, "Well, not *all* your fault. Say about
ninety-eight percent."

"Why?"

"Because you've let her down too. That makes it unanimous,
doesn't it? Only you were the one who mattered most to her,
so that if you hadn't let her down, it would have made all the
difference. I suppose," David went on conversationally, "that
you've been doing it nice and gradually, a bit of letting down
here, and a bit of letting down there, so that she really had
nothing to hang on to, while she was fighting her family . . ."

"Shut up," said Marc, suddenly.

"I thought you wanted to know why she's changed so much,
and whether what has been happening to her is quite as
inevitable as you seem to think it is. You said that you couldn't
do anything to make things easier for her; all you could do was
just go on making it harder. I don't agree."

He paused, looking across the stream at a pine which had
fallen down the bank and was lying with its upper branches in

the water. "Must have been a bad electric storm lately," he remarked. "The split's quite fresh." Then he said deliberately, "You and I weren't brought up to play games at other people's expense. You're old enough to know better, and you're starting too late to be able to get away with it. Don't fool yourself, laddie, you won't get away with it. You're going to find out that for every person who's stepped out of line and lived to regret it, there are two people who stayed in line because they got their values mixed and lost their nerve, and who have lived to regret it still more. You don't hear about those people because they're still in line where they don't show. You only hear about the others."

"Do you believe that?" asked Marc, startled.

"I wouldn't say it if I didn't. From my own experience, that is, from what the people themselves have told me, I'd say the proportion was somewhat higher than two to one. In the old days, the difference in religion was probably a real barrier to mixed marriages, but you don't take your religion that seriously and I don't suppose Erica does either, so what you'd be up against would come chiefly from outside. That makes it a lot easier, and if you and Erica are really in love with each other, then all you have to do is figure out what matters most to you — whether you'd rather be out of line with Erica, or stay in line without her. You can't have it both ways."

"I wish Eric could."

David said sharply, "She hasn't been getting it either way so far, has she?"

"I guess not."

He saw Marc's expression and said, "Sorry, but sympathy is not what you need at the moment. What you need is a good swift kick in the pants."

It seemed to Marc that what he needed most at the moment

was time to think, and he said, "I wish you'd shut up."

"All right," said David, settling back with his shoulders against a log.

He wanted to think about Erica, and with a shock he realized that in the end, it had taken David to get him to listen to her. Only a few days before, when she had been trying all over again to tell him what mattered most to her, she had said, "I wish you'd believe me," and when he had protested that he did believe her, she had answered hopelessly, "No, not quite." Like her father, he had always assumed that Erica did not know what she would be letting herself in for, and again like Charles Drake, he had considered himself to be in some mysterious way better qualified to decide what would be best for her in the long run than Erica was herself.

In refusing to believe her, he had placed himself beyond her influence and relegated her to a position where all she could do was to stand back and watch him being influenced by other people and in effect, being influenced against her. He had shut her out, although now he remembered exactly the way she had said, "Give me a chance to understand, and if I let you down, well then you can shut me out. I guess I'll have deserved it. It's not my fault that I'm not Jewish and I can't do anything about it, but surely, surely the fact that I love you so much makes up for it!"

The day he had met her he had asked her what she wanted most and she had said, "Just what every other woman wants; I'm afraid I'm not very original," and the last day, three months later, he had asked her again, for somewhat different reasons, and she had said, "I want you to *believe* — to believe in us. I don't care how long I have to wait, that isn't what matters. I don't think I matter much either. What does matter is you, and what I can't bear is the idea of your going overseas with nothing to come back to at the end of it but a world in which there is no place for you and me."

"What's wrong?" asked David, watching him.

"Nothing," said Marc. "I was just thinking."

They were silent again and finally David asked, "Mind if I ask you a few questions?"

"Go ahead," said Marc without interest.

"Is there anyone in this collection of people who are so dead against your marrying Erica, or her marrying you, who happens to know both of you?"

"No."

"Is there anyone who knows both of you who's in favour of it? I don't mean people who just know you casually."

Marc thought for a moment and then answered, "Yes, there's one. Erica's sister Miriam."

"Good," said David. "That makes two of us."

Marc almost missed it at first, and then he demanded, "What do you mean, two of you?"

"Miriam and me."

"You don't know Eric . . ."

"Well," said David, "not intimately, but I did spend last Saturday night with her from six o'clock till my train left at eleven."

"You did *what*?"

"I told you I was in Montreal for a three-day clinic."

"Yes, but . . ."

"You told me about her that night we ran into each other at the Rosenbergs' in Toronto, and then when you wrote to say that you were on draft and going to Petawawa, you sounded even more depressed about the whole thing, so I figured that since I didn't have anything to do from five until my train left at eleven, I might just as well have a look at her and see what it was all about."

"How did you find her?"

"I just picked the Drake with the fanciest address. Got the right one first shot," he added with a certain amount of pride. "Anyhow, I rang up, and when I got her, I said I was your brother from the backwoods, and would she care to have dinner with me. She sort of gasped and then she said, 'You're David,' as though I'd suddenly dropped down from Mars. I don't know whether she was crying or not, it sounded like it anyhow. There was a longish silence, because I couldn't think of anything to say, until finally I asked her if she'd mind if I called for her at six so that we could have a couple of drinks . . ."

"You called for her?" repeated Marc.

"Naturally," said David. "I don't make it as easy for people to dictate terms to me as you do."

"Go on," said Marc, staring at him.

"Well, she said she'd be ready at six, and I got a taxi so much sooner than I expected that I arrived there promptly at a quarter to."

"Did you meet any of the family?"

"Yes," said David. "I met Drake." He picked up a flat stone and sent it skimming out over the surface of the water upstream. "I was standing with my back to the door looking at that picture over the fireplace when someone said behind me, 'Mr. Reiser, I'm Erica's father.' As soon as I turned round and he saw my face, it was obvious from his expression that something was wrong somewhere . . ."

"I'll bet it was," said Marc grimly.

"No, not the way you mean," his brother answered him immediately. "He was just puzzled. I said that I was afraid he'd got me mixed up with you, and that I was Dr. David Reiser, so we shook hands and he gave me a cigarette and then asked if

I'd like a drink. I said, 'Yes, thanks very much,' so he got one for each of us and one for Erica when she came down. He said he'd just heard the maid say the name Reiser, when she'd gone up to tell Erica I was there, so naturally he thought it was you."

He paused and then added deliberately, "The next thing Drake said after that was, 'I'm sorry to say that I've never met your brother.' And there was no doubt he meant it."

"He said that?" asked Marc incredulously. "But why? Why after all this time, for God's sake? I don't get it."

"I gathered from Erica, that her father's opposition had collapsed, the day after he heard that his son was missing. I don't suppose he felt much like going on with it after that. He looked pretty well shot when I saw him. Anyhow, he asked me what I was doing in Montreal, and I told him that I'd come down for a clinic. He wanted to know where I practiced, and I told him that too, and he seemed genuinely interested and kept on asking me questions, so I kept on talking. It may seem funny to you but I liked him. And by the way, the last thing he said to me was to tell you that he hoped he'd have a chance of meeting you when you're in Montreal on Wednesday."

"That's the day after tomorrow." He was still trying to believe it, when he heard David asking abruptly why he had allowed Drake to get away with it.

"Get away with it?" said Marc.

"Yes. Why didn't you go and see him at the very beginning, before this whole mess had a chance to develop?"

"I couldn't do that."

"Why not?" asked his brother. "I know what happened, or at least I've got a pretty good idea, because Erica told me the whole story. The point is that it takes two to play the game Drake was playing, and he couldn't have got away with it at all if you'd behaved like an ordinary, intelligent human being, instead of like a Jew with an inferiority complex. I know," he said in a different tone, "it's easy to talk, particularly at this distance."

In the intervals of silence they could hear the wind stirring in the trees overhead, the sound of running water, and sometimes the rustling of an animal in the underbrush.

Staring unseeing at the tangle of trees, bushes, and vines across the little stream, Marc said at last, "I almost did see Drake once. I got as far as his outer office."

"And what happened?"

"I guess I just lost my nerve."

A moment later he burst out violently, "O.K., go ahead and tell me I've made a hell of a mess of it!"

"Give me time, laddie," said David imperturbably. "Don't you want to know how Erica is?"

"I already know how she is," he said under his breath.

"I wrote her a prescription for some stuff to make her sleep — my idea, not hers. I hope she got it filled. She didn't seem to be very interested in herself, all she could talk about was you. She did say that she was going to enlist this week, but she hasn't a hope of passing her medical till she's put on ten pounds and had a good rest."

David changed his position, sitting higher, with his back instead of his shoulders against the log, and said dispassionately, "As I've already remarked once, you're old enough to know better. This whole mess, as you call it, is your fault from start to finish, only having started it, you haven't got the guts to finish it; all you do is listen to a lot of people yapping about a situation they don't know the first thing about, and refusing to listen to the one person who does. And then you let those other people finish it for you."

He said, "If you think God is going to hand you another

Erica Drake on a platter, only tailored to measure according to a lot of cockeyed theories about 'Jews' and 'Gentiles' you're going to find that you're wrong. There isn't going to be another one."

"I know that." He had already made up his mind, but he had more faith in his brother's judgment than in the judgment of anyone else he knew, and he said, "Go on."

"You're a queer mixture of a weak character and a strong one. I've always thought you'd be up against something like this sooner or later, so that you'd be forced to make a choice, and if you made the right one, then you'd be somebody, and if you didn't, then afterwards you'd just let yourself go, and say what's the use, and subside into complete mediocrity. If you allow a lot of other people to talk you out of doing something that you know is right *for you*, and talk you into letting yourself and someone else down as badly as this, then you'll never amount to even half the human being you ought to be. Maybe it's a question of sticking by your own principles, I don't know, but you don't think like they do. If you did, you might be able to get away with it, but you don't, and neither does Erica. The difference between you is that she seems to realize it and you don't . . ."

"I do realize it."

He glanced swiftly at Marc, and after scrutinizing him for a moment he said, "Yes, I guess you do, but I'm going to finish my speech anyhow." He paused and then went on, "People have been trying to type us ever since we were born, Marc. I know it hasn't been easy, it's been tough as the devil a lot of the time, but we've stuck it out this far, and neither of us can afford to give up now." He paused again and said finally, "You can't quit."

They both got up and started down the road toward the

town. The sun was setting over the bush and the Algoma Hills were slowly changing from burnished gold to deep purple, but Marc did not look back. He did not look back until they had passed the last farmhouse and were nearing the row of run-down cottages on the outskirts, and he heard the first whippoorwill calling from the bush. He turned and his eyes swept over the line of hills as they caught the last rays of light from the west, and then he began to walk faster, looking ahead of him again.

The Reisers were at dinner, his father at one end of the table and his mother at the other, and David sitting across from him, when the telephone rang in the hall, and Marc, who was near-est the door, got up to answer it.

It was the girl who worked in the telegraph office down on Main Street and because she had known Marc all her life, instead of going through the usual formalities, she said, "Marc, is that you?"

"Yes. Oh, hello . . ." he began, and then realized that he had forgotten her name. "Hello," he said again, more firmly.

"Where have you been all afternoon, for goodness' sake?"

"Well, I . . ."

"There's a wire for you from Ottawa. You've got an extra week's leave."

"What!" gasped Marc. "What did you say?"

"Here, I'll read it to you. 'Captain M. L. Reiser, 32 Elm St., Manchester . . .'"

"All right, you can skip that part of it. Read me the rest."

She read him the rest and asked him if he would like a copy delivered. "We're pretty short handed now, but Tommy comes in after school, and he should be back from dinner in a minute."

"All right," said Marc dazedly. "Send Tommy along with it."

He put down the phone and stared at the panelled wall above the telephone where he had once carved his initials, M.L.R., Marc Leopold Reiser.

"What is it?" asked David from the doorway.

"I've got an extra week's leave." He said suddenly, "I'm going to phone Eric and ask her to marry me."

He could hear his mother and father talking in the dining room and looking up at his brother he said, "Go and explain to them, Dave, please."

"O.K.," said David.

"Tell them . . ."

"O.K.," said David again. "I'll do my best."

He disappeared, and into the phone Marc said to the long distance operator, "Montreal, please . . ."

There was a wait while she was getting the number and he went on looking at the initials M.L.R., until finally a woman's voice said, "Hello."

"Manchester calling, just a moment please."

"Hello," said Marc. "Hello, may I speak to Miss Drake, please — Miss Erica Drake."

"Yes, I'll get her. Can you hold on a minute?"

"Is that you, Mrs. Drake?"

"Yes . . ."

"This is Marc Reiser speaking."

"Oh," she said. "I'm sorry, I didn't recognize your voice."

"Is Eric all right?"

"No, not exactly. She — she's badly overtired . . ." The voice dropped into silence and then he heard her say, "I'm glad you telephoned, Mr. Reiser. I hope — I hope there's nothing wrong?"

"No, I've just been given some extra leave . . ."

"I'm so glad! Just a minute, I'll get Erica."

He heard Miriam's voice somewhere near the phone asking, "Mother, is that Marc?"

"Yes, thank goodness."

"Marc!" said Miriam into the phone.

"Hello, Mimi." He was beginning to be thoroughly frightened and he asked, "What's the matter with Eric?"

"She seems to have cracked up. She came home on Saturday night, after your brother left, and just sort of went to pieces. Mother's kept her in bed ever since. You are coming tomorrow, aren't you?" she asked anxiously.

"No, I think I'll probably leave tonight. Mimi," he said quickly, "is there any news of Tony?"

"No," said Miriam.

"But there's still a chance, isn't there?"

"I don't think so," she answered after a pause.

"Where was it?"

"The Mediterranean. He'd been transferred to Malta." She said, "I'm glad about your leave, Marc."

"Thanks, Mimi."

"Here's Eric . . ."

And then he heard Erica's voice saying, "Marc — Marc, is that you?"

"Hello, darling. Eric," he whispered, swallowing. "Eric, darling . . ."

"Is it true about your leave?"

"I've got another week."

"Marc!"

He said in agony, "Don't cry, darling — you mustn't cry any more."

"It's getting to be a habit, isn't it? I'm sorry." There was a brief silence and then she said, "There, that's better. When are you coming?"

"I'm going to try to make the train tonight. It's the Vancouver train and it's due in at Windsor Station at 11:15 tomorrow morning. Do you think you can meet me?"

"Yes, of course . . ."

"Are you sure you're well enough?" he asked anxiously.

"There's nothing the matter with me, really, I just . . ." She stopped and then said, "I'm just a fake."

"Eric . . ."

"Yes?"

"Eric," he said. He suddenly got to his feet, kicking away the telephone stool, and gripping the phone with one hand and the frame of the door leading into the back hall with the other, he said, "Eric, will you marry me?"

Her voice was suddenly very faint as she asked, "Do you mean now or afterwards?"

"I mean now — tomorrow, or the next day, as soon as we can get a license." He drew in his breath and said with a great effort, "Of course, if you like you can — well, you can think about it and tell me when I . . ."

"I don't have to think about it, except that I guess — I guess I can't quite believe it!"

"Neither can I," he said rather unsteadily.

After a pause he heard her asking, "Marc, are you . . ."

"Am I what?"

"Are you *sure*, darling?"

"Yes," said Marc. "I'm quite sure now."

There was a long silence and finally he said still more unsteadily, "I'm going to hang up now because I . . ."

"It must be catching. Goodbye darling."

"Goodbye, Eric."

"And give my love to David!"

He put down the phone and after a while he turned and found his mother and father standing in the door leading to the dining room. Whatever it was they had intended to say to him, when they saw his face, they did not say it.

He looked from one to the other and finally the words came out, wrung from his heart, "Please . . . give us a break!"

His father was the first to answer. He said, "Don't worry, Marc. We'll give you a break."

Later, as he was standing on the steps of the train looking down at the three of them, his mother and father and brother, his father said, "Tell Erica to come and see us sometime, Marc."

"I'll tell her," said Marc. "If it doesn't take us too long to get a license, we might come and see you together, after we're married."

"No," said his mother, shaking her head. "We don't want you spending most of your last week on trains."

The train began to move and David said, smiling up at him, "Good luck, laddie."

His father raised one hand in a little gesture of farewell, and then his mother cried out suddenly, "Marc, come back!"

"I'll come back, Mother."

And the last he saw of his family, they were still standing together under a lamp and a sign which they had first seen thirty-five years before, when the three of them, a mother and father and a little boy of five, had come from Austria.

It is five hundred miles from the little town of Manchester, on the edge of the mining country in northern Ontario, to the city of Montreal in Quebec, but Marc had been over the line so often since he had first left home to go to university seventeen years before, that lying awake in his berth he could call off the name of every town and every village through which they passed, and he knew the look of every lake and river, every forest and every stretch of field and pasture, invisible in the darkness.

When the train crossed the river at St. Anne's, he was already standing on the platform, looking out. Also standing on the platform was a middle-aged naval officer who told Marc that he had not seen his home in Montreal since the beginning of the war, and that the train was twenty-six hours late.

"We're running on time now, aren't we?" asked Marc.

"Depends on what you call 'on time.' We're still twenty-six hours late so far as I'm concerned. Got stuck in Alberta. Alberta," he repeated in disgust. "What a place to be stuck." He took out his pipe, put it away again, and went on staring out the window. He got off at Montreal West.

After Montreal West, Westmount, then six minutes to Windsor Station.

"What track are we on?" Marc asked the porter who was piling luggage on the rear platform.

"I don't know, sir."

"Never mind, it doesn't matter."

They were in the railway yards now, passing a row of freight cars, then a dining car standing by itself, and finally they were there.

The porter opened the door and said, "Stand back, please sir."

"I'm not going to fall off," said Marc from the bottom step. Just before the train stopped he jumped. The platform was clear for a few moments, then people began streaming from all the cars ahead and he had to slow down. Sleeping cars, coaches, two baggage cars, then the coal car, and just as he came up to the engine, he saw Erica standing by the barrier waiting for him. The moment he caught sight of her, he began to run.